EISWOLF

QUEST FOR A HERO

an adventure with dragons and a Princess

BY HC JOHNSTON

Copyright © 2021 H C Johnston
All rights reserved

No part of this book may be reproduced, or stored in a retrieval system, or transmitted in any form or by any means, electronic, mechanical, photocopying, recording, or otherwise, without express written permission of the publisher.

First published in 2021, HC Johnston

newstanestreetbooks@btinternet.com

ISBN-9798525662469

Cover design by: hejo

1: Quest for a Knight

The drums begin. A slow, funeral beat fills the castle courtyard, echoes from stone wall to stone wall like a dying heart, shudders through the rough wooden platform standing at its centre. Six tall towers, dark against the fading day, cast cold shadow. This citadel is harsh and stern; no fanciful tracery prettifies the windows, no amusing gargoyles spout water. No turrets, gaily fluttering flags or crenelations trouble the walls. Cannon are not yet an instrument of war; this place demands blood and bone, sword, muscle and grit.

The people of the Kingdom assemble, and wait.

The setting sun glances off the gilded spike at the top of the highest tower. For a second, light burns like a falling star.

(Oh, all right, one flight of fancy. The spike has no function, but the architect swore it added romance. Everyone agreed the new castle looked overwhelmingly grim, which the architect blamed on a brief with too much stone minimalism and not enough whimsical fantasy. So he was given some extra money and artistic leeway. But when he was found fiddling the building fund, the five other spikes and the gilded hell-mouth entrance gates were axed. As was he.)

Wind whistles across the stones.

A girl, bare-foot and dressed only in a white shift, appears at a huge ironbound door. She steps into the chill air of the courtyard. Slowly, reluctantly, she walks across the cobbles, followed by a grim-faced captain in chain mail. At the foot of the scaffold, the girl hesitates but then, in time to the drumbeat, she climbs the steps. She is a Princess. She is the Eternal Rose.

A middle-aged man in blue court robes signals to the drummers. They cease. The silence is as freezing as the wind.

The Princess bends forward, delicate as a snowdrop. Her long silver-gold hair falls over her face, as if she mourned. A last shaft of the sun illuminates her slight figure; her shoulders shake. The Princess weeps. The King, in his golden crown, watches from a window in the tallest tower. He covers his face with his hand.

The man in blue, the King's Herald, bellows his challenge. "A Hero! We cry out for a Hero to pass the Seven Tests of Kolras! Who will save us all?"

Trumpets bray. The crowd rustles with unhappy muttering. This time, will there be a Hero?

"Hear ye!" The Herald yells. "For the Hero who passes the Seven Tests shall marry the Princess, and receive half our Kingdom! We pledge this!"

The Princess holds her arms wide, exposed to the merciless cold in her thin linen shift. She cries out through her silken hair, "I pledge this!"

The King, in his tower, bows down and echoes her. "I pledge this!"

The people sigh, many in tears. But no Hero comes for the challenge.

The sun sinks behind the citadel. Darkness fills the courtyard. The captain of the guard helps the Princess down from the scaffold and she walks, head lowered, her hair streaming like a comet, across the cobbles to her father's tower. A thin-faced man in grey stands quietly at the door. He bows and steps back to let her enter, then follows her inside.

Where she straightens up and parts her hair. "Phew! How did One look?"

"Ravishing as ever, Your Majesty."

"Ha!" She wiped her nose, which had been running as freely as her tears in the cold wind. She shook the raw onion out of her handkerchief. "Next time SHOES! It's MARCH, for pity's sake! AND a woolly vest AT LEAST! FREEZING to death is NOT on Our agenda." A lady-in-waiting brought rabbit-fur slippers and a pink velvet mantle. The Princess dived into them. "And those drums! So doomy! Liven them up, Hegemon, they're positively morbid. And slow! As if One dawdles like an imbecile. All for a no-show. Wine!"

But what really annoyed her was, what the devil happened to Plan A?

***

So that was everything done and dusted for another March.

The crowd dispersed into the City, troubled and quiet. The ceremony had taken place every Spring Equinox for the last nine years, but no true Hero had passed the Seven Tests of Kolras and nowadays, few turned up for the challenge.

The mighty Sir Eiswolf, who knew the City well, had watched with his squire Perry from a good vantage point, perched high on a stable roof. But, like the rest of the audience, now they needed a drink, a snack and a place to sleep.

Perry slid down the tiles into a convenient dunghill and landed almost gracefully. He was slight, neat and dark-haired, if older than usual for a squire. "Good show, that. Very gripping. Fancy your chances, boss?"

"Not a lot." Eiswolf, a big man, landed more heavily. "The odds are as cruddy as…" He looked down. "My shoes. How many 'heroes' they had?"

"Marejah the baker says eleven, as of last year."

"Exactly." Eiswolf adjusted his hood over his rusty, shaggy hair. "All pushing up daisies. No thanks."

"Ah, but, that makes it a real challenge, doesn't it?" Perry trotted along beside the tall man, cheerful as ever. "Coz if you win, there's no question. You get the girl and you get to be King."

They walked to a tavern and what they hoped would be flea-free beds for the night, with their usual optimistic disposition. But they had little money and no horses, after Eiswolf's incident with a landlord, his wife, her daughter, and a terrible misunderstanding. Inside the tavern, the ceremony was the main topic of conversation: specifically, the lack of heroes, which had rather put a downer on the jollifications. But hope springs eternal, as Perry found when he went to buy the ale.

"Big lad you've got there," said the tavern-keeper. "Hero, is he? Big enough."

"Just passing through, mate. What's your best brew?"

"So why's he not up at the castle? Hog-gobbler. Five pennies."

"Each! You're a bandit. No, he's taking a rest from the knight stuff."

"Ah." The landlord's eyes narrowed. "He got the law after him, then?"

"No. But you will if you pour short measure. That's more like. He's going to see a relative, doesn't want a big to-do. "

"If you say so." The landlord sniffed. "How about paying me right now, Sir Squire."

Perry grumbled and paid. He took the beer to Eiswolf, who was sitting on a bench surrounded by space, like a negatively charged magnet in a heap of iron filings. The other drinkers watched carefully, if surreptitiously.

"Cheers," said Perry. "Here's to crime."

"You a Hero, then?" One of the regulars had decided, on the strength of a flagon of ale too many, that tonight's sport was Prodding the Big Stranger.

Eiswolf smiled, tightly. "Not so much. Cheers."

An older regular chimed in. "We run out of them. It's breaking the King's heart."

An ancient crone looked up from her mug of posset. "The Princess, lovely girl! Kept in a dungeon, such a shame! I mind the day she was born!"

"I know the story," said Eiswolf. "But you can't have any old hero just dashing in willy-nilly." He took a slug of ale and announced portentously, "They must hear their Call. Or it don't work."

"Oh," said the crone. "Is that why the others is all dead?"

"Could be," said Perry. "Proper preparation prevents piss-poor performance, as I always say. When I'm sober."

The younger regular frowned deeply. "You mean there's rules?"

Eiswolf settled in beside the tavern fire to explain Advanced Heroic Procedure.

"Well, every Hero has his Quest but they're, you know, specific, pointless going after the wrong one. You train in knightly - doings - and face impossible dangers and overcome deadly enemies, like, prove your worth."

"And get some money behind you," Perry added. "Expensive business being a knight, horses and armour and all."

Eiswolf hacked his squire on the shin. "Heroes are not mere mercenaries! True knights care nothing for lucre."

Perry ignored the kick. "But their squires do, because someone has to pay the bills."

"Shut up, Perry. I will pay you back, I said so. Anyway. Then you wait for the Call, and then you reject it."

The regular frowned. "Why?"

"I, er…" Actually, Eiswolf was not too clear on that. "Sort of a tradition. Anyway, you do that twice. Then Fate forces you into your True Quest, for honour and righting wrongs and defending virtue and all that stuff. But you still need a good horse, proper gear."

"And the right magic," said Perry.

"And the right magic. Like, for a werewolf, you need a silver dagger."

"Well, you'd know all about that," said the older regular. "So you've got a Quest, then?"

Perry shifted uncomfortably, and Eiswolf studied his beer.

Eiswolf was big, strong and skilled; he had earned his knighthood the hard way by courage on the battlefield. But he had not heard his Call. He had no Quest. So he had no way to show how virtuous and worthy he was, no story for the troubadours to sing, no tale to make his fame live forever. A Knight without a Quest was no true knight at all.

The younger regular laughed. "So what about the Seven Tests of Kolras? You could do that."

Eiswolf shrugged.

Perry stepped in. "Not his bag. He's a knight erroneous."

"Errant." Eiswolf hissed. "The word is errant. As you well know."

Perry muttered into his ale. "I says it as I finds it."

The crone leered at Eiswolf. "What about the Princess? She's a natural blonde, suit a big lad like you."

Perry made a wide gesture with his mug. "Well, on a true Quest, you fall in love from afar, don't ya, just with her picture or her name. Or the first time you see her face. Otherwise, it's not True Love, is it?"

The crone sighed. "I remember when I first saw my Phil, starkers he was. Oh, that was love at first sight all right, hung right down to - "

"Shut up, Gammy," said the older man. "Blimey, put me off my ale, you will. So, didn't you see her face?"

"Hair got in the way," said Perry. "Right, boss?"

"Alas, yes," said Eiswolf. The landlord came up with a jug of ale and nodded to the older regular. "Oh, thanks. That's very generous of you. er…"

"Bobbet." The older regular winked. "Now, about this Hero lark."

***

Black. The sky was black, without fathom. Stars scattered across space like gems thrown by a god's hand, white and sharp and burning. A movement on the far horizon: deep blue shadows, shapes in outline, angular, unnatural, mathematical, unloving, all in motion… Crystals? Clouds? A mathematical projection?

The creature on the snows beneath moaned, roused itself, sniffed the air, the harsh life of the wind, the stars, knew the shapes, now run and run and run - Howl in the joy of blackness, vivid existence, the ecstasy of the hunt, Night, and Blood, and Death, and only the sharp stars to share the rapture of the moment under the shifting green fires of the lights in the endless sky -

The sleeper turned and moaned, thrashing, kicking, whimpered as the vision faded. So sad, so sad. All gone, gone, no more. The sleeper turned back into the warmth of the bed, and snored.

***

"Six is too many." Perry grunted. Morning light forced its way through the cracks in the attic's shutters, and the dust-motes danced, golden. Not that Perry appreciated them. "Three's too much of that stuff." He sat up gradually, scratching his head through his short dark hair. The fleas had been active most of the night. "You all right, boss? You were making that noise."

Eiswolf rasped his hand over his stubble. He sniffed: the room stank of old beer and unwashed men. "Mouth like the bottom of a swill-bin."

The attic trap-door crashed open. A voice yelled, "Make way for the King's Champion!"

Eiswolf ran for his sword, throwing his hunting knife to Perry. He twisted in the air like a cat, sword-point towards the intruders. "Stand!"

The King's Champion, the grim-faced man who was also captain of the Palace Guard, had been tipped off about a potential Hero at the tavern. Having an entrant for the Equinox ceremony, however late, would surely please the King. But was this the man?

Eiswolf snarled savagely, swishing the bright sharp sword. He was tall, if not a giant: strongly built, although not monstrously so. His hair was gingery-brown, shaggy and sun-bleached from travel. He was scarred and unkempt. And that made him a standard soldier of fortune.

Until you saw his eyes: the colour of mud but glittering like steel. And he stood lightly, like an eagle ready to scythe through the air, as if gravity was simply a rumour. The first soldier literally did not see him move. Eiswolf's blade was at his neck in less than a heartbeat. "Do you want to die?"

The King's Champion, generally called Black Al, put his hand on Eiswolf's bare shoulder. "Sir Knight! We mean no harm. Please!"

Eiswolf looked deep into the Champion's eyes. But Al was a seasoned soldier. He stared back. "You are commanded to the Palace. We heard that a Hero was here. The Kingdom has need of you."

"You need lessons in manners." But Eiswolf put down his sword. "I am no hero, sir."

"That is not our information. This is a royal command."

The soldiers drew their swords. They looked very determined, all eight of them: too many to take on, Eiswolf judged.

"I assume you want me to wear clothes? Or is it come as you are?"

Perry handed Eiswolf his shirt and breeches. He turned round to dress.

The Champion took in a breath and swore quietly. For Eiswolf had a long crest of shaggy hair running down his back. As he straightened up to put on the shirt, the crest ruffled, as a dog's might when shaking itself. Eiswolf was a marked man in many ways and his had not been an easy life.

The soldiers escorted Eiswolf from the room, followed by Perry. The Champion looked about and found a jug of water. He washed the hand that had touched Eiswolf's skin with extreme care.

***

The Great Hall of the Castle was the biggest room that most people knew. Limestone walls soared up to a complex timber ceiling, gilded and painted with beasts, angels, fairies and demons. Sunlight shone over the assembled lords and ladies through tall, glazed windows. The light reflected most brightly on a raised dais at the far end, glinting on the King's golden throne and the silver chair for his daughter the Princess. The crowd rustled with anticipation, for word had it, despite the disappointment of the previous day, that a Hero had been found.

Drummers and trumpeters lined up behind the throne to play a fanfare.

The King's Herald, in blue, led the royal procession. The man in grey followed, a small, sober figure holding a tall black staff topped by a silver mace-head. A shiver went through the crowd, for he was the Hegemon, lawgiver and judge, the incorruptible and unmerciful.

Now came ladies in waiting and gentlemen of the bedchamber in rainbow-bright silks. The King's Champion, in chainmail, paraded a spear with the King's banner of deep blue. A young squire in crimson came next, his lance carrying the red triangular pennant of the Princess. Five pairs of pages marched behind, each carrying a lightweight hunting lance, on which was a small flag embroidered with knightly symbols. A single page came behind them, and another with an empty lance brought up the rear.

The royal couple finally entered, gleaming in gold, silver, satin and brocade; the court bowed and curtsied, in a whispering shuffle that spread from the dais through the hall, all the way back to the public entrance doors. The trumpets sounded again.

"All rise!" cried the King's Herald. "Hear ye your King!"

But the King did not speak. Instead, the grey Hegemon stepped forward, his eyes darting from side to side. He was very irritated indeed.

"Our beloved people!" He almost snapped his speech. "Far and wide do we seek men of courage, to face the Seven Tests of Kolras! We offer the highest reward, honour and reputation!"

"Try money," muttered Perry. He was crushed behind Eiswolf at the far end of the hall, a soldier gripping his arm. Eiswolf was squeezed firmly between two guards.

The Hegemon rattled on. "But a true hero deserves more! Behold our Princess! Our Eternal Rose!"

The Princess, exquisite in dawn-pink silk, her silvery-blonde hair in fine plaits under a little cap of gold wire and pearls, raised her blue eyes.

She spoke sweetly. "Beloved lords, ladies and those of lesser degree, One is a willing sacrifice. For what could be higher, or more noble, than to serve One's people! One awaits One's Hero so impatiently! Who shall rescue One, and fulfil One's greatest desire!"

A ripple of applause went through the crowd. This lovely girl, so heart-catching, offering herself so readily to any man who could save her realm no matter what she might feel. Tears ran down a few cheeks.

The Princess dabbed her eye with a delicate silk square. "One shall withdraw to One's chamber for quiet prayer and contemplation, while these noble men decide the terrifying, crucial matters of the Quest! Be wise, my brave people!"

She'd had a little spat with her father that morning. He had insisted she make an appearance at court because apparently there was a late entry. It seems Black Al had been busy and dug something out of a dunghill, but Daddy was taking it seriously, heaven knew why. She pointed out she'd done her bit in the freezing cold yesterday, she had things to do, people to see, total waste of time, she'd been through this little performance ELEVEN TIMES ALREADY FOR NOTHING! He told her to at least look as if she was on-side, and she agreed to a short speech. If the man was a real challenger (unlikely) the Court people could catch up with her after, and if this was Plan A turning up late, she knew all about that anyway. So, nobly, she swished out of the hall and back to her dungeon.

The Hegemon raised his black staff. "Where is our Hero!"

A soldier gave Eiswolf a mighty thump between the shoulders, and he stumbled forward a few steps. The King's Champion decided this was good enough, yelling, "Here he is!"

The entire court turned around to look.

And the Hegemon went even greyer.

Well, this is insane, thought Eiswolf. What sort of idiot do they take me for? I'm not holding my hand up for a chance to get dead quick, I told that bloke in the pub, I told the soldiers, she's pretty, maybe if you were madly in love, like a Hero on their Quest and his Fate commanded him.

Oh.

Ah. Right.

Princess, half a kingdom, Fate, two refusals –

Eiswolf was a man of his times and had been brought up on tales of great deeds and heroes. And, sometimes, you can be trapped in a story, just by knowing a story.

All the nobility of the Kingdom were watching him. Was that pounding in his chest really Destiny knocking? A tingle ran down his neck; a shiver went over the hair on his back.

A Princess, and half a kingdom. Wake up, man! Now. Now. Now. Time to be a Hero.

"Who calls me!" Eiswolf's voice boomed down the hall, firm and strong.

Behind him, Perry struggled and hissed, "Are you nuts?"

Eiswolf turned calmly. "It's all right, Perry. This is all right."

The Hegemon cried, "The Kingdom calls you! Come forward, Sir Knight!"

Eiswolf started to stride towards the dais. A guard stepped in smoothly and stopped him after five paces. The trumpeters came out with a blast, and the drummers gave it a one-two. In a flash, the King's Herald unfurled a ceremonial scroll. The whole business was choreographed to the second. And very well-practised.

Now Eiswolf understood the eleven standards the pages were carrying and why one had an empty lance. Eleven dead knights' worth. And space for the next.

The King's Herald declaimed, "We must know four things, Sir Knight. First, your true name and lineage!"

Well, that was easy.

"My Lords, I am Eiswolf, the last and lost, descended of Rime and Storm, the North Wind and the Northern Lights, faithful to the Gods of Ice! I have travelled far and long to come to this place, for this Quest!"

The crowd whispered gratifyingly. A stranger knight with a romantic tale!

The King's Herald read out Clause Two. "What device do you fight under, sir?"

"My squire has my banner."

It was Perry's turn to be shoved between the shoulders and stumble to the dais. "My lord! I bring your most noble - urk!"

Two soldiers grabbed his bundle and unwrapped a black battle standard, a diagonal shaft of green and red shimmering from corner to corner. In the centre stood the Snow Wolf, which brings the winter storms and one day will eat the Moon. A terrifying 'device' for a true Hero.

The King stared at Black Al's surprise package. The King was not a superlative judge of character, which was why he had the Hegemon, but he'd been in the job long enough to trust his intuition. One glance at Eiswolf made him uncomfortable: actually, suddenly slightly itchy. Still. Had to be done.

The Herald came to Clause Three. "Sir Knight, swear allegiance to our King! Will you fight without reserve, defend him without hesitation, set your own life at naught? Do you so swear?"

True loyalty. "I swear." Eiswolf swallowed, his mouth suddenly dry.

"Will you undertake the Seven Tests of Kolras without doubt or reluctance, to be proved in the fire of danger and the crucible of terror?"

True courage. "I swear."

"Do you swear to marry our Princess, that she may be fruitful, and bring forth a kingly line of strength and virtue?"

True Love. "I swear."

Now for Clause Four, sometimes called the Black Clause. "And will you complete your quests within a year and a day? Know that if you fail, you shall be deemed a traitor, and executed accordingly."

The court fell silent. It's not often you hear a man pronounce his own death warrant.

"I swear." But even Eiswolf could not control a bead of sweat on his upper lip.

The Herald turned to the King, "Your Majesty, do you swear that if this knight should succeed, that half your Kingdom will be his, and in due time, through your royal blood, he may become king and a father of kings?"

"I swear."

"Then let Fate decide!"

Another loud fanfare rose to the roof. The King bowed to Eiswolf and processed out, followed by the King's Herald, the King's Champion, the pages, the ladies and gentlemen of the household, and the trumpets and drums. The hall began to empty.

The Hegemon was extremely annoyed. What the blazes was Black Al playing at? Out of the blue, late, no notice, who the hell - That creature would never, ever set a finger on his lovely Eternal Rose. Never! He sniffed, taking his place at the end of the procession.

Eiswolf, Perry and the soldiers were alone. Perry carefully folded the black standard. "We're for it now."

The soldiers relaxed, and laughed. One grinned. "You said it, pal."

Perry stuffed the banner under his jerkin. "How does it feel to be a doomed knight?"

"Don't exaggerate," said Eiswolf. "Have a little faith."

But Perry had also seen the eleven standards, and the empty lance, and one of the palace servants surreptitiously sketching Eiswolf's snow wolf.

Eiswolf went up to the dais to look at the royal banners. The King's was in rich sapphire silk, embroidered in gold and silver thread, a crowned knight on horseback pointed his glittering sword forward. Eiswolf looked closer. The eyes seemed blank.

The red pennant for the Princess had a pearl-white rose at its centre. Perry frowned. "What are those silver squiggles? Thorns?"

Eiswolf squinted. "Any of you boys know?"

"No idea," said a soldier. "Not our business, is it?"

The captain of the guard yelled. "Eyes right!" More soldiers entered the hall, led by Black Al.

He saluted the first captain, and shouted, "I, King's Champion, by command of the King, require the Hero Eiswolf to appear before the Eternal Rose!"

"I come, sir," said Eiswolf.

He recognised the design on the girl's banner. The squiggles were not thorns. A wreath of scorpion tails surrounded the white rose.

***

"Got to look good!" Eiswolf was beginning to bounce around again. He had been taken back to the tavern – under armed guard - to dress more fittingly for a personal meeting with the Princess. "Like, heroic. Well, not too grungy, anyway."

Perry frowned. "Are you bright and noble or glowering and scary?"

"Dunno. What've I got?"

They sorted through his sparse collection of clothes, all travel-stained and not in the best condition. Perry picked out a clean-ish linen shirt, a brown kersey tunic, and a mantle of black worsted.

"Mail or not?" Perry held up the mail coat. "Mail says warrior."

"Or that I don't trust them."

"Well, you don't."

"True. But there's no need to show them right now, is there." Eiswolf was not a courtier, but he was a man who had worked in courts. "What do women like? Should I come in, sort of, sweaty from the fight?"

"What fight?"

So Eiswolf took a swing at Perry, and they scrapped half-heartedly for a few minutes.

"Nah," said Perry. "Frankly, you're coming over a bit ripe."

"What if I burst through the door and roar?" He threw back his head and gave a huge growl, and pounded his chest.

"You're a shining hero, not a bear. Touch of hairy chest, maybe? Urk. Maybe not."

"But I'm a fighter, right? The Tests will be all tourneys and battles and single combats. Got to look like a winner. Women like that."

So they settled on a long dagger with a gilt-leather scabbard at his belt, as swords were not fitting for a lady's chamber, a touch of cleavage through his shirt, and his sleeves half-rolled to show the strength of his lower arms and a few scars.

"Give me a head-toss," said Perry. "Swear like you don't care."

"Bloody hell," Eiswolf muttered.

"Not like that, you pillock. Strong and bold. Give them your best thousand-pace stare. No, that's too scary. Erm. Distant longing?"

"For what?"

"Imagine there's a big venison pasty over there - That's it!"

So the knight set forth to meet his Princess. In a bold, heroic, devil-may-care sort of swagger –

"Don't mince," said Perry.

In a bold, heroic, striding sort of way.

"Better," said Perry. "Knock 'em dead, boss."

***

The Princess, like most people in authority, did not like surprises.

Damn. Where the hell did this one crop up from? What the blazes happened to Plan A? And now Daddy said she actually had to meet this out-of-towner. Unbelievable. She'd have words with Black Al, too, about the limits of initiative in the court of today.

She sat in her silver chair in her dungeon, and fumed.

To be clear, her 'dungeon' was not a cellar, or even below ground. It was a set of chambers at the end of the corridor leading off the courtyard. This was officially a dungeon, because that's what she called it. Glazed window-slits gleamed with sunlight, tapestries hung on the walls, rushes covered the floor. In a modern touch, there was a large fireplace. But the huge ironbound oak door clanged shut every night. And her ladies or the guards always accompanied the Princess.

Actually, she had the best security in the castle.

The Princess signalled to Lady Dorcas to arrange the royal skirts for artistic effect. Lady Chloe brought her a single white rose (a silk one, as real roses were unavailable in March, even for princesses). A royal wave told Lady Hebe to pour two goblets of wine for the toast. Lady Iris hid some full cups behind a table, for the girls' after-event slurp. Lady Tillet and little Lady Mally arranged chairs in a semi-circle facing the door.

As the Eternal Rose, the Princess glowed, a vision of white and pink in the deliberate gloomth of the dungeon. Her six ladies took their places on the chairs, each holding a silk flower in their hands.

A loud triple knock on the door: a guard. "We bring your Hero!"

Lady Dorcas replied. "Enter, faithful guards!"

Eiswolf strode in behind the soldiers. The air was thick with expensive perfume, and he could see what the Kingdom no doubt thought of as Seven Beauteous Maidens. He knew that a true Hero could pick out the Princess straight away because of her exceptional loveliness and general all-round nobility.

That, and the socking great clue that she was holding a white rose and wore a necklace of pearls worth, literally, a king's ransom. But this was a game for the Court, only a game ... He had his pretty speech. "My ladies! Never have I seen such loveliness! Not heaven itself has such an array of the Flowers of Paradise!"

The Princess took a deep breath. Big. Rough-looking. Slightly whiffy. But - vocabulary of more than ten words. Who knew.

Eiswolf prowled around the girls, touching their hands as he examined the flowers. They curled up and giggled. Having given each lady the appropriate amount of attention, he strode towards the Princess and went down on one knee.

"Your Majesty, there is no concealing true Royalty!" He bowed his head.

The girls all gasped as if this was the most terrific surprise.

The Princess declaimed, "Sir Knight, take wine with Us, for your courage in accepting Our challenge!"

Iris leapt up and grabbed the toasting cups. She gave one to Eiswolf, who was still balanced on one knee, and the Princess took the other.

The Princess cried out, "To the Seven Tests of Kolras!" and downed her wine. She needed it.

"To the Quest!" Eiswolf drained his cup. So did he.

The Princess stared dramatically into space. "Go forth, receive instruction in your Quest from our most loyal Hegemon! Fail Us not, in your courage and devotion! Let all here present know that

We will weep every night and pray every morning for your successful return. Go, my Hero, bring Us release from this most dreadful confinement, bring Our realm to safety through your valour!"

Eiswolf bowed his head. "Your Majesty! I shall complete this Quest, or die in your service!" Then he stood, bowed gracefully, and left the room feeling quite perky.

Back in the chamber, the Princess exhaled. Duty done for another year.

"Whoa! Well, that one's a world-beater. Weird, weird, or weird?" She shuddered. "Hairy neck, for heaven's sake! Ugh!"

Iris joined her mistress in a shiver. "The way he snuffled around!"

"I'd do him," said Dorcas, and winked. "Big lad, you can tell."

The Princess shuddered again. "Anyone have any idea who the hell that was? Sorry, WHAT that was?""

"Seemed all right," said Chloe. "As these types go. Drink?"

"Thought you'd never ask," said the Princess. "Is this the same wine? That stuff's bit rough, Iris."

"Like our knight?" said Iris. "No, this is the good one."

Hebe snorted. "I didn't know whether to shake his hand or tickle his ears."

"If you tickle his tummy, he might wag his tail at you," said Dorcas.

Iris called the meeting to order. "Come on, then. I'd say three weeks."

"Fifty gold ones on three weeks, any advance?" cried Chloe. "Ladies, place your bets!"

"Ooh, three months!" said Dorcas. "He's got more about him than the last two!"

And so, betting on the life expectancy of the latest hero to grace their chamber, the ladies amused themselves harmlessly. They'd had a lot of practice.

***

In the top chamber of the second-tallest tower, the Hegemon met with the black-robed Conclave of Scholars, who advised the King and his council. All were men, most were middle aged or older, and none were athletic by nature, so there was a lot of wheezing after the long climb up the tower. Their mood was resigned. The Tests were annual, and Conclave's presence was primarily ceremonial, but there were procedures to follow. They signed off the last few documents.

The Hegemon rubbed his hands. "Right, who did the quick recce on legalities? Nothing's changed, has it? No signs in the sky or sudden divine revelations? We're clear to go?"

The eldest scholar raised an eyebrow at this lack of respect, which normally quelled the most unruly student, but the Hegemon took the usual amount of notice: none. The old man whiffled a little. "All is in order, my lord."

"We had better welcome the lucky contender. Bring in, er…"

"Eiswolf, my lord," said a third scholar.

Clatters and bangs followed: the soldiers on the stairs went into their ceremonial salutes, then came a waft of chill air.

Eiswolf rattled in and stood foursquare in a heroic position, filling the doorway. The room smelled of old leather and old men, not valorous deeds. "My lords, you have instructions for me?"

Conclave shrank back but the grey Hegemon stood his ground. "I do, sir. Please, we are all friends here. First, let me record our huge gratitude that you have accepted this Challenge." Even if you are a poser.

"Sir, I am thankful for the opportunity." Eiswolf also found grace cost nothing. Even to a little skinny weasel.

"Our noble Princess tells me that you are most acceptable, Sir Knight. This favour is for you, to wear next your heart." You oaf. The Hegemon held up a gold chain, ornamented with a rose set in pearls and enamel bluebirds.

Eiswolf swore to himself. Damn, didn't think of that.

Knights who quested in the name of their lady could be known by her favour. A blue ribbon could make him the Knight of the Azure Band. If, playfully, she gave him a bunch of flowers, he would be the Knight of the Rosebud and get a terrible ribbing every time he went into a tavern. God knows what the lads would make of a cute little necklace. "Ah, my lord, so fragile a jewel may get damaged on my Quest."

The Hegemon frowned. "Send this to the Kingdom if ever you are in mortal danger, and we shall bring two hundred men at arms to your aid at once." Suck it up, big boy.

So Eiswolf put on the necklet. Whatever. He stood heroically again. "Sir, my sword is ever at your command. What foul beast must I slay, what dread enemy must I defeat?"

For a second, the small man almost laughed. "Sir Knight, the Seven Tests are not merely of physical strength. The Kingdom requires a man who is wise and patient as well as strong and courageous." Get that, thicko?

"I am your pupil, sir," said Eiswolf. Pen-pusher.

"The Tests in the Manifest must be undertaken in order."

The which? "The manifest what?"

"A list, sir. On completion of each task, you must send word to this court. Not just a messenger, they get killed. A short letter will do, in ink on something robust. Parchment for choice."

Eiswolf frowned. What the hell was wrong with your enemy's head on a spike, all of a sudden?

The Hegemon was still talking. "And do remember to sign it, please."

"And date it?" said Eiswolf. "Maybe a copy or two?"

The Hegemon ignored him. "Written proof will be verified by the Conclave." The old men nodded. "Complete the Seven Tests within a year and a day. If you fail we shall pursue you with utmost - I believe the term is prejudice." Now, he smiled. "The Manifest has been lodged for safekeeping at Bladbean. To access it, you must ask the Newts."

Newt, toad, frog, stickleback, Eiswolf did not care. At last, he had a Quest.

***

Eiswolf bounced down the bleak woodland path. "What did you think? I could be a King. I've been Called! What did you think of her? She's like a snowflake, she smells of jasmine, I can do it! What do you think?"

"She's a looker," said Perry.

"Natural blonde. A real Princess."

Eiswolf could not put off a visit to the Good Witch Bess any longer. At least he had good news. Bess was not his real mother; she was many things, but she was definitely nobody's mother. But she was the closest he had.

Eiswolf and Perry picked their way down steep tracks to the Witch's hovel, past terrified peasants and cattle that refused to take the magic-haunted path. The wood fell silent. Only the breeze shivering the leafless branches showed they were still in the land of the living. No bird sang. Eiswolf smelled acrid smoke, way before Perry spotted a roof thatched in heather and bracken.

"Wotcher, cock." A figure appeared from nowhere, startling both men. "You're late."

Eiswolf stopped bouncing. "Bess, you could give a bloke a blue fit!"

"Surprised, eh, Sir So-Important-Knight?"

Bess was a small woman, dressed in scraps and wraps of fabric. Her long, dark, grey-streaked hair fell in elflocks down her back; her eyes were as sharp as pins in her weather-beaten face. "Been in town long?" she said. "Don't answer that. Two weeks."

"I was coming to see you." He muttered, embarrassed.

"Yeah, right." Her steely gaze bored into him.

Eiswolf looked down and half-mumbled. "I wanted to show Perry the challenge thing. The Princess and half the Kingdom and all."

"Right." She was still annoyed.

Eiswolf was profoundly grateful to the Good Witch Bess. She had rescued him when he was a boy, more or less brought him up, gave him a home when he wanted one, and good advice whether he wanted it or not. But. There was a but. Every visit turned into a trial. Recently these had become unpleasant.

"Er, yeah, actually, I've got to tell you something." He took a deep breath. "My Quest. I'm doing it."

"What?" Her glare was like a blow to the stomach.

"The Tests. Kolras. And the Princess. And…" He ran out of words.

"You what?" Her voice was edged like a saw.

"I heard the Call." He tried to stare back defiantly but failed.

"I see." Her eyes burned. "Perry, where were you when he was hearing voices?"

"Trying to stop him, Bess," Perry said, miserably.

Bess's tone sharpened to a razor. "So what happens to your real mission? The one I've been training you for?"

Eiswolf tried to laugh it off. "If I'm a Hero, I can do both, right?"

"No!" Bess exploded. "Swan off on a ludicrous, pointless - You do know they're all dead? All the idiots who've tried this?"

"Well, I wouldn't say no to half the Kingdom, would you!"

"Which half! The useless half with marshes and mountains? Eiswolf, you have a far greater task." She tried to grasp his arm but he pulled away.

"Bess, I felt it. In the Great Hall, I felt the Call! I did!"

"The call!" She almost laughed but restrained herself. "You still swallow all that?"

"Yes!" His colour was rising, along with his voice. "A true knight must follow the call! That's what makes me a knight! What am I now? Some bumpkin with a sword!"

She hissed at him. "Better than a dead bumpkin!"

Explosion time, his turn. "This mission of yours, oh so secret, don't tell the idiot boy, far too important to tell me what I'm risking my life for! How long am I supposed to wait? Until I'm too old to fight? This is now, Bess! This is mine!" He glared, sweating with fury. "I swore to the King. They'll kill me if I go back on it."

"That's right, blame them!"

She was beside herself. Every boy in the Kingdom played the game about the Princess and half the Kingdom, dressed up in cooking-pot armour and fighting with wooden swords. And every man who had tried it, was dead.

But her boy was fidgeting with energy. She had never seen him so excited. If she denied him, he might turn his back on her -

Calm down, she told herself. He was alive, and strong, and skilled. She could assist with her hidden knowledge. A doctorate from Imperial College, project-leader at Caltech and five years at DARPA had to count for something, even in this god-forsaken medieval dimension.

Anyway, he had a year and a day. Plenty of time. She could bring him round. She smiled: hard, uncompromising. Eiswolf felt a chill down his spine.

"Well. My lad will be a hero and win a Princess, eh? These things are not straightforward or any numpty could do it. Come to me when they give you the Quests? Swear."

"Yep."

Eiswolf and Perry made their way back to the City. At its darkest, dampest and most flea-ridden, Eiswolf was more comfortable there than with his foster-mother.

***

The sky echoed with the screams of the ravens that tumbled through the air around the Black Tower. The Glimmer Lord tapped his fingers on the arm of his chair. So much to plan, so little time.

"My lord, your messenger has arrived from the Kingdom."

The Lord scowled. He did not like to be interrupted. "Who?"

"Mirak, my lord."

Ah, good. A remarkable lad: so young, so bright, so subtle and so corrupt, a mind made for conspiracy, and a heart for deceit.

Mirak entered, silent and graceful as a leopard. He bowed beautifully. "Great Lord, I have seen the ceremony of the Equinox. A man has agreed to undertake the Tests."

"Oh? Who's that suicidal?"

"A knight from nowhere, my Lord, called Eiswolf. Rumour associates him with the Good Witch Bess."

"Does it, by Jove." Pestilential woman. "So what's he like?"

"He's tall. Strong." But the boy stopped.

"Spit it out, lad, what's your opinion, you've seen him."

"He's strange. They say he's a werewolf."

The Glimmer Lord snorted. "Unlikely. And?"

Mirak did not raise his eyes, as if ashamed. "He seems a true Hero, my Lord, although you said they do not exist."

The Glimmer Lord laughed. "I never said a man couldn't make you think he was a Hero. I'm sure he comes across as very heroic. My old friend Bess knows about all that. We shall watch this situation. Now go and amuse yourself how you will."

The boy grinned widely. "Anything, my Lord?"

"Use your imagination, my boy."

Laughing, the lad ran out, the light of utter licence in his eyes.

A Hero? What was Bess playing at? The Tests were a pointless ritual, if intriguing in their obscurity. Utterly irrelevant to his own plans, of course. But uncertainty in the Kingdom? He liked uncertainty. Uncertainty was useful. Maybe use that to resolve an irritating question of strategic balance? Well, if Bess was in the game -

"Let battle commence."

The ravens screamed.

2: Neuts

A couple of days later, reality started to break in on Eiswolf. Such as, the meaning of the Hegemon's expression. That had not been a good smile.

The Palace had been generous with equipment: Eiswolf had his choice of armour, boots, and saddlery. Perry had new linen and, better, a bag of gold to finance their travels. Most important of all, they had horses.

Given the pick of a King's stables, do you go for speed, endurance or comfort? For tournaments, the high-accelerating courser was the animal of choice: but a questing knight needed all-terrain capabilities, reliable and robust. The Master of Horse had tried to palm Eiswolf off with a charger, a huge animal that had seen too many miles and frankly, looked a bit dim. Eiswolf picked a destrier of just under sixteen hands, squarely built with good load capacity and strong hindquarters for those steep hill-climbs, in a suitably impressive glossy black. The horse was bred in Maffersdorf and trained by the great Terbaud, so Eiswolf put aside the fact that Pepper was a gelding.

Perry was offered a plain old rouncey. "Blimey, I can't be seen on that!" He wanted a palfrey for their 'ambling' gait, more comfortable for long distances. But they were expensive and normally reserved for nobility. A pretty jennet was small, light and manoeuvrable, but Eiswolf pointed to their reputation for fragility: repairs on the road could be a problem. The hobby was out because

Perry associated those with low-rank bandits and again, there was a question over stamina. Also, the only one they had was piebald.

"You'll be lucky to get a bloody mule at this rate," said the Master of Horse, after a tense hour or so. "Very picky for a squire, you are."

"He'll take that one," said Eiswolf. So Perry ended up on a small bay mare of no particular type at all. He tried to give her an air of mystery by calling her Corsaire, but the docket from the Master of Horse had not been big enough.

Eiswolf and Perry rode out towards Bladbean, a small town two days' journey away. The dawn was cold.

"Newts." Eiswolf muttered.

"Surely he was joking?" said Perry. "Little slithery whatsits?"

"I don't think he makes jokes." And that was not the only thing annoying Eiswolf. "Do I have to wear this bloody trinket all the time?" The necklet caught on his chest hair, uncomfortably.

"Well, if the Princess gave it to you…"

"Makes me look a bloody prat."

Perry smirked. "Don't complain, oh Knight of the Flashy Jewellery. I think it's pretty. Especially the little birdies!"

And here he discovered that his mare, now called Corsa, could not be roused into more than a reluctant canter, even when a large man in armour riding a destrier galloped up behind.

"Ouch." Perry clambered to his feet. "Not fair, you know."

"Bloody hell." Eiswolf sighed. "Can't I put this thing in a bag?"

"No, because you'll lose it and the Princess will not be pleased. She wants her favour to be close to your manly bosom." Perry remounted. "Oh glorious Knight of the Glittery Bluebirds - Ouch!"

***

The Princess and her ladies watched from the third tower as Eiswolf and Perry rode out through the courtyard: the knight halted and waved to her before leaving the castle. She graciously waved back.

"He looks really good on that horse," Dorcas had said.

"The squire's not too bad, I suppose," said Iris.

"Hm. Seems old for a squire for me," said Dorcas. "And, well. Too nicely-groomed, if you get my drift."

"The knight is a proper man," said Chloe. "Seems a shame."

"He volunteered," said the Princess. "It's not our job to play nursemaid. Now, have the leases on the Wardur transfer been sent over?"

So they, like the rest of the Palace, went back to their day-jobs.

What does a princess do all day? This rather depends on her. The King was sharp enough to recognise that he had a bright daughter, so after she had become bored with sewing fine seams and playing arcane, non-strenuous ball games with her ladies, she had joined the King's circle of advisors. She drafted diplomatic messages, and looked over legal transactions like the Wardur property purchase. She suggested Royal visits and wrote to local dignitaries, always under the seal of the King's private chamber.

But what she could not be, under any circumstances, was an official member of the King's Chamber. And she could never inherit the Kingdom, however bright, capable and ambitious. To get her hands on real power, she had to marry. Then she had to hope that the new King would not murder her or anything.

She was not the kind of girl who thinks that hope is a strategy.

The Dungeon had been her idea. A Princess kept under duress in a Dungeon, as she told her father, sounded a lot better for the Quest than one who wanders about in a pretty dress playing those dratted ball-games. But her real reason was to monitor the Court and keep away from other people's plots, because plots meant trouble. She kept an eye on the Hegemon, the barons, foreign diplomats and spies, and any over-ambitious captains of the guard. Her only card was her position as Princess: without that, she was disposable. So her father had to stay King until her marriage, then he could die because she would be Queen. But if he died too soon –

"Your sweet brow is troubled, my child." The King entered the Dungeon.

"Not at all, Your Majesty. We ladies are so tender of heart. Why, Chloe shed hot tears for the brave knight as he rode away."

Chloe giggled into her embroidery.

The King smiled indulgently. "Ah, dear Chloe, all my pretty flowers, you make this court a garden of delights! But I must take counsel with my daughter, so pray excuse us, and ornament some other fortunate part of my palace."

The girls bowed their heads and left, taking their embroideries and musical instruments with them.

The King faced his daughter in private at last. "Well, another contender."

"Where did Black Al find this one?" The Princess was beyond pretty phrases after nine years.

"Apparently one of the guards heard about him. A genuine hero, eh? "

They stared at each other. She was fuming, because Plan A seemed to have evaporated into thin air, but he was happy because another year taken up with the (eventually) fatal adventures of a knight was a year - gained.

"Just a word, Daddy. They did more or less have to drag this one in kicking and screaming? What happens when one doesn't come at all?"

"My dear angel, you have no need to concern yourself."

"Daddy, I am twenty-four! How long…" But she did not finish her thought or her sentence.

Because a Princess who is too old to have a child is no Princess at all, either.

The King's face clouded. "We will make sure that a suitable King is found in due time, and you will marry. I know how dearly you desire children, and I would have no greater pleasure than to see you hold my grandson in your arms."

"Well, if it's fathered by the one that just rode out, prepare to put a leash and a muzzle on it!"

"What?"

The Princess was deeply peeved. "That - knight - is a werewolf. Don't tell me you don't know, Daddy."

The King tried being apologetic. "But my sweet…"

"AND I'M NOT HAVING IT!"

She stamped her little foot. The King knew there was no arguing with her in this mood. He left, as gracefully as he could.

She was right, of course. They were scraping the barrel. But then, Wise Kolras had developed the Seven Tests as a stalling mechanism, not a selection system.

***

The Kingdom's fairy-tale was a useful concept. Everyone knows where they are with a good King, a Princess locked in a dungeon, 'impossible' tests and the noble knight who gets half a kingdom as his reward. In the days when kings sorted everything out with a few swipes of their battle-axe, that might have been enough.

But, the King sighed to himself, certainly not now. The enemies of the Kingdom were powerful, but also subtle. The people might think they needed One Strong Man to lead them to victory in battle, but the King knew, from the true records of his grandfather and father, that being a Fighting King or even a Splendid King was not sufficient. Fortunately, wise Kolras had left a full play-book of options.

Kolras was a commoner, but he had been the Kingdom's greatest servant under three mediocre kings, Fighting, Hermit, and lastly, Splendid: when Kolras had spent most of his energy managing a man who was grossly unfit for high office. Kolras knew, for the peace of the Kingdom, that the crown must pass smoothly to the most suitable candidate. Suitable. Not some random offspring or the baron with the biggest army, both of which struck him as foolish neglect. But to bypass the legal succession, he needed a good cover story.

So he did the (to him) obvious thing, and asked the Conclave of Scholars to suggest a plan for if the Kingdom, by chance, ran out of male heirs. And Conclave came back with the Tests, to be held every Equinox until a winner emerged, with all the unnecessarily obscure, fantastical impossibility he could have desired. The safety-net was in place.

At first, this was unnecessary. The crown had passed peaceably to the current King, after the Splendid King fell off his horse, and all seemed well. Kolras knew the young King to be fond of peace and quiet, and died content. But alas, the young King's son, the Prince, grew older, and began to show every sign of being as impetuous, spendthrift and dangerous as his forefathers, plus a disturbingly cruel streak. The King prayed for guidance.

God moves in mysterious ways. A gang of pirates came upon the Prince and his hunting party and seized them, presumably for ransom. But this was followed by silence. After a year and a day, the King, barely speaking through his tears, declared that if his son were no more, then the Seven Tests of wise Kolras would choose the next heir. And so began the ritual of the Equinox.

After a couple of years, and six deaths, word got around among potential heroes. Originally the ceremony was in both spring and autumn but with fewer and fewer candidates, this was knocked back to annual. Even so, last year produced only one challenger, who lasted a month. If the old man in the pub had not told the guard about Eiswolf, this year there would have been none.

The King knew the Tests were losing credibility, and with no suitable candidates, might even be seen as a curse on the Kingdom. He needed to identify real contenders for the succession.

Because, werewolf or not, he did not expect to hear from Eiswolf again.

***

Bladbean was a small town with the usual taverns, cattle-market and bridge, and a few places where newts might be expected to hang out. The knight and his squire went from the horse-pond to springs by the cattle-market, to where the river curved into water meadows. But having plodged into all of them, neither Eiswolf nor Perry had seen even a flash of a newt. Now they were at the end of a drainage ditch near the bridge.

"Nope," said Perry, who had been volunteered to wade in as far as he could. "No newt activity that I can see."

They had drawn a festive crowd of children and the otherwise unoccupied, watching the strange Knight and his squire with unalloyed curiosity. As Quests went, this was a rum one.

"What about under them reeds?" said a crone.

"Been there," said Perry.

"I've caught you a frog," said a small girl, helpfully.

"Thank you, darling, has to be a newt." Perry splashed into a new part of the ice-cold pond.

"What're you going to do with it when you've caught it?" said another crone.

A very good question. Eiswolf rather hoped the creature would be magically empowered with speech, or have instructions on its skin. He did not want his first message back to the Palace to read, 'Caught one, what do I do next?"

"What are they doing?" said a calm voice behind him.

"Looking for newts," said a small boy. "It's a Quest."

Perry rummaged around in the gloopy darkness for a few more minutes. "You know, I think the little bastards heard we were coming. He did say newts? You did hear right?"

"What's going on?" said another calm voice behind Eiswolf.

"They are on a Quest for newts," said the first.

"I heard perfectly well," said Eiswolf. "The Hegemon may be a creep but he is clear-spoken. The Manifest of the Seven Tests of Kolras is held by the Newts of Bladbean."

Suddenly, the crowd gave a large collective sigh of "O-oh!" A few giggled. Eiswolf spun round to find out who was disrespecting him, to be faced with two slight figures in grey monk's habits, their hoods up. A third joined them.

"What's so funny?" he snapped.

One of the monks stepped forward. "Sir Knight, I fear you are under a misapprehension. We are the Newts of Bladbean."

"Pardon?"

***

Bladbean College was square, solid, and plain, a stone quadrangle housing fifteen colleagues. Eiswolf and Perry, now dried off but still very, very annoyed, sat on stools by the fire in the gatehouse.

Perry fumed. "You and your cloth ears! Why didn't you ask?"

But all he got for that was a thump on the head.

A monk entered, dressed identically to the others but for a lightweight metal chain around his neck. Eiswolf and Perry stood up and bowed.

The monk shook his head. "Please, we have no such useless ceremony here."

Eiswolf started into his speech. "Sir, we thank you for your hospitality."

"Please do not call me sir. We have no need for such useless hierarchy."

Eiswolf was stumped. "What do you want me to call you?"

"The community refer to me by my usefulness. I am Pontifex."

"Ah, I see," said Perry, who did not see at all but felt he should register his presence.

Eiswolf tried again. "Well, er, Pontifex, we are here on a Quest that only - Are you sure you're the Newts?" He had a strange feeling this was a joke by the Hegemon, or possibly even Kolras.

Pontifex let down the hood of the habit, revealing a brown, lined but calm face, completely without hair. Not an eyebrow. "We are the College of Bladbean. Some local people call us that, I believe as a jocular contraction of 'neuter'."

A light began to dawn. Not newts. "Oh. Ah. Neuts!" Neuts? Eiswolf tried not to stare. That was why they smelled so clean. This was a new one on him but introductions could fill in a second or two. "Ah, my manners, where are they, I am Sir Eiswolf and this is my squire, Perry. I seek the Manifest of Kolras." He found himself bowing automatically but commuted the bow to a nod of the head.

The Neut nodded back.

Eiswolf reviewed all the possibilities for a community of bald neuters, and did not get far. But they wore habits. "Um. And is this a religious foundation?"

"We follow a philosophy, knight. We are a refuge, a focus of contemplation and a centre of learning."

Perry had to ask. "So what's the neuter bit about, if you don't mind me saying?"

Pontifex smiled a little: at least, his mouth broadened. "This life requires sacrifices, but the fleshly part is of no true importance. We deal with all such matters. First, you will eat. You will stay this night. Our librarian, Bibliotect, has retired to meditation and will not be available until the morning. Then we may discuss the Manifest."

He turned on his heel and walked out, without farewell.

"Well, that was easy," muttered Eiswolf. But he shivered.

***

Perry suspected he knew how the 'fleshly part' might be dealt with but was surprised to discover that this also applied to the Neuts' taste buds. Supper was a bowl of light beige gunk. The monk had been short when Perry asked. "Soup." The bread was simultaneously dense and spongy. The meal did not go down without a fight.

Pontifex intoned, "We give thanks to Coquus for our food." A row of brown, bald, totally clean-shaven heads nodded. "Cantor will bless our sleep."

One of the monks began to sing in a reedy soprano, pleasantly enough, but Eiswolf's polite smile began to set in stone by the fifth verse. The song drifted into a quavery diminishing sequence, an eternal question, or perhaps mere uncertainty on how to stop.

"Thank you, Cantor. Accompany our guest Perry to a cell. Eiswolf, will you follow me."

Light conversation was a tough call with the Neuts.

"Been here long?" said Perry.

Cantor stared ahead. "We take no note of the meaningless passage of time."

"But you like it here?"

"We do not concern ourselves with transitory satisfactions."

"Right. Er - your family, do you come from round here?"

"Such connections are of no importance to us."

After which, Perry gave up. The sleeping cell was a square stone box, but as a guest, he had a special treat: a sack of straw and a blanket. Cantor pointed them out. "We have no need of such comfort. You will rise with the dawn." And then left.

"And a good night to you," Perry muttered, already shivering.

Eiswolf had little more success with Pontifex. "I am curious why Kolras chose to entrust this document to your College."

"That is a matter which Bibliotect must answer, not I."

"Oh. Have you been head of the College for long?"

"Will that contribute to your Quest?" Pontifex stopped and looked at Eiswolf, with, just possibly, a tinge of irritation.

"Well, you must have seen other knights come here for the Manifest. Can I learn from them, I know they're all dead now but…"

"Nothing. You can learn nothing. "

Eiswolf heard a definite tone. He grasped the monk's arm, but it felt as slender as a twig, so thin he might break it by mere carelessness. He let go immediately. "Sir, I go to my death if I do not understand this quest. What can you tell me?"

Pontifex raised calm grey eyes. "Your survival is important to you, but has no meaning for the continuation of the College. Bibliotect will decide if you should be given the Manifest. I do not have that ability."

Eiswolf deeply, deeply wanted to grab Pontifex by the throat but could see this would be completely useless. He must wait for morning.

***

There were noises in the night. The monks lay open-eyed, wondering what demon had arrived with the winds that suddenly blew so strongly over the college. The voice was distant, almost a whisper, then a song, then a yell, a scream. then nothing, then circling as if trapped, battered at the shutters of the windows, retreated as if to regain strength, then with a bang, blew out a massive door, shattering the hinge. After that the air was quiet.

***

Perry, who had given up on the idea of sleep when the blackbirds started singing at four, was kicking around the herb patch in the dawn. A monk came out and started hoeing. His face was not quite as lined as the others, so Perry judged he must be younger and, possibly, more approachable. "Hi," he said.

"Hallo, guest," said the monk.

Perry tried for flattery. "Admiring your work. Nice spot you have here."

"It is sufficient," said the monk, and hoed on.

The obvious question still burned in Perry's mind.

"Neuts. So, tell me, are all of you, er, without? I mean, lost your bits? I know the Barons of Elderton have a nasty way of doing that to their prisoners."

"Not all. Some chose the path. Some had no need. And you?"

Perry took a step back. "What?"

"You would be welcome here, if you wish for calm. "

The monk hoed, then weeded, then straightened up and stretched, while Perry stood with his mouth open. "I don't need - Thanks but no," he said, in the end. "But I suppose it's a kind offer."

"We are not kind," said the monk. "That is a meaningless conception in a community without harm. You will discover that many concepts in your world are meaningless at the deepest level. Fear. Love. Loyalty. Hope."

The bloodless tone of the monk's voice grated on Perry. "Ah. Well. Thanks for telling me."

"Thanks have no meaning in this community. You could lay aside all loss, all sorrow."

The Neut's eyes bored into Perry. He squirmed. "Right. "

"Your life is a deception, squire. One day the truth will have to be told."

"Must go, breakfast." And Perry almost ran to the refectory.

***

Bibliotect the librarian was old, very old. He looked like an aged turtle as his bald brown head crept out from the neck of his habit, swaying a little from side to side as he tried to focus on Eiswolf.

"A knight?" he quavered.

"Yes, Bibliotect." Pontifex spoke loudly and clearly. "From the Palace, one who seeks the Manifest."

"The what?"

Oh, hell, thought Eiswolf. What if he's forgotten where he put it?

"A knight, you say?" A flicker of memory crossed the clouded blue eyes. "Has he a banner?"

"Perry, the banner," said Eiswolf.

"It's in the saddlebag," hissed Perry.

"Then go fetch."

Perry bowed and scraped out of the room.

Eiswolf took command. "And while my squire brings forth the banner, I shall tell you of my lineage." Because that had to be good for five minutes and would keep the librarian occupied and focussed, hopefully. "I am Eiswolf, the last and lost, descended of Rime and Storm, the North Wind and the Northern Lights, faithful to the Gods of Ice! I have travelled far and long to come to this place, to rescue the Eternal Rose and to save this Kingdom!"

But even as Perry dashed back into the hall with the banner, he could see that Bibliotect was not an easy audience.

"It made no more sense the third time," said the old man. "Rime? I know of no family called Rime. I do know people called Frost."

"It's a metaphor," said Eiswolf, through gritted teeth.

"That won't do, you know, calling yourself after the weather. Very untidy, young man. Although I did know a chap called Snow, once."

"Look, I'll start again. My name is Eiswolf."

"Strange sort of name," said the old man. "Where do you say you're from?"

"Banner," muttered Eiswolf.

He and Perry unfolded the flag. Bibliotect peered at it.

"What's that white smudge in the middle? Looks like a sheep."

"The Snow Wolf, Bibliotect," said Eiswolf.

"What about the Ice wolf. Are they different?"

"No," said Eiswolf, very, very patiently. "My name is Eiswolf. My device, on this banner, is the Snow Wolf.

"Very untidy," said the librarian. "Calling yourself one thing then showing something else. Very sloppy. "

Maybe if he changed tack. "I have come for the Manifest, Bibliotect."

"What? Be specific. Pontifex, you bring me a lamentable standard of acolyte."

"The Manifest of Kolras!" Pontifex almost shouted in the old monk's ear. "That list! This knight wishes to take up the challenge."

"Knight? What Knight?"

Between Eiswolf and Pontifex, they managed to get the old man to understand that the document they wanted was the precious one in safekeeping. Pontifex's expression of studied calm was beginning to freeze on his face.

"The list! The one on vellum!" Pontifex almost shouted.

"Vellum? We never write lists in vellum. Very wasteful."

Eiswolf tried. "A wise man called Kolras gave it to you!"

"No need to yell, young man, I still have my wits and my hearing. That chap was most particular."

"Which chap?"

"Are you the ice chappie or the snow chappie? I thought you had a sheep?"

As security systems go, Eiswolf had to admit, this was pretty well foolproof. No fear or pain would unlock the old man's memory: no force had any meaning for him or the College. He wondered how many knights had given up right here and made a run for it.

"Look, Kolras gave you a Manifest, a kind of list. On vellum. You are to give it to any knight who asks, and then, after a while, the Palace sends it back. And you look after it until the next knight asks."

A slight frown crinkled the old brown face. "Oh, that! Damn nuisance. Back and forth, back and forth! If they don't want the thing why do they keep asking for it?"

"Yes!" cried Pontifex, "That!"

"Oh, I'm sitting on it, hee-hee-hee!" He tapped the side of his nose. "Closest to what's dearest, eh? Eh? Not that'd you'd know," he said, sharply, to Pontifex. He leaned forward to whisper to Eiswolf. "No crown jewels, turns 'em jealous, proper old biddy, that one. What's that thing? Why is he wearing that necklace? Pontifex, you're getting very odd ideas about the acolytes, you know how Sculptor came to a bad end."

Pontifex and Eiswolf lifted the old man off his chair and, in a cavity beneath the seat, found the Manifest. Pontifex was still outwardly calm, but Eiswolf caught the glint in his eye and tightened lips. Even devotion to meditation and all that good stuff was no defence against life with Bibliotect. And as they both carefully put the old man back, Eiswolf saw something totally unexpected.

***

"So is that it?" said Perry, as they trotted away.

"Bought with my blood," said Eiswolf. "I'd rather fight a hundred battles."

Their trip out of Bladbean was faster, partly because they knew the way and partly because neither wished to stay longer than necessary in the land of the Neuts. For the sixth time, Eiswolf looked at the Manifest to see what all the fuss was about, but the language was incomprehensible. Nor was the Manifest a list; clumps of words were scattered all over the page. He put the leaf of vellum back inside his tunic.

Worst of all, now they were on another journey. Pontifex had broken the news that this Test was not over until they found the Enchanted One, deep in the Old Forest, who would set the Tests in order. Perry objected that this was not in the original brief, but Pontifex replied that this was how the game was played, so like it, squire, or lump it. Patience with their visitors was running low at the College, and their farm had just lost a sheep and two chickens to some animal in the night: they had other concerns.

That evening, as Perry lit a fire, Eiswolf played with the necklet.

"Do not, on your life, break that thing," said Perry. "Hell to pay if you do."

"What do you make of her?"

"Who her?"

"The Princess."

Perry unpacked the saddlebags. "Probably a spoilt brat. Foot."

Eiswolf stuck out his leg, so Perry could unlace the boot. "Been thinking and, well, I get a princess out of all this. But she only gets Me. So what does that …"

"Let's take this one adventure at a time. Other foot." Perry took off the boot.

"You know another really weird thing," Eiswolf lay down, wrapping himself in his cloak.

"What?"

"Some of them are women. The Neuts."

"What!"

"When we were lifting that old man. Pontifex slipped out. He made a boob. Ha-ha."

Perry shuddered. "No, don't want to think about that. Oof. All that meditation and study stuff? Do you think they really discover anything useful?"

Eiswolf stared at the sky. "I suspect they don't. Not enough energy there. Well, maybe the next Test will be more up my street, fighting has to come into it, surely?"

Finally overcome by sleep, he snored. Perry did not.

***

The King was in private conversation with the Hegemon. "This knight has begun to trouble me a little. My daughter tells me he's a werewolf. Hm?"

The Hegemon smothered his irritation. He did not like surprises, he did not like unknowns in the game, and he definitely did not like Black Al, the King's Champion, going off on his own finding contenders. But his job was the smooth running of the Court and that mean a relaxed King. "Your Majesty has no need to worry. The werewolf business is a myth, I'm sure the man puts the tale about to scare his opponents." He smiled, comfortingly.

"Hm. Odd, though, don't you think?" The King's vague eyes peered down into the Hegemon's unreadable face.

The small man blustered. "He's big, bold, fights a lot, blah di blah, absolutely from the pattern-book, just like the others, your Majesty. And they failed. All the sorceresses, dragons, mystical swords and Rings of Power, nobody's ever got past Test Four."

The King nodded sadly. "I'm sure you're right, Hegemon. But I would like to give the situation serious consideration. Whatever happens with this knight, we need to think forward to settle matters, just in case people Ask Questions or get Unhappy - or if I - if I were…" The King chuckled nervously. None of his forebears had passed their fiftieth birthday, one way or another. He was forty-nine.

"I will set my mind to this, Your Majesty. Please be assured, your reign will continue in glory for this Kingdom, and grow in renown to be the marvel of the world!"

That was more like it. The King smiled. His ultimate aim was to be known simply as The Great King. Or, failing that, the Very, Very Old King.

The Hegemon smiled, too, as he returned to his study. Actually, he did not have to think long at all about what would happen if the King should die. The Conclave would find their new King very quickly. Sitting in his study, at the top of the second-highest tower.

***

The Eternal Rose was also deep in scenario planning, in her dungeon.

"Shall we embroider a new banner for him?" said Iris, who had a romantic nature. "We could do a wolf with a rose in his mouth."

"Urk," said the Princess. "Bad enough to be slobbered over in real life without putting it on flags." Moodily, she moved a backgammon counter.

"We need to recognise his courage," said Chloe, today's opponent. "Looks kind of mean-spirited if we don't."

"How about a gilded muzzle," muttered the Princess. "He makes me feel scratchy just being around him. Ugh."

The girls exchanged glances. Dorcas came in. "My lady, he really looks the part when he's on that big black horse, and the people are happy. You know, that we still get the pick of the best heroes."

"I agree he'll make a fine corpse," said the Princess. "And if it's up to me, the sooner the better. She moved another counter. "I win."

"But that means another year," said Chloe. "And there's no guarantee - " She stopped, realising she had left herself no polite place to go.

The Princess laughed. "There's no guarantee a better one will turn up, or that he'll succeed, or that he'll marry me, or that I can provide an heir, or that the whole teetering mess does not collapse because our enemies invade." But she said that to herself, not her ladies.

She had worked that all out a long ago. Her ladies were the nearest she had to friends, but no Princess ever has a true friend, so she had not confided in them. And, over the years, as the parade of doomed knights went by, she began to design Plan A. But Plan A might not work.

Maybe it was time for Plan B.

"Look, if we didn't have these blessed Tests, who would you see as a contender?"

"But he has to pass the Tests," said Iris. "It's the Custom of the Kingdom."

"Customs can change," said the Princess, who was well versed in how and why the Tests had been created. "Girls, I need your imaginations. Dorcas, pin that piece of parchment up on that tapestry, maybe we can do a kind of map. Chloe, find the marking chalk. Well, if we write 'BATTLE' along the bottom, from bad to good, then 'JUDGEMENT' up the side, then Prince Adolf of Bechstein would be there, right? Hopeless loser and completely gaga. Hang on, not so fast, let's put him on another piece. Might be handy to have a manageable candidate. Right. What about Gregory of Petzold?"

***

Eiswolf could not put it off any more. He'd had a terrible night, and knew he had sleep-walked not once but three times, because Perry had woken him at the doorway of the hostel, then by an open window, and finally crammed into a corner of the room. Perry did not tell him about the three dead rats; his boss was no worse than usual, nobody was harmed, why disturb him?

The time had come to see Bess again. Eiswolf and Perry picked their way down the woodland track, their palace-bred horses not concerned in the slightest by any eldritch vibrations from the Good Witch. As ever, she knew they were coming. She met them a hundred paces from her hut.

"I could have told you," she said, before Eiswolf could even say hallo. "You should have asked me."

"What about?"

"Our bald friends. I know Pontifex quite well." Her stare challenged him.

"Can't I get off the horse first?" muttered Eiswolf.

"How you'll keep that thing fed, I don't know. Couldn't you have picked a practical one?"

She marched into the hut. Eiswolf dismounted and trailed behind her. Perry picked up Pepper's reins and hoped he would not be dragged into yet another domestic drama between Eiswolf and his foster-mother.

"So where now?" said Bess. "If you deign to tell me. If I'm important enough to know, this time."

"Don't go on at me, Bess."

"Well, don't treat me like a village idiot. Where are you going?"

"Um. I have to find the Enchanted One. In the Old Forest."

Bess frowned. "The Enchanted One what? Why?"

"Don't know. To put the Manifest in order." He shrugged. "Do you know about that?"

Bess stared up at her extraordinary - Boy. Stubborn, arrogant, overconfident. Although Eiswolf was a warrior who was head and shoulders taller than she, what she actually saw was the young lad who had arrived at her door years ago, beaten up because he was strange.

She flared up. "You're going into this blind? You fool! I taught you better than that!"

"I'm asking you, right? Do you know?"

Bess threw down a cup on the floor in sheer temper. "Who cares? This is lunatic, Eiswolf!"

"It's the Quest!" he yelled. "Can't I get it though your head, this is my Quest!"

"Don't yell at me, boy!"

"This is what I was made to do! I follow the Quest and I get…"

"I know! A princess and half a kingdom? It's just a story, Eiswolf! Nobody ever gets the Princess! Have you ever, ever heard of a knight winning a Quest? Have you? Name one."

They were shouting themselves to a standstill again.

"Then I will be first," he said.

"I need you - I need you to…" But she could not tell him why. He was not ready.

"Right. No answer. So pardon me if I follow my Call. With or without your help."

She put her hand on his arm. "Wait! The Quest isn't for real! It's silly and pointless, it's all lies!"

"So the King and the Princess and Kolras are all liars? And what about you? You're only not a liar because you won't tell me anything."

He was almost sneering. These days he was not so fearful of her. One day, he might not be afraid at all.

"That's not fair." Suddenly, unexpectedly, she felt a wound, heard a quaver in her voice. She turned away in case he saw her weakness.

"Fair. You expect me to be fair but you!" He strode angrily through the door.

"Take care!" she called after him. But his rapidly diminishing figure simply marched towards the large black horse.

And when he was out of sight, she allowed herself a sob.

***

The Hegemon finished reading the last tome on the Seven Tests. He sat back in his chair, satisfied.

Absolutely watertight. Old man Kolras had been a skilful writer and a better lawyer. In between all the heretofores and whereasmuches was a rock-solid, brassbound, impregnable box of puzzles. The twist of the Enchanted One was a case in point. Most kingdoms set Tests that show which man in armour is crudely powerful enough to hit other men in armour with big bits of metal harder than they hit him. But these Tests had style.

For example, if you ran the tests in the same order every time, then Knights Three or Four would not only know what they were well in advance, but might find ways to fix them. But if the tests were randomised? Now that was a touch of genius.

A soft knock at the chamber door disturbed his good mood. Damn, what had the King found to mess up now?

"Sir, you have a visitor," said the guard. "Marejah the fancy-baker."

His good temper returned. "Please send her in."

Marejah was a young woman, rounded and pretty, her black hair in ringlets under her clean white linen cap. She carried a large wicker basket over her arm, also covered in a white linen napkin, and she was smiling.

"My lord, how good to see you in health!"

"And I you, my dear. Please, let me help you, that must be heavy." He took the basket by the handle and lifted it on to a table.

Then, catching the half-smirk on the guard's face, he signalled to the man to close the door.

"My dear Marejah, it's been too long. Much too long."

She made such a picture in that plain stone room, her bright hair, her fresh complexion, the blue of her skirt, the softness of her bosom -

She almost giggled as she drew back the napkin over the basket. "Well, I have this new recipe, my lord, up from the coast, with cherries!"

"Cherries? Oh, you spoil me!"

"See? Under the almond paste, I knew you must try one at once!"

And, laughing innocently like schoolchildren, the Hegemon allowed Marejah to feed him a cake.

***

The King was meditating on the nature of heroes. On the whole, he didn't like them.

The knights who turned up for the Tests were typically big: some were battle-scarred brutes, some, mere ambitious boys. Most had been glory-seekers, but that was what knights were. One peasant had hoped to make a fairy-tale come true but Black Al got rid of him very quickly.

What they had not been, the King considered, was men who had the slightest idea of how to run a modern kingdom. Of diplomacy, negotiation, the ebb and flow of political power, they knew nothing. Couldn't negotiate their way out of a flour sack. None of them was a patch on -

Oh, dear. If only, if only. Why was life never simple?

How to find a man who was, how could one say, like the Hegemon, but - sexier.

The King had to admit that the Hegemon was grey. Weedy, really. Unfortunate voice. Not a lot of presence on the large stage, although effective enough in cabinet. Useless on a horse. He made a great Hegemon but as a king, no. The King sighed. No, he would not do.

Anyway, marrying him to the Princess was not a good idea. They might produce a child through an alchemy that the King did not want to consider too deeply, but once the baby was born, the Hegemon would be history. The King had few illusions about his daughter.

"She'd eat him alive," said the King to himself. So the Kingdom would lose a great servant, who might carry on for decades, for what? A flirtation with a circlet of gold. The King thought too much of his minister to do that to him.

Which left the werewolf.

Uneasy lies the head that wears the crown. The King muttered, sighed, and pulled out the tables of genealogy again. In among all these inbred, power-mad, over-muscled idiots, there had to be one half-decent candidate, surely?

***

The Old Forest was windless, quiet, dark even in an April noon, reminding Eiswolf strongly of Bess' place, actually. For that reason, he was not alarmed at all. He rode calmly between the massive oak trees. Perry was not so relaxed.

"So what do you have to do? Are you supposed to kill it? You don't know what an Enchanted One looks like."

"I'm sure there will be a Sign." Because if Eiswolf knew one thing about Enchantment, there would be Marks of the Chosen, who were Set Apart. Because there was not a whole lot of point if they weren't.

And he did see a Sign, as they rode further under the trees. "Look. Mistletoe."

"So what? There's loads in the orchards."

"Not on oak trees, Perry. This is special."

A white ribbon was tied to one of the bare oak branches. Eiswolf spotted another, then another. "Wishes," he said. He rode towards a large tree whose lower branches fluttered with ribbons.

Perry hung back. "Any clues?"

"Follow the trees."

The festoons of white led them through the wood up the side of a hill, to a clearing of scrubby grassland.

"Nothing here," said Perry.

"Yes, there is. Look." Eiswolf pointed to the centre, where twisted bushes grew between large rocks. In the middle stood a small, lopsided apple tree, still holding a few wrinkled yellow fruit from the previous autumn.

Perry cantered towards the tree, then stopped dead. That was not a natural arrangement. The stones formed a rough chamber: three large flat slabs as walls, a capstone over the top. He turned and galloped back, pale and scared. "Fairies. Let's get out of here."

"I think that might upset our host."

Perry turned his horse, and saw a tall, slender figure beyond the stones, a man in a black hooded robe, whose face could not be seen.

Eiswolf rode towards the man, then dismounted and bowed. "My Lord."

Perry gasped: now he could see the stranger was unnaturally tall.

"Welcome, Sir Knight." The man's voice was clear, and rang through the cold air.

Eiswolf made his speech. "I bring greetings from the King. I am Sir Eiswolf. I have come for the Enchanted One, in pursuit of my Quest to pass the Seven Tests of Kolras."

"As have many brave knights before you. By what right do you claim the One?"

Eiswolf knew this was a trick question. The hair on his back hackled, for this was no ordinary man. A strange, almost metallic odour hung in the air. This was, as Perry said, a place of Faery power. Fairies were notorious for playing games with humans, as cats toy with a mouse. Go carefully.

"I do not make a claim in the name of the King, for human kings have no dominion here. I do not claim at the point of my sword, for I know you do not fear the weapons of men. I do not claim in the name of the Tests, for these may have no meaning to you."

"Indeed not," said the man. "The matters of your kingdom are of no concern to us."

So what did fairies value? Gold, because they buried pots of coins in odd places. They stole children, bewitched travellers, called up storms, spread disease if you slighted them, in fact, you should always pay your respects in strange places –

Respect.

"Forgive me, I do not claim the One at all, my lord, for this does not belong to me. "

"Better," said the man.

"I request, with the greatest humility, to become its guardian for a while. I pledge to protect the One and return it safely to your care. And whatever else you desire of me, I offer freely."

"Anything? That's a bold offer, Sir Knight. What if I want your head?"

Eiswolf swallowed hard. "I know that the nobility of your race will protect me from harm."

The man stood motionless for a minute, then laughed. "Sir Knight, Eiswolf, is it? You should be called Felix. Or Scelus. I shall give you two gifts. You shall have your Enchanted One. Come forward, Sir Knight, for your other gift."

So Eiswolf took a couple of steps towards him.

"Closer, man, I won't bite."

Eiswolf came within touching distance. The man held out his long, slender, ivory hand and tapped Eiswolf on the forehead. "I give you the gift of seeing who you are. That's more valuable than some people think."

"Thank you, my lord." Eiswolf bowed. Now for the fast get-away with the Enchanted whatsit. "But where …"

He straightened up. The man had vanished. On the grass where he had been, was a small black box with a golden padlock.

That, it would appear, was that.

***

On the way back to the Palace, Eiswolf and Perry found a nice, noisy, smelly, busy, extremely human tavern, to wash the forest out of their systems with plenty of ale.

"So how did you get it?" said Perry. The black box sat on the table in front of them.

"I asked nicely." But Eiswolf could still feel where that ivory hand had tapped him between the eyes. He shivered.

Perry prodded the box. "I vote we take a look at our Enchanted One,"

"Might be dangerous. What if it's a demon?"

"You ought to know in case the Hegemon tries to pull a fast one."

Which was true. So Perry picked the golden lock with his penknife. Very carefully they opened the box to find -

"A toad," said Eiswolf. "Maybe it's eaten the enchanted cricket or whatever." He shook the box gently, but the only contents were a pad of moss and a very dopey, semi-hibernating toad.

"Sounds like it's a very dangerous toad," said Perry. "Don't upset it. Sorcery and stuff." In his defence, Perry was on his fourth mug of strong ale.

Eiswolf looked at the toad. The toad stared back. "No, don't think so. Just a toad."

The toad woke a little more, swallowed, and croaked. Eiswolf took a small horn cup of water and sprinkled some over the creature.

"Well, toad, here's where our adventure really starts," he said. "I wonder what Conclave will do with you."

That night, he had one of his dreams of black sky, and sharp stars, and ice: the sort of nightmare where you cannot wake up, no matter how much you shout. Eventually Perry punched him hard enough to get through, but he was shivering and wringing with sweat, and had no more sleep.

***

In his Black Tower, word came to the Glimmer Lord. The Enchanted One had been brought to Conclave. Soon the next Quest would be decided.

Matters were trotting along pretty fast. Bess seemed to have chosen her creature well.

This was annoying. If her Hero gained a Princess and half of a reasonably wealthy kingdom, Bess would have the resources to become a nuisance. So the Glimmer Lord set his mind to the problem.

How could he turn this creature to his own account? What would this Eiswolf want? What gift could he give, which would hook him into this man's soul?

***

The trumpets sounded the fanfare. The Hegemon, the Princess, the King, and all the ladies in waiting and gentlemen of the bed chamber crowded into the Great Hall, a glittering scene.

"Good people!" cried the Hegemon. "Welcome our hero who brings the Manifest and the Enchanted One! In public, so that none may doubt us, show them forth!"

Eiswolf waved the sheet of vellum. "The Manifest, sir!"

"Sir Knight, place it on this table. You, squire, bring forth the One!"

And so, to a confused murmur of "Oh, a frog! No, a toad, isn't it? No, a frog, honestly, any idiot can tell the difference, no warts." (courtiers are town people, unfamiliar with natural history) Perry tipped the toad, now named Albert, onto the table.

The Hegemon announced, "Place the bowl of paint. Squire, can you get the thing…"

"He's called Albert."

"I don't care if it's called Persephone, get it to walk through the paint."

So Albert paddled through some blue water-paint, then over the vellum. As each blue foot touched a piece of writing, one lawyer from Conclave wrote the phrase down in order, and another made a fair copy.

"We have our Quests!" cried the Hegemon.

Eiswolf frowned. "But I still can't read what they say."

"Sir Knight, your second Quest is to travel to the land of the Dark Sorceress, for only she has knowledge of all languages."

Eiswolf had no chance to say any more, because the court went into full celebratory feast mode. Perry rescued poor Albert to wash his feet: a small boy in the Palace stables had agreed to be a toad-sitter.

Eiswolf spotted the self-satisfied expression on the Hegemon's face. Fit-up. Eiswolf knew this in his bones. Well, maybe they were all in for a surprise, this time.

3: The Eternal Rose

In her dungeon, the Princess glowered. Werewolf or no werewolf, the Tests of Kolras had outlasted their usefulness.

For nine years the Princess had waited. Her world had changed the day the Prince was kidnapped: suddenly, she had become the key to the Kingdom. And now, with the damned Tests of Kolras not working, surely she should have some sort of say in what happened next? But the flurry of parchments pinned to the tapestry displayed how difficult the next step would be.

One list ranked princes by ability, one by wealth, and one by general diplomatic usefulness. Needless to say, they did not match. Plan B was a tough nut to crack.

Elite warriors might be problematic. Take Eugene of Bezier. Top three tourney knight, but a fearsome temper and a habit of killing squires, lovers or indeed anyone who stood on his toe. Sons of emperors were out: imperial courts were swamped with ambitious families trying to get their princess in line. The Kingdom, although rich, was not in that league.

The Kingdom did have one prize: the great port of Cymenshore was dripping with wealth, a tasty morsel for any ruler. As a result, the town was in permanent danger of attack; the last pirate raid had been eight years ago, a nasty business with a thousand casualties. But the pirates were defeated, trade resumed quickly and the wharves and warehouses were replaced within a year.

Plenty of kingdoms were eager to acquire Cymenshore by a cheap, low-impact marriage rather than a difficult and expensive war. In theory, because the port was a palatinate (it had a high degree of self-government), change of ownership had to be cleared with the local noble family, the Vendants, who would take a new oath of fealty. But the last Count died a while ago and the other Vendants were lost in the raid. A council currently ruled the town. The situation was a little untidy, but that was not a deal-breaker.

The Princess went through options. "Hamo, Indlett of Deepheim, Ebrein of Rossendale. Hamo's in talks with the Blankenfeldts, Indlett is thirteen and Ebrein is on his fourth wife. Not exactly a splendiferous array."

But marriage was the only way she could access power.

Dammit, that's what Plan A had been designed to do! She really would have to track down what had gone wrong there.

The problem was that Plan B needed a candidate who was both politically acceptable and who did not make a habit of executing, murdering or otherwise disposing of his queens. Or at least, not before she got at him first.

After all, Daddy had killed Mummy.

***

The Hegemon sat at the great table in the King's Chamber, in a modest position between the King's Attorney and Baron Venmoor. Not at its head. The Chamber was in session.

But he could have sat on a stool by the fireplace, and everyone would still have known he was in charge. He did not go messing around with battles and swords and armies, because he did not have to. His public persona combined anonymity with hidden power: as if all he had to do was snap his fingers, and his enemy would be borne off by brutal soldiers to unknowable torments in a deep-buried dungeon (which was approximately true. He had working arrangements with the King's Champion, Black Al, and Walbrect, the King's jailer).

Although born a commoner, the Hegemon had risen further than any in the Kingdom. As negotiator, conciliator, he was the trusted intermediary whose primary concern, everyone agreed, was the welfare of the Kingdom.

But that was as far as he could go, because as a commoner, he could get no further. Even if the King made him a baron, he would be no nearer the throne, because hereditary nobles took precedence. That had also been one of Kolras' ideas, to prevent foolish kings bypassing his painfully negotiated aristocratic power-system.

Unless, somehow, the Hegemon married the Princess.

Which was so sensible! The King would get a safe, secure succession. And the Princess would get a husband who truly respected her, who worshipped the ground she trod, who had never seen a more perfect, lovelier, more angelic creature -

Who would definitely not kill her. That had to be a major point in his favour, surely? The only action of the King's Chamber that haunted him was the last Queen's trial for treason. He still saw the woman's desperate white face as she fell on her knees stretching her hands out to men who had once been her friends. None aided her. They could not, because she was guilty, her lover had confessed; the barons who had sent armies to overthrow the King were all imprisoned. The King had wept and the Hegemon tried desperately to think of a punishment that would be less - final. But the needs of the Kingdom came first.

And the Princess, then a girl of twelve, had to be a witness, to show that she supported the rule of law.

But no more of that. If he were to marry the Eternal Rose, she would be safe for all time. Her royal blood trumped any succession going through the barons. He would rule with justice and precision, she would be the glowing heart of the people's devotion. And if he became King, what reforms! What modernisation, what development, what improvement. And he'd get to have sex with a proper Princess.

"Hegemon, your thoughts?" The King's Attorney was polite but the Hegemon recognized the wounded-sheep bleat in his voice. An unhappy man.

"My lords, it benefits no-one to be precipitate," he said.

The Earl of Whitfall frowned. "But this matter has been judged in Session and in Camera already. This appeal is simply wasting more time."

Now for a little wheeze. Nobody ever loses friends by suggesting that a problem is so weighty, more time is needed for consideration. Especially if you co-opt any objector onto a high-powered committee.

"My Lord Whitfall, naturally I - meaning, the King's Chamber - would wish that this should be addressed in full. If I may suggest that, as one with such deep experience, you bring this matter to a session of the Private Cabinet, so that these issues can be aired properly?'

Whitfall, as a relatively junior earl, was not entitled to address the Private Cabinet. If he impressed, maybe he could be elevated to membership.

Bull's-eye. The Hegemon watched the man flush slightly. Really like falling off a log. Odd how easier these things get, the higher up you go. He presumed that at some point, he'd have to find out what they were supposed to discuss. But most things were not that urgent. Certainly not compared to the future of the Princess and the Kingdom.

As long as that hairy brute with the sword did not get in the way.

The Hegemon snorted. The Quests would sort him out. And if they did not? He smiled, thinly. He would rescue his Princess from this Eiswolf.

Who was a wholly unsuitable candidate as King, anyway.

Having squared his patriotic, romantic and sexual duties, the Hegemon hummed to himself as he went to prepare for the Private Cabinet meeting, to flatter Lord Whitfall.

***

The time for wine had arrived. This was a time when women talk about men.

"Well, what about Indlett?"

The Princess almost yelled. "He's a kid, Chloe! How am I supposed to get pregnant? No, don't even suggest that!" She could see that Chloe was thinking about the 'discreet good friend' option. The one that had got her mother executed. "All right, think outside the box."

"What box?" Iris was a literal girl.

"The box we've created!" But Iris looked even more confused, so the Princess changed tack. "These princes all have problems. I know you like Roland of Gretsch, Chloe, but he landed on his head in his last tourney and he hasn't been the same since. What if we think beyond the nobility?"

This did not go down well: the girls squealed and shuddered.

"Urk," said Dorcas. "You mean, a commoner? Gross."

"We have precedents," said the Princess, who had done her research. "The Whitfalls trace back to a merchant tailor. The Earls of Passfield were horse-breeders."

"Yes, but they're not very noble," said Chloe. "And they're certainly not royal."

"But for a man of true ability…" said the Princess.

"Like who?" said Dorcas. "You mean, like, clever?" Her voice held all the suspicion of 'cleverness' that is the aristocratic birthright.

The girls exchanged glances, and shrugged. "Nobody comes to mind," said Chloe.

"The cleverest man in the Kingdom is the Hegemon," said Iris. "Everyone says so."

The girls all stared at her. So did the Princess. It was her turn to shudder. "Are you serious? That runty little squirt? I'd be the laughing stock of the realms! "

"But, my Lady, if there's only a choice between the Hegemon and the Knight of the Wolf?"

The Princessing lark, the Princess mused, was definitely not all it was cracked up to be.

***

Bess was in her usual position on the track to the hovel. The riders raised their right hands. As if she could not already see who they were, by that ludicrously big black horse and the underpowered brown mare. They had come about the next Quest. Perhaps Eiswolf had learned his lesson at last.

"Hallo, Bess. Um."

"You came to ask me what I know." She tried not to sound too annoyed, but could not stop herself. "Not the pleasure of my company."

"Don't be like that, Bess."

Eiswolf dismounted. He looked tired. A rough night. Or more likely, an evening of rough drinking and rougher women. That's what these idiot heroes were supposed to do, carouse.

In the dim hovel by the light of her modest fire, she poured them weak ale and gave them fresh flatbread.

"How are you, then?" said Eiswolf.

"Waiting for you to ask about the Dark Sorceress," said Bess.

Eiswolf very nearly sighed, biting his lip hard. "You're well-informed," he said, instead.

Bess was still annoyed. "You've been back over a week. I know."

Perry chipped in. "We had to wait for just before the Full Moon, apparently."

"But now we're clear to go," said Eiswolf. "Happy now?"

He had not had a lot of sleep, and his patience was wearing thin.

She still wished he would give up the Quest. But, under the insane rules of the Kingdom, he had started, so he had to finish or die in the attempt. And at least she could still influence him, look for the moment to suggest that, as well as winning his princess, he could do something for her. She poked the fire. "So now it's Dark Sorceresses? Why her, why Jocasta?"

Eiswolf almost snapped at her. "Bess, the Quest fails here and now if I can't get a translation of the Manifest, and they get to hunt me down and kill me like vermin!" He stared at her, then his eyes narrowed. "So any pointers, which will probably save my life, would be very helpful." Then he paused. "Jocasta? You know her, too? By name? Is she dangerous?"

Bess shrugged. "She's batty. But that's what you get when you rely on the left-hand path. Which tends to let you down when you need it most." She could not stop herself. "Like men."

Bess was in one of her moods. Eiswolf regrouped. "They say she has the gift of tongues. She's supposed to talk to birds and beasts."

Bess snorted a laugh. "Any fool can talk to the beasts. Old Barmy Brian down the village talks to birds and sheep. And logs and carts and gates. Don't make him a sorcerer. It's not the talking, it's when they start answering back you need to worry. Especially if no-one else can hear."

"So she's mad?" said Perry.

"As a March hare."

Eiswolf tried one last time. "Is there anything useful you can tell me?"

Bess gave in. "She's got a nice little earner with the prophecies, so cross her palm with silver. Actually, gold is better. She's out of her skull on weird potions a lot of the time, so don't expect a straight answer, but she only lives by the clemency of the King, so if she gets arsy, remind her about that."

"Anything else?"

She's a mixed-race ethnobotanist and biochemist from Miami? A wild-child hippy chick? None of the words had any meaning in this world. Bess shrugged again.

"Not that would help."

Perry declared that he would hit the hay, and went out to the shelter where they had tethered the horses. The shadow was darker in Eiswolf's face, and Bess forgot her irritation long enough to worry about her boy.

"I've got mead," said Bess. "A cup to help you sleep?"

Eiswolf sipped the strong wine, staring into the glowing embers. Then, after a few minutes, he spoke. "It's the dreams."

"Oh? I thought you'd got rid of those."

"They've come back. The snow, a black sky, a sharp wind. And I feel different." He squinted into the wine. "I feel strong and alive but like I'm pulled apart, I get so hungry, but not for food and I -" He started to sweat. "I have to kill…"

"In a dream, boy. Only a dream." She refilled his cup.

"But it feels - You know when I'm fighting - I know the way people look at me, like they see something terrible, even Perry, but to me it's just grey fog - I become what I am in the dream, don't I? I'm a wolf. A wolf, right?"

He raised his gaze to her face, sharp and deep. A golden light flickered in his eyes. Or reflected flames?

She looked away. "You have a condition. It's like the falling sickness, you know that."

"At the stone chapel, the Faery Knight said I would see what I really am." He took her arm. "Is that a wolf?"

She could not tell him. "No," she said. "Just a dream."

"Damn you!" he yelled. He threw the wine in the fire. He stood, tall and threatening in the darkness. She knew he wanted his sword, the one she had hidden as he came into the hovel. "Don't lie to me! You know! Why won't you tell me!"

"Eiswolf! You are set apart! You have power inside you. Ignore the dreams."

But he was desperate. "Bess! You don't know how I feel, it's all wrong! How can I be a hero! This isn't clean!"

What could she say? What did he expect, power never is? Heroes are measured by what they go through as well as what they win? That no real-life hero has clean hands?.

He went out into the night, as he always had, to wander under the cold white stars and breathe the sharp north wind, his place, his birthright, his solace. The place of a wolf.

***

Dawn came damp and grey to the hovel.

"Does he love her?" said Bess. This seemed an odd way to say 'good morning' and Perry was not prepared.

"Who?" said Perry.

"The Princess. Love at first sight, like the stories say?"

The witch was stoking a fire, heating the breakfast pottage to the boil. She did not raise her eyes from the cauldron, and her voice was carefully controlled.

Perry hid behind his bannock for a second or two. "Well, he's seen her."

"So have I, Perry, I know what she looks like. But is there any evidence of romance?"

Well, no. Apart from what Eiswolf reported as a perfunctory explanation by the Hegemon of the relationship between kingship, marriage, power and the Quests, nobody appeared to have mentioned love. Eiswolf knew no more about his future wife than he could see. The Princess had barely exchanged fifty words with her Knight.

"The Princess seemed to be looking him over," said Perry. "I mean, at court. And she did send him the favour, the necklace."

"And did he 'look her over', as you so delicately put it?"

"Well…" Actually, not in any serious fashion. "Well, he said she's pretty. And a natural blonde!" Perry perked up.

"But no lightning bolts or rainbows?"

Perry shook his head.

Bess was genuinely puzzled. The Princess seemed to be just a concept to Eiswolf, rather than flesh and blood. Did he want power? Or just to spite Bess by ignoring her mission in favour of his own Quest?

Or sex? "And has he no other fancy at the moment?"

Perry almost blushed. "I don't get involved in any of that, Bess. He can look after his own needs. You know, me and my, um…"

"Problem," said Bess. "No, I don't suppose he needs a pimp. Even one like you."

Perry did blush this time.

Bess took pity. "That sounded much worse than I meant. I was going to say, with your, um, disability."

"No, he doesn't." Perry was now bright red.

Bess laughed. "You are such a prude, Squire Perry. Well, someone's got to rouse our mighty knight and potential stallion from his slumbers. That snoring's new? Maybe a deviated septum. Has he broken his nose recently?"

Perry ran to where Eiswolf was indeed driving the pigs home to market. The conversation had been uncomfortable. Because if Eiswolf did succeed, and become king and marry and all that, what would become of Perry? Usually, squires were younger sons of the gentry on the way to full-fledged knighthood, but Perry was different. His disability, as Bess put it, debarred him from knighthood and there were few openings for a squire of his advancing years. But if Eiswolf did not succeed -

The future was unknowable. He stood over his master and, not thinking, shook him by the shoulder. Eiswolf lashed out, and the next few minutes were an unequal hand-to-hand scrap until Eiswolf woke up enough to realize that the squawking thing was Perry.

Outside, Bess stirred the pottage. So, not love. And if Eiswolf did try to find love again he would be…Miserable. Betrayed. Just like before. Bess could see no good future for her boy in the embers of her fire, in love or fortune.

But that was irrelevant now.

***

The Glimmer Lord had his reports from the Palace..

"Madame has no great liking for her pet wolf, it seems," he said to Mirak. "Not that God Almighty would be good enough for that girl, I fear Eiswolf is in for a chilly marriage bed, if he ever gets that far."

"According to my sources, he has been seen with women of the town," said Mirak. "But no sweetheart, all the girls he knew seem to have married or gone away."

The Glimmer Lord chuckled. "Ah, dear lad, you must learn to read between lines. Now, I see a man who sought love but was disappointed. Unsurprisingly, many families are not happy to have a werewolf as a son-in-law."

And that gave him a really good idea.

"Mirak, my boy, the tradition of your people, the dancing and so forth. Can you show me?"

"It's much better with costumes." But Mirak put on a little display anyway. "This is the Crane-dance. And this is the Hawk. And this is the Flight of Butterflies."

"And how quickly could you teach these dances to another, say, a girl?"

Mirak simply scowled. But the Glimmer Lord smiled.

4: The Dark Sorceress

The crowd outside the Palace was marginally smaller as the brave knight and his trusty squire set out again, etcetera etcetera. A few declared that they weren't breaking off from work to watch any more departures unless 'something interesting happened'. Also, the Dark Sorceress was not much of a draw: she lived about two days' journey away so the Quest had little mystery.

The Princess and her ladies waved from their tower. Eiswolf waved back. Then the town, and the Palace, returned to their daily occupations.

Did no-one think to follow the brave knight? Did no half-grown lad or servant girl, seized with a spirit of adventure, try to join them? Did no guard or Baron want to keep tabs on Eiswolf, as this affected the royal succession, possibly creating the opportunity for a Palace coup or a military overthrow? Did no-one plan an assassination, from the Hegemon down to the landlord of the tavern where Perry had passed a counterfeit coin?

Well, the crowd was right in one way. Nothing would really change until Eiswolf fulfilled the Quests, because otherwise this was still situation normal. Yes, in previous years, the lads and spirited girls, spies, assassins and rogue barons had tried various romantic and daring exploits with the eleven previous knights. Teenagers, guards and assassins were usually buried in the people's cemetery by the southern gate, assuming there was enough left to find and bury, and the barons were in the aristocratic necropolis by the north entrance. The Hegemon ran a tight ship.

**

The Forest of the Dark Sorceress lay deep and silent. Ivy smothered the trunks of the trees: a faint miasma from the foliage of the yews sank down on the riders beneath. No birds sang in those black glades: no sun penetrated to the damp, dank moss of the path. Daylight itself seemed scared to enter, fearful of a trap in the twisted, ancient branches and contorted roots. As if to create a suitably respectful atmosphere, every now and again along the path there was a post with an animal skull fixed on top: bear, stag, badger.

"So did she kill them?" said Perry. "How could she kill a bear?"

"Maybe she didn't," said Eiswolf. "Maybe they're sacrifices. The landlord at the last place said she likes to be paid her tribute."

They trotted on, until Perry noticed a change in the skulls. "That's a horse, boss."

They stopped to look more closely.

"Sure it isn't a donkey?"

"Nope, definitely a horse. Look, Corsa won't go near." The little mare was spooked, without question. Pepper, the big destrier, whinnied but stood his ground.

Eiswolf dismounted and went to investigate. He examined the skull, now naked and bleached; the remains of a fine bridle clung to the bone. A war-horse. "It smells quite fresh. See the marks on the pole?"

Perry nodded. "If it's kind of runes, like cuts along the edge, they're like letters, I can read some. Um. Pray. Brave. Knight. Gift. Hell. So where's the knight?"

Eiswolf swept away the leaves at the base of the pole with his boot. "Well, the good news is, I've found him. The bad news is …"

The pole had been driven into the ground through a human skull. Eiswolf could see by the way the bone had broken that the knight had been alive at the time.

Beyond were two more horse-head totems. The skulls were more recent. Eiswolf looked about and caught the glint of more white bone through the wood. "How many knights have come this way?"

"No-one knows, boss. Are you sure she's the only one who can help?" Perry tried not to let his voice quaver, and failed.

"So they tell me." Eiswolf remounted and they picked their way down the darkening path.

"Eight so far," said Perry, when they halted again. "You sure you want to go on, boss? Eight men down."

He said this, not because he was a coward, or to cast doubt on Eiswolf's courage, or unsettle the knight. His duty as a squire was to alert his knight to all factors, in case he had not spotted them, or chose to ignore them for foolish reasons, like pride. Eiswolf and Perry were still alive after years of questing because of the way Eiswolf, with Perry's assistance, calculated the odds in each situation. There are old knights, and bold knights …

Any idiot can charge into a sorceress' den, yelling and waving a sword. Walking out again without a decorative pole through your forehead is the hard part.

They stopped where the path fell away into a ravine, crossed by a single rickety wood and rope bridge. The horses would need careful leading: there was no other path. Difficult to cross, impossible to retreat over at any speed. A perfect trap.

"On we go," said Eiswolf. "So far, this is all a tale to frighten kiddies."

"Apart from the corpses," Perry pointed out. "If she's that deadly…"

"If she's what killed them. Maybe they were unconscious already, there's lots of ways to get knocked out."

And the other reason Eiswolf still survived was that he did not always believe his eyes. Eiswolf had met many women, some of whom claimed to be sorceresses, but had yet to meet one who could single-handedly overpower a mounted, armoured knight by strength. Not to say that she could not exist: but so far, he had not met her. The knights might have been overcome by poison, or sickness, or ambush, or distracted by the stage-managed uncanniness of the place long enough to be the target for a well-placed arrow.

When he and Perry got back to the tavern afterwards, the tale would be all about how Eiswolf bravely charged over the bridge without regard and conquered the black-hearted witch by his might. But then, who could contradict them?

To make sure they got back 'when' and not 'if', Eiswolf checked the bridge before setting foot on it. The ropes were old but thick, with no signs of the crude booby-traps that villages used to defend themselves. The ravine below was deep and rocky but not covered in sharpened stakes.

"We can cross," then he waved at the squire to go first, with Corsa. That might seem harsh, but squires were there to protect their knight, not the other way around. Perry, sweating, led Corsa carefully over the planks to the far bank. She was not much happier, being a mare who liked solid ground under her hooves. Then Eiswolf started to lead Pepper, leaving as much room as he could between himself and the heavy war-horse: Pepper was replaceable so if the bridge did give way under his weight, Eiswolf did not want to be near.

At the middle of the bridge, a flash caught Pepper's eye on the far bank. He stopped and snorted, then whinnied.

"Great," muttered Eiswolf. "Come on, you stupid bastard. Easy, now."

But Pepper's eyes rolled up, showing the whites. He started to paw the bridge. The planks shuddered.

"Perry, can you see what spooked him." Eiswolf spoke in a very calm tone of voice.

Perry tied the shivering Corsa to a tree. "Just more path, boss. More skulls, too."

"Right." Eiswolf could not leave the horse. If Pepper bolted once off the rein, Eiswolf might be taken out too. They could stand still until Pepper calmed down, but as the bridge moved, the horse was more frightened by the second.

"Boss, I'll come and hold Pepper while you get off. I'm lighter than you."

"Not if we're both on the bridge together. Nice try, you don't die a hero today."

Something moved in the wood on the other side. Eiswolf caught a glimpse, almost a glitter, among the black glades. Bigger than a fox but not as big as a stag. The gait was not a deer's, either, but he could not catch a scent.

"We might have company, Perry. Quiet, Pepper, quiet there. Behind you, about fifty paces, off the path, my left."

Now Pepper neighed and threw up his head. Thick white sweat foamed on his flanks and he chewed his bit.

Perry ran down the path and saw colour. Not black or green. Or ivy, or yew, or root, or trunk, a golden flash. Which vanished.

He raced back to the bridge. "Not a soldier, no idea, gone. "

Corsa whinnied as Perry came back towards her. And then, Pepper whinnied in response. The mare snuffled, reaching out her long head towards the bridge and the horse. He shook his mane.

"Good," said Eiswolf. "Perry, bring Corsa to the end of the bridge. Gently now, my man." He pulled on the rein. Slowly Pepper took a step towards the mare, then another, until Eiswolf eased him off the planks. On firm ground, Pepper and Corsa sniffed each other's muzzles, then Corsa chewed Pepper's mane.

"Must be love," said Perry. "But I thought he was a gelding?"

"She doesn't care. That's friendship," said Eiswolf. "Be grateful."

Then he mounted and they continued along the death-strewn path into the night.

***

As she stared up at the curtains around her bed, it struck the Princess that if she did not want Plan C (for Cringe-making), where Wolfie-thingy won, C would have to be superseded pretty damn fast by Plan D, especially if Plan B, for Backtrack, had really been knocked out of court.

The King had not been happy with her list of candidates.

"My dear, I appreciate all the work that went into this but, well, none of this has any relevance during the Quest. I can't go against the Tests of Kolras, the people expect us to follow the rules. If we don't, who will?"

"But, Daddy, the Tests have to end eventually! How much better to have an idea of who we really want for the job?" She almost pleaded.

She reminded the King uncomfortably of her mother. He coughed gruffly and looked away. "The people would have to be prepared. I'll consult the Chamber. You need not worry. Go and play delightful games with your ladies, my Rose."

He might have got away with that when she was fifteen and green, she muttered to herself, but not at age twenty-four and eleven knights down.

She had not always been so cool about the Quests. The first two knights had been handsome Errol and bold Walther. She had fallen in love with each. And when they died, she wept for months, blamed herself, then her father, then Kolras for making the Tests so difficult, then herself again. Next came burly, smelly Tomas of Waldstein, who slobbered over her and called her 'little girl'. She had been profoundly grateful when news of his death came through.

That was when the penny dropped. The knights were similar in some regards; ambitious, bold, brave or foolhardy, and usually rather arrogant. But in all other respects, they were random. Anything might turn up. And in Eiswolf, anything had.

Her mouth pursed. Plan C was just not acceptable. If Daddy would not be sensible, then she had to have a plan D. For Death. She stared into the dark folds of the curtains for inspiration.

***

"I want you to keep an eye out." The Hegemon pushed the bag of silver coins across the candle-lit tavern table. "And an ear to the ground. That's all. The King's Champion here tells me you're reliable, that's why we're talking."

The man on the other side of the table, tanned and lined, appraised the Hegemon with sea-bright eyes. "So what's the poor bastard done to you?"

"Now, Izak, none of that," Black Al came into the conversation. "You take your money, no questions, you know that."

The tavern stood out by the western gate, a filthy, smelly, ill-lit place where dark deeds were planned and dirty business arranged. Every town needs at least one. This was a main recruiting station for Black Al, a natural choice when the Hegemon needed to find an operative. As was, seeing that he was in town, Izak.

Izak was an independent trader with an expert group of support staff and international connections. Or, to be brutally plain, a pirate. He was shore-bound until the harbour-master down at Skralingshaven, a small boat-yard and lay-up dock, decided that his credit was good for the repairs on his ship. The Hegemon's bag of silver could go a long way.

"So he's a hero? I hear he's more than that." Pirates like Izak succeed because they listen to gossip that others dismiss.

"What have you heard?" said Black Al, calmly.

"He's a werewolf."

"And what difference will that make?" Black Al smiled condescendingly.

The pirate grinned. "None at all, but I'll need silver to make a blade."

"But I don't want you to kill him," said the Hegemon. "I simply want a report on what the Wolf is doing."

"Really," said Izak. "So why the interest? You in love, then?"

Black Al brought a heavy fist down on the table. "None of your business. Can you do it?"

Izak shrugged, and drank his ale. "Yes, why not, no problem. What if he turns wolf on me?"

"He won't," said the Hegemon. Because that was what he firmly believed. A romantic tale had been embroidered over the years, but Eiswolf was no more and no less than a man.

The pirate laughed, this time. "You been at long at sea as I have, my lord," his sarcasm was acid, "you learn not to dismiss these things so lightly. I'll take your silver. I'll turn some to a blade. If he comes after me man-like, then I hear what you say. But if he comes wolf-like," he drew a finger across his throat. "Only one way for that kind, my lord, money or no money. Deal?"

"Deal." Black Al shook his hand quickly, before the Hegemon could add any lawyers' conditions as he had with two previous contenders, who had then declined the job. The Hegemon glanced at the Champion, annoyed, but he nodded. Izak grabbed up his money and left.

"He's right in one way," said Black Al. "Might be simpler just to kill him, that forest is nice and quiet. Not many go there and fewer come back, as the old tales say."

"No, he has to be seen to fail in such a way that I can discredit the whole organisational apparatus." Black Al appeared to be listening, but his eyes were glazed and the Hegemon knew the soldier was not up to his complex politico-strategic approach. "It's about restructuring the system." No, still too many long words. "Assassination is not - The King would be very displeased."

The Hegemon knew that if he were to be heir presumptive and engaged to the Princess, being a mere commoner who murdered his way there was a bad idea. He would not be legitimate, and the barons might get ideas. He tried again. "The Conclave has to agree, you see."

"Oh, I leave all that office stuff to you," said Black Al. "You've got the patience. Got to see a man about a horse." He winked, obscenely, at the Hegemon. "You want a guard to walk you home?"

"No, thank you," said the Hegemon, through tight lips. "I am quite competent - " but he talked to the Champion's shadow.

One day, thought the Hegemon, I will take that ignorant, crude, inept… He felt a sharp blow on his head.

"Sorry, mate. Didn't see you." The militiaman stared down at the Hegemon, disdain as plain as if it was written on his forehead. Other men started to stare. The protection from Black Al, a man they knew and respected, was gone, leaving the Hegemon, whom they did not know, alone in a very hostile place.

"Fine," said the Hegemon. "Just leaving."

"Oops," said the militiaman, and tipped a slug of ale on the Hegemon's sleeve. The small man stood up and pushed his way out of the tavern, then drew his cloak about him. A clear night. Perhaps Marejah the baker would be home?

***

Sleeping under the stars is all very well, in a place you know with a nice campfire and a decent tent when rains. Anything else is a recipe for rheumatism, paranoid dreams and a tendency to wake suddenly because something has just screamed. Perry would have traded any amount of manly bonhomie under Night's starry cloak for a decent, dry, mattress. As soon as he saw a glow of dawn, he got up to sort the packs for the horses, because the sooner he started, the sooner they could get out of there.

Eiswolf snored. While that was better than his yelping, thrashing nightmares, every snort raked down Perry's nerves like chalk on a blackboard.

And that was another thing. Squires and knights, for practical reasons, travelled very closely together. Perry was quite sure that if he snored as voluminously as Eiswolf had started to do, his knight would give him his marching orders. How was anyone supposed to get any sleep at all? He tightened Corsa's girth a little enthusiastically, and the mare squealed.

Eiswolf muttered and spluttered, then finally woke. "Any chance of a fire? I suppose I should shave before we meet this witch."

Perry darted a glance of pure, dark evil. Internally, the conversation was on the lines of "Fire? He wants a bloody fire? What does he think I am, Fifi the Fire Fairy? Why can't he get his own bloody fire, but no, he's too grand to go and collect a few sticks and remember where we put the flint and she won't notice if he's shaved or comes ready-stuffed with sage and onion, who the Hell cares?" A sleep-deprived Perry was a savage and unforgiving creature.

"Tell you what, I'll get the water, the stream where I took the horses last night." Eiswolf got up and grabbed a leather flask from Corsa's pack. "Do we have enough kindling? I saw dry moss down there."

And that, Perry sighed, was the problem. Eiswolf was not a usual knight. He did not beat his squire, or starve him, or treat him like a slave. Every time Perry thought of splitting from his brave but disconcerting master, he was reminded why they stuck together. Eiswolf valued the partnership because he had been alone for so long before they met up. Perry knew how it felt to go unprotected. Knights and squires were not usually exactly friends: the disparity in status was too great. But Perry knew that, at the push, he'd sacrifice his life for Eiswolf and he knew, well, he hoped, that Eiswolf would put himself out for Perry.

The knight came back with water and moss. Perry started a small fire. They boiled water in a tough leather bag by dropping red-hot stones into it, and then Perry shaved Eiswolf because it's not the sort of thing you want to try with a sharp knife without a mirror or a good reflection. Perry, of course, was known to have been a prisoner of the Barons of Elderton, so did not shave.

***

The Hegemon did not shave, because Marejah, although her kitchen had sharp knives, did not run to a razor and he felt awkward about using a valuable steel blade that must have cost several week's takings. The sun crept under the eaves into the room and the man slid out of the pretty baker's bed; she had risen hours earlier to fire up the small brick oven and start the dough. The smell of yeast rose up through the trapdoor from the little shop-cum-bakery below her chamber. The warm bed, the bright light, the comfortable scents. This was the happiest part of his life, had he been brave enough to accept it.

But the Hegemon's ambition hemmed him in. He had nursed it since he was a spindly, difficult, snuffling adolescent in a small market town, completely unremarkable except for his talent for numbers. When his parents died of spotted fever, the parish made the orphan boy a school assistant as he could barely draw a bow or lift a sword. But neither bow nor sword was needed in the counting houses of his uncle, a cloth merchant, where young Bevis, not yet the Hegemon, went next.

The merchant had been a second father, considerably more positive than the first. He sent the boy to an expensive school, telling the lad that with his brain and the older man's experience, the world of commerce lay open. Why, with enough money, becoming a Lord was not unknown. The merchant winked. "Listen, young Bevis, there is nothing you cannot aspire to. Let these bumpkins knock each other about with staffs and swords, we know better where real authority lies!" He tapped the side of his nose. And eventually the merchant had been elevated to a baronetcy, despite never having been a knight. A few years later he died; rich, titled, and with a very handsome estate, which he left to Bevis.

Over the years, Bevis built his fortune, became a trusted advisor to the nobility and was invited to Court (Invited! How he wished he could wave that in his father's face!). And now, he might marry a Princess and wear a crown. What man could want more.

Right?

"My lord!" Marejah's clear voice rose up through the trapdoor from her bakery below. "My lord! Would you care to try the fresh honey-rolls?"

"Would I!" Laughing, he clambered down the ladder into her small, happy world.

***

Dawn broke over the forest, and made not the slightest difference. Beneath the boughs of the yews, the path was as shadowed as ever. But after a couple of hours, the riders reached a clearing where a sickly light penetrated. Posts stood in a circle, each with its skull, maybe a dozen in all. A skein of smoke rose from the forest beyond.

Eiswolf dismounted and drew his sword. This was the place. Who else would choose to live here but the sorceress?

Perry decided to stay on Corsa in case of sudden action. "Give me your horse." He took Pepper's reins from Eiswolf.

"Ho! Ho!" yelled Eiswolf, to the trees. "I am come on the Quest of Kolras! I am Eiswolf, the last and lost, descended of Rime and Storm, the North Wind and the Northern Lights, faithful to the Gods of Ice! I have travelled far and long to come to this place, in my Quest to rescue the Eternal Rose and to save the Kingdom! Show yourself to me, that my Quest shall be fulfilled!"

No echo returned, no answering call.

"Ho! I am Eiswolf! I am the hero who will save the Kingdom! Come forth, show yourself, do your duty in the Seven Tests of Kolras!"

A shadow moved in the woods beyond the posts.

"Easy, boss," said Perry, quietly.

"I've got them."

The shadow moved again, quietly, then stepped into the light.

She was slender, black-haired, of middle height, in shimmering green and purple. Her hands sparkled with rings and bracelets. A charm the size of a man's palm hung around her neck, glinting in the pale light.

"Who are you?" Her voice, quiet but piercing, carried like birdsong through the glade.

"I am Eiswolf, lady." He bowed low to her.

She came closer. She had once been a beauty, Perry decided, and was still notable despite her years. Her eyes, black and liquid, flashed like jet: her mouth was strong. Perry could smell her patchouli scent.

Eiswolf made his speech. "My lady, I am told you have knowledge of all languages, the tongues of men and beasts, the forbidden, the unnameable and the unknowable. In my Quest I must find one who can tell me of the Tests Kolras has set. Can you help me, a humble knight?"

The witch came up to Eiswolf and trailed her slim brown hand over his strong face, then his deep chest. She threw her head back and chanted.

"Snarfle-dred-flimshaw, endia-boojum-doof!"

"Pardon?" said Eiswolf.

"Oh, blimey," said Perry. "Bess was right."

"Silence, slave!" the witch hissed. She stepped back and began to twist and spin in a dance. "Olly-vanny-maker-lanny-unta-poot!"

Eiswolf was rooted to the spot. "Actually, all we want is a translation."

She slithered back to him. "Brave knight so free, I need my fee? Each man must pay, and pay he must, for those who cannot pay are dust!"

Then she -

Well, Perry thought, you don't often hear a good witch's cackle these days.

Eiswolf recovered himself. "We have gold and silver in plenty."

But the witch had wound her slim arms about his neck, playing with his chest hair. "Gold and silver pay their way, but I demand a deeper play! Three nights at my call with me, and all your wishes granted be!"

"Er, boss," said Perry.

"It's all right, Perry." He smiled down at the witch. "My squire frets about me."

She gave Perry a glance of the archest evil he had ever seen, which made him start and unsettled Corsa.

"I shall take your challenge," said Eiswolf, "for I am a knight in the lists of love as well as war. Let us begin our tourney of passion, my lady."

Things, he thought to himself, were looking up.

The witch peeled herself off Eiswolf and nodded, then beckoned to the woods. Out came five men, peasants by their clothes, and unquestioning initiates by their expression. All were armed with staves and long forester's knives. She called out.

"Take this squire and these horses, let them be housed and stabled! For tonight is the First Night of the Full Moon!" She turned back to Eiswolf. "Know, knight, that like the Moon, I shall change my shape, and you must master me! On the Second Night, you must go into the Moon's Shadow for this belt of gold and silver! And on the Third Night, if you seize this talisman from me," she held out the charm, a translucent bluish stone with grey marks that did indeed look a little like a full moon, "I shall give you whatever your heart desires! But if you fail …"

"I end up a garden ornament, I know." Eiswolf had a limited capacity for airy-fairiness. Six to two against that he could see. Even if the servants were not trained killers, they had the weight of numbers.

As Perry, still on Corsa, was led away, he muttered to Eiswolf. "Three words, boss. Box. Mad. Frogs."

Eiswolf smiled to himself. If this had been easy, there would not be so many skulls along the path.

***

The First Night was bright and starry. At least, Perry told himself, they got a meal and a fire. The witch lived in a hovel, which was not a criticism but the usual term for a small cottage with no upper floor, very like Bess' home, standing about fifty paces from the clearing. A fire burned outside, where Perry and the men sat to stay warm. Beyond stood a shelter where the horses chewed decent hay.

The servants, who seemed to act only as a group and would not stir without a direct order from the witch, were quiet if not exactly friendly.

"So who is she?" said Perry.

Groupie One, as Perry thought of him, frowned at this lack of respect. "Our Lady is from beyond the Moon, a strange land full of wonders. She came to us on a shooting star. One day she shall return, and we shall all be blessed!"

"Bless the Lady." Groupie Two intoned, followed by the others.

"For she knows all tongues," said Groupie One, "And the secrets of men's hearts are known to her."

"All of them," said Groupie Two. "Down to the darkest."

"Ugh," said Perry. "Enough to turn anyone's brain. So what's this with all the skulls?"

"They were not worthy," said Groupie Two. "They failed in her test of Love."

Well, love was one way to put it, thought Perry.

Eiswolf had spruced himself up and came towards the fire.

Perry quietly went over to him, not happy with the deal. "You do know if you were a girl, there's a name for what you're going to do?"

"Getting my end away? Don't be such a bloody puritan. The test of love is a well-known quest. She's not that bad looking. Shush, here she comes."

The witch appeared at the door of the hovel, through a tinselled curtain. She wore veils and scraps of black, gilt, silver and purple: her hands were painted with complex designs in brown, her eyes outlined in black. In the light of the fire, she was an extraordinary sight. She held a gold cup in her left hand.

"Drink with me, Knight! Drink the Cup of Passion!" She put back her head and poured a big gulp down, then wiped her mouth with her hand and passed him the cup. He smiled bravely, and took a good drink.

"Follow me, Knight!" She made strange gestures with her hands, hopped up and down a couple of times and hissed. Then Eiswolf followed her into the hovel, to be tested.

Now, squires get to see and hear things that others do not; so being outside the door while Eiswolf entertained a lady friend on the other side was not unknown to Perry. This normally meant a lot of squeals and giggles, thumps, squeaks and groans, and possibly the collapse of the bed.

But what Perry heard was an unearthly hoot, followed by caws, whistles and hysterical laughter.

"What's all that?" he whispered to the Groupies.

"She speaks in the tongues of beasts," explained Groupie Two, his eyes glittering. "Blessed be the Lady!"

As the evening wore on, Perry and the Groupies heard moos, a passable imitation of a stag in rut, oinks, what was probably intended to be the roar of a lion, tweets, cackles and the short sharp bark of a dog-fox, followed by the ear-splitting screech of a vixen. The sound effects grew quieter towards dawn, to Perry's relief. The whole business had been thoroughly unsettling.

At dawn, the witch emerged, smudged and definitely the worse for wear. She waved at her Groupies. "Bring me wine! And let my Hero sleep, for he has laboured mightily!"

So that probably meant he passed muster, thought Perry.

Eiswolf woke around one in the afternoon, and came out groggily.

"Good grief, boss, what did she do to you?"

"You want the blow by blow?" Eiswolf was tetchy and scratching. "I've got a mouth like the bottom of a pigsty. Any clean water around here?"

"Sure, boss. So, did you master her as she changed shape? We could hear a lot of squawking."

"Presumably." Eiswolf took the jug from Perry and poured the water over his head. "God knows what's in that wine, though. Weird stuff. Really weird stuff."

Muttering, he made his way rather gingerly towards Pepper, as his clean linen was stowed in the saddlebag. The Groupies bowed as he passed. Perry got back to cleaning harness and darning shirts.

At dusk, the men lit the fire again. The witch appeared from wherever she had been all day. Eiswolf was uncharacteristically quiet about the first night, apart from complaining about a sort of sprain in his back and getting Perry to find a salve for scrapes on his shin. But Perry could tell by his face that the 'test of love' had not been what he expected. He looked more grim than excited.

"Hey ho, off to the races," whispered Perry. "Here comes your lady-love." Which is when Eiswolf clouted him over the head.

"Now is the Second Night!" the witch cried. "Are you prepared for your Great Test?"

"As I'll ever be." Eiswolf stood up and hitched his belt higher.

"Then share the Cup of Shadows with me!"

"Just remind me?"

"Moon shadow, gold and silver belt," said the witch, who could be concise when she had to be. "Drink with me!"

She took a deep draught from the cup, silver this time, Perry noted. Then she passed it to Eiswolf. Now, a Hero should have laughed wildly and tossed back the eldritch brew without a qualm, but Eiswolf looked into the cup, sniffed it, gave her a glance of deep suspicion, and took a very careful sip.

"That enough?"

"It'll do." She led him into the hovel once more.

The night was dark and a troubled wind blew, so Perry and the Groupies took shelter in a couple of tents. Perry, ears alert for any sign that he should intervene or make the horses ready for escape, would have got little sleep anyway. As well as sounds, this was a night of strange lights. The smoke from the hovel's fire glowed green: behind the building, later on, someone lit a bonfire out of which flew sparks of blue and violet. Then the noises started, a low murmur at first, developing into zooming and yodelling in a woman's voice.

"That would be an unknowable tongue or a forbidden one?" said Perry.

"My Lady speaks to the Void."

Well, I hope the Void has good hearing, thought Perry. If I was the Void, I'd want better enunciation.

Then came a much deeper, louder sound, which could only be Eiswolf: but a noise Perry had not heard him make before.

"My God, she's hurting him!"

He sprang to his feet, but Groupie One laid a hand on his arm. "It's her way."

They dragged Perry back to the ground. He mentally worked out exactly how many seconds it took to untie the horses, break into the hovel, and get that bloody man out of whatever mess he was in this time. That, too, was what squires did.

Dawn broke. The witch came out, called for her usual jug of wine, and sloped off into the woods.

Eiswolf appeared at mid-morning, looking rough. Really, really rough. Three jugs of wine and a few tumblers of brandy rough. "Water." Perry had foreseen this and set up a couple of pitchers in advance. "Bath," he then said, somewhat unexpectedly, as Eiswolf, like all his people, thought excessive bathing weakened you.

"The river's a few paces down the track. Do you - Do you want soap?" If he did, Perry thought, he must really be ailing.

"Nope."

"Do you, um, need a hand?"

Eiswolf stared at him, hard, then seemed to reconsider. "That salve. And drying cloths."

"Yes, boss."

Perry followed him down the track. Eiswolf limped slightly, winced and coughed, and certainly took his time.

"Tough night, eh, boss. What was that all about, the shadow stuff?"

But Eiswolf simply stripped off and walked into the river to wash. He had acquired a few bruises, Perry noticed. The crest of hair down his back was matted and uneven, and seemed to have lost a few tufts. He kept standing up to stretch as if his back pained him. Perry handed him a linen towel, then his clean shirt and other clothes.

"Never done that before," said Eiswolf. "Oof." He sounded more irritated than concerned.

"What, exactly?"

"Don't know. Can't remember. That damn stuff she gives you scrambles your brain. Ouch." He stretched again, carefully.

"Then how do you know…"

"I don't. Just a feeling that some things will never be the same again". He inspected the interior of his breeches as he spoke, so Perry assumed this was not a deep spiritual insight. "I seem to have a rash. Is that salve any good?"

"Yes, but put it on yourself," said Perry, quickly. There were parts of Eiswolf that he was content to know existed without getting too close to them. "I wonder what she has in store for you tonight?"

"Not half as much as I do, friend," said Eiswolf, bitterly.

***

In the heights of the Black Tower, by the light of many candles, the Glimmer Lord considered the detail of his strategy. He had a southern dukedom in his hand already: the eastern empire was ready to talk; the northern islands were softening up. The Kingdom was not the largest territory but could be a key to the rest.

On one side of his table stood his prized chess-set: a gift from a mighty and unexpected power. He picked up a queen, carved from rock crystal and inlaid with gold. "Ah, Bess, my Bess, what we might have been."

Beside her was a knight, a tiny figure in white quartz streaked through with a dark stain like a lightning bolt. Behind them were bishops, castles and pawns in ivory, marble and alabaster, but no king. On the opposite side were pieces in porphyry, bloodstone, serpentine, amethyst: and a king of carved ruby.

"Bess! I wonder what you really want from all this Test nonsense? Don't put too much hope in your Hero, my dear, you've been disappointed before." He bent down to whisper to the little queen. "He's only a Man!"

The Glimmer Lord took down one of his great tomes of ancient knowledge, termed a grimoire by those who like a strange foreign word when they wish to cast an air of mystery. The book contained, among useful charms against warts and hypothetical ways to summon a demon, insights into the Kingdom and its neighbours. The lists of nobles covered not only the realms but also major earldoms and principalities. Some would dearly like to add a piece of Kingdom to their estates. The Glimmer Lord's strategic plan depended on weighting risk factors in each combination of man, royal house, and possessions.

The key was undoubtedly the port of Cymenshore. The other realms all needed the port: if he possessed it, they would come into line. But to extract the port from the Kingdom was not easy. The Glimmer Lord had no intention of getting involved in the knightly charade of the Tests himself, but if Bess' boy was really a contender and won, the Kingdom would be broken in two, because the prize was half a Kingdom. Not the whole lot. The King would not hand Cymenshore to his new son-in-law on a plate, you could bet on that. But with only half the Kingdom's army available to them, the port would be vulnerable, unless a wealthy, powerful lord assisted them against a weak King and an unknown upstart.

Of the personalities involved, the King was a man propelled above his natural limits by an accident of birth. The Prince, the young psychopath, was not in the picture, and had not been for several years. The Princess was a prize in a raffle.

And then, the unknown quantity. The Glimmer Lord picked up the flawed figure of the white knight. To back the wolf, or destroy him? Would he play the Lord's game?

The Glimmer Lord sat back in his great high-backed chair. His big idea was almost fully formed. He watched the full moon rise behind storm-wracked clouds through the tower window. But on the topic of strange nights, he wondered how Bess' lad was getting on with that batty woman Jocasta down in the forest.

He grinned. "Better him then me," and replaced the piece on the board. As he did, he knocked over a pawn. "That damn thing keeps getting in the way." He grasped the little white cone, about to fling it to the floor. But that would have broken the set, a careless act that might displease the set's giver. So he put the pawn back.

One piece that, for some reason, has never appeared on a chessboard is a Princess. Well, no analogy is ever perfect; that's why they are analogies. Not reality.

***

" 'Tis the Third Night of the Great Moon," said the witch. "Tonight, you must wrest this all-powerful charm from me to gain your heart's desire and I warn you, knight! You shall not find that easy. Many have tried, all have failed."

There seemed to be a lot more Groupies around. Perry had counted about a dozen, maybe more in the shadows of the forest. Making a break would be messy.

The knight declaimed to the crowd. "I hear you, witch! But know that I, Eiswolf, last and lost, have travelled many leagues for this favour and I will not fear nor be denied by you! Let us enter the Lists of, um, Dread?"

Well, a good guess. The Groupies applauded their appreciation. Perry had his copy of the Manifest ready for a spot of instant translation by the witch, and no idea at all what he would do if Eiswolf failed and died. That is, other than die as well.

"Come, Knight! Drink of the Cup of…" she paused for effect as usual, "The Cup of Terror!"

The cup was black and shiny. Even from a distance Perry could smell the potion: whiffs of creosote and marsh-water topped off with a wrackingly sickly sweetness. Only a brave man would drink that.

The witch sipped the potion cautiously, then quickly passed the Cup to Eiswolf, who did not look at the drink, or her, but simply poured the concoction into his mouth. And spluttered, coughed and heaved.

"Boss!"

"Leave me, Perry. Look after the horses." Straightening up, Eiswolf gave the other heroic speech he had prepared. "Send word to my love the Princess, the Eternal Rose, that what I do, I have done for her, and for the Kingdom! But if I am found wanting, none should mourn, for I died as I have lived, in pursuit of glory!" He took a heroic pose. "Let my squire bear this message!"

"Afterwards," said the witch. "Don't want him accidentally running into any soldiers and bringing them back here, do we?" Occasionally the mist in her mind cleared for a while.

So Eiswolf entered the hovel for the third time. Perry saw that Groupie Two had thoughtfully brought a pole and was carving runes, ready for the last act.

The hoop-la started almost as soon as the tinsel curtain fell behind Eiswolf. The noises were not just animals but a symphony of wheezes and cackles. Glowing green lights seemed to spark and leap from one part of the roof to another, then the witch began to sing.

The Groupies, to a man, looked terrified and put their hands over their ears. "The Forbidden Tongues!" hissed Groupie Two. He pushed Perry's hands to his head.

"No!" cried Perry. "Whatever my knight undergoes, so must I!"

"You are truly brave!" cried Two, and put his own hands in place.

The witch made a hell of a racket, true, high, impossibly operatic swoops followed by baritone growls and yelps. Once again Perry found himself considering the boundaries between unknown, forbidden, incomprehensible and plain bonkers. But the stakes and their skulls had come from somewhere.

Drumbeats. A single drum, presumably, accompanied by a rhythmic grunt. Then a wail, then back to the beats and the grunts, but under this Perry could hear a groan. And he knew Eiswolf's voice.

The smoke from the chimney turned deep purple. The singing and drumming rose, then came another groan, deep and desperate.

Perry stood, itching to get to the horses. Half a dozen Groupies pulled him to the earth again. The witch sang and yodelled by turns, drumming ever faster and louder.

Eiswolf screamed. Perry half got to his feet before the Groupies seized him, and this time did not let go. The man screamed again, followed by a deep wail. The others died this way, Perry knew that as well as if he were inside that damned place himself. Paralysed by that infernal potion, tortured beyond imagination, then dragged out and executed to the glory of the witch. Perry sweated and trembled; he knew he had to rescue his master. But he was held fast by four strong men in a grip of utter obsession.

The drum rhythm changed, slowed, became a heartbeat. The witch sang quietly. Perry strained every nerve to hear Eiswolf. Nothing, no sign that he was still alive.

Until the howl. All the Groupies froze in astonishment. Eiswolf howled again, sharp, assertive, for the Snow Wolf was there and he was master. Another howl, and a ferocious growl. Then came a ghastly, half-swallowed sound, as if the Wolf savaged its prey.

"Let me go!" cried Perry.

But before he could rush into the hovel and rescue/restrain/kill his knight, Eiswolf appeared at the door. Blood splattered across his bare chest and dribbled from his mouth: his eyes glowed with a golden light that was not of this world, he howled horribly. He held up the pale charm, glinting under the night sky, then ran into the black forest.

The witch came to the door panting, her dress torn, her eyes wild. "He conquered me!" she wailed. "My dark love has conquered me!" She gave a strange, wheezy little cry and collapsed. The Groupies rushed to support their beloved mistress.

Perry was truly scared; he could hear distant howls, whether from Eiswolf or a wolf-pack across the hills, he could not tell. The men persuaded the witch to drink wine, but she wept like a fountain and made even less sense than usual.

But life, and bureaucracy, goes on, Perry told himself.

"I understand this is a difficult time for you, madam, but in line with your agreement," he waved the sheet of parchment, "If you could translate these Quests? Then we'll be out of your hair."

"My only love! My dark-hearted hero!" She did look desperate and for a moment, Perry was almost sorry for her. Eiswolf could be a real bastard with women.

"Look, plenty more fish, sweetie. Another knight will be along soon, you can impale him, that'll make you feel better. Keep your snarf-taradiddle up." He smiled at her, and she smiled through her tears, then he handed her the list.

***

In the morning, Perry waited for Eiswolf in the clearing but saw no sign of him, so saddled Corsa up anyway and began to make his way back, leading Pepper by the reins.

Eiswolf stood beside the bridge, still shirtless but slightly cleaner, with the moon charm around his neck. Perry threw him a shirt. Eiswolf started to take Pepper back over the rickety bridge. However, horses are learning animals. Pepper had only crossed the first time against his better judgement, and had no intention of being fooled twice. So the men had plenty of time to catch up with what exactly had happened.

Well, there would have been, if Eiswolf had remembered anything. "God knows. Those damn potions. I get flashes and dreams but I can't actually remember much at all. Oof. Come on, horse."

"Sprain?"

"No, scratches, like a cat? And I've got a sort of nagging left shoulder."

Eiswolf was confused as well as aching. Try as he might, he could not fit what he had been through, or thought he had been through, with any sexual or romantic flings he had previously experienced. Or heard of. Why, for example, did he have three bruises in a triangle under his left armpit? The usual places were rather sore, but why –

"Pepper!"

The horse now stood rooted to the spot, in a calm, 'I'm not going anywhere until I've chewed my bridle some more' way. Also, he did not know he was called Pepper. His previous owner called him Mystery. Not that he knew he had an owner, either. The two-legged creatures came and went. Some of them sat on him. Of the current Herd, Big Two Legs smelt funny and made a flap, but seemed all right. He just did not see why he had to walk over the thing-which-moves-over-deep-falling-place until he was good and ready.

"Pepper, count of three, then we all go together! Perry, lead Corsa, will you?"

Well, thought Pepper, She's Herd, so that must be all right. He tossed his head and followed Her and Little Two Legs, quiet as a sheep. Once on the other side, the riders mounted up again.

"So what was all the shouting about?" said Perry.

"No idea, it's sort of blurry," said Eiswolf. "Ouch. You got any more of that salve? And what about the Quests?"

Perry consulted the copy of the vellum sheet, now scrawled over with translations. "First bit looks standard enough. We need an archer that can hit the tail-feather of a lark, a man who can outrun the sun, one who can lift a mountain and one who can hear the grass grow. Then business about a dragon. Then it's not so clear. A sword, a ring, but that bit's all jumbled. You up for all that?"

"Suppose so. Yow."

"So how did you get out? Surely when you drank all that stuff…"

Eiswolf laughed. "IF I had, you mean."

"But I saw you!"

"Did you?" Eiswolf tapped his nose.

"You took a swig, then you spluttered and coughed and –oh." Perry replayed the scene: Eiswolf, doubled over and retching. "You spat it out."

"Most of it. Old trick a fire-eater once showed me when I was in the circus. I couldn't get rid of all of it, so I was woozy but I could still move, so I had to lay low until she, um, and then I grabbed this charm."

"So what was all the howling? You spooked me."

Eiswolf grinned happily. "Now, what is the use of a reputation as a werewolf unless you can use it?"

"Bastard," said Perry, admiringly.

"Thank you," said Eiswolf. "Still wish I could remember it all because I'm bug…" A twinge made him shift in his saddle. He decided not to pursue that thought.

***

The spring sun was bright on the Black Tower, and in a lower chamber, the apprentice was perfecting his craft. His master entered, and laughed. "How goes the training, my friend?"

"Testing, my lord." Mirak paused in his dance exercises to wipe sweat from his brow.

The Glimmer Lord smiled. "They say this takes more energy than a bout at rapier and dagger. Well, let's see?"

Mirak went through the passes. "These are the first five in the sequence, then there's another four, with more complexity."

Technically, he was perfect. There was a kind of chilly beauty in his movements. But that would not be enough. The Lord looked him in the eye. "I think you need more practice."

Mirak flushed with annoyance. The Glimmer Lord shook his head and smiled.

"Don't let your pride get in the way of learning, my friend. You do the physical side very well. Absolutely to the point, I cannot criticise you. But now I want to see your heart."

Mirak, still pink, went through the third sequence again. "Well, my lord?"

"Better. As a wise man in my country once said, the secret of success is sincerity. Absolute sincerity. If you can fake that, you've got it made."

He started to leave the room, chuckling at his own joke. Mirak ran after him, and caught his sleeve.

"My Lord! My Lord! I need things!"

The Lord smiled. "Of course, lad. Whatever you require, my treasury is open. I only criticise to help you improve."

Mirak bowed, and the Lord left.

Old bastard, thought the boy. He'll pay for that, through the nose. Then he did the fifth sequence, with added rude gestures.

"I'll give him from the heart. That sincere enough, my Lord?"

He threw the props to the ground in a fury. Then, after a few seconds, he picked them up again, and began to practice the sixth sequence. Mirak was a disciplined apprentice.

5: Grand Tourney

After delivering the translated Manifest to the Conclave, Eiswolf and Perry had to find men of extraordinary talents.

Knight, squire, quest, setting forth. The whole town knew the form.

A scrappy crowd gathered outside the Palace and a couple of old women raised a cheer, but frankly, the novelty had worn off. Maybe there would be more excitement when Eiswolf's body or miscellaneous bits were sent back, but nobody was holding their breath.

Except for the Princess. This Quest seemed to be low risk, so Plan D had to be put in motion, preferably before Eiswolf won the hearts of the people or whatever. One more dead knight was not suspicious: the death of a hero might be. She waved, he waved back. She turned to what she now called her Planning Hanging. Just in case any of her ladies sprouted a few extra brain cells, she had replaced the written notes with representative scraps of fabric. Connecting them up by tapestry wool worked quite well. Now. Where could Death come in?

***

"You know," said the King, in a very mild voice, "I suppose we have to consider the possibility that we might have found our knight? We have not examined all Kolras' procedures, have we? In case of …" The King trailed away, as if putting the idea into words was too, too distressing.

"No, your Majesty, that has never been necessary before." The Hegemon tried to sound reassuring.

Because the Tests were not meant to be difficult: they were meant to be impossible.

In the seclusion of the King's Chamber, they nodded at each other. A cold hand laid on them both. The Kingdom was one and indivisible, and had been so for three centuries. Actually splitting the Kingdom in half was unthinkable: Kolras had added the idea to the Tests as a reward that sounded good but would never be put in action. Apart from anything else, this set one terrible precedent.

"What of the Princess?" said the Hegemon. "Her Majesty has been most gracious and yet I perceive a quietness about her."

"Ah, Hegemon, this has been so trying for my little girl. To be so close to her heart's desire, to every womanly ambition, love, marriage, a babe to call her own, so cruelly snatched away so many times. What other lady would have shown such fortitude. And yet, one day, the wisdom of Kolras will be revealed and there will be a new heir. She herself has asked how we might ensure a peaceful future, for if this brave knight does not succeed, we may have to consider what other paths Kolras has left us."

Has she, by God, thought the Hegemon. He admired the Princess beyond reason, but had never thought of her as a power-player for the simple reason that she would not choose her husband. Queens did not rule, and were replaceable. "And would your Majesty wish her Majesty to be involved?"

"Good heavens, no! What can such a delicate creature know of the great matters of empery and governance? Let her realms be those of delight and comfort, let her play with her ladies and be an example of beauty and gentleness to all, but to be sullied by the rough necessities of diplomacy? No, my dear Hegemon. Never!" And the King laughed.

Just possibly, thought the Hegemon, he does not know his daughter at all. Or he chooses not to see, or he does, but chooses not to believe. But maybe the game was changing. If she had decided to become a player -

The King's watery blue eyes met his. "These are testing times, Hegemon. Most testing. Who knows what fate has in store? But I am the most fortunate of men in my Princess, and my faithful advisors in this Chamber, and in the Conclave of Scholars, and my closest counsellor, yourself. Together, we shall steer this Kingdom to safe harbour, no matter what storms we encounter. And you," he leaned forward and tapped the Hegemon on the hand, "you are our helmsman. Be assured of my utmost faith in you."

He smiled, then rose and left the Chamber. The Hegemon allowed himself to glow a smidgeon. With a little more pressure in the right places, and attending to the Princess, how might the winds of fortune be persuaded to blow? The wolf was merely a distraction.

***

The Grand Tourney was five day's ride away, and the road was clear and straight. As Eiswolf and Perry got nearer the tourney-ground, more and more parties of knights, squires, ladies and general hangers-on joined the throng, a festival atmosphere. Tradesmen set up roadside stalls for ale, bread, and cooked meat. Musicians piped, strummed and warbled at them; young ladies waved and cooed, occasionally disappearing into the bushes for a quick, efficient dalliance. At night, tents were to be had for a few pennies, the fires of the campsites glowing like stars. Armourers hammered and blacksmiths clattered as they made last-minute adjustments to various pieces of equipment, reminding everyone of the excitement to come.

But Perry was very, very unhappy. "You're mad to enter the Grand Tourney! It's not in the Quest! Just find the types from the Manifest and get out! We've got a dragon to slay!"

Perry was right: the Quest asked for a team of specialists and the only reason for going to the Tourney was that this seemed the obvious place to recruit. So why, given the random risks in any battle, and that the Manifest did not require it, was Eiswolf so committed to fighting in the contest?

One reason, that Eiswolf would not admit, was that he was really, really spoiling for a good, clean punch-up. He was two quests down and the sum total of his achievements to date was a sheet of vellum with unreadable writing, a toad called Albert, and a rash in a personal place that would not go away. This was not what knights were about. Knights won renown in battle and by God, he was going to have some of that.

"It's how I draw men to my service. You can't ask a man to fight a dragon if he has no confidence in the leadership. It's a gut feeling."

"But what if you get beaten?"

Eiswolf simply rode on towards the huge temporary town that was the Tourney. Tents for the knights were set out in rows, each bearing a coloured pennant at the top. As a knight of the Kingdom, Eiswolf was in Blue sector. Each tent contained a truckle bed and a stand for armour, with space for the squire to attend to domestic necessities. Outside each tent, the knight's banner was raised: as glory was the object of the Tourney, everyone had to know your name or at least, the name you fought under. You could not enter the Lists without identification, although this could be as vague as 'the Black Knight' if you wished.

The sumptuous pavilions of the lords and ladies who had travelled simply to watch and feast were at one end of the encampment, well away from the noisy, smelly business end (which would get noisier and smellier over the next few days). That was where the saddlers, farriers and blacksmiths had set up, plus a horse-fair to replace animals killed or injured in the lists. A hitching area for the battle-horses was on one side, but Corsa was led up the hill to the mare's enclosure, as any mare in season would cause mayhem among the battle-stallions. Corsa was far away from her master, so she whinnied all the way. Beyond the hitching area were booths with more food and entertainment for those who could pay. They even had latrines.

"It's well organised," said Perry, grudgingly. "We're third row from the entrance, five along to the right."

A servant came to their tent and told them to wait for the Herald of the Lists to bring the order of battle. With so many knights, if all tried to approach the tourney officials at once it would create an unseemly crush.

The Herald was obviously marked for a future life as the sports director of a country club, for his system was remarkably close to a squash ladder, with added blood and guts. In the main tourney, each knight fought in a knock-out division (preferably not killing their opponent) not only on horse-back, but also, in the Herald's own little wheeze, wrestling, archery, and a sword-fight on foot. Winners went into the first melee, where knights would be divided into two teams and battle for a symbolic silver circlet. The lucky team would go into the second melee, a true free-for-all, and the champion would be the last man standing. Or limping, or lying on the ground, groaning, as the case might be. The ultimate prize was Honour, signified by a circlet of gold.

But there were many other contests for those of lower status, or too old or missing too many bits for the main tourney: stone-lifting, foot races, quintain, target archery, display horsemanship and signalling. This added interest, broadened the potential entrants, and helped to spread the crowd around the site.

One sport that was not represented was jousting: the Herald of the Lists thought this an effeminate business, as the opportunities for mayhem were so limited. Building a specialised tiltyard and viewing platforms was both expensive and inconvenient. His audience wanted to be close to the real action, which was why so many came. Jousting, he had decided, was too sanitised.

The Herald of the Lists, followed by a small detachment of three pages, marched smartly into Eiswolf's tent. "Sir Knight, you'll fight the Knight of the Swamps, then Sir Leodigras, then either The Lord of Macintree, who might scratch as he has a lame horse, or Sir Dauntless, I think that's a pseudonym. Tomorrow morning, second bell, please be at the battleground with all your equipment ALREADY prepared, we allow no time for armouring at the ground, squires may assist you to mount but must retire behind the rope when the horn sounds for battle. After battle you must wait to be assessed before your squire can drag you away, we did have an Incident with a grudge match and a man playing dead. The next sessions will be in the afternoon. If you are unfit to proceed, I or one of my men must be informed by the noonday bell. Weather permitting, the first melee will be in two days' time. Any questions?"

"None," said Eiswolf.

"What name do you fight under?"

"I am Eiswolf, last and- "

One of the Herald's pages began to write in a small ledger. "Just the name, if you please, Sir Knight. How do you spell that?" Perry told him.

The Herald swivelled to see who had spoken without permission. "And you would be Squire who?"

"Perry, Lord Herald." Perry bowed.

"And do we deliver the body to you, if necessary?"

Eiswolf and Perry exchanged a controlled glance.

"I suppose so, Lord Herald," said Perry.

"Delivery is free, but my page will take a gold piece to cover burial costs as a surety, to be returned on live departure. Sir Eiswolf, please show me your device?"

One of the Herald's jobs was not only to call out the name of the knight in the lists but also to describe their coat of arms. This was for the simple reason that you might not know Sir Leodigras, and his own mother would not recognise him in a full helmet from a distance, but you could certainly see what colour his shield was. Most knights took the colour theme into their surcoats (the loose tunic they wore over their chain-mail), the horse-trappings and any other bits and pieces made of fabric or dyed leather.

"My knight fights under this sign." Perry took the canvas wrapping off the brand new shield.

The Herald squinted, then dictated the 'device' to his page in heraldic-speak. "Sable (*black*), bend dexter gules and vert (*right-handed red and green stripe*), that's not strictly legitimate, should be tincture on metal, you know, (*you should only put a colour on a gold or silver background*) charged with a rampant argent (*silver*) - Is that a sheep?"

"What?" said Eiswolf. He had not inspected the shield on its return from the armoury and by Perry's shame-faced expression, neither had he. The page smirked.

"It's a wolf," said Perry.

"Is it," said the Herald, as the page wrote a note on his ledger. "I'll have to remember that." Meaning that 'if you're stupid enough to have a high-falutin' symbol painted by the village idiot, don't blame me if I get it wrong.'

Then he bowed and moved on to deflate the next knight with over-mighty expectations.

Perry laughed. "Gold as a surety against burial costs? Hey, I'd bury you for sixpence."

Eiswolf grinned. "Dead bodies all over the place are just SO untidy."

Then another Herald entered and besought that the brave knight should feast mightily with the Lords of the Tourney, so that sorted out his social diary. Perry, as usual, was left to amuse himself.

***

Actually, this could be very useful. In so large a gathering, although Eiswolf might have fought some of the knights before, the majority were unknown. With a little judicious chatter, Perry could get useful information on Eiswolf's opponents, and the tourney favourites.

His secret weapon was his age. Squires were usually teenage lads, sent by noble families to learn the business from a famous knight. The expectation was that in due time they would show, by expertise in arms or an act of valour, that they were ready for knighthood. And knights needed squires, because this was not a one-man business. A lot of work went into armour, horses, travel arrangements and domestic needs, all the behind the scenes planning to make sure the knight appeared, gleaming and heroic, in the right place at the right time. Rich knights might have a couple of younger boys as pages as well.

Some fourteen-year-old boys took to this, but some did not. Failure could be punished brutally. Families had to leave their teenage son to a stranger whose primary job in life is killing people. Once a squire rode over the hill with his knight, who knew when, or if, his family would see him again.

So new squires were absolutely grist to the mill for Perry, because a lot were lonely, afraid, and only too happy to talk to a friendly stranger. Those who weren't, wanted to show off. He had to explain how he, a slight man with a couple of grey hairs, was still a squire, but now had that speech down to a fine art.

"My name's Perry, I am squire to Sir Eiswolf, last and lost, descended of Rime and Storm." He raised a mug of ale to the other squires grouped around a fire about three tents down.

"Bit old for this game, arncha?" said the first squire, named Benet.

"Well, truth be told, I'd have been a knight years past, but, well, I was captured and I'm not whole any more." Perry sighed, dramatically but not too tragically. "The Barons of Elderton, you know."

Those squires who knew the Barons and their reputation, all winced.

"Ah, that's a bad business," said Benet.

"What's he mean?" hissed a young squire to Benet.

"Well, a true knight must be whole and hale, for the honour of the whatsit, so if you're missing, um…"

"Bits," said Perry.

"Exackly, you can't be knighted. When was that, then?"

"Oh, a long time ago now. Water under the bridge, really."

"What bits?" said the young squire. One of the others took him aside to explain, and he went a gratifying shade of green.

"H'm," Benet was still suspicious. "So how did you end up with," he pointed at the shield, now set up outside the tent, "the Knight of the White Splodge?"

At this point, Perry had a cunning ruse. "A long tale. Cast your minds back twenty summers since."

Cue deep sighs and mock-groans from the other squires. Perry grinned and shook his head. "Another time, maybe."

"Right," said Benet. "Here. Have some ale."

Perry took the plunge. "So what's yours like? Mine can be a right madam."

***

Knights at the feast were seated without regard to title, for the only honours that mattered were those to be won at the Tourney. Ideally, the table would have been round but practically, that would not have fitted in the large marquee that acted as a hall, so trestles it was, as the Herald of Lists explained. So knights were seated at long tables, without regard to title.

Unless you were very famous, like Sir Dietrich of Metzen, who had to be where everyone could see him, as the name knight of the Tourney. Or you were notorious, like Sir Ulrich the Knacker. Or very rich, like Sir Cadwal, who had a full set of gilded metal plate armour and no fewer than six high-bred battle-stallions. Or you were a previous Champion, or high up in the seeding, or the son of a friend of one of the Heralds –

Eiswolf found himself shuffled towards the bottom of one of the long tables, quite a distance from the famous knights and also from the best food, like the roast venison that scented the air so teasingly. A lugubrious man in a dark brown mantle sat on his left side on the bench. On his right was a very young knight, probably no more than eighteen, who fidgeted and chewed his nails by turns.

"Sir knights, may I introduce myself? I am Eiswolf, last and lost!"

"Ah, the werewolf." The lugubrious man spoke without malice. "How do."

"I am called Sir Dauntless," said the edgy lad. "I fight for the honour of my lady."

"Oh, who's that?" said Eiswolf. But the boy went red and would not say. He tore into a roast pigeon instead and yelled for more wine.

"No manners, these young ones," said the man in brown. "Doesn't know how to use his napkin." Table manners were important to knights, at least in the early stages of a feast. "I fight for the love of my lady."

"So do I," said Eiswolf. "I fight for the Princess of the Kingdom."

"Nice one," said the man, approvingly. "Mine's a duchess. Here's to the ladies, God bless 'em." He toasted Eiswolf, and Eiswolf toasted in turn. A servant with a lined face and sea-bright eyes placed another flagon of wine on the table.

The boy sniggered. "Ask him about his favour."

The dark man frowned darkly, and shook his head.

Eiswolf was a little puzzled. "I bear a favour from my Princess."

"Bet yours isn't embarrassing," the man muttered, swigging more wine. The food might be average but the drink was flowing well, and the knights took proper advantage.

Eiswolf spoke carefully. "It's not what I would have chosen."

"Go on, show him," said Sir Dauntless, who could live up to his name when full of alcohol.

The dark man leaned over confidingly, slurring slightly. "Sometimes I do wonder if our dear ladies are having a laugh at our expense. So what's yours?"

There was nothing for it. Eiswolf parted his shirt to show the little necklace with the roses and bluebirds.

Sir Dauntless collapsed in giggles. "Wow! Cute!"

The dark man nodded gloomily. Carefully, so that no-one beside Eiswolf could see, he parted his own shirt. "White satin, next to me 'eart. She was very particular."

Eiswolf pieced the clues together. "So you are the Knight in White Satin?"

The boy laughed helplessly. "Tell him! Tell him!"

The Knight leaned over to Eiswolf's ear. "Intimate nether garments."

Eiswolf was fully occupied in not laughing, because the knight was already shouldering a tremendous burden.

"Mind you," said the Knight, "at least she's not my Mum." Which is when Sir Dauntless went bright red and might have started the Tourney early, but for the fact that he fell backwards off the bench.

And indeed, Eiswolf got a little blurry after that, although the feast seemed to involve arm-wrestling, getting onto the table and singing, making an unsuccessful pass at a serving wench, and tying Sir Dauntless' breeches laces to the bench and then challenging him to stand up.

However, before getting too far into the third flagon of wine, so attentively provided by the bright-eyed servant, he noted a middle-aged man at one of the upper tables, in the black fur-trimmed robe of a doctor. He was watching rather than feasting. Behind him stood a young squire with red-gold hair, patient and quiet amid all the ruckus. The man had a very piercing expression.

"Who's that?" he said to the Knight.

"Him? Don't want to get mixed up with him." The Knight actually shivered. "That's the Glimmer Lord."

Then Eiswolf saw the man talk to one of the servants, and the servant pointed his way. The Glimmer Lord looked at Eiswolf very hard for a couple of seconds, before taking up a conversation with his neighbour.

Eiswolf went back to jollification, but part of his mind filed away the image of the man, and his stare, and the name.

* * *

First light was a cruel time. The entire encampment seemed to have a hangover, which took the edge off the adrenalin-fuelled men who were due to fight. The Herald of the Lists went about his business, humming happily, because he had found from experience that it could all get very messy very quickly if everyone was pumped up too early. The ladder system needed a supply of winners from the lower rounds, not a row of corpses.

Eiswolf staggered out of his tent with fifteen minutes to go, Perry still stuffing him into his coat of mail, then Perry threw him his helmet and spurs and raced to the hitching posts where Pepper had to be saddled. At least he had no time-consuming plate armour to fit. Eiswolf, like most knights, fought in studded leather breeches and a gambeson, a padded linen jerkin, with a coat of mail over that, topped by a padded mail 'coif' over his head and neck. His helmet was like a metal bucket with a slit for the eyes. Leather boots completed the outfit, but no gloves – they were too expensive and clumsy. He and Perry got to the tourney ground with about thirty seconds to spare, along with quite a few others. The Herald took the opportunity to give them all a dark look and a dressing down.

The first fights were in mounted swordsmanship. Eiswolf despatched the Knight of the Swamps, a goose-farmer, very swiftly with a big backhand blow to his shoulder. The man fell off his horse and was bruised but not damaged. Next up was Sir Leodigras, whose mount was not battle-hardened and very over-excited: he lost the fight when his horse bucked him off before Eiswolf struck a blow.

The last bout of the morning was with the lad who called himself Sir Dauntless. Eiswolf knew that though the boy's skills would not equal his own, a hard-driving, reckless amateur could take a professional by surprise. Sir Dauntless was determined to live up to his name and made a series of aggressive charges at Eiswolf. He put all his energy into massive swipes at the head and upper body, intended to knock Eiswolf out of his saddle. As Eiswolf was taller than he, this meant he raised himself on his stirrups to sweep his long sword and that created a point of imbalance. Eiswolf kept out of the way of the wilder strokes and parried the ones closer in, but held back from attacking until he could see the boy sweat.

As Sir Dauntless began to get tired, Eiswolf went in and unhorsed him in two strokes: one to the head, the other to mid-body. The boy sailed over his horse's crupper and landed heavily but not dangerously so. He would live to fight another day.

And, as he had planned, Eiswolf got through his allotted fights in just over an hour, without falls or any significant injury, leaving plenty of time for recuperation before the foot-fights in the afternoon. He and Pepper were both still fresh as a daisy. The small crowd who had watched this low-ranking round applauded politely, then moved to the main arena where Sir Ulrich was living up to his name with the unfortunate Knight of the Silver Horn. Shouts and yells told Eiswolf this was a considerably bloodier affair. But that's what the crowd liked.

***

"Which of these knights do you consider the most brave and noble?" said the Glimmer Lord. He was taking a comfortable glass of wine with the Lords of the Tourney, otherwise known as the Earl of Dugdale and Baron Eims, in their tent near the main arena.

"Oh, Sir Dietrich has to be in the reckoning," said the Earl. "Finds his opponent's limits quickly, a very elegant way with him. Has to be a good bet for the prize."

"But can he do a fourth year?" said the Baron. "He's been at the top a long time, this could be the opportunity for new blood."

They were middle-aged men who had been middling fighters themselves, with no particular skill or ambition. Then came the happy day when the Baron, at yet another poorly-managed, lacklustre event, decided there had to be a better way, for the knights, for the crowds, and for Baron Eims and Earl Dugdale. They started out with very little apart from unfarmable land near a major road but over the years, the Grand Tourney had grown into its name: this was definitely the premier event in these parts. Business was going swimmingly well, and was, through earls and barons were not supposed to care, extremely profitable.

The Glimmer Lord had made himself known a couple of years previously as a connoisseur of knightly skill and courage. Once they had checked that he was not a competitor, as occasionally a foolhardy type tried this on, they welcomed him. He brought other rich and well-connected men and was generous in his support. The Lord marked out the most promising knights (not always the winners, for that can be a matter of luck) and took them into his very well-paid service.

"Any wild cards?" said the Glimmer Lord.

Baron Eims sucked his teeth. "Sir Phobos, the Knight of Fear. Big rep out East, good armourer, ruthless bastard."

"Ah, yes," said the Glimmer Lord. "The Fright Knight. Yes, heard of him."

"Or Sir Alberich, they say he sees the fate of every man he fights."

"Arse-up in the sand, most of them," said Earl Dugdale. "He's got this oogie-woogie thing he does, puts people off. But all credit to the bloke, works for him."

"Yes, the Psychic Knight," said the Glimmer Lord. "But have you heard of a werewolf?"

The two promoters stared at each other. "We don't hold with your actual supernatural creatures," said the Baron. "Very difficult to handle."

"Awkward buggers," said the Earl. "Throws the prize money scale as well, they all want more to fight a giant or a troll or whatever."

"I meant the man known as Eiswolf," said the Glimmer Lord. "What do you know about him?"

"Well, come with us and take a gander," said the Baron. "He's through to the ladies' excuse-me."

"Big, arsy, mouthy," said the Earl. "Is that white thing on his shield supposed to be a wolf, then? Looks more like a sheep."

Laughing, they made their way to the hand-to-hand fighting rings.

***

Eiswolf worked his way through a series of reasonably fit but not very skilled opponents at wrestling, archery, and sword-fighting on foot. Perry saw to the horses, then went off around the rest of the Tourney. This was the place to find the latest in maps, lucky charms, saddlery, weapons, armour and all the technology that the modern questing knight might need. After an interesting but exhausting shopping trip, Perry returned to the tent to help Eiswolf out of his kit.

"How was your day?"

"Not so shabby," said Eiswolf. He and Perry peeled off his mail. Eiswolf had had a very sweaty few hours. As soon as he was down to his shirt, he dashed outside the tent for a couple of minutes. Some men were not so picky but if you wanted to wear the same breeches the next day… He came back more slowly. "I may have found an archer. Called Flowers, beat me hands down at the long shots but hopeless at the near stuff, in fact, he seems almost blind. Weird. He has to be able to take the tail feather from a lark, right?"

Perry shrugged. "That's what the Manifest says. What about the man who can outrun the sun?"

"Watch the footraces tomorrow morning, the melee doesn't start till after noon. And we then need an all-hearing type. Any water around?" Eiswolf poured the jug over his head and struggled out of his damp and very dirty shirt. "Strong man. Wrestler today, I didn't fight him, he was in the side competition, name of Meroens. Check him out. More water?"

Perry frowned. "What, washing again? It's getting to be a habit."

The Herald arrived with his invitation for the Knight, now the winner of his division and elevated to one of the teams for the melee, to sup with the Lords of the Tourney. Eiswolf's star was rising.

***

The night was black and the moon was bright when Eiswolf staggered back into the tent with the help of a couple of servants, laughing uncontrollably. "These men know how to drink!" he told Perry, unnecessarily.

"Yep. Sure, come on, let's be having you. God, you're heavy, you do know it's the melee, thanks, guys, here's silver for your trouble."

The larger man scratched his nose. "Will you need us tomorrow night?" Eims and Dugdale were not the only locals to make a good thing from the Tourney.

Perry dumped Eiswolf onto the bed. "I should think so. You know where we are."

"Yeah, the Sign of the Sheep."

Perry sighed deeply. It was too late tonight but tomorrow he had to see if anyone could make that damn shield look like a wolf. He did not want Eiswolf going into the melee as the Knight of the Sheep, however rampant.

"Thanks, guys."

Eiswolf sang happily to himself, because he had now met his side in the melee. They were good enough to beat the others but not, in the knockout afterwards, good enough to get past him. He was also still bouncing around with the adrenalin of success in the hand-to-hand sessions.

"Hey, you should have seen me this afternoon! Did I tell you about the wrestling?"

"Yes, over your shoulder in one."

"Ha! No sweat! The hand to hand, that new twist and thrust move, didn't know where I was coming from! I can win this, I know I can!" He danced around the tent, somewhat unevenly.

Perry led him back to the bed. "You need to be fresh tomorrow.".

"Did you find Meroens?"

"Yes, he's up for a spot of dragon-slaying, as long as there's money in it. He's a wrestler, not a knight."

"Good. Good! And Flowers?"

Perry paused in the complicated business of getting Eiswolf out of court dress, with all the buckles and laces and points. "I don't know. I do have a problem with an archer who needs a dog to guide him round the camp.'

"He's an ace at three hundred paces. Believe me. Ow."

"Is that the rash? Sorry. Ooh, that's nasty, maybe Bess should look at that."

"Over my dead body," said Eiswolf. "So did you sign him up?"

"Yes, And a bloke called Fittle, he hears stuff." Perry had gone with a creative interpretation here, because, frankly, being in tune with gossip was a damn sight more useful than hearing a cockroach fart from a hundred paces. "What about tomorrow?

"I need you, we're allowed to re-arm and remount. Youch!"

"Sorry. That's a new bruise. Can you move your shoulder freely?" Perry helped Eiswolf manipulate the joint.

"Yes, no problem. I heard a rumour about the Dogstar Knight?"

Perry paused again. "I saw him. They say …"

"They say he fights in honour of the Queen of Faery. What do you think?"

Perry had spotted the man in practice. His armour was black-patinated in the finest workmanship, his glittering black shield adorned with a ten-pointed silver star; he rode a huge black horse. But only when he dismounted could you see how extraordinarily tall he was, at least a head taller than Eiswolf. His face was ivory, his eyes sharp and grey. On his helmet he wore a crest of black feathers wound about with emerald green ribbon, the colour of Faery.

Perry took out a clean shirt. For a moment he had thought he recognised the man who gave them Enchanted Albert. But no. How could that be? "He's very tall, pale, a skilful fighter but then it was mid-day."

"So all that could be true?" Everyone knew fairies, as creatures of the sun, were at their strongest at noon. "They say he is five hundred years old. Went down to feast Under the Hill with the Queen and when he came up again …"

"Well, he does have white hair. And he has white hounds with him, the ones with red eyes."

Eiswolf shivered. "Gabriel hounds. Well, he's not in the contest so hopefully I don't need to worry." But even Eiswolf, so commonly believed to be a supernatural creature himself, went cold at the idea of a Faery Knight.

Which is probably why he dreamed so vividly all night of being part of the Wild Hunt chasing the moon. At least until Perry thumped him and made him turn over, to stop the yelping noises.

***

The First Melee involved twenty knights on each side, the Side of the Leopard versus the Side of the Bear. They entered the arena to huge applause, each knight called out in turn by a herald. Ladies fainted, wept, or lusted, according to their temperaments: men cheered, clapped or scowled, according to theirs. (A few probably lusted but, in this society, it might not be wise to show that.)

The Side of the Leopard bore gold ribbon armbands: the Side of the Bear had black ones. Having sorted out who they were supposed to knock on the head and whom they were supposed to defend, the two sides joined battle for the Honour of the Silver Circlet.

Working out what's going on is hard enough in a modern rugby scrum or polo match. Now put the two together, and add clouds of dust from a dry battle arena. The spectacle was glittering, loud, exciting and visceral. You could feel as well as hear the thud when the knights collided with each other or clashed shields. But ultimately, it was confusing. Few moves were illegal. When blood started flowing, the knights could barely see the side they were on, not that they cared very much. By this time they were all well into red mist territory, where anything that moved got swiped, anything that got up got knocked down, and anything that came towards you got thumped.

Pepper was having a good day. The other battle-chargers were stallions, because in theory they would fight the other horses and so add to the power of a knight, but a tonne of stallion is a handful at the best of times and not every knight could control them once the horses, too, got to the red mist stage. Pepper, the gelding, bit and kicked and reared with the best, but always reacted to his rider, who got him out of trouble as needed and placed him well for the next attack.

After forty minutes, the knights had been reduced by half. The Herald called out as each injured man was removed from the battleground, and their squire and the paid locals came to carry the man out, or drag the horse away, or both. Eiswolf unhorsed two knights by sheer force, fighting another to submission on foot. Then he bravely assisted two other knights on the Side of the Bear (and, inadvertently, until he saw the glint of gold, one of the Leopard knights). The Herald called a five-minute truce for those who wished to change horses or attend to their armour.

Eiswolf rode over to Perry.

"Blood injury on your left calf!" the squire called out. "Blood on your right gauntlet. What about your helm?"

"That's fine!" shouted Eiswolf. He had a cut across his brow that bled into his left eye, but did not stop him fighting. He could not feel if the other injuries were his or blood from another knight. In his excited state, he could hardly feel pain at all. But nothing affected his movement so he assumed injuries were not serious. "How's the horse?"

"Minor cuts, bridle looks fine, cut to your left stirrup-strap, saddle good to go."

And then Eiswolf was off, back to the battle. This is what knights did. This was his destiny.

In the second half, the Bear took the ascendancy. In the thud, clash, clatter of metal and men and horse-flesh, Eiswolf was at the heart, he struck, he parried, he parted man from horse and knight from dignity, Eiswolf won, Eiswolf was a hero!

The Herald called an end after fifteen minutes as the Bear was so clearly the better side. He awarded the Circlet to Sir Dietrich, the senior knight, and a loud cheer went up. This almost made up for the death of Sir Dauntless, the fearless lad who had fought in his mother's name, who snapped his neck slipping off his horse when the saddle-girth broke. He was one of three fatalities in the melee.

"They died fighters, and heroes!" said the Herald. He meant it.

Back at the tent, Perry managed to get Eiswolf out of his armour and into his court clothes but when your subject insists on demonstrating all his finest moves, catching him for long enough to lace up a robe is not easy.

"Hold still, for the love of -"

"Did you see me? Did you? Nobody! Nobody got close! Am I right? Am I right?"

"Yeah, you're right, you're the greatest. Hold still!"

And Eiswolf went off to the feast, confident that he was the premier knight of the Tourney.

***

The feast began in an orderly fashion, with brave speeches from the Earl of Dugdale and Baron Eims, and special mentions for those who had distinguished themselves in the melee. But around about three flagons in, a certain amount of grit entered the conversation.

Boasting was an established part of the ceremony: having won your battles, you were allowed (actually, expected) to stick it to the losers about what a bunch of pussies they were, and give fair warning to your opponents about how you would rattle their bones. Eiswolf was quite good at this; possibly too good, because he had a natty line in insults which the average half-cut knight could not riposte, at least not verbally.

As knights were defined by their reputations, and those without lands depended absolutely on a good reputation to get a position in the court of a duke or earl, if you go about separating a knight from his dignity and then stick it to the losers in a witty way, well, you have to expect blowback.

Eiswolf was a man of exceptional fighting ability, but he stood out for other reasons. He should have taken the clue when he flirted with the servant maid, yet again, and yet again got nowhere, because the girl said the rules might be different round his way but round here, decent people did not have sex with dumb animals.

"Sir Knight!" yelled one of the Side of the Leopard. "You fight well! For a man without balls!"

"What!" shrieked Eiswolf, leaping to his feet.

The knights of the Leopard laughed mightily. "Sir, you cannot abide a pair of balls! Why, neither your horse nor your squire has any! We only have your word," he leered, "that you have. Sir Eunuch, we will find you out tomorrow!"

Eiswolf swallowed his anger. "Sir, my horse and my squire cannot defend themselves here but I assure you, I have enough balls for all three of us! While you had not enough for yourself, Sir Runalot!"

Another knight joined in. "We have a trophy for you! A fine deer's paunch! Set the deer's liver before him!"

The deer's paunch, the guts and internal organs, was the traditional reward given to hunting dogs so this was an unusually sophisticated insult, especially after two flagons of wine.

"Sir, why bother with the deer? Let me see your own liver. I will wager it is white. You have no need of it to fight tomorrow!"

Or in other words, 'loser'. Another point for Eiswolf.

"Here, sir, I have a good report from your mother that the moon is not in your favour." A third knight chose to be witty.

"My mother?"

"Sir, you may hear her howl outside the gates, as she scavenges through the rubbish!"

Now Eiswolf did not know who or, to be brutally frank, what, his mother was, but this was not the sort of insult to parry with words. So he leapt across the table, so did the other knight, then one of the Knights of the Bear decided to join in the fun, flagons were broken and benches thrown but no swords were drawn: the Herald of the Lists had a very strict no-weapons policy at the feast, for exactly this reason.

Quietly, in a corner, the Glimmer Lord and his flame-haired squire watched all, noted all, said nothing. And further back in the shadows, the Dogstar Knight watched everything.

***

The Lords of the Tourney had a problem. They were having a quiet drink in their own tent, away from the hullabaloo of the knights.

"Tough one, this, Jonno," said Baron Eims. "I see where he's coming from. Could turn very nasty on us."

"He's got a point, Nev," said the Earl of Dugdale. "He's made this Tourney what it is. Be fair to the guy, he is the big draw."

They were facing an uncomfortable possibility: that their name knight, Sir Dietrich of Metzen, might not win the melee the next day, and could be beaten by the Knight of the White Smudge.

Sir Dietrich had brought this to their attention before the feast, wanting to know what they were going to do about it. Actually, what he said was, "You spike this bastard and spike him good! Or I don't play! You want me at the Tourney next year, you fix this!"

The promoters stared into their wine.

"Would Ice-thing take a dive?" said Jonno. "He's got no land, gold usually works."

"He looks enthusiastic to me. All mouth and puff."

"Maybe a word in his ear? We could promise him a big purse next year. Or an appearance fee? Dietrich can't go on forever."

Nev sighed. "Well, maybe Colin could come to a generous decision in the melee."

Jonno shook his head. "Not in front of everyone. Anyway, you know Colin. All straight and above board, or we don't get the good names signing up." Now it was Jonno's turn to sigh. "Maybe his luck will run out. If it don't, I'll round up the lads. Dangerous places, tournaments. You can have an accident."

***

"Bloody stupid," said Perry. "You might have wrecked everything, don't twitch, it's only salve."

"Hmph," said Eiswolf. He was never at his best at first light. Today he also had a crashing hangover, possibly a broken nose, a split lip, bruised knuckles and a lucky punch on the ribs, as well as his previous battle-scars. Not to mention the rash.

Perry was in one of his tight-lipped moods. How stupid did Eiswolf have to be, to take such ridiculous risks just before the

Grand Melee! Against Sir Dietrich! He was already half-beaten. How could his reactions be sharp and his eyesight clear with a four-flagon hangover? "So are you going to concentrate? Or will you kind of play it by ear and see what turns up? And where do you want me to take the body? Bess? Or the Princess?"

Eiswolf stood in silence, then took his sword and shield from their racks. Perry, still angry, picked up a practice shield and let Eiswolf get his eye in with a few swipes and thrusts. Perry went to collect Pepper and saddle him up, then led the horse back to Eiswolf. They were still not talking when they arrived at the arena. Then, as Eiswolf mounted up, Perry muttered to his master. Eiswolf rode into the line of knights who would take part in the Grand Melee. All twelve of them.

Eiswolf spotted the Knight in White Satin, who seemed pale and nervous: this was the first time he had progressed so far in the Tourney. Sir Dietrich, in his distinctive blue and yellow colours, gave Eiswolf a very dirty look. He heard another knight whisper "Here, doggy, doggy!" as he rode past. The Lords of the Tourney seemed very unhappy.

Then the trumpet sounded. Eiswolf was a marked man: he was fighting two knights before the last note faded away. Sir Dietrich obviously waited his turn because he did not engage with any other knight, until the Knight in White Satin charged at him. Sir Dietrich swiped the man from his saddle almost contemptuously, but did not dismount to take him on foot. White Satin made a very sensible decision, removed his helmet, and retired.

Eiswolf cracked one assailant on the side of the helmet with the pommel of his sword. The man was knocked silly but did not fall from his horse. The other man decided to come in closer but Pepper snapped and kicked at his mount and the animal was less committed than his rider. The horse reared away from Eiswolf, who got in a very handy blow to the man's back, putting him safely on the ground. The man was limping, so Eiswolf did not pursue him.

Three down. Of the seven knights left, a man in red fought one in blue and white. They did not look too dangerous to Eiswolf so he let that go on without him, he'd mop up the winner later. Two more knights sized each other up, one in purple, one in the chequerboard design called vair. They were interrupted by a knight in red and green, who rode Purple down and dismounted to defeat him on foot. Vair then cracked Purple's helmet. He fell, bleeding. Five down. Sir Dietrich was still waiting.

A blow clouted Eiswolf heavily from behind on his shoulder, then his thigh. He swivelled Pepper to face a knight in red and white who charged into his side, trying to knock both man and horse to the earth. Eiswolf turned Pepper out of the charge and came back in, slashing beneath the man's shield and catching him in the gut. Red/White groaned and slumped forward. Another blow landed on the back of Eiswolf's helmet: Vair was taking his chance. Eiswolf made Pepper rear and kick out: one hoof caught on the other horse's muzzle, making it jink, but the rider drove back again and fitted in a couple of heavy blows to Eiswolf's right arm. A knight in yellow appeared from the side and sliced at Red/White, distracting

Eiswolf's attacker long enough for Eiswolf to get away. Red/White joined battle with Yellow.

Eiswolf looked for Vair, as his horse appeared to be injured. Any knight was at a disadvantage on the ground. He galloped towards Vair but Red cut across, having seen off his opponent. Eiswolf attacked and spotted Sir Dietrich dealing efficiently with Vair on the lame horse. An easy win: but that is how Sir Dietrich had become champion four times. Eiswolf tried to be as swift and effective with his own opponent, bringing the man down with a blow from his shield, hitting the helmet so hard, the impact wrenched his neck backwards.

Yellow now rode at Eiswolf, but Eiswolf and Pepper jinked and Eiswolf knocked him down in a side-blow as he went past. The man did not fall cleanly. His spurs caught in his stirrup, his horse dragging him to the edge of the arena.

Sir Dietrich was still waiting. A silence fell across the crowd, apart from the wild neighing of the horses and the groans of the injured. Eiswolf knew he had fought too much: he should have preserved his strength, like Dietrich. This was a fight he might not win and if he did not win, he would not survive.

Sir Dietrich made his horse rear. Slowly, with enormous control, he raised his horse to a gallop towards Eiswolf. He should have been easy to sidestep, but Dietrich's horse made a sudden side-step of its own at the last second. The mounts crashed chest to chest. Dietrich stood in the saddle to bring his sword down on Eiswolf's head but Eiswolf kept his nerve and thrust towards a weak spot under Dietrich's arm. He made contact but did not break the mail-coat. Dietrich twisted his horse out of the way, then came in close for another blow to the head. Finding this defended, he crashed his sword down on Eiswolf's wounded thigh. Eiswolf felt himself weakening. He had to be Cold. Efficient. Effective. Remember Perry.

He rode Pepper away for a few paces. Dietrich shouted, presumably about cowards. Then Eiswolf turned to face the Champion of the Tourney and rode straight at him. The horses crashed heavily, shield grated on shield. Eiswolf could smell Sir Dietrich's breath. He could see the man's eyes through the slit in his helm: they were hard, blue. The knight leaned forward, hissing at him. "Animal!"

But Eiswolf did not lose control. When Dietrich leaned forward, Eiswolf saw a small gap above his collarbone between the mail of his headpiece and his mail coat. Eiswolf went for a slicing stroke. The blood ran in a trickle at first, then a flood. The crowd were silent.

Sir Dietrich fell from his horse.

***

The final feast was generous, if a little subdued. The Herald announced that the new Champion was Sir Eiswolf, descended of Rime and Storm, under the device of the Snow Wolf. Much valour had been shown, many champions named, but those who had not succeeded this time should nurse their bruises (cue audience laughter) and come back next year, more determined than ever. But some knights would not ride home. They should remember the fallen, the three knights in the first melee, the four in the Grand Melee, as well as two stone-lifters, a couple of archers and three unfortunates in the wrestling competition. The doctors had told him, however, that Sir Dietrich would recover, and be back next year! This brought a round of applause.

Eiswolf could barely hear anything. He held the trophy in his hand, a simple circlet of gold, almost in a state of shock after three days of solid fighting. After the melee, he had passed the mortuary area: how had so many died in a game? Looking at the corpses laid out without their helmets, he realized he had laughed, had feasted, with all of them.

"Good going, boss," whispered Perry, as he poured Eiswolf's wine. He had also made sure to pick up the bags of gold which changed hands as the unofficial prize for the Tourney: honour was mighty fine, but knights who endangered their lives in these contests wanted cash as well. Corsa was now laden with a fortune.

"I remembered what you said. Thanks," said Eiswolf, quietly.

"Needs to be said, sometimes," Perry folded his arms. "So let's go and slay a dragon."

***

Nev and Jonno had less to smile about, later in their private tent.

"Had to happen," said Nev. "One day."

"But why that? God, he's hardly an advertisement for chivalry, is he?" Jonno was deeply depressed.

Nev leaned back on his chair and searched for a silver lining. "Well, he's on this Quest and none have survived so far. Look on the bright side, he's off to fight a dragon. And the Glimmer Lord seemed pleased. Never seen him crack a smile before. More wine?"

"One more year, we could have had Dietrich. It'll be hard work, getting back to that." Jonno gloomed.

"Too many deaths as well. We want winners, not to wipe out all the knights in the realms. We'll have to get Colin on-side about jousting. It'd cut the casualties. "

"You know what Colin's like. That's your job. Here he is! Colin! Talk of the devil!"

And the Herald of Lists entered and removed his tabard. "I'm gasping," he announced. "Well, what a turn-up, eh? Could be a good story for next year, though."

Jonno winked. "Nev's got an idea about that."

***

Eiswolf and Perry rode quietly away early in the morning. Perry had arranged for their new 'team' to meet them the next week at the Palace before setting off in search of dragons, because he wanted his knight to have a couple of days rest, and for Bess to check over his injuries. Eiswolf was subdued, but he always was after a tourney: the physical and emotional cost was high.

"Sir Champion!" A clear voice rang out.

Eiswolf swung Pepper around, ready to attack.

"Not so hot, sir!" The Dogstar Knight was under the trees at the side of the road, his white, blood-eyed hounds sniffing to and fro in front of his great black horse. "You fight bravely, but not foolishly. That is rare. I salute you." The giant man took off his black helmet, revealing the ivory face and white hair beneath. "May you succeed in the Seven Tests of Kolras as well. If that is your desire."

"What do you know of me?" Eiswolf was thoroughly unsettled.

The fairy knight laughed. "That you are unique. You are marked out, but maybe not the way you think, Sir Knight. Give my greetings to your good Lady Bess."

Then he turned to ride into the greenwood and was gone.

"Oof," said Perry. "The sooner we get back to the Palace…"

They rode on at an amble, until Eiswolf started to feel more like talking. "Where did you hear that, what you said?"

"A very wise old woman told me, I ignored her, and I've regretted that ever since."

"Odd thing to say. 'Win Ugly'. Is that what she meant?"

Perry snorted. "Who's the guy with the pretty necklace AND the circlet? Maybe if you try hard, you can get matching earrings."

Eiswolf laughed. They made their way back to the safety of the Kingdom.

6: Dragonslayer

The King sat on his gilded throne in the Great Hall: his faithful Hegemon stood alongside. The Princess sat on her glittering chair. All the nobility of the Kingdom were there, in gold, silver, and rainbows of velvet and brocade. Both King and Princess stood to lead the applause for the mighty Champion of the Grand Tourney. Here was a hero! Here was a man fitted to pass the Seven Tests of Kolras! Here was a future King!

The King, the Hegemon and the Princess shared these thoughts, although not, perhaps, the same celebratory tone.

Dammit, thought the King, what is this man? A cockroach?

The Hegemon simmered. That lumbering, crude, rough - I will not let this happen to my lovely lady!

Oh, poo, thought the Princess. Plan D, here we go.

"Welcome, Sir Knight! Our Champion!" The King knew how to make an elegant speech, so he did. Wine flowed, the feasting table groaned with roast meats and fine pastries. Music filled the air, as troubadours sang of the legendary exploits of the knight.

Eiswolf was approached by many of the mighty in the land, assailed by earls and positively drowning in dukes, all wanting to grasp his hand and look deep into his eyes to assure him of their utmost loyalty and devotion. Their ladies, too, pressed silken fingers on his sleeve, or tried to whisper in his ear. For this man was in line for half the Kingdom, and everyone wanted him to know they were on his side. This man could now do favours.

The Hegemon snarled internally. So quick to forget their true King, so foolishly obvious, so trusting that the creature they wooed so brazenly would listen! Or live long enough to grant their wishes, ha! The wine turned sour in his mouth, and he made mental lists of the most blatant turncoats.

The Princess also suffered many congratulations. Ladies made witty asides about how lucky she was. A true hero! So strong! So virile! So determined! So unusual! How relieved she must be, after so many disappointments that a man worthy of the Tests had finally been found! And not before time …

Oh, poo, she thought, again. This Really Will Not Do.

Then the hall rang with calls for Eiswolf to make a speech. He stood, strong, foursquare and confident. "I am a man of few words as I'm sure you are all hoping." Some laughed. "I appear before you as a plain knight and the humble servant of this Court. I bow before my liege lord the King and my lady the Princess! In the name of this Kingdom, I was granted victory in a great contest: and now the prize must go to its rightful owner."

He pulled out the golden circlet from his jerkin. "This is the Honour of the Grand Tourney. But, Princess, you can give me a greater reward. As I wear and will always bear your favour closest to my heart, please accept this small token in return." He knelt in front of her silver throne, holding out the circlet to her with both hands so that all could see.

The Princess smiled modestly but winningly. She seemed too shy to take the trinket from him, but reassured by her ladies, she leaned forward to grasp it. "Sir Knight, We accept this gift with all Our heart!"

The ladies applauded.

But he did not let go straight away. Quietly, he said "Lady, many brave men died so that you may wear this. But however much death this brings, I will pursue the ultimate prize. I swear this."

A cold sweat ran down the Princess' back. Did he know what she planned? Or had he really fallen in love with her and was doing the total commitment bit? For the first time, she was a tad uncertain about whether she could overcome this ... wolfie-thingy.

She smiled, tightly. "Sir Knight, We shall treasure this above all other favours, We shall wear this at our highest and most joyous occasions!" She pulled the circlet away from him, and put it on.

The whole court applauded. Eiswolf returned to his place, the feasting resumed. Happiness was all around. Along with plots, alliances, affairs, side-deals and secret agreements, because after all, this was a court.

Eiswolf toasted the nobility, and the King, and even exchanged a glance with the Hegemon. But every time he looked at the Princess, all he could see was blood dripping from the circlet into her silver-gold hair.

***

Bess welcomed Eiswolf back to her hovel in her usual manner, declaring that she hoped he had got THAT out of his system now. He grunted, but grinned, and limped off to hunt hares for the pot.

Bess and Perry took advantage of the early summer sunshine to lay Eiswolf's kit on the ground, looking for wear, repair or replacement. Bess tutted. "How he doesn't catch a terrible disease I will never know. Ugh, throw that one away, Perry. So when are all these miscellaneous men arriving?"

"Should be a couple of days. We're got far-seeing, all-hearing, strong as an ox, I found a swift runner in the market yesterday, a Southron called Zadab. Then we can go off and kill a dragon." He grinned cheerfully, digging more linen out of a saddlebag.

Bess looked at Perry very carefully. "We? What part do you expect to play?"

Perry subsided. "Team support. I'm supposed to keep everyone happy. Bess, have you ever seen a dragon? A real one?"

She shrugged. "Depends what you mean by a dragon. Have I ever seen a scaly critter with four legs and wings that breathes fire and only eats virgins? No, because they can't exist. For lots of reasons."

"Then how do we fulfil the Test?"

"Creatively," said Bess. "Urk, don't touch - What was that before our mighty knight got his hands on it? A shirt?"

Sorting out the fighter was a tougher business.

"I'm fine, Bess, honest."

"Don't be a baby. Take off that tunic. Oh, for the love of - What is it, man? What have you found that I've not seen before?"

Reluctantly, Eiswolf removed his tunic and shirt, revealing bruises and scrapes from the Tourney and his adventures before. "Perry's put salve on already," he muttered. "I'm fine."

Bess inspected him and moved his arms about. "What's wrong with your shoulder?"

"Twisted it."

"What's this?" She prodded the little triangle of bruises under his armpit.

"The witch. I dunno," he said, before she could start her inquisition.

At heart, she was relieved. At least Perry had kept him out of the clutches of the doctors. The salve, a mix of beeswax, olive oil, honey and oil of thyme, might not have done any good but did no harm, either. Sometimes Bess thought if she could only get people to leave well alone, not 'doing' things, plastering cures all over and digging around to 'purify' the flesh, that would be her greatest medical gift to this society. And, unfortunately, about as likely as persuading them that 'bad smells' and 'night air' did not cause disease.

Perry returned with a clean shirt. "What do you think, Bess?"

"I think he was very lucky and he has a very faithful squire," said Bess.

"What about the rash?"

"What rash?"

So after a confused but heated exchange of mumbling between the knight and his squire ('Show her!" "No!" "You said you'd show her!" "No!" "Go on!") Eiswolf, very reluctantly, dropped his breeches.

"Dear God, man, what have you been doing?"

Eiswolf muttered to the air. "A curse, by the witch. I'm cursed."

"No, Eiswolf. That is not a curse. Dear oh lor', what did I tell you when you first started out?" She tapped him on the chest, accusingly. "So which floozy was this, Perry?"

Perry tried to stare into space and failed. "Well, the witch, I think. He - he laboured mightily for three nights."

"I contended with her," said Eiswolf.

"Is that what they call it these days. Oh, you mean Jocasta? Well, if you've been sleeping with Jojo, you'll be lucky if a rash is all you've got. Bizarre woman. Wash that thing and I'll get a salve." So Bess went off to find a potion in the hovel. Eiswolf did insist on putting the salve on for himself. It stung.

***

The Land of the Dragon was seven days' journey. The first part of the road also went to Cymenshore, so was clearly marked and well-travelled. On mounts from the Kingdom's stables (including the dopey charger; the Master of Horse finally managed to palm the animal off on Meroens the wrestler), Eiswolf's troop of experts rode steadily towards the land devastated for so long by this supernatural beast. Eiswolf led, riding on Pepper, followed by Perry on Corsa, then Fittle the all-hearing on a cob, Meroens on his charger leading the archer Flowers on his horse, as the man was too far sighted to ride without assistance. Zadab the runner, at the rear, dozed on a mule.

By the second day, Eiswolf had established that no-one had ever seen a dragon, although Fittle had heard tell that they were huge but not, as the stories would have it, scaly like a snake. "Sort of knobbly, they are. The man what told me, what saw one, or maybe his brother, he says they run fast but not like a horse. And they're brown."

"But what about breathing fire?" said Perry.

"He didn't say about that."

On the third day, Flowers the archer, a short-tempered man, had taken a severe dislike to Meroens, as the wrestler came from a town where Flowers' cousin had been swindled. As Meroens had the task of leading Flowers' horse, this gave many opportunities for low-level curses and accusation. Fittle was also working his way around to asking for a bigger purse, because at least he'd heard of the dragon and he could get close to those as had seen it for more information, unlike the blind bastard Flowers, the thicko Meroens, or the foreigner Zadab.

"No," said Eiswolf. 'The purse is the same for all of you. And nobody gets a penny until I fight the dragon."

"Well, maybe I'll have to reconsider my participation," said Fittle, tartly.

"You'll have to reconsider your occupation if you do," said Eiswolf. "How will you get on with no ears?" He showed the man the sword by his side. Fittle subsided.

By the fourth day, Meroens had taken a couple of swipes at Flowers, Fittle constantly muttered to himself and Zadab quite clearly lived in a world of his own, assisted by dry leaves which he kept in a small bag, chewing one from time to time. But finally, as they stopped for the night, they saw a sign that they were getting near.

Well, the tavern was called The Green Dragon, for a start. The landlord was only mildly curious, for many travelled to see the dragon and this was not the first group intent on slaying it.

"So is it, like, big?" said Perry.

"Big enough to kill a man," said the landlord.

"I heard they was knobbly," said Fittle.

"Maybe so. It's got an evil temper," said the landlord. "I'd think that was more important."

"What does it eat?" said Perry.

"Nosey travellers," said the landlord, tiring of questions.

Perry settled back on the bench and nursed his ale. If there was one big lesson from all this, he told himself, he travels fastest who travels alone. He was also very uncomfortable being so close to Cymenshore. The road branched off towards the Valley of Swords in about another mile, where the merchants who had shared the road would split off. He had asked the other travellers about how matters were in the big port after the devastating raid eight years before. They said normality had returned fast: the town had been rebuilt, the harbour repaired and its walls strengthened. If anything, Cymenshore was richer than ever, under the inspired leadership of a man called

Richard of Clifton, who had stepped into the breach left by the deaths of so many in the Vendant family, the traditional aristocracy of Cymenshore.

"Best thing that ever happened to the place," said one trader. "And a family to come after him, too. Three fine sons. Why not come down and see for yourself, we're staying for a month or two."

But Perry shook his head and regretted even thinking about Cymenshore.

***

The Princess sent out a call across the Kingdom for the sagest and most expert wise-women, for she had decided to become adept in the skills of healing, to bring relief to the sick and the dying. This was to be her womanly Quest, while her knight fought dragons and - and whatever else was on that ruddy Manifest. Try as she might, the Princess had not been able to persuade any member of the King's Chamber, not even the love-struck Hegemon, to show her the list. So if the dragon did not fix Wolfie-thingy, and she could not pre-rig a Quest, Plan D needed a more direct approach.

A motley collection of women came to the palace: midwives, dressers of corpses, toothless hags who'd lay a curse for a penny, vague sorts who collected dew by the light of the moon, and a few brisk bone-setters. Bess, curious to see the object of Eiswolf's quest, left her hovel and joined the gathering in the courtyard.

It was the sort of crowd where, when you look around, you sincerely hope you do not fit in. Talking to your invisible friend/demon/dead grannie was popular, as was glowering darkly while grasping an ancient book, preferably bound in the skin of a murderer. Bess gravitated towards the bonesetters, tough women with strong hands and a very firm idea about how skeletons ought to work.

The King's Herald came into the courtyard to bring order to the chattering crowd. He stood by the dungeon door and announced, "Her Majesty the Princess has no interest in those who only commune with spirits, nor those who depend for their wisdom on the intermediary of a demon or familiar."

"Eh? What's he say?" said one toothless crone.

"Dunno," said her companion. "Speak up, man!"

"NO SPIRIT HEALERS!" yelled the Herald. One of those days, alas.

"What about cats?" said a young White Witch, tinkling with the bells and crystals of her craft.

"NO CATS!" yelled the Herald.

"She's missing out," pouted the White Witch. "Cats can be very potent."

"Nor!" the Herald tried to get back on track. "Nor does her Majesty wish to lay a curse or any form of spell with words, nor to purchase …" and here he gave a meaningful stare to the glowering book-carriers, "any spell-book, grimoire, occult manuscript, wisdom of the ancients, or secret ceremonials of a hidden cult!"

"What?" yelled another crone.

"NO BOOKS!" yelled the Herald.

A bonesetter sniffed. "She's not leaving herself with much, is she?"

Crones and spell-makers began to leave, muttering that women of their special expertise were plainly not valued in a modern court. Maybe, some whispered, it was not the brightest idea to upset so many people who laid curses for a living, whether traditional or text-based. But if that's what Her Majesty wanted -

"Now," said the Herald. "Those who can demonstrate true skill in the healing arts, with knowledge both of simples and compounded medicines, may remain."

"What's a compounded medicine?" said one of the bonesetters.

The Herald sighed. "If you don't know, sweetheart, you've no chance." And a few more women trickled out of the courtyard.

About a dozen candidates were left: Bess recognised a couple of women who, in another society, would have been doctors, a very experienced midwife, and a famous White Witch from the far west. Bess suspected she came as much to be seen as selected. A page took their names and ran in to the Princess; they would be announced and interviewed in order. Bess was about half-way down the list. Light rain began to fall. The Herald generously allowed them to shelter under a pent-roof at one side of the courtyard: of course, they were not allowed into the Palace itself. One of the 'doctors' obtained a small stool from a palace servant for the White Witch, who was in her seventies.

They went in one by one. The Princess dismissed some swiftly, but took her time over others: the longer, presumably, the better. The midwife came out again and Bess beckoned her over.

"So what is she looking for?"

The midwife frowned. "I'm not sure. Be careful of that one, Bess. How's your boy?"

"Oh, off slaying a dragon. Questing, it's his thing. He gets to marry the Princess if he wins."

"Well, keep me posted," said the midwife. "If anything comes of it, I'll put you in for nine months' time. Assuming the baby's human." She had the grace to look apologetic before she said, "But I do know a very experienced master of hounds. Just in case."

The woman meant well, Bess told herself, as she forced a smile. They all meant well. Except for the ones who didn't.

"The Good Witch Bess!"

She went through the entrance into the long, cold stone corridor, towards the huge iron-bound door of the dungeon. A guard glared at her as she went into the royal quarters.

The Princess, attended by her ladies, was on her silver chair. Her red pennant hung above. She wore pale pink brocade glittering with silver threads, and pearls, lots of them, in celebration of her virginity.

Bess curtseyed deeply and took careful note. Under the glamour and glitter, the Princess was a confident girl… No. Bess corrected herself. Too old to be a girl. The blonde hair looked natural. So what was this sudden urge to improve the lot of humanity?

"Good Witch Bess," said the Princess. "Please stand, in this chamber all are members of Our Court. This may be a dungeon, but We breathe royal air." She sighed, dramatically, arranging herself on her throne.

"Thank you, Your Majesty."

"And what of your skills, Bess?"

"Your Majesty, I am practised in the ways of herbs, salves, unguents and tinctures, compounding of elements and extraction of virtues from salts and minerals. I am present at birth and death, and at all stages between. I dress wounds and soothe fevers, bring restful sleep and guard against the evil airs of the night."

The Princess smiled graciously. "Well said, witch. And in all of this, do you use spells?"

Tricky one. "If my patient wishes. If they find an incantation comforting."

The Princess looked at her a little harder. "We would talk with this woman in private." Her ladies curtseyed, and left. "So, Bess, you seem to find little use for spells. What is the source of your knowledge?"

So Bess told her about years of study in a college of the healing arts, taught by great professors, because her homeland made much less distinction between the capacities of men and women. She had become proficient in drugs and minor surgery, but most important of all, in diagnosis and –

"Diag-what?" The Princess leaned forward. "You use strange words, allow Us to catch up with you."

"Diagnosis. Finding the exact disease or condition, Your Majesty, because if you don't know what the problem is, you cannot give the right treatment."

"Is it not enough to balance the humours, heat with cold, or wet with dry?"

"Well, no. Inflammation, for example, can have many causes. Although symptomatic relief might help, stop you feeling sore, that won't cure the problem."

"Oh," said the Princess. "The doctors of this land do not share that view."

"I know, your Majesty," said Bess, grimly. The doctors of this land killed more than they cured.

"Interesting. And what of the spotted fever which assails the people of the lower town?"

Bess gave her own reading of the outbreaks of typhus and sepsis that occasionally swept through the overcrowded and insanitary poor quarters.

"Rats?" said the Princess.

"The fleas from rats, Your Majesty. And some think the Pest itself may be connected."

The Princess shivered despite herself. "It is many years since our people have been visited by the Pest. So what must be done? What banes shall we use?"

This was a chance to tell authority how to control at least some infectious diseases, so Bess took it. "A new approach, your Majesty. Kill all rats, naturally. Remove harbouring places for fleas such as unnecessary tapestries, and the rest beaten or cleansed regularly with soap and doused in essences of peppermint and thyme. While we're about it, remove old floor rushes before laying the next set. Actually, you don't need rushes at all, really, on a washed floor. "

"But what about the dogs?" said the Princess.

"They can be trained to go outside. And so can the men," said Bess, firmly. "Then wash your hounds in those essences every day for a fortnight, then monthly after, and get your washerwomen to boil the linens."

The Princess looked down at her linen underdress, finely woven and delicately worked. "Even this? It'll be ruined."

"Alas, spotted fever knows no rank, your Majesty. Linen is tougher than you'd think. "

"You can't boil wool, though. Not unless you're outfitting a troupe of dwarves. And silk would just die." The Princess stroked her pink brocade.

"You may dress them with a drying dust from the East. A trader in the City can obtain some, ask for sharp white earth. A simpler form of costume may be preferred. And," in for a penny, "Limewashing walls is beneficial, it poisons bacter - um - many harmful things."

"Like peasants do?" The Princess was unenthusiastic, and she drew the line at requiring the whole court to bathe daily. "We'd need an entire regiment of servants just to bring water from the river, the well would run dry in a week. But interesting, interesting. Now, Bess, they say you are a companion of Our brave knight, Sir Eiswolf?"

"I have helped him since he came to this land as a boy, yes, Your Majesty." Bess could not prevent herself from smiling.

The Princess was on this like a hawk. "We see the pride in your eyes. He is unusual, is he not?"

"When he first came to me …" And Bess, softened up by finding a listener for her medical theories, launched into the story of her boy, outcast even by street beggars because of the ridiculous idea that he was a werewolf. She looked after him, as far as he let her, taught him, sent him to sword-masters and riding-masters. And then, in a skirmish about seven years ago, he had won his spurs and been knighted on the battlefield. "He has overcome so much, despite what they all say about him, and he won his knighthood for courage, not favour at court,"

"And you are quite sure he is not a werewolf?" said the Princess. "You understand how important this is to Us." A tiny shiver of distaste went down her back but she controlled it.

"Quite, Your Majesty. I can assure you he is a man as other men." Bess grinned to herself. If not more so, if the other day was any evidence.

"Thank you," said the Princess. The woman was plainly besotted with her strange, adopted son. Although she had useful ideas and seemed skilled in the right sort of medicines, the poisonous ones, she might have a mother's protective instinct for her creature. "One suspects you would not wish to relinquish your comfortable hovel and live at Court just yet. But We hope to discuss these matters again, soon."

Bess left, happy to have seen the Princess, an intelligent woman if somewhat remote, and taken a first step to introducing modern medicine. She waved happily to the other women in the courtyard. Bess did not see the late arrival, a woman in purple and green, long black hair straggling over her shoulders.

But the Herald called her, and the Princess received her.

"I am called Jocasta, the Witch of the Wood, Your Majesty! I am mistress of shadows, the caller of the dark spirits, a dancer under the moon." Jocasta curtseyed dramatically.

At last, thought the Princess. A poisoner. "And are you prepared to assist Us in Our tasks, no matter what the danger?"

Jocasta's liquid black eyes flashed and her voice rose. "My lady, my life is no longer of value to me! My heart has been broken by an evil knight! He came to me and for three nights we were in Paradise, then he betrayed me through his sorcery. He took from me that which was most dear!"

The Princess frowned doubtfully. "Your virginity?"

That put Jocasta off her stroke. "Er, no, my Lady, that which was, er, second, er, most dear." She got back into wailing mode. "My power, he struck down my power!"

"Oh. So you haven't got it any more?"

Jocasta paused. "It came back. When he went away. After a bit. But assist me to pursue this knight and revenge my …"

"Power-cut," said the Princess. "Must have been nasty."

"Yes, well. And I shall care not what is my fate! I am in your hands, Lady!"

The Princess sat back on her throne. Mad, mad and mad. But maybe useful. "By the way, what is the name of this dastardly deceiver?"

"Eiswolf!" growled Jocasta, who had not really tuned into Court gossip and completely forgot why Eiswolf had come to her in the first place.

How convenient, thought the Princess. She leaned forward. "That'll be our secret, Witch," she said.

***

The dragon-slayers were getting closer to their prey. They must be, as the road to the citadel where the Dragon wreaked its destruction was lined with stalls offering genuine dragon scales, dragon-shaped gingerbreads, a variety of little dragon flags and pennants, and guaranteed, battle-tested, never to be repeated offers on dragon-proof armour that still had the dents (not holes, mark you) from the last bloke.

"So he's dead?" said Perry, to one of the hopeful armourers.

"Yeah, well, not by the dragon," said the armourer. "He caught a nasty chill hanging about, gets cold up here in winter."

And still there was no agreement on what the dragon looked like. Perry tried. "Could be green, that's traditional. Wings seem to be optional."

"This is not helping." Eiswolf was becoming unsettled. "Maybe it's a shape-changer."

Meroens laughed, the deep-throated chuckle of a strong man who knows no fear. "Sir Knight, I feast on dragons! Let it see my mighty fist, and tremble! For I shall rip the beast from nape to crotch, and damn its fiery breath!"

Perry leaned over to his knight and whispered. "He's not in the same world as the rest of us."

"None of them are," said Eiswolf. "We've lost Fittle again." The ear-wigger was also a sneak thief, so this was exactly the kind of crowd he liked: distracted and dense.

The walls of the citadel rose up: serious, old, massive stone watch-towers, with guards standing between the crenellations. Above the main gate was a stone carving of a dragon, this time a long, low-bodied creature with a forked tongue. Each traveller to the city had to stop to give their name and business. A strict curfew operated at sundown, so Eiswolf's group needed to stay together.

"I am Sir Eiswolf, the last and lost, descended of Rime and Storm, the North Wind and the Northern Lights, faithful to the Gods of Ice! I have travelled far and long to come to this place, in the name of the Eternal Rose and the Kingdom!"

"How do you spell that?" said the guard. "And are you here on business, for pleasure or visiting friends and relatives?"

"I'm here to kill the Dragon," said Eiswolf, slightly bemused.

"Business, then," said the guard, marking his roster. "Gernit, any room at the Dragonslayer's hostel? Oh, right, sir, your lucky day, we do have a couple of rooms left. So that's you and a squire, then."

"And a team," said Perry. "Fast-runner, far-seer, all-hearer and a strongman."

"Oh, full set," said the guard, approvingly. "Well, I'm sure we can squeeze you in. Ten gold pieces for the entry permits, team discount, and that'll be three silver coins per night per team member, livery extra."

They rode into the ancient citadel. Around them were small shops and stalls selling all that the discerning traveller and dragon-fancier might want. A horn sounded to announce the curfew: the huge gates locked with a clang. Instantly, the town glowed with torches set in iron holders in the walls. A boy in a green costume and a strange hat, which might be interpreted as a dragon's head, dashed in front of their horses. "Tickets for the show!" he yelled. "See the Dragon! See the Dragon! The only official tickets for the show!"

Perry looked at Eiswolf. "I suppose we better had. Boy, two tickets."

They handed over six silver pieces and dismounted, giving their reins to Meroens with instructions on how to get to the hostel, then followed the boy. In the centre of the citadel was a high curved wooden wall, breached by a carved gateway. Once inside, Perry and Eiswolf saw bank upon bank of benches, which rose up and away from a large sunken arena, as deep as two men were tall. At each end of the sand-covered arena, huge, iron-banded gates led under the benches. Torches burned all around.

A man came to collect their tickets. "Dragonslayer or non-dragonslayer?"

"Er, slayer," said Eiswolf. Perry and he took their seats a couple of rows above one of the gates. The benches were packed.

A small door opened in the side of the arena. A man in glittering black and silver armour and a complex silver helmet walked forcefully into the centre, followed by a division of guards. At a signal, pages in silver brocade ran forward carrying small torches, some swinging them about their heads, others hurling them up and catching them in rhythm. Deep music throbbed, distant horns and drums. The man raised his helmet, to applause from the audience.

"Once!" cried the man, his voice echoing around the arena. "We were at peace! We were rich! We were content!"

The music began: the simple songs of the happy peasant, chirpy and clumsy, as interpreted by a court musician. Pages strewed flowers and mimed general cuteness, while the man intoned a pocket history of the land. Apparently, this was remarkable chiefly for a lack of noteworthy knights, artists or events, and mainly famous for cheese (cue comedy turn from three pages). The music rose in intensity.

"But then!" cried the man. "Came … The …"

At a stroke, all torches were extinguished.

"Dragon!" cried the man. Drums, horns and trumpets went crazy. Torches flared, this time in ghastly reds and oranges. The pages moved around in general imitation of tortured souls.

"In the deep south, men heard a rumour," the man intoned. "But who knows its secret origin. To us came," pause, blackout, ghostly glimmer behind the man, a pale shape, huge, growing bigger and bigger, "An Egg!"

Oohs and aahs from the crowd.

"This Egg, we warmed on the breasts of our virgins, surrounded in silks and washed in the finest perfumes." The Egg got brighter as he spoke. "Until one day …"

Thunderclap. A black mark appeared on the Egg, which now glowed red.

"It Hatched!" Blackout, rising moans and lamentations, drummers started up a frantic crescendo. The torches were lit once more, huge and fizzing with sparks, and the pages dashed about in terror.

To doom-laden choruses and drums, the man cried, "We fed the beast, night and day, until our city starved and our children were sold into slavery to buy meat, more meat, for the creature."

"Meat!" repeated the pages, lumbering about on all fours.

"Many tried to kill the dragon, but none succeeded!"

"Meat!" said the pages, dying artistically all over the arena.

"Brave men came to save us, but all were destroyed."

"Meat," growled the pages, gnawing on each other's arms and legs.

"I think I get the picture," whispered Eiswolf to Perry.

"I think they're hanging it out too long," said Perry. "Losing dramatic momentum here."

"And tonight!" cried the man, "Yet more brave men are here! Sir Frithwald, stand for us!"

A thin man about four seats along stood up awkwardly, to take the cheers of the crowd.

"Bloody hell," said Eiswolf.

"Sir Ignatius!"

A dark man in the row in front of Eiswolf bounced to his feet and bowed.

"And finally, the Champion of the Grand Tourney himself, the one, the only, Sir Eiswolf!"

Perry kicked his knight who stood, then turned on the 'I'm the real champion' bit by clasping his hands above his head.

"No getting out of it now," said Perry.

The man hushed the crowd to silence. "But what are we really waiting for?"

Voices in the audience yelled, "The Dragon!"

The man nodded, and bowed. The pages ran out of the arena. The man signalled to the guards. "Take your places. Ladies and gentlemen, no sudden moves, no unofficial torches. Do not provoke the beast or we cannot guarantee your safety. Lights, please."

His men withdrew behind shoulder-high panels. The music stopped. Some of the torches were dimmed. Heavy growls and thumps rumbled across the sand, as if a creature was trying to get out -

The gate beneath Eiswolf and Perry swung open. Even from a good five metres above, the stench was indescribable. The growling got louder, this time not a dramatic interpretation by the pages.

The man called out. "The Dragon!"

A growl shook the arena's seats.

"I can see it!" whispered Perry.

A huge head showed through the gate beneath them, dark and roughly arrow-shaped, swinging heavily from side to side. A long pink slit tongue darted from the mouth. Then, slowly, with an odd, sideways gait, the dragon walked into the arena: four-legged, about as high as a man, dragging a heavy tail at least as long as its body, grey, rough, vast.

Eiswolf swallowed hard. "I was expecting two blokes in a dragon-suit."

The dragon raised its head, saw the man in the helmet and waddled towards him, then raised its nose into the air, flicking its tongue to catch his scent. And then ran towards him. Very, very fast.

"God Almighty!" cried Perry.

The man dashed behind one of the barriers and a guard waved a torch as a distraction. The dragon crashed into the wooden panel with a shock that ran through the sand and echoed up into the seats above.

"The dragon is hungry!" cried the man. "Feed the beast or we will not leave this place alive!" While the dragon sniffed around the barriers, a couple of guards at the other gate entered dragging a goat on a halter. They tied the halter to an iron ring in the arena, then ran out again. The dragon picked up the motion, turned, saw the goat, started running and –

"Oh God," cried Perry.

End of show. The drums, muffled now, beat as the crowd left the arena in silence.

"Who knew?" But even Eiswolf could not stop the catch in his throat.

***

Back at the hostel, the atmosphere was tense. A kerfuffle had erupted just before Eiswolf and Perry arrived, as Sir Ignatius' servants tried to throw their weight around. Several broken benches, noses and a few loose teeth later, Sir Ignatius' men declared that this stinking hovel was no fit place for their master to sleep, and withdrew. The knight himself had not deigned to make an appearance.

"Blow-hard," said Eiswolf, looking at the wreckage. "Get him without his squad, he'll cut and run, I'll make a bet."

"Takes some of them that way," said a serving man, as he put the benches upright again.

From a corner, Sir Frithwald watched them with oddly blank eyes. He seemed to be operating automatically, barely speaking to anyone.

"What's with him?" said Perry to the serving man.

"Marked," said the man.

"Like how?"

"Like, he sees death. Takes some of them that way. He's on his own, no money, that's not his own horse. One last throw for him to make his name and win his lady. You've seen the type."

"Fey," said Eiswolf. "God, can't you talk him out of it?"

The knight who saw his own death appeared to register their presence for a moment, then went back into another world of terror.

"Not that sort," said the man. "More ale?"

They drank in morose silence. But on the third flagon, Perry felt bold enough to ask. "So how exactly do you plan to kill that thing?"

"Not a clue," Eiswolf's mouth was grim.

"But you must have an idea!" Suddenly, Perry began to worry. This was not the careful knight that Perry knew. Was he, too, fey? "You never go in without a plan! Ever!"

Eiswolf grunted, shaking his head. "I need a better look. In daylight."

"But if it's a creature of magic, maybe it's only visible at night?"

"Idiot!" Eiswolf banged his hand on the table. "That thing is flesh and blood! It's killable!" He glared at Perry ferociously.

Bravado, Perry decided. The stupidly fatal sort. "I don't think anyone can kill that! Not the knight's way! Let's just get out!"

Eiswolf grabbed Perry by the arm. "Do you doubt me?"

"No! But…"

"Do you doubt me!"

The tavern was silent.

Perry whispered. "I don't want you to do this. We'll find something else!"

And that was the only spark the fire needed. "What! WE? Are WE fighting that dragon?" He roared. "Who are you to tell ME!"

Perry tried to pull away from Eiswolf's grip. "This is suicide!"

But Eiswolf, in his fury, dug his hand harder into Perry's arm to pull the squire face to face. "Do tell me, squire, what clever underhand piece of tomfoolery do you suggest? Listen to me! I will do this with honour. Honour!"

Perry hissed back. "Then you'll be a very honourable corpse!"

"Silence! You tell me about honour? You half-man, you nothing!" Eiswolf shoved his squire away roughly. "I must do this, and I will. Be ready to arm me, then your duties are ended." White as a sheet, he drained off his beer and marched out.

Perry shook, barely able to hold his cup.

The serving man swooped by and offered up a flagon. "Free refill. Takes some of them that way. You'll be all right, always a job for a good squire, there'll be another knight along when that one gets - "

Which is when Perry threw the beer in his face and ran out.

***

Fittle had managed to get Eiswolf an interview with the Keeper of the Dragon the next morning. Out of his black and silver armour, the Keeper proved to be a tall man in late middle age, with dark hair whitened in a badger-stripe over one ear. He was heavily scarred: his hands were criss-crossed with fine lines, and he had two large cut-marks on his face, one on his chin, the other across his brow above his eyes.

"Sir Knight, we welcome all who would rid our land of this curse!" He seemed genuinely friendly.

"I would not wish to interrupt your essential preparations." Eiswolf managed the courtly words despite his hammering hangover. "But if I am to contest your beast, I must familiarise myself with its ways."

The Keeper smiled. Not many knights took the time for this: not that many stayed after seeing the dragon and giving the whole concept a good night's thought. Sir Ignatius was already looking shaky.

"This way, Sir Knight." They went down a ladder into the arena, then across the sand to the far gate and into a timber-lined corridor. Through another gate of iron bars, they came out into an open space lined with huge metal cages. In the centre, men in stout leather aprons offloaded a cart of ox carcasses. Caped leather hoods covered their neck and shoulders, and they wore chain-mail gloves.

"If you will follow me?" The Keeper led Eiswolf to a platform at one side, reached by a ladder the height of two men. The Keeper climbed up, then Eiswolf, then one of the men in leather. The man pulled the ladder up after him. A bell rang. The men ran from the cart into the corridor and closed the iron gate after them. Then, at another bell, panels in the cages slid to one side and out came the Dragons. Not one, not two, but at least eight or nine, some mere striplings the size of a man, others the size of a donkey and then came…

"Ah, yes," said the Keeper, with satisfaction. "Mavis."

"Who!"

"Called her after my wife's sister." The Keeper smiled.

Eiswolf could not believe his eyes. The huge dragons began to rip the carcasses apart, snarling and hissing at each other, making vultures look like creatures of refinement and elegance.

"Her?" said Eiswolf. He had never put his mind to it before. But then, who had? He had assumed dragons were - well, the sort you fought were - well, male.

"They are all ladies," said the Keeper. "You can tell by the way they squabble." He smiled tolerantly as his ladies ripped into flesh, bone and each other.

"But to release your land from its curse, do I have to kill all of them?" Eiswolf's voice went up an octave despite himself.

The Keeper laughed. "The challenge is against the oldest dragon. The one you saw last night. We call her Ethel. After my auntie."

Eiswolf looked as hard as he could for areas of weakness. The creatures were covered in rough, thick, heavy skin and seemed to have little sense of pain. Their run was ungainly, unlike a horse as Fittle had said, but lightning fast, their jaws could crunch through the skull of a bull like a man eating a pie.

"So she's not here?"

"Working up an appetite." The Keeper waved to a gate to another yard where, by the sounds of low growls and squeals, Ethel was getting light exercise with something that was not dead. "They smell fear. Gets them all excited. If they seem a touch sluggish, I get in and ginger them up." Which explained the scars.

"Thank you," said Eiswolf. "Now I must return and -"

"I'm afraid we're stuck here for a while, till the girls finish," said the Keeper. "Can I offer you refreshments?"

"Ah, not at the moment," said Eiswolf, as the stench of the dragons and the rotting meat rose towards the platform.

***

"Where's Perry?" Eiswolf marched into the hostel, a man with a mission.

"He's talking to the horses," said the serving man. "I've seen that before."

"Takes some of them that way. I know. The stables, you say?"

He found Perry grooming Corsa. The mare had been grateful at first but was now wishing Little Two-Legs would go elsewhere to mutter and shed a few tears, because every time LTL started crying it got too enthusiastic with the curry-comb.

"Squire," said Eiswolf. Perry looked up, reluctantly.

Eiswolf put on his best heroic knight voice. "I have searched this land long and hard, for I have need of a clever underhand piece of tomfoolery."

"Pardon?"

"I've seen the dragon and I need all the help I can get."

"Oh. All right, boss."

And that was that: as close as Eiswolf ever got to an apology, and as close as Perry ever got to a fulsome declaration of devotion against all odds. After five years together, that was all they needed.

***

The next day, the team wandered about the market for a while. Perry negotiated more supplies. Eiswolf examined weapons, while Meroens caught up with a man from his own country. Flowers followed Fittle for a while but got lost and had to be guided back to the hostel. Fittle returned later, mysteriously richer than when he went out. Zadab snored in a corner.

That night was Sir Frithwald's turn with the dragon. The Keeper dispensed with the song and dance show, as everybody wanted to get to the main event, but kept the drums and torches, because they helped to bring Ethel up to speed. Eiswolf and Perry watched from the same place as before. Sir Ignatius sat about ten paces away, staring fixedly, taking no part in the excitement of the crowd.

The atmosphere felt different this time. There would be blood on the sand soon. The crowd's anticipation could almost be tasted: men, women and even a few children were pale, concentrated. Hungry. That was the best word Eiswolf could find. They were blood-hungry.

Sir Frithwald rode into the arena on his borrowed horse and took his bow, to applause. Then the drums rose, the gate slid back, out prowled Ethel. Immediately the horse panicked, screaming, and bolted towards the opposite gate, shrieking, bucking, almost climbing the guards' barriers in terror. Sir Frithwald could do nothing. Ethel picked up the commotion, and raised her dark triangular head, the long slit tongue darting in and out. Then she ran. The dragon seized the horse by a hind leg and dragged it to the ground, snapping the animal's neck with a bite. Then she turned to the man groaning on the ground beside his mount -

Both Eiswolf and Perry had seen death before, in many shapes and forms. But never had they seen a man eaten alive to the cheers of a crowd.

***

Back at the hostel, the team assembled. Eiswolf and Perry were pale and quiet. Finally, Eiswolf spoke. "One chance. I get one chance at this."

"You can still walk out," said Perry.

"Our knight is no such coward!" boomed Meroens.

"Like you'd know about courage," said Flowers.

"The odds they're giving ain't good," said Fittle. "I suppose you wouldn't pay us now?"

Zadab giggled a little, then sighed happily.

"I get one chance," said Eiswolf. "Believe me, courage has very little to do with this. I have a plan, and it's the only way you get your pay. Right? For God's sake listen carefully."

But Perry had another concern. "Boss, a thought. What happens if you do kill the dragon? They seem to get a lot of business from it…"

"This is about getting out in one piece," said Eiswolf. "Let me deal with the upshot, all right?"

So Eiswolf laid out the plan. They did a group handshake, all brave men together, and swore an oath, then each went to find his own place to grab a few hours' sleep.

***

Time is peculiarly elastic. Whatever you want to last forever, the first night of a honeymoon, your child's first steps, the day you win the championship, passes in a flash. When you could really do with not hanging about, the night before fighting a dragon, for example, time limps like a wounded dog. Eiswolf stared at the ceiling, then at a wall, then at another wall, got up from the truckle bed and stared out of the small window, considered waking Perry, decided that was not a good idea, chewed a fingernail, checked his sword for sharpness yet again, then lay down on the bed. His stomach churned but he dared not eat: throwing up before the fight might be seen as cowardice, so if he survived –

He turned on his side. All this for the love of a princess, and half a kingdom. Well, not the love of a princess. To marry a princess and be a king and the father of kings. He could barely remember what the girl looked like, although he still wore the little necklace. How would they divide the Kingdom, anyway? He would not get Cymenshore, that was a certainty. Mountains, probably, marshes and useless moors. But the title was important. And as he started assessing noble estates and dividing them into a logical order, one for him, one for the King, he did indeed fall asleep. Counting your chickens does that for most people.

***

Blackness. Cold. A rising wind. Blue shadows across the snow-field, sharp as a knife, clear as water. Above were the whirling stars. If he stared long enough, he could see them circle around the central star, like lords and ladies dancing about their king. Bright, white, beautiful, he could stare at them for hours. But the wind cut across, spraying a sharp scatter of ice in his face and bringing the warm scent of blood -

Eiswolf muttered in his sleep, and turned on his side.

***

The morning passed in a blur of preparations. Eiswolf had a series of practice fights against Perry and Meroens. Zadab, parted from his bag of leaves for the duration, began to wake up enough to look scared. Fittle went off to do what he had to. Flowers, still cursing, arranged his arrows and strung his bows, all by touch. Perry went to retrieve the horses from the livery stable to find he had to pay in full upfront, on the ostler's basis that trying to get paid after the fight was not a good idea. Sir Ignatius had indeed done a runner, and left a big bill behind.

At the arena, a meal was available at mid-day for the knight and his entourage, but nobody had any appetite. Fittle came back from another tour around the markets and guard-posts to confirm what Eiswolf suspected. Then Perry tried to get his knight to go off for a quiet snooze, and failed.

"Time enough later."

"If you're not totally sharp…" but Perry could not complete the sentence, so Eiswolf did.

"There might not be a later, I know. I know!"

So Perry let him alone.

Afternoon led into evening. The team were as ready as they would ever be. Perry armed his knight, then attended the horses. Flowers collected his bow and arrows, Meroens loaded up with spare weapons. Fittle, his part now completed, whistled through his teeth casually and wandered towards a tavern. Zadab watched in increasing alarm, until Meroens grabbed him by the shoulder and marched the man into line. "You're with me, pal."

The horn sounded for curfew. In the arena, the torches sprang into fire. The crowd started to fill the benches, then the musicians got into place. The drums and trumpets began. Eiswolf, Meroens, Flowers and Zadab were led into a dark side-chamber behind the small door where the Keeper and the pages made their appearance. They could see nothing, heard only the feet pound on wooden benches above their heads, a hubbub of crowd chatter and intermittent cheers.

The Keeper arrived in his dress armour. "I salute you, Sir Eiswolf. Are you sure about this? On foot?"

"Absolutely," said Eiswolf. No horses. Sir Frithwald's death made that an easy decision.

"Your men may assist you and your person but cannot touch the dragon. If they do, they will be killed by my men. You must kill the dragon single-handed. Anything else is a foul stroke and will be punished. Is that clear?"

"Yes," said Eiswolf.

"Then, sir, by God's grace, we shall proceed."

The door opened and the noise from the crowd hit them like a punch. The Keeper strode out into the torch-light and made a speech, but Eiswolf was not listening. Then the Keeper stopped speaking and turned, beckoning them.

Eiswolf marched out, carrying his shield, his arm raised in salute. The crowd roared. Behind him, Meroens, Zadab and Flowers stood in line. Then the drums fell silent.

Eiswolf turned to his men. "What we did this morning. No more, no less. One chance only. I trust you."

Meroens gave Eiswolf a stout spear. Eiswolf judged that the skin of a dragon was too tough to be slashed: only stabbing would get through. He also had a short, pointed sword at his side, over his chain mail. Then, after a moment of consideration, he handed Meroens the shield. What he lost in protection he would more than gain in agility, but the crowd saw this as an insane demonstration of courage. They shrieked and yelled their approval.

Then Meroens and Zadab took up their positions behind one of the barriers, with Flowers behind another. The torches flared, the drums announced the main attraction, the iron-bound gates swung open. Out came Ethel, cautiously expectant of a tasty, crunchy morsel or two.

Eyes, heart, brain, blood, belly. Every creature has vulnerable points. Eiswolf had trained since a boy to find them on men and horses. Concentrate. Eyes. Small, in a massive, armoured skull, too small to be a target. Ethel lifted her head, the pink tongue darted in and out.

Heart! No creature can survive a blow through the heart, but the dragon, its body slung low between wide-spread front legs, had no chest he could aim at, unlike a horse or a bull. The heart might be a long way inside those ribs. How big was a dragon's heart anyway? Brain. Not unless he had a hammer to crack that skull. Blood. But where were the veins, what could he hope to reach with his spear –

The dragon watched him, tasting the air. Then, appetite overcoming caution, she started to run. Eiswolf stood his ground until the last moment then leaped aside: but the dragon, an intelligent hunter, swept her long tail at him, catching him at knee height. The blow hit him like a brick wall. Eiswolf went down. The Dragon turned, ready to grab a meal, but Eiswolf yelled and Meroens sprinted out to help him to his feet. The dragon geared up to run again.

"Now!" yelled Eiswolf. The wrestler put his hands under Eiswolf's foot and boosted him into the air. He landed a dozen paces away from where the dragon expected. Then Meroens ran like hell to his barrier.

Eiswolf faced the dragon head-on. A stroke sideways through the ribs was too dangerous, far too close. Through the neck or mouth, maybe the belly. He waved at the dragon with his spear, catching a glint in the torchlight. The animal followed the glitter, he was pretty sure. When she charged, he dropped on one knee the way he did in a boar-hunt, so that she would impale herself on the spear. But the force of the creature was like an earthquake: his spear stuck in a little way, inadvertently putting space between his body and the flailing claws and teeth, but he was carried backwards by twenty paces until he hit the pit wall. The dragon tried to swish her tail again.

As she turned, Eiswolf dashed forward and stabbed beneath the ribs with the short sword. Contact! Blood, red blood! The creature flinched! What can be wounded can be killed! The crowd shrieked. And in that second, Eiswolf took his eye off the dragon. Irritated, she rose up on her back legs and tail, up and up, to twice the height of a man, and lashed out at him with long front claws. This time she caught his mail coat, ripping right through from neck to waist, snapping the spear's shaft.

Eiswolf yelled. Meroens waved the replacement spear at him, but the dragon was almost on top of the knight. Zadab's moment of glory had come. Meroens threw the runner in the air into the arena, shouting (unnecessarily), "Run, you stupid fool, run!"

Zadab, now fully awake, waved at the dragon. Distracted, the creature turned. Zadab, terrified, sprinted like lightning past the creature, dodged scything claws, leapt over the flailing tail, desperately looked for the wooden ladder out of the arena - which was not there - vaulted at a barrier, scrambled on top of the panel and balanced, wobbling, for a second. The dragon ran towards him, so he turned towards the pit wall and leaped. He caught the edge, just, but was left dangling. The dragon speeded up, trying to work into the narrow space between the wall and the barrier to grab this rather lively snack. But Zadab managed to heave himself up over the wall's edge, ran through the benches and out of the stadium. And disappeared.

Which gave Meroens enough time to reach Eiswolf, hand him the heaviest spear, and set him on his feet. Then the wrestler seemed to hesitate but Eiswolf pushed him away. "My kill!" he yelled.

Now the dragon was properly annoyed as well as peckish. Keeping a few paces from Eiswolf, she watched him with a dull eye, waiting for the inevitable moment when dinner began to lose strength and make feeble movements. Eiswolf knew he had to act soon. The only weak spot for the harpoon, which is what the unusually heavy spear was, would be the animal's throat, preferably near the jaw where blood vessels are bunched together. Even that might not be the killer.

So he grabbed all of his strength and hefted the unfamiliar weapon onto his shoulder. He threw the spear the way he had been shown by the bright-eyed old sailor in the market.

The blade went in, and stayed in. The dragon clawed at the shaft, but the blood flowing from her neck showed she had taken a major wound. Now, how long before the creature weakened and Eiswolf could finish her off?

Meroens looked up at the Keeper on the benches above. The man was frowning. The Keeper made a small signal to his guards. Meroens did not need hearing like Fittle to catch the distant sound of iron gates drawing back. Movement flickered in the gate at the other end.

"Flowers!" yelled Meroens. "Can you see them?"

"Pretty as a picture," cried the archer, came out from behind his barrier, and loosed three arrows down the arena, through the opened gate, down the timber corridor, into the leading guards of the small detachment in the yard beyond as they made ready to come in, to kill the knight and end the dragon-fight.

"Call off your men!" yelled Meroens to the Keeper. "Or you're next!"

The dragon scrabbled at the harpoon but could not dislodge the blade. She turned one way then another to get rid of the irritation, then lashed out at Eiswolf, who was almost pinned to the wall, but could not get past her claws and legs and tail without walking into her mouth. The fight was not over yet.

Meroens ran into the arena, clattering on Eiswolf's shield with a sword. The Dragon turned to the commotion, allowing Eiswolf a fraction of a second to run away. But he could hardly put one foot in front of another. Suddenly he felt as if turned to lead. Meroen's brave gesture was wasted. He was so tired, so tired, to lie down and –

He snapped awake again, face to face with that dark grey head and long pink tongue. The only way out of the arena alive was through the dragon. He lunged, grabbed the harpoon shaft, pulling himself up over the dragon's leg into the creature's neck. The dragon scratched at him with her claws but was too exhausted to rear up again. Eiswolf drew his short sword, climbing up past that terrible mouth, inches from that dull eye, the stinking breath, and stabbed as hard as he could into the junction between jaw and throat. Blood spurted.

The thud as the Dragon fell could be felt through the arena. The crowd were silent: suddenly Eiswolf realised they had been silent for a few minutes. He rolled off the creature into the sand. Meroens ran to help him up. Then the wrestler hoisted Eiswolf onto his shoulder, shouting, "Dragonslayer! Dragonslayer!"

And after a few seconds, the crowd joined in.

***

The Keeper was very helpful. He suggested packing Ethel's head in a barrel of salt to prevent decay on the way back to the Kingdom. He promised to keep a bag of gold for Zadab, should he ever reappear. He signed Perry's chitty to confirm that Eiswolf had indeed slain a dragon, fair and square. When Eiswolf rode out the next day, the crowd cheered him and his group. The livery stable actually waived the charges.

Perry found this all quite odd. "Haven't you just killed their main source of business?"

"Smile to the people," said Eiswolf. "I'm sure they can work things out for themselves." He waved and looked heroic, blowing a kiss to some girls.

At the city gate, they bade farewell to Fittle and Flowers, who took another road. Any other road, as long as it did not include dragons. Fittle's information on the standing orders to the guards, should a dragon fight ever look like succeeding, had been invaluable, as had Flowers. Eiswolf handed over their horses and bags of gold with real gratitude. Meroens, in charge of the donkey with the salted dragon's head, did not seem upset to see them go.

Then came a nine day's ride back to the Palace, because as soon as Eiswolf was a day away from the citadel, he almost fell off Pepper. Perry discovered he had a possible broken leg where the dragon's tail had hit him, as well as more damage to his shoulder, bad bruises and very deep cuts to his arms and chest, none of which he had mentioned after the fight or while they were within the city walls. Perry patched his knight up as well as he could: Meroens was helpful because as a wrestler, he was used to dealing with injury, and he also had the strength to lift Eiswolf on and off his horse, which

Perry could never have done. They travelled slowly, but they travelled on.

At the Palace, the people rejoiced at the return of their hero. Eiswolf summoned up the energy to ride into the courtyard with some of his old bounce, but his pale thin face told everyone that this had been a difficult Quest, and that the price of a dragon's head is high.

The King came out to meet him. "An astonishing feat!" he declared. "Our land shall ring with your name! Bring the best, bring wine, fresh linens, call our greatest doctors!"

"No need, your Majesty," said Eiswolf. "I shall go to the Good Witch Bess and regain my strength. Then we can celebrate. But let my Princess know that I returned with a gift that cannot be equalled." He gestured at Meroens, who dismounted and lifted the barrel off the donkey, then knocked away the lid. The stench was extraordinary but the head itself was unquestionably a real dragon. Or at least, as near as anyone sane would wish to get. Then Eiswolf and Perry and Meroens rode out towards Bess. They did manage to get half-way before Eiswolf blacked out.

***

The Keeper declared two days of mourning for his favourite lady, Ethel. The show in the arena now had a new twist, being about the life and the death of the dragon. But there was no longer the same edge, everyone agreed.

However, the Keeper was not wholly unhappy. For Ethel, in the way of her kind, had left a nice clutch of eggs maturing under a heap of rotting stable-muck in the outer courtyard. Soon would come the cheep of little reptilian voices. And until they grew up and became parthenogenic lizards like their mother, Mavis could go on the billing. For according to the tale, which was spreading so fast, as soon as the Dragon was dead, a sibling had flown through the night in storm and tempest, arriving miraculously to take revenge for the murder.

Personally, the Keeper blamed letting Ethel take the edge off her appetite with Sir Frithwald for her lacklustre performance. That would not happen again. Whistling happily, he went to see Mavis and scratch her nose through the bars of her cage, promising her many nice new crunchy knights to come.

7: Half a Kingdom

This Really Would Not Do.

The thing watched you, wherever you put it.

It did not fit. There might be a style and a place where it did, but the Princess was jiggered if she could think of one.

Insolent. Drawing attention. You had to explain what it was. And everyone always said the same.

"No! A real dragon? He must be very brave! You are so lucky!"

Even boiled down to a skull and mounted on a decorative stand, the thing - presumed.

"Daddy, do I have to keep this in here? Can't you put it on a wall? Or wherever?"

"My angel, the knight will want to know how much you admire his courage. Hiding the, er, thing, will seem disrespectful. By the way, what have you done with the floor rushes?" The King's vague blue gaze wandered around his daughter's empty apartments and bare, echoing stone floors.

"Unhygienic."

"But what abut the dogs?"

"We're training them."

"Is that why they smell of peppermint?"

And had a haunted expression. Royal hounds were unused to a scrub-down, and house-training was a real shock to the system. The hound-master had complained, loudly, that he had not come into his trade to look after fluffy scenty ladies' darlings. He would have given notice had he not been an indentured servant.

"New ideas, Daddy, one has to keep up with the times."

"Ah. My sweet, I hear that the noble knight recovers well from his injuries, and -" The King paused and cleared his throat, carefully not looking at his daughter. "I propose a feast to celebrate your betrothal."

What? WHAT?

"Oh, isn't that rather early? He's got a few more quests first, surely, I was thinking of next Equinox, myself." Drat, drat, drat! "What's the hurry?"

The King smiled reassuringly. "I wish to present our knight to our Court as a sign of our honour and faith, to reassure the people that we will fulfil our side of the bargain in the Tests of Kolras. His fame has already begun to spread. A betrothal is a fitting public act, don't you think?"

Now this REALLY Would Not Do.

***

"Idiot," said Bess.

"Get off me!" said Eiswolf, for the umpteenth time. "Ow."

"Well, don't move," said Bess, also for the hundredth time.

Eiswolf was a quiet, well-behaved, sweet-tempered patient - Oh, please. Of course not. He was a vigorous man, primed to achieve great acts of valour and honour. Lying still while his foster-mother adjusted his bandages was not in his playbook. He had been sore, bored, and in a deeply bad mood for three weeks. Bess was not much better.

Perry quietly scoured chain-mail, listening out in case he was needed, for example, if Eiswolf and Bess decided not to speak to each other. Being stuck between Eiswolf's temper and Bess' grim determination was no novelty, but this time was harder, because of Meroens.

The wrestler was handy about the hovel. He chopped wood and looked after the horses when Perry went off to buy supplies or negotiate with an armourer. He was cheerful and willing and as strong as an ox, respectful to Bess and in deep awe of Eiswolf, and very hard to criticise. Not the sharpest tool in the box, perhaps, but he had fitted into the household very easily. Bess liked him.

He also had a major role in restoring Eiswolf's fitness. Meroens understood a lot about strength, and injury, and training. He had already taught the knight a few useful moves. Eiswolf's day began with light exercises to stretch his sore muscles and build up strength without putting too much strain on his shoulder or his leg, then went into technical training with sword, or dagger and mace, or hand to hand. Meroens was a good partner, strong enough to resist when Eiswolf started hitting with full force, a patient but direct and uncompromising coach.

Perry could not do any of this, and he knew.

But he tried not to let it get to him.

A lot of the time, he failed.

"Good God, woman, what are you doing!" Eiswolf roared. Perry drooped: nearly time to be a go-between again.

"What's all the noise!" called Meroens cheerfully, as he came back from the forest, a massive load of firewood strapped on his back. "Killing a pig, then?"

Bess ran out of the hovel. "Thank God you're here. Can you tell His Lordship that I have to take the old bandage off or he'll turn blue and die? Beat some sense into him, please?"

"Yes, no problem, Lady Bess." Meroens threw his load down lightly and went inside. "What's all this, then, Princess?"

Perry heard the two men laugh together, vigorously, deeply, manly.

His heart sank.

***

In the King's Chamber, the Hegemon and the King looked at each across a large table full of maps. Ivory counters with spots of coloured paint were placed at strategic points such as cities, rivers, or mountain passes. The maps were representative rather than quantified. they showed distance by days of journey, not miles. Where there was nothing of interest, the mapmaker put a blank space, or imaginative flourishes such as giants or dragons or flowers. Maps were about how to get to places and what to expect when you got there, not geology. The King was now using them to work out who owned what.

"Earl Passfield is blue." The King placed a counter with a blue spot on the map. "And Whitfall is yellow and blue. Orange?"

"Bezant," said the Hegemon. "And Earl Mortfeld is red."

"And we have twenty-four earls in total?"

"Twenty five, your Majesty. You granted Piermont an earldom last year."

The King sighed. "An even number would have helped. One for him, one for me. But I suppose that would be too easy." He smiled, to show that he knew this was a joke. The Hegemon smiled back.

Half a kingdom. The phrase slips off the tongue. A princess, and half a kingdom.

But kingdoms are composed of estates, and farms, and towns, and farms have farmers and towns have traders. Above them are local warlords who, after the passage of a few centuries, are dignified with titles like Baron and Earl and Duke. And they all have opinions. A kingdom is a balance of power, because if earls or traders become over-ambitious, civil war can easily result, and while all wars are terrible, only civil wars can be utterly destructive. A successful kingdom needs to know the opinions of the farmers and traders and earls and to balance their jealousies and grievances and dreams.

Half a kingdom is not the same as a kingdom, halved. Cutting the map in two was not the answer.

Eiswolf was much further through the Tests of Kolras than any previous challenger. There were rumblings among the traders and farmers. They wanted to know what the King would do. The Kingdom had never suffered a full peasant's revolt, but neighbouring realms had. The King knew that even with Black Al and his military forces, they could not easily be contained.

On top of it all, the knight was increasingly seen as a hero: he had a witch, a tourney and a dragon under his belt. The Tests had created a potential Pretender.

"I had a word with the Princess," said the King.

"Indeed," said the Hegemon.

"About the betrothal. Red for Mortfeld, eh? It's not until you see this all on a map. He's awfully powerful in the north-west, isn't he. Yes, the betrothal."

The Hegemon blanched, and held his breath. "And what did her Majesty say?"

"Oh, you know the ladies. She has nothing to wear, wants to ask all her friends, charming girlish bashfulness."

The Hegemon seized on this. "Bashfulness?"

"Oh, nothing to be worried about. She will do her duty, as do we all." The King put a green counter beside one of the red ones. "Do you think Mortfeld would accept an exchange of castles with Piermont?"

The Hegemon assisted his King, but his mind was elsewhere.

Duty! His only duty was to save the Princess. She had no appetite for this marriage, he had seen her disgust at the feast of the Tourney, when she took off the gold circlet using a napkin and scrubbed her hands after. When Eiswolf returned with the dragon's head, she asked after the knight's health formally at meetings of the Chamber, but without passion. She sent linens, wine and food to

Bess' hovel, but had not visited. Duty! She did her duty, but no more.

She would be very grateful to the man who saved her from this unnatural, cursed marriage. Together, they would rule justly and well –

"Yellow is Whitfall, you say? How did that little upstart get hold of the Snowfell Pass?" The King examined a counter.

The Hegemon snapped back into the present. "A dowry, I believe, I think he married well."

"Ha! Good luck to him, then," said the King. "That's a very uncertain road to power, if I may say so. Had to kill all three of mine, you know."

To which there was no easy answer.

"Yes," mused the King, placing a counter with each thought. "First one gave me a son but turned out to be a spy, the next one was a traitor and the last one was a lovely girl, lovely girl, but very free with her favours. You do know," he fixed the Hegemon with his vague blue eyes, "Royal marriages are different. Royalty is brought up to a different way."

"Absolutely, your Majesty," said the Hegemon. "Shall I call the Conclave in now?"

"Do so, dear fellow, do so."

The Hegemon left the chamber. He would rescue her, no matter what.

The King watched his disappearing shadow. Poor fool, he thought. Poor fool.

***

In the Princess' dungeon, a curtain of blue silk covered her Planning Hanging when other people were there. Now she was alone, she drew the silk back, unlaced her heavy rose brocade overdress, which dropped to the floor, hitched up her shift, and twirled her silvery hair into a plait. She put the little ladder against the Hanging and climbed up with a length of green wool to link the scrap of fabric representing Earl Bezant to the scrap that was Earl Dugdale.

Then she came down and took in the wider picture. A nexus of activity was visible around younger, junior barons like Whitfall, while established men like Bezant were holding back. Eiswolf scenarios were playing through, slowly. If he succeeded and took half the Kingdom, there was no advantage in supporting the King from the wrong side of a new border. As a new ruler, Eiswolf could award estates and power. But if - No! When! - Eiswolf did die, no-one wanted to be caught looking treacherous to the King, either. The older men had been through this before, the younger ones probably did not see the danger.

She heard a scratching noise at the door: a sharp scrape, three times. "Come in, creature!" she called.

"My lady! The stars are in alignment!"

"Oh, they're always aligned somewhere, somehow," said the Princess. "Well, Witch, what's the problem."

Jocasta had struck a dramatic pose, but this was of no account if there was no audience of impressionable ladies. She straightened up, because the Princess was about as impressionable as granite.

"My Lady wished to know of my success with the sleeping powders of the East." She flourished her hands. "Long and hard did I -"

"Just give me the results," said the Princess, in no mood for the full presentation.

"They work, but they taste very bitter," said Jocasta. "There's no concealing them. I hear that the knight gets stronger by the day. If he's to waste away, we must act soon, or he will not seem to have been killed by the dragon's blood."

"H'm, I wonder about that. Wasting away might take a while and I may need a faster resolution."

"That's a risk," said Jocasta. "Looks bad if he's jousting one day and on his deathbed the next. Anyway, you need the replacement, don't you? The disposable prince?"

This was shorthand for a suitor to occupy the role of prince in waiting, the next to be ready for the Tests of Kolras but only 'when the time was right'. The Princess had worked out that she could mourn for Eiswolf for a year, get legal grounds for delay for another six months, then, with ideas from the Planning Hanging, well, who knew what might happen. She still had hopes for Plan A.

"We need to deal with our furry friend," said the Princess, "But if it's fast, it doesn't need to be painless, right?" She grinned brightly.

"We have to get past Bess," said Jocasta.

The Princess frowned. "So that's true?"

"Yes, your Majesty. Not one morsel of food, one drop of wine, or thread of the linen you've sent has been used. The big squire's been burying everything in the forest."

"H'm," said the Princess. Dammit.

***

Black Al was splashing the cash down at the tavern on the western edge of town, which was busier than usual. Great lords had come to the City for meetings with the King's Chamber, and each had brought bands of retainers and mercenaries. Black Al took full advantage to listen to the scuttlebutt: which lords were late paying their men, who had bought new horses, whose lady played him false, who had a feeble-minded son. All pure gold, much more valuable than the coins Al threw to the landlord.

The Hegemon slid in, muffled up in his long grey cloak. The regulars looked at him suspiciously, barging into the small man as he made his way to Black Al.

"Make it quick," said Black Al. "I have to be back at the Palace before the Barons of Elderton arrive."

The Hegemon ignored the lack of pleasantries. "Your man has his report?"

Black Al waved at a corner, and Izak appeared, with a truly piratical grin. "My lords!" he cried, coming to them with open arms. He was a fair few brandies to the good.

"Sit down, man," said Black Al. "What are you so cheerful about?"

"Why, telling the tale, my lords! For I was there when the knight did kill the Dragon!" He dropped to a confidential tone. "I was in them parts, you see," and he tapped the side of his nose with his finger.

Inwardly, the Hegemon sighed. This is what you got when you used amateurs. "I know, Izak, I sent you. You were to watch him and report back to me."

"Ah," said Izak, focussing blearily on the Hegemon. "Well, my lords. He's a well-made man, of great fighting strength, big-hearted, oh, he'll make such a Prince, my Lords!"

"No doubt," said the Hegemon, patiently. "But that's not what I want to know. I want to know what his weaknesses are. Does he drink, gamble, make free with women?"

"Why, my lord, all of those, like a king he is!" Izak's eyes glowed. "But not too proud to listen! Why, he was like a lamb when I showed him the harpoon, as quick a man to learn as I have ever seen!"

"What?" said the Hegemon. "What's a harpoon?"

"Why, 'tis how the seal-eating folk of the Far North deal with their mighty leviathans! For such a creature may be killed by a man, if he but know where to put a blade! Full forty fathoms long, some of them, brought down by a single stroke!" Izak stood up to demonstrate, nearly overbalanced, and sat down again. "Coz' it's not just the strength, you see, it's the cunning!" His eyes narrowed. "You must think like the creature itself! So you put all your weight behind -"

The Hegemon had finally caught up with the implications. "You mean, you showed the knight how to use this harpoon?"

"Why, yes, and sold it to him, too." Izak grinned.

Black Al chipped in. "And this is a -"

"A big heavy spear, oh, you need shoulders for the throw." Izak broke off to mime a weight-lifter's build. "But flew like a hawk, it did, straight to the mark! And boom! Down she went!" He giggled.

Black Al leaned forward. "You sold him the spear that killed the Dragon?"

"Oh, yes. No other weapon is strong enough."

The Hegemon and Black Al exchanged desperate glances. Black Al sighed. "In the name of God, man, why?"

Izak sucked in his breath. "No man could go in against that creature and live, else. I don't hold with suicide."

Amid his rising panic, the Hegemon noted that next time he hired a spy, he'd be more careful about checking out their moral viewpoint. "You were only supposed to watch him! Look, does he have any weaknesses at all?"

"None," said Izak, cheerfully. "Wolf or no wolf, he's a proper man." And back he went to the crowd on the other side to tell the story once more, with gestures.

Black Al and the Hegemon looked at each other. This was getting out of hand.

"I'll see you later," said Black Al.

"Yes," said the Hegemon. He watched as the King's Champion left the tavern. But would it be wise to trust that man?

Black Al, oddly enough, was thinking exactly the same.

***

Above the far land, where swifts screamed and the first and last rays of the sun struck, the black tower loomed: and within the uppermost chamber, its Lord mused.

The Glimmer Lord was a huge fan of romance. The way it bypassed all the logical circuits in a human being, no matter how intelligent or aware, never ceased to amuse him. The biggest impact was often on those who thought themselves immune, like monks, or generals, or professors. But the best fun was with knights brought up in the tenets of strict chivalry, where romance was the whole point (after success as a warlord).

Knights were pre-primed, but to really get to them, you had to set up an unresolvable conflict between love and duty. Ideal scenarios were (in no particular order) falling in love with your king's wife; falling in love with the daughter of your enemy: going to collect a princess to become your king's wife only to fall in love with her yourself; and falling in love with a stranger knight on the battlefield (weird one, this, slightly dodgy but hang around for the denouement) who turns out to be a princess in disguise! Ta-da!

Well, the King currently had no wife. His track record was poor, so a replacement was not likely soon. Although the Kingdom had enemies, the daughters of the leading ones all looked like a reflection in a spoon. Acting as a princess-collection service was out, see reason one. And God only knows how you could set up number four.

Which left the straightforward maiden in peril scenario, an old one but still a good one.

A messenger knocked at his door. "News from the Kingdom, great Lord." The man bowed, holding out a parchment scroll.

A letter from his contact in the Palace. Everything was cooking up nicely: the Kingdom was in a ferment of expectation. Men questioned their futures under this new, unknown prince. He grinned as he read the letter:

'The merchants of Cymenshore are troubled. For they have always depended on the strength of the Kingdom, but if the Kingdom be split, then who will pay for the army? There is also unhappiness in the North, that they be slighted, and great lords in the west are affronted and may seek to combine in a principality, to assign their loyalties as they desire.'

The Glimmer Lord allowed himself a smile. Fat cats wanting a bail-out, Northerners with a chip on their shoulders, and down in the West, an awkward squad wanting self-rule.

"Plus ca change, c'est plus le meme chose," he muttered. But this was good news. The Kingdom was becoming vulnerable, and Cymenshore was dangling like a ripe peach.

The letters also told of the growing legend around Eiswolf, not vague tales of wolves and ice and snow, but as a true hero. This, too, was ripening nicely. The Glimmer Lord had seen Eiswolf fight at the Tourney, but being impressive in the lists did not signify any great intellect or uncanny abilities. Killing a dragon showed Eiswolf was brave, strong, and lucky. No more, no less.

And on the plus side? The man was weird, but that could change from a disability to the sign of a Chosen One. He was plainly ambitious, or why follow the Quest at all? Ambitious men often do not look too closely at how they achieve their goals. They are open to a deal. And all men can be blinded by their own desires. Now was the time to make Eiswolf useful, to put him in thrall to the Glimmer Lord.

The Glimmer Lord had a very good idea of what Eiswolf's desires would be, and how they could be fulfilled.

In short, Eiswolf could be managed.

He called the messenger over. "Call Mirak. Time to act."

***

Eiswolf was getting stronger. Meroens found their sparring was getting harder. If Perry was bold enough to volunteer to be a target (behind the shield) for sword or mace, he got clattered.

Eiswolf's spirits were also returning, a good thing in one way, because a morose Eiswolf was a difficult man to live with inside the little hovel. But a chirpy Eiswolf was almost worse: he itched to get out and do great deeds. So he badgered Bess to declare him fit, wrestled with Meroens to the peril of Bess' domestic arrangements, pummelled Perry or turned him upside down for fun, and generally bounced around as if he had too much energy to keep in his skin.

"You're not fully recovered yet," said Bess. "God help us all, but you're not back to full strength. You only need to pull that shoulder again when it's not healed and your fighting days will be over. Go out with Meroens and annoy the village."

So Eiswolf and Meroens roamed the area, drinking in village taverns and chasing local girls and getting into minor spats with the lads, but careful to pay for damage and to leave no lasting grievances. The village was quite proud that Eiswolf, king in the making, had chosen to recuperate there.

Perry stayed behind at the hovel and found things to do.

Meroens was now a friend to Eiswolf as well as a boon companion. Eiswolf liked his direct ways and open-hearted manner. Meroens was a farmer's son, but had been left without lands after a baron's skirmish, forcing him on the road. He had not become a mercenary as he had no great appetite for killing, and anyway, had seen the other side of their cruelties.

"I couldn't do to anyone what they did to my old mum," he told Eiswolf. "I don't hold with that. When you're King, you won't do nothing like that?"

"I hope not," said Eiswolf.

"Good," said Meroens. "You're a true knight. And I shall serve you always."

As Eiswolf got stronger, he and Meroens rode together. The knight started to show himself in neighbouring towns, so that all should know Sir Eiswolf. He greeted the mayors and local lords, they entertained him in their halls, and he impressed them greatly with his noble manners and intelligence. All were agreed that he was more, much more, than a werewolf or a lucky chancer.

Perry stayed behind and helped Bess.

Finally, the time arrived to think of Court once more. This meant a set of Court clothes, surcoats, crests, and a caparison for the horse. Bess sent out for a tailor and a leather-worker, while Meroens reviewed the state of Eiswolf's saddlery and armour with Perry.

"No offence," said Meroens. "But seen better days, right?"

"It's very serviceable," said Perry. "And it was free, from the Palace."

"Yeah, but, well, compared to the stuff at the Tourney this looks, well, not the best, is it?"

Perry, despite himself, got irritated. "If we had an infinite amount of money, of course we'd get new! Fighting that dragon was bloody expensive. And there's other quests to do. We've spent about fifty gold pieces already! Gold doesn't grow on trees."

Meroens laughed, which irritated Perry even more. "He's a knight! What do they care about money!"

"One of us has to!"

"Oh, my poor little penny-pincher, think big! He's going to be a king!" And Meroens patted Perry on the head. Perry was sorely tempted to take a swing at him but - but - but - Meroens was three times his size and head and shoulders taller. So Perry had to be content with a dignified retreat.

The next day, a saddler from one of the local towns arrived bearing a magnificent set of horse-trappings, for free, because he wanted his work seen at Court and to be known as the man who supplied Eiswolf, the great champion. He was followed by an armourer and a swordsmith.

"See?" said Meroens. "Money's not important."

Then Pepper was dressed up in his caparison for Meroens to give him the once-over. The wrestler sucked his teeth.

"What's the matter now?" said Perry. "I think he looks very good."

"Yeah, fine," said Meroens.

But later, alone with Eiswolf, he gave his true opinion.

"Boss, that horse."

"Yes, Pepper's a good ride."

"Well, boss, like, no offence but -" Meroens paused, chewed his lip, and stared to Heaven.

"For God's sake, man, spit it out!"

"Well, you know, to be blunt, he's got no balls, has he."

"He was the pick of the bunch when I chose him, balls or no balls. He came from the Palace stable. Anyway, stallions can be untrustworthy, they have a temperament."

"Yes, but boss," Meroens' voice dropped to a low whisper. "If you turn up at Court, like, on a horse with no balls and, saving your pardon but that's the truth, right? And a squire with no balls and, well, I heard, didn't go down well at the Tourney, did it? Not the right, um…" Had Meroens understood the modern term 'image', he would have used it. "Well, makes you look a bit, well. Elfin."

"What!" Eiswolf almost drew his sword at this insult.

While fairies were indubitably real and very dangerous, as the Dogstar Knight proved, elves were different. The Kingdom had many legendary supernatural beings, from gnomes to sprites and elementals, but elves were definitely a literary invention to entertain the court. Nobody left a saucer of milk outside to keep an elf happy. Elves were said to be bright and beautiful, until you crossed them. They sang and danced most prettily, and laughed gaily as they tricked poor clod-hopping humans. And they had a mortal following, who declared themselves Elvish or half-elves, who dressed most fashionably, and sang sweetly, and also played slightly vicious personal games, and were often men.

Elfin was not an ethnic group, but a way of life.

"Well, look at it like, plain, boss. Perry's a nice little bloke, with all his problems, but, you know it looks… Odd." Meroens got bolder, "And I don't think you need any more oddness, if you know what I mean."

That gave Eiswolf pause. Locally, he had managed to overcome the werewolf idea once the lords and mayors had seen him and spoken to him, but he knew this was still a problem. A reputation as an Elfin wolf might not be overcome by talk or fighting.

In all-male societies such as travelling knights, homosexuality happened, of course. Nobody with any sense got upset at what chaps got up to with other chaps when they were out on quests that might last many months or even years, as long as they were discreet. The 'elfin' problem was not sexual orientation but, in a society that only prized aggressive masculinity, the perceived effeminacy. You could be as flamboyant as you liked, that was not illegal; but it was despised. The Kingdom had no laws against bestiality, either, but romancing your sheep was hardly acceptable behaviour at Court.

But Perry had been at Eiswolf's side for five years, unfailingly loyal, ever-inventive, self-sacrificing, prudent –

"I hear what you say. I should think a knight on such dangerous Quests could have need of two squires, don't you? As for the horse, if you find a stallion with Pepper's disposition and strength, then maybe we will consider a change." Eiswolf smiled, so they clasped hands, as manly men do.

***

The Princess, in her echoing chamber, had decided to receive the Hegemon. "My lord, how pleasant to see you. Please, be seated."

"Your Majesty does me much honour." The Hegemon sat on a stool. A minty-fresh hound slunk by.

The Princess posed in the glory of her beauty, her silver-gold hair arrayed in a complex series of ringlets and plaits, the silvery gauze of her gown draped over an under-dress of the sweetest pink, pearls wreathed into her hair and around her neck.

"My lord, it is too long since we spoke," said the Princess. "Our meetings in the Chamber are too brief and impersonal. We have need of advice from the Kingdom's greatest servant."

Well, if that didn't soften him up, nothing would. But he was already practically melting at her feet.

"I am Your Majesty's slave," he said, in a slightly strangled voice.

The Princess launched into her carefully-prepared speech. "Know then, my Lord, that although We are most willing to undertake the duty required of Us in the matter of this betrothal - You do know about the betrothal?"

The Hegemon nodded.

"That We will marry the knight who passes these Quests with a joyful heart, nonetheless We must be assured of the good repute and intent of this knight, for the protection of the Kingdom. For what disasters might follow should We fall into the hands of a juggler, a scoundrel or a creature unearthly?"

He did not look startled, or act astonished, or deny her fears. He knew. He knew, all right, and she'd place a very big bet he was already on the case. He had as much to lose as she did, maybe more.

The little man bowed. "Your Majesty's wisdom is a lesson to us all." And his heart leaped in his chest.

"Your enquiries must begin at once. And until they are complete, no ceremony can take place, for We would not put Our Kingdom in such peril."

"Your Majesty, your caution is exemplary." Heated by her trust, the Hegemon dared another step. "But, your Majesty, if this knight is unmasked as a thing unworthy, then the people will be gravely disappointed, for there will be no answer to the question of the succession. Who then would sue for your Majesty's hand in marriage?"

The Princess blushed, a trick that had taken a few day's practice, but evidently worth it, because she could see the Hegemon's eyes glisten. "Sir, We must choose from men close to us, long known to us, those we know to be of dignity and experience, not merely those with a thick arm or a hard head. We will choose for the good of the Kingdom."

And that was as plain an offer as she could make. Fix this wolf, and you get a shot at the (literal) title.

The Hegemon smiled blissfully. "Your Majesty, my every breath is at your command!"

"Ah. About Daddy - His Majesty - if you could calm his most worthy desire to see this betrothal? We understand the knight himself has made no demand. We see no need to be precipitate."

"As your Majesty pleases!"

"We can still have the feast. People have been looking forward to that. Wouldn't want to be a kill-joy." She stood. The interview was over.

The Hegemon bowed, backing out of the chamber. She favoured him! She had seen sense! Of course she had, she was a woman of intelligence and refinement. She had looked about and of all the potential - say it, kings - he was her choice! She did not have the final say, but get this wolf out of the way and his path was clear! What was the alternative? A brainless warlord? His heart sang, the world a brighter place.

Right, thought the Princess. Plan F in motion, assuming Plans D and E don't work. Plan G is a rerun of Plan D with the

Hegemon as target, but that's for the future. It's a shame, in a way. He is a useful little man.

***

Eiswolf had decided to go out riding, having recovered enough to be able to get out of trouble, or at least back to the hovel. Attacks by bandits were unlikely as his spreading fame as a dragon-slayer meant few would take the chance. In fact, he was quite used to cheery peasants and foresters waving to him as he rode forth. Women brought their small children out to see him. He drew the line at kissing babies, however. (And they drew the line at offering them to him. No sense in putting temptation in the man-wolf's path.)

Through the summer greenwood he set Pepper to a trot, breathing in the scent of growth, hearing the rustle of young leaves under a southern breeze in the flickering gold and green light, a good time to be alive. He realized how close he had come to the alternative. He raised his head and sniffed the scents of life, newness and decay, each worthy in itself, felt the urgent twittering of the birds, mating, fighting, dying, all music to the everlasting pageant of colour and energy and change around him –

And then he heard the scream. A human. He had no choice.

He galloped as fast as he could through the wood, over streams and gullies, beaten by branches but unyielding, to rescue a helpless one.

He found the girl in a clearing, on her knees, weeping, scratched and dirty as if she had run through brambles, her shift ripped over one shoulder. She looked up at him and screamed, scrabbling away through the leaves and twigs.

"Be of good cheer, lady," he said, as calmly as he could. "My name is Sir Eiswolf, and I would be of aid to you." He dismounted, approaching her carefully on foot. "I bear no weapon, I have no ill-will towards you."

The girl looked up and although plainly terrified, she did not try to run away. She looked about sixteen or seventeen. Under the grime her skin was fair but freckled, as if gold had been flecked over her face with a careless hand. Her eyes were huge, and glass-green. A cloud of exotic perfume hung about her, a heady mix of lemon, anise and camphor-wood.

Eiswolf got closer. "My lady, tell me your name."

"I - Oh!" And then she burst into tears again. Eiswolf strode towards her and swept her up in his arms. She seemed hardly more than a child, a lost child in the forest. He set her on Pepper's saddle, then mounted behind her.

"We will go to my mother's home, my Lady. She is a wise woman and will see to your hurts. What is your name?"

"Mifanna, my Lord."

"Tell me your tale."

And as they rode through the greenwood, she gasped out her story, getting closer and loser to the strength of the knight's body, until she finally twined her arms about his waist.

"My Lord, I am an orphan of noble blood. I come from the Black Fells, my father was a lord of good repute and I am Lady of many lands in my own right, but my parents died when the Barons of Elderton made a quarrel with them, and their men over-ran our castle. I escaped with my ladies, running through the snow in our bare feet, we found sanctuary with the people of Wardur. But the Barons would not be swayed, and set siege to the town until they released me, for Baron Robert would wed me to gain all the lands by right that they had stolen from my father."

She swallowed hard and caught her breath. "I could not marry the man who had killed my parents! So I took neither bread nor water from them, then they locked me in a high tower, and said I could marry or die, for I had no other choice, and I stayed there for four days, but the thirst, my Lord! The thirst undid me. So I agreed to the marriage, and they allowed me down to the hall, but as their ladies set to array me in fine robes, I slipped out and cast myself down the garde-robe, not caring if I lived or no. But by grace, I landed in the dung-heap and ran out of the town, and I was so filthy and stinking that none thought I could be a lady."

"Then I travelled for many days to come to ask for justice from our great King, but the Barons, when they discovered my escape, set their men and their hounds and their horses after me, and their guards had discovered me and Baron Robert said…" She gasped. "Baron Robert said if I would not wed him, he had ten good men who would take my maidenhead, and he told them to - dig a grave and then I screamed, and I heard your horse, and those cowards ran!"

He clasped her to him a little more closely, feeling the fluttering beat of her heart, her warmth, her fragility, her trembling. "Lady, there is no need to be afraid. I will take you to Court, our King will give you justice. But first, we have to tidy you up, don't we?" He looked down at her in his arms, she looked up at him, her fiery-golden curls spread across his shoulder, and suddenly she darted up and kissed his cheek.

"You are my true knight!" She snuggled back in to his chest. They rode on, in a curiously happy silence.

A while later, Eiswolf spotted dark shapes moving through the forest behind him. "We have company." He took Pepper up to a canter. She clung to him as if he was her last breath.

But not a mile from the village, the pursuers took advantage of the thinning wood to charge at the knight, surrounding him. With no sword, he fought them off as well as he could with fists and his long knife, but with Mifanna in his arms, he was hampered. One of the men grabbed the girl, tearing her from his grasp, then the others closed in on Eiswolf. The last thing he remembered before being knocked from Pepper was her voice shrieking "Save me! Save me!"

***

Fortunately, a forester was walking back from his day's work with his donkey when he spotted the loose horse with its fine saddle, and then the man unconscious on the ground. Even more fortunately, he was the sort of forester to save an injured man rather than slit his throat and make off with both horse and saddle. He set the man on the horse and led them back to the village, where a tavern-keeper recognised Eiswolf, and took Pepper and his load back up to the hovel.

Bess was beside herself: so much so, she neither cried nor spoke. She and Perry got Eiswolf on to the truckle bed. Meroens checked him over, but Bess, pale, took Perry to one side. "He's been knocked out. If it's a brain injury, I can't do much. Watch him. If he starts taking fits - "

"He hasn't," said Perry, firmly. "I'll be right there, Bess."

And he sat by his boss through the night. Meroens stood guard at the door.

Slowly, groggily, the next day Eiswolf came to. Bess started doing all sorts of strange things like sticking pins into his hands and feet and passing a lighted candle in front of his eyes, but he pushed her away in irritation. "Where is she? Where's Mifanna?"

The tale of the orphan gripped both Perry and Meroens. "You have to find her," said the wrestler. "If it's not too late."

"I know," said Eiswolf.

"You're due at Court," said Bess. "Or have you forgotten that wretched Quest?"

Eiswolf fell silent. His great Quest. How could he forget? And yet those glass-green eyes, those freckles, the exotic scent, that trilling heart, seemed a hundred times more real than the icy Princess. And Mifanna truly needed him: she was an orphan, like himself, lost in the forest, like he had been, pursued without mercy, as he was. He had to rescue her.

"I will find her. Or revenge her death. But I will go to Court for my next challenge, for I have also sworn this, my King and my Princess expect it. I am a man of honour. I do not give my word lightly."

But Bess could see the love-light burn in him like a candle in a horn lantern.

"I'll tell the lads at the tavern to listen out," said Perry. "She's not a fairy and neither are the men, they have to be somewhere. We'll find her for you, boss. We'll sort this out."

He grasped Eiswolf's hand, but the man did not seem to register he was even there.

8: The Sword of Destiny

At the royal feast, earls, dukes, ambassadors and merchants all declared themselves mightily impressed with Eiswolf's achievements, although the knight himself seemed subdued. The public betrothal to the Princess had been quietly shelved, but the Court definitely expected signs of royal commitment. So the Princess assiduously tried to make a toast to Eiswolf, but he seemed to have little appetite for wine, even the very special vintage that she had procured with great trouble from the far south.

The King smiled. "Our Knight is abstemious! A trait not often found in fighting men, but welcome in any King! Come, daughter, Sir Eiswolf would be in good heart for his next Quest and not fuddled like a common soldier!"

"My Lord, We are most gratified simply to see Sir Eiswolf in health and We will have much time to rejoice together later, when We are - " she did manage to squeeze the word out. "Betrothed." She also found a sweet smile for her knight.

Nope. Nothing. Not a twinkle in return. She might as well not have been in the room. Whatever preoccupied him, marriage was not the subject. Well, that knocked one idea on the head: no luring him to a secluded place for a little dose of poison. She kept her eye on the 'special wine' and managed to get a serving boy to take the flask back to her chamber before it wiped out half the dukes in the Kingdom.

"She's a looker," said Meroens to Perry. They were at the foot of one of the long tables, but as Eiswolf's squires they were among the few commoners with the right to attend at all. "A real Princess. I see why he's fighting, now."

"H'm," said Perry. "She's got a very glinting eye. Noble ladies are different."

Meroens had his own ideas about where ladies of the nobility might indeed have a difference and entertained their end of the table for a few minutes with anatomical impossibilities.

"Anyway," said Meroens, "How did you come to be this expert on noble ladies? You're not exactly equipped." He thumped Perry lightly on the crotch.

When a few flagons in, Meroens forgot to be as polite to Perry as he was when sober, and he did like his horseplay.

"I was a page," said Perry, patiently. "I was a page in a noble house."

"Oh, where?" said the man opposite, a reeve from Scything.

"In Cymenshore."

"Well, you'll know this Richard of Clifton, then. He's the man of the future, nothing moves down his way without him knowing."

The reeve waved towards the King and the nobles. At the head of one of the tables, Perry spotted a well-built man in a grey robe, clean-shaven, with thick, dark, curly hair. He was in animated debate with Earl Dugdale, and surrounded by men who wanted his favour, for they laughed and joked with him, or fell silent when he spoke.

The room suddenly seemed incredibly hot and noisy. Perry swallowed hard, trying not to faint. Because the last time Perry had seen Richard of Clifton, he was Dickon the steward, a servant in the Vendant household, the secret love of the Countess of Cymenshore.

"Not a noble, I hear," said a merchant to Perry's left.

"No," said the reeve, "but a man of abilities. And we all know titles can be arranged, eh?"

Perry took a slug of wine and tried not to feel sick. "Wasn't there a noble family in Cymenshore? The Vendants?"

"Was," said the reeve, shortly. "Most of 'em were killed in the raid. Not popular, very grasping they was, not many folk stood in the way to protect them when the pirates came calling. He was quite high up in the household, and he took his chance afterwards. Married well, too."

"Really," said Perry. "Who to?"

"Magret, I think her name is. Merchant's daughter, I believe. She brought plenty of money with her, that I do know."

Magret. Well, that explained a lot.

"Here, Perry, you all right? You look green," said Meroens.

"I'm fine."

Meroens' attention was caught by a shuffling noise across the room. "Hallo, what's that?"

The King's Herald marched towards the high table carrying a scroll on a purple velvet cushion, followed by a train of black-robed scholars and academicians from Conclave. The time had come to reveal the next Quest.

Eiswolf raised his head and started to pay attention. He had drifted off among the chorus of formal congratulations and the pleasantries of court conversation. The girl with freckles and huge green eyes haunted him. Every second he sat eating roast boar and drinking wine, she was a prisoner - tortured - worse - but he could do nothing about it, because of Duty, and his Quest. He glanced at the Princess; she smiled back, a vision in pink and gold and silver. That was what the Quest was about: fame, power, wealth. No longer would he be the boy from nowhere, pursued by the suspicion of wolf's blood. Ruling from a hall like this, surrounded by nobles like this, with this Princess by his side, surely that was enough of a prize for any ambitious man. How could he be so distracted by a glimpse, a cry, a tear, an echo of love?

The King's Herald presented the scroll to the King, who nodded. The Herald stood and declaimed, "Our most puissant King! Mighty Princes and Lords of this Kingdom! Know that Conclave have examined the Manifest, with great learning and patient endeavour" And a lot of four syllable words which were lost on most of the crowd.

"Blimey, they do hang it out," said Meroens.

"We have ascertained that the next challenge shall be a Test in fair fight against knights of all nations, a trial of virtue and of strength! You!" Unexpectedly, the Herald swivelled towards Eiswolf and stared him hard in the face. "You must win the Sword of Destiny!"

A great cheer rose, the lords drummed their fists on the table and their boots on the ground. Eiswolf smiled and nodded, clasping his hands above his head. No, he did not have a clue what the Sword of Destiny was. On his experience so far, he could not even be certain it would turn out to be a sword.

***

Bess was in a truculent mood.

"Another idiotic tourney! Well, what am I going to say. That leg needs rest and if you injure that shoulder again, I can't do anything. If you feel dizzy or see double, get the boys to bring you back, I'm not happy about that crack on the skull. Keep away from the bad drink and if you're going to whore around, at least pick one that isn't covered in sores. Washing helps."

"Yes, Bess."

"Meroens, keep him out of trouble. What he gets up to in the tourney is his look-out but get him safely in and out. I don't care how, but bring him back in one piece, alive."

"Yes, Lady Boss."

"Perry. Just look after him. And yourself." Then Bess patted Perry on the shoulder. Something about her manner made his stomach turn over.

Domestic duty done, the men mounted up and rode away from the hovel.

Bess went inside to her books. She wept for a while, then opened a volume of parchments, which had been carefully scraped to remove the old ink, and began to write.

Her boy was on a Quest, but not the one for which she had spent so many years preparing him. The Tests had killed all the knights so far. He could easily die, not even in a Test, just an unlucky blow to the head or falling from his horse. She mastered herself and did not cry. If he died, her mission was in ruins. But If he succeeded and became a Prince, what then?

"Them's the rules," she muttered.

In the early days, she had thought finding a killer in the Kingdom would be easy. But unexpectedly, although death by battle or accident was frequent, the law of this land took murder very seriously indeed. Only the rules of chivalry made the difference between a knight and a murderer: but this was the difference between white and black. Among these people, knights went out to fight themselves into a public reputation, because riches and promotion followed. She had not really understood this at first, just seeing the carnage of skirmishes and tourneys.

And then she found she needed to set up a good story: that was how this world understood their history and politics. So, she needed a tale of how an evil man was to be killed by a man of virtue. A hole and corner assassination would do absolutely no good, would not remove the poisonous ideas the man was spreading. She could not kill the man herself, because - Because she knew him and she had never killed anyone and he was well-guarded and - he'd kill her first - but she could not trust anyone else, his bribery and threats and sorcery would be too much for them. And she was a doctor! She could not kill.

Then the boy had arrived at her door all those years ago, and she saw the strange golden light in his eyes. She knew he was a gift, her weapon against the great evil, strong and determined and implacable. A killer for the taking. Or he could have been, if she had filled his head with enough fictitious wickedness and poisonous lies. But she was not like that. She had him trained in every battle skill, but lying to him? No. When the time was right, when he was ready, she'd explain, and he would understand, and he would –

The boy was bright and funny, and exasperating and unruly, and he made her lonely life more bearable, and she had never believed in the argument about the 'greater good' trotted out by extremists,

Until now. She loved her strange boy, but the end-game was approaching. "Get a grip, Bess Mulholland." This was social surgery, the removal of a fatal cancer. Even with - she swallowed hard - collateral damage, everything would be worth it. Eiswolf, she forced herself to say through gritted teeth, was a means to that end.

For heaven's sake, he wasn't even human. He was her tool, a weapon. And no more.

***

The Princess and the Witch shared a confidential flagon of wine, but not the one intended for Eiswolf.

"Real shame," said the Witch. "I'd have liked to see how it worked. Supposed to be quite quick, coldness spreads up your limbs, reaches your heart, end of story."

"Well, keep it by, no telling when it might be useful," said the Princess. "What do you think of the Oriental costume?"

They inspected the silken clothes spread out on a bench. "Different," said the Witch. "Not very warm, though. So where does this come from?"

"Iris saw them at a trader's in the market. You're right, silk's no good here in winter. So, back to the subject. I have a preference for Plan D, part two. Which at least removes the problem permanently."

"I beg to differ," said Jocasta. "It removes this particular manifestation of the problem, but not the problem itself."

The Princess smiled. "But what about your revenge."

"Your Majesty's progression to the throne is more important. And for that, we still need a prince." Jocasta, now she was in the Palace and away from her drugs and potions, was clearer-headed than she had been for a long time. By accident, she had landed in a position of power. Taking out her frustration on Bess' wolf was still on her agenda, but as part of a much more entertaining web of events.

They looked up at the Planning Hanging, now gloriously flagged and beribboned from one end to the other. The Princess smiled again. "You know, I'm rather proud of this. Really quite clever."

They laughed.

***

The Hegemon sent out his trusted messengers to the four corners of the Kingdom, to solve the mystery that was Eiswolf. By fast horse, the news came back.

1   He's a werewolf.
2   He's a bloody good fighter.
3   What do you think I am, loony? See points 1 and 2. No way am I taking that on –

So the Hegemon sent forth to the lords of the border lands for knowledge of this creature. The news took a little longer to return, by beacon and pigeon as well as swift horse.

4   A what? You don't believe in those, do you?
5   Never heard of him. Who does he say he is?
6   Aha! The ancient prophecy!

For a second, the Hegemon got quite excited, until he read the rest of the message.

6 (continued) For the Signs are in the Sky, the Owl does hoot, my little finger hath pained me these three nights, and the song of the eel is heard in the land –

"They do spend a lot of time on their own up there," said the messenger. "I think that one has his own whisky-still."

"Unbelievable," said the Hegemon. "He can't come from nowhere."

"Unless…" said the messenger.

"Unless what?"

The man shuffled a little. "Well, unless he comes from, well, Under The Hill."

"A fairy?" The Hegemon was taken aback. The tales of his childhood were full of fairies. Once he thought he heard the Gabriel Hounds chasing the moon through the night. But he had never seen one.

"He looks right," said the messenger. "Big, uncanny."

"I prefer the werewolf theory," said the Hegemon, firmly. "Let's find out all we can, assuming that."

Because curiously enough, frightful though a werewolf might be, they were a lot easier to cope with than a fairy.

***

Eiswolf was unusually quiet on the way to the Cloister of Westerings, where the Sword of Destiny had been held for five hundred years. He rode at a good pace, neither Meroens nor Perry could spot any new injury: but there was no banter. If you were lucky, he grunted.

Perry rode ahead to check the way and listen to the gossip. Many ambitious knights were making their way to the Cloister to display their abilities, if not fight for the Sword itself. The Sword guaranteed victory to anyone of pure heart (insofar as you can kill people if you have a pure heart), but asked a terrible price. Sir Devlas, for whom the Sword had been forged, used it to defend the Castle of Virgins against the evil forces of night, and had been transformed into pure light as his reward (although others held that he slept in the Crystal Catacombs, until the day when he would be called forth once more).

But although the stories might be fanciful, the Sword was real, paraded through Westerings every July on the anniversary of Sir Devlas' battle. The weapon on display was a long-sword of steel worked in the eastern fashion, the gilded hilt inset with stones of power, by which Perry's informants meant magical talismans like bezoars and jacinths, and the stone from the head of a toad. (Perry had a sudden sentimental twinge for Albert, still happily in his bucket in the palace stable).

The contest for the Sword only ran occasionally, when the signs and portents were right. The winner had not only to beat the living daylights out of other knights, of course in a pure, virtuous and valorous way, but also get the Sword to accept him as its new master. That was the hard part, because the Warden of the Cloister plunged the blade into the winner's heart, on the basis that the Sword would turn aside and refuse to injure its true new lord. And, as the Sword had never left Westerings, the answer to the next question was obvious.

Meroens and Eiswolf rode behind Perry at a comfortable ambling pace. Meroens finally asked the question he had been ruminating over for a while.

"So how did Perry get to be your squire, boss? He's not the usual, is he?"

"Neither am I."

More than a grunt, so Meroens felt free to pursue his thought. "Yeah, but plenty of young lads want to be a squire. Why pick him, nice bloke and all." Meroens shrugged. "But he's old."

"He's no older than me. That's not important, anyway. He made himself useful and we get along and, well, five years ago, I was on my own. It's worked out well."

Sometimes Eiswolf was not very good at lying and even Meroens could pick that up. But even Meroens knew when to leave a topic alone.

The true answer was that, after the battle when Eiswolf had been knighted for saving the life of a duke, he found himself with the title of knight but none of the support structure. He had never been a squire, for no knight would take him even for money. Bess had invested in his fighting skills, but he had no training in other knightly ways. His previous occupation as a 'free lance', a security escort or general man at arms for hire, was no longer open. Knights were supposed to be above all that. The duke's gratitude did not extend to inviting him into the ducal household. He did not have wealth to pay for horse or fine armour, and definitely could not support the expense of a squire, who would need to be fed and lodged, and expected to be educated.

And that did not count the werewolf thing. Even when he won his spurs, another lord had objected that only humans could be made knights, or else his horse would be a candidate too. Eiswolf ended that argument by hitting the man on the head. An undercurrent of muttering followed him; he found it difficult to find tailors to clothe him or barbers to shave him and trim his hair. A lot of people seemed very keen to wash their hands after they touched him, or kept tight hold of a hex charm when he was nearby. Or the purple-blue flower called wolfsbane.

As a poor knight wandering the streets, Eiswolf had little chance of gaining a squire, or a livelihood, even if the rumour of werewolf-dom had not followed him. Then he had found Perry. To be exact, he spotted a group of lads, who had no better sport than to kick anyone weaker than themselves half to death, hacking into a small heap of dirty clothes. And then he saw a hand in the heap, and the hand moved. When challenged, the boys yelled that Perry was a nonce, and a crip, and peculiar. They spat on him. Eiswolf didn't know Perry, but he knew the lads by type, because when he had been younger and smaller and not as strong, he'd been kicked half to death himself. So he beat them off without mercy.

"Sir, I can never repay you," Perry gasped through a split lip.

"You speak like a- " Eiswolf had been about to say 'gentleman' but the timbre of Perry's voice was not quite right. "Like an educated person."

"And you have the manner of a - Whoa!"

Perry had finally seen what had rescued him. Wow. Weird, really odd, like a distorted glimpse of a reflection. What the hell? But whoever and whatever that was, it had saved Perry's life. "A man of valour. I can never thank you enough."

"Let me help you. Where do you stay tonight?"

When not groggy from concussion, Perry turned out to be bright and cheerful, full of ideas for Eiswolf's progress as a knight. Knowledgeable about the ways of courts and chivalry, Perry finally gave Eiswolf the training in etiquette and courtly procedure that he had lacked. Eiswolf was grateful for his company, too.

Perry considered that, strange though the whole deal was, it was considerably better than anything else on offer. Being a squire meant a title and a place and, not least, protection. Eventually, he told Eiswolf about the Barons of Elderton, and Eiswolf told him about the wolf thing. Matters worked out reasonably well, after that.

Meroens had been ruminating for a while. "So, when you're a King, like, what happens to Perry?"

"I've got a few impossible tests to do first, Meroens."

"Yeah, but, you won't need a squire, will you?"

"There'll always be a place for a man as talented as Perry."

"Yeah, but, you know, odd and all that." Meroens squinted towards the sky again. "You got to be careful, boss. You need to look impressive, like a proper king, leading your men into battle and winning victories and stuff. Now, I've got nothing against our King, he's a good man, but you know that little weaselly Hegemon, like, he does him no favours. Makes him look like he's, you know, not the real ruler. Looks iffy."

"Iffy?"

"Not quite right." And having delivered his political analysis, Meroens went quiet.

Eiswolf did not want to think about any of this. He wanted to get to the Cloister, let the dice fall as they will, then work out what to do when and if he survived. Because the more Eiswolf mixed with the higher nobles and lords of the lands, the more obvious it was that

Perry, streetwise oddity, competent squire and entertaining companion for a landless knight, did not fit the profile of royal retainer.

***

Westerings was a small town with a large religious establishment; not only the Cloister and associated assembly halls, barns and offices, but also the headquarters of both the Weeping Nuns and the Zachoritic Rite. The town council was quite happy as all paid their taxes and employed local tradesmen. Unlike trade guilds or brigades of fighting men, they caused no trouble in the town. However, all the sects had holy days when they marched in the streets or held open-air services, so two men were employed by the council specifically to make sure that nothing clashed.

The contest for the Sword had taken the council by surprise, disrupting the carefully arranged diary. Some very unhappy nuns were, frankly, spitting tacks (weeping was kept strictly for their services). The Zachorites were more into silent protest and had blocked one of the main roads by lying down. But even they could not prevent the tide of horses, knights, nobles, ladies and hangers-on as the tourney circus hit town.

The crowd wound its way through Westerings, up steep cobbled streets towards the high-walled bastion that could be seen for miles around. Here were taverns and lodgings and a beacon-tower around a piazza, where the battle arena had been set out. As the crowd rode up the steep hill, they passed statues on each side: knights in white stone, their heads bowed, holding their swords before them. A few were crowned with fresh flowers: at more than one, a woman sat at the statue's base, mourning. For these were the knights who had attempted the challenge, and failed.

"Now that would put me right off," said Nev (more formally, the Baron of Eims). He and Jonno, Earl Dugdale, never missed a chance to size up tourney competition. This was a rare chance to see Westerings in action. "Morbid, I call that."

"Yeah, but these types, it's all glory, isn't it," said Jonno. "Who have they got? Dietrich's still not a goer."

"He should be happy to be alive. Oh, the usual bunch, I think. Our wolfie friend seems to be nap. No money to be had on him."

"Nap for what? Winning, or going home in a shroud?"

They laughed.

It was true that many of the knights who had been at the Grand Tourney were now in Westerings. Perry had spotted the Knight in White Satin, the Fright Knight, and about half a dozen others.

"But they're not here for the Sword," he said to Meroens. "Now, him." He pointed at a wild-eyed knight on a prancing white horse which snorted and whinnied with anger. "He looks the type."

"Nice horse," said Meroens. "So what, like last time, they have to get through rounds to get a shot?"

"Suppose so."

But as this was not strictly a tourney, in fact Perry was wrong. The gathering at Westerings was really a religious festival. The display of the Sword of Destiny was for veneration, not to show off the prize. The central battle for the Sword was overseen by the Warden, designed to prove the valour of the contenders, not as a knockout winner-takes-all.

But Nev was right that the betting (or the opinion of the wise, because money was not supposed to change hands on such a serious topic) was with Eiswolf. Correction, some were of the opinion, which they were prepared to back, that he would survive.

Eiswolf and his squires were greeted with great ceremony and lodged in a house on the piazza. The Warden himself welcomed Eiswolf to Westerings in the name of his rite and all the town. Eiswolf was gracious and mannerly in return, promising to seek after the Sword with all his strength, determination, and honour. (And, he said to himself, wits).

A commotion started outside: cheering! Eiswolf poked his head out of the door. Young girls in white danced by, throwing flowers onto the street, pages gambolled and sang, a joyful assembly of lovely women rode on dappled ponies, their bridles tinkling with golden bells.

"What the hell's all that about?" said Perry.

"He has come!" cried the Warden, clasping his hands in joy. "He is here!" Then he, too, dashed into the piazza to join the rejoicing.

At the end of the procession Eiswolf could see a knight. His horse was large and creamy-white, with the heavy neck and curled mane of the royal breed from the southern mountains. The man glittered in silver armour. His shield had a simple device, a gilded 'sun in splendour' on a sky-blue ground. And the man himself –

Tall. Probably taller than Eiswolf. Young. His golden hair gleamed like a halo. His eyes were blue, brighter even than his shield. His profile was noble, he smiled modestly, sweetly, as the crowd welcomed him. On one arm, he bore a ribbon of blush-pink, picked out with pearls and silver.

Perry called out to one of the girls. "Who's he?"

She giggled. "Sir Adelbon! The True Knight! For he is pure as well as strong, the finest knight of all!"

Suddenly Perry was aware of a strange sound, a deep, grating noise, and felt a sort of rumbling through the floor.

Eiswolf growled.

***

That evening, a deputation from the Kingdom arrived in Westerings, led by the Hegemon and accompanied by the Glimmer Lord, who came at the King's own invitation to see this important event. The Hegemon was most attentive to the Glimmer Lord, treating him with huge respect: and the Lord was gracious in response, taking the small man aside for quiet conversations and sharing a joke or two.

Eiswolf fully expected the Hegemon to call on him, because he fought for the honour of the Kingdom, but no visit materialised.

"I don't like this," said Perry. "He can't have forgotten you."

"Bloody rude," said Meroens.

Then a message arrived that the Glimmer Lord craved an audience. Eiswolf, unsure of the man and his importance, agreed with no great enthusiasm. The Lord was all smiles and congratulations, bringing gifts from the Kingdom.

"And especially, the Princess has sent you this fine wine of the southern realms!"

He gestured at a female servant, a dark woman in her forties, who did not look Eiswolf in the eye. But then, she was only a servant.

Eiswolf dismissed her. "Thank the Princess, but I have sworn that until I have won the Sword of Destiny in her name, no strong drink shall pass my lips!" Because according to Meroens, rumour was that Adelbon did not drink, carouse, or hang out with wild women. If Adelbon could, so could he. So the sealed wine-jug was returned to the servant, who left the room, muttering what sounded like dee and part two.

The Glimmer Lord smiled. "Sir Knight, this will be a great day for the Kingdom, and for yourself."

"Like to be my last, if the stories are true," said Eiswolf, cautiously.

The Glimmer Lord smiled again. "A few men have been made the poorer by betting against you. I have seen you do battle, I know of your humble beginnings. I am here to say that, despite everything, I believe you to be the truest challenger for the Sword, and thus, for the great Tests of Kolras themselves."

"Despite everything?" said Eiswolf.

The Glimmer Lord looked embarrassed. "Oh. You haven't heard?"

The roar was postponed until the Glimmer Lord had left, with many courtesies and compliments. Actually, it was more of a howl.

"THEY GOT SOMEBODY ELSE! THAT PREENING PRETTY-BOY, THAT GIRL!"

Perry managed to calm him down long enough to get sense out of him, but the tale did not improve with telling. For Sir Adelbon had come to the Kingdom. Hearing of the call for a Hero to win the Princess, he had been delayed by saving three queens from a swamp-monster and defeating an army of trolls, (as you do, many apologies) and asked if he, too, could undertake the Tests of Kolras. This was unprecedented. The Conclave considered his request for three days and nights, before declaring that due to his exemplary virtue and courage, he would be allowed –

"They can't do that!" said Meroens.

"It gets worse," said Perry.

Because not only was he allowed into the contest, but he also got a bye.

The Manifest was at the Palace, so no need for Adelbon to go to the Neuts of Bladbean. Albert was in his bucket in the stable, but the Conclave explained that obtaining the Enchanted One was not part of the Seven Tests as such, just clarification of their order. And winning the Tourney had not been the quest: recruiting the team of men with special powers was the quest. Adelbon was able to point to his own runner, hearer, archer and strong-man. The translation of the Manifest was declared to be faulty, for the requirement to kill a dragon should have read 'a man skilled in killing monsters' and Adelbon was already well-known for that, latest being said swamp-monster. So Adelbon could proceed straight to the Sword of Destiny.

And he wore the Princess' favour upon his arm. She said she wished there to be no sign that she preferred one knight over the other.

Any uncertainty Eiswolf had about his quest disappeared the second he saw a competitor. And for that pink-faced idiot to get through without so much as raising his sword! Now, Eiswolf wanted nothing in the world more than to win.

That, and to smash the smug little princeling into the ground.

***

The Glimmer Lord supped with the Hegemon in private.

"What think you of our contender?" said the Hegemon.

"The perfect knight, or the other thing?" said the Glimmer Lord. They laughed.

"Well, we must plan on the basis that either might become our new sovereign," said the Hegemon, carefully. "In the interests of the Kingdom, a man brought up in a court has to be preferred. But it would not be the first time that such a prize went to a man of war."

The Glimmer Lord poured more wine for the Hegemon. "I see your problem. But there are other considerations. What sort of ruler will our wolf-like friend become? How would he behave towards your Kingdom when he has the command of, permit me to assume, the less desirable half?"

The Hegemon paused. "He's not stupid. We have reports on him, the Good Witch Bess did her best with his education, we gather. Sharp enough, no known atrocities. We could negotiate with him." As long as it was in a large room, at the far end of a very long table. In daylight.

'You don't believe the werewolf business, then?"

"A tale to scare the superstitious."

"And the other man? The gilded darling of the crowds?"

The Hegemon smiled. "Pure, gentle, innocent, guided by the pure light of truth. He might kill you, obviously, but there's always a very good reason for the death of his enemies, for they are the enemies of Light."

"And what do you really think?"

They laughed, again.

"Hard to tell. He's a real wild card, not known at Court. Not a lot of information, but the Princess did insist. I can't get near him without a phalanx of ladies and retainers in the way. He looks right and he says all the right things but…" The Hegemon grimaced.

The Glimmer Lord examined the small man, now eating a piece of pigeon. The Hegemon was not just a jumped-up steward; he had genuine ability. Even insight. To have risen from commoner to Court was not just machination. Perhaps he was just very good at organisation. Another piece slotted into the Glimmer Lord's considerations.

"Well, my lord Hegemon, a third road. What if neither man succeeds? On the record so far, no knight walks away from this contest."

"We have considered this," said the Hegemon, a mite too quickly. "Her Majesty the Princess cannot be condemned to eternal spinsterhood. We are examining the rulings of Kolras to find his wisdom on this set of circumstances."

I have you, thought the Glimmer Lord. Men can conceal much, but the love-light shines like a beacon.

So that made three possible- He allowed himself to use a word from his old life. Scenarios. For Eiswolf, the plan for his management was in hand. Adelbon was a lad without experience, who could be persuaded to follow a mentor. Or there was the small, grey functionary, who knew how to be grateful - Ah, love, love. How useful that emotion could be.

"A toast to the future of the Kingdom," said the Glimmer Lord. "And to you, Hegemon."

"And to you, my Lord," said the Hegemon. "May we have many more such meetings of the mind."

"After the outcome of this battle, we may need them," said the Glimmer Lord.

***

A commotion outside rattled the lodging-house with music and laughter, so Perry went to the door. He found three pages in sky-blue, who bowed and smiled sweetly.

"Our Lord would parley with the great warrior, Eiswolf!"

"Oh," said Perry, mind running fast but not quite fast enough. "I'll see if he's in." And shut the door.

"You know he's ruddy in," said Meroens.

"Yeah, but is he receiving guests?"

"He's a knight, not your granny!"

"There's dozens of them out there." Perry peered through a small, dim window. "Like rats in a granary."

"I'll do it." Meroens opened the door and declared loudly, "Whoever would parley with our master Sir Eiswolf must show themselves and enter singly, without weapons or men at arms."

"That I shall do," said a strong, clear voice, "For I have no fear of treachery."

Sir Adelbon stood on the threshold, filled the door, and glittered. Points of light from his armour danced about the dimly lit room. His brilliant blue eyes bored into Perry. "Tell your master I am here," he announced.

"Um," said Perry. He ran into the back room, where Eiswolf dozed in front of a small fire. "Boss! Boss! He's here!"

"What?" said Eiswolf.

"Tidy yourself up! And look threatening!"

But while Eiswolf might have needed reminding to adjust his dress, threatening came by nature.

"Sir Adelbon," he said, trying to keep the growl out of his voice. "We are honoured by this visit."

"Sir Eiswolf, I have heard of your achievements."

"Have you," said Eiswolf. He could not resist. "Remind me of yours?"

"I shall send you a troubadour, many songs have been composed in my honour," said Adelbon, nobly but modestly. "But we are not here to contest the half-told tales of long ago! Sir Knight, I am here to assure you that if the Divine Right should favour me, I will look after your household, and be a most loving and dutiful husband to the Princess, and steward of the Kingdom!"

"Half the Kingdom. Boundaries yet to be decided."

"Indeed," said Sir Adelbon. "But I swear by my own renown, that this shall be a fair fight, for honour above all! And to bring peace to the Kingdom!"

"Right," said Eiswolf. "I hope you've studied up on Cymenshore, in that case."

Perry gave a sharp glance at his boss.

"Where?" Sir Adelbon seemed genuinely confused,

"The flash-point in the Kingdom. The port-town. Full of rich men who don't care a lot for noble blood. The peace of the Kingdom, and the land which you will receive with the hand of the Princess, depends on this place."

Sir Adelbon went pink. "Why, sir, I expect their fealty, as any King does from their subjects! For lords and those of low degree will see that Right has prevailed! Those who do not, cannot be of the Light!"

Eiswolf smiled. "Ah, sir, I'm sure the lords of Cymenshore will be most grateful to hear that! And what of Scything?"

"Where? I, um. All lands which come under my rule, shall be assured of my most careful and tender care! For I shall be a King!"

"Prince. You're not king until your father in law dies."

"Prince of most gentle and powerful renown!" Sir Adelbon went even pinker. "For guided by my Lady the Princess and wise men of her counsel, I shall be a ruler the like of which the Kingdom has not seen!"

And he marched out.

"Plonker," said Eiswolf. "But he might be handy with a sword, I suppose."

"What's all that about Cymenshore?" said Perry.

"Do you think I'm a total idiot?" Eiswolf was laughing. "If, I know, a huge, huge if. If I get through all this, I'll be taking over a big chunk of the Kingdom, and it doesn't run itself, does it? Even I know enough to keep my eye on Cymenshore. I think I could do with a drink. Join me, Perry."

Just when Perry thought he knew his boss through and through, he could still surprise.

***

The first day of the contest dawned. Assuming that the knights survived that long, fighting for the Sword of Destiny would take place over three days, culminating in the moment when the winner faced the final test, as the Warden of the Sword plunged the blade into the breast of the man who would be its master. The Warden prepared with many hours of meditation and prayer, for as a man of peace, the only way to justify an action which might kill another was belief that this was for the Divine Good.

Now the knights would put on their armour, unfurl their banners, bridle and caparison their horses, and reveal the full glory of their chivalric majesty.

"What's that horse?" said Perry. "Where's Pepper?"

"He came available," said Meroens, leading the snorting white charger. "One previous owner who's not got a use for him right now. He's called Storm. Thought I'd give the other feller a rest."

Meroens held Storm while Perry covered him in the black caparison slashed with red and green. Perry unrolled the banner. Then came the time to reveal the new shield.

After the last unfortunateness, Perry went back to the Armourer and complained strongly about quality of depiction of the Snow Wolf. The Armourer listened and shrugged. He was a chap who mended bits of metal, not a limner, so there was no point in appealing to his aesthetic sense.

"Look, I got pots of paint in five colours, and one gold and one silver, I can do lines or quarters or halves, or you can 'ave one of them." He pointed to the sample shields hung on the wall behind him. "For your hanimals, we got a lion, a unicorn, or a bear, and you can 'ave one in small, medium or large."

"But we need a wolf!"

The Armourer sucked his teeth. "Well, wanting to help you out, like. You want a wolf that looks like a lion, or a wolf that looks like a bear?"

"A wolf that looks like a wolf!"

The Armourer, not being an artist, used stencils. He did not have one for a wolf. He shook his head, sadly. "Sorry, you're out of luck, there, pal."

So Perry left the shield with instructions to make the white thingummy look more ferocious, and crossed all his fingers.

Once more, the shield came out of its canvas cover.

"Bloody hell!" said Meroens.

Eiswolf heard the exclamations, and came in. But words failed him.

"Well, it's got a good set of gnashers on it," said Meroens.

"It looks ferocious,' said Perry, defensively. "With the crossed eyes and all."

"Yeah, well, it frightens me," said Meroens. "Kind of striking out at the enemy, like with its little hooves."

"Paws," said Perry, desperately.

"Since when did sheep have paws?" said Meroens.

"Oh, God," said Eiswolf.

But it was far too late to do much about it. Eiswolf mounted up and rode to the piazza. The crowd cheered him on, although "Here's to the Knight of the White - er - What is that?" did not quite have the ring of "Here's to Sir Adelbon, the True Knight of the Shining Sun!"

The first bout with Adelbon was fairly normal, by Eiswolf's standards. Swords sparked off each other, shields clashed and the knights rode their horses vigorously and skilfully. Adelbon was strong and a good horseman, his fighting skills as practised as anyone from a noble household, if lacking battle experience. But his youthful strength carried him through. Eiswolf knew the winner was the one who walked away, not the one who looked prettiest.

The judges declared a draw, not a popular decision among those in the crowd who knew what they were looking at, but Eiswolf bowed his head and accepted the ruling. He had got the measure of his opponent, a reasonable result.

When he returned to the house with Perry, he found the Knight in White Satin. "Good to see you again, sir."

"And you, Sir Eiswolf, you look well. I heard about the Dragon." The Knight paused. "Was it real?"

"As real as you'd want to see. Does your lady send you here?"

"Here, there and everywhere," said the Knight, sorrowfully. "She's very keen on honour. So is Chummy." He jerked his head towards the piazza. "You know about him, then?"

"Not as much as I'd like."

So the Knight told him that Adelbon was famous for deeds of derring-do, who rescued virgins (and left them that way) and extricated small children from lions, blocked a dam with his bare body to save a village from flooding and –

"Give me a break," said Perry, who was beginning to have Adelbon overload. "Is this guy real?"

"Oh, a model to us all, he is," said the Knight. "According to his troubadours, anyway."

The more useful information was that he was the younger son of an earl of a distant territory, who had been spotted as a potential tourney knight and given the full training, but, frankly, as dim as a half-wick lantern.

"He looks good and all," said the Knight, "but you get him into a difficulty and he panics."

"So how did he get here?" said Perry.

"Right. Well, word has it, and I've got no proof." The Knight squinted, as befitting a man telling a terrible secret. "Some say the Princess sent men to find him and made him her knight so he could win half the Kingdom and marry her. But she is too gentle a lady for such goings-on, so that's a rank slander."

"Absolutely," said Perry. "Have another drink."

***

The second day's battle started out as much of a piece with the first. Adelbon was young, with good powers of recovery, so Eiswolf knew he would not be overcome by strength alone. Now was the time to use a little - Eiswolf did not know the word 'psychology' but he understood the concept very well.

"Aha, Sir Knight!" he called out, as they grappled with sword and shield in the middle of the arena, their horses snorting and whinnying. "Any thoughts on the Scything situation?"

"The what?" gasped Adelbon, swiping at Eiswolf's helmet.

"Scything." Clang. "Boundary dispute." Crunch. "Lord Maslett or Lord Crowdale?" Then Eiswolf turned and rode out to the barrier to get a longer run-up on his approach.

Adelbon shook his head, and did likewise. They met in a mighty crash of man and horse and metal, many great strokes were made, many blows landed.

"But - Oof - The question with Cymenshore - Aha!" Crash. "The question is - urk - what about the reeve?" Bang.

"The what?" Adelbon missed his blow and was nearly unhorsed in return.

"The reeve! Ambitious man!" Clunk. Eiswolf rode out to the barrier again, to pick up a mace.

Adelbon, still shaking his head, rode to his seconds for a spirited discussion. The judge by the barrier noted his protest, then walked to Eiswolf and his men.

"Sir Eiswolf, Sir Adelbon complains that you keep talking to him."

From the other side of the arena, the glittering knight gave Eiswolf a look that would certainly have killed if he could.

"If it troubles him, Sir Adelbon must learn to keep his ears closed.".

The judge frowned. "Sir Eiswolf, is this the way of a noble knight?"

"It's the way of a knight who intends to win," said Eiswolf. "The boy has a lot to learn. You can tell him that, if you like."

Perry grinned. "Win ugly!"

So the knights crashed together once more, with Eiswolf giving Adelbon tips about the taxation status of Wardur, the proposed freeport at Hydon, and the rights of foresters in the Weald of Snave.

"Shut up!" shrieked Adelbon. He made a mighty swipe that could have cut Eiswolf in two, had he still been there. But Eiswolf was already ten paces away. Gathering Storm up for a final assault, he got in under the boy's guard while still unbalanced from striking the blow. Adelbon sailed through the air and landed on his back.

Eiswolf raised his sword to the judges. They signalled the end of the bout. But they declared a draw, because of Eiswolf's 'unorthodox technique'.

"You was robbed," said the Knight in White Satin, on the way back to the house. "You should appeal."

"Makes no odds. We're all square, just tomorrow to go." Eiswolf was not worried about the battle, but why Adelbon did not seem unduly concerned; the boy was definitely not suicidal. Although Adelbon threw ideas like Divine Right around quite freely, he did not seem the martyr type, so he must be assuming he would survive the Sword. What did he know that Eiswolf did not?

Back at the house, the serving woman from the Hegemon's party waited for Eiswolf and his men.

"My lord! Many congratulations! Now drink the health of your Princess, for she would celebrate your victory with you in spirit if not in body!" She held up the richly engraved flask full of rare wine from the southern realms.

"Give that to my squire, we will enjoy it later. Now I must salve my wounds."

Perry took the flask and tried to get a better look at the woman because she seemed somehow familiar. Not a palace servant, but –

He took the wine into the small buttery at the rear and was about to pour a cup when a thought came into his head. When Eiswolf had been injured after the Tourney, Bess had accepted nothing, not food nor drink nor clothing, not even from the Palace. He smelled the wine and suddenly he was back in the clearing with that mad woman and her groupies. So he took the flask into the back yard and emptied the wine over the refuse piled by the drain channel in the alley.

When Eiswolf asked for wine later, Perry gave him a perfectly decent clairette and he was none the wiser, if slightly confused by what passed for the best wine from the southern realms. And when the woman came that night, Perry was able to return the flask with a clear conscience.

She looked about the room. "And your master? Is he well?"

"Oh, very well. That's him singing with his companions!" He pointed upwards: tuneless catch-singing could be heard from the room above between Eiswolf, Meroens and the Knight in White Satin.

"And he drank the wine?"

"Every last drop!" Perry grinned. "Be sure and tell the Princess!"

"I most certainly shall," said the woman.

But as she walked back to her own lodgings, Jocasta shook her head. What on earth was the man made of?

***

Black. The dream always began with black. Then flaring, sparking, blinding white, crossing and recrossing, trails of light across the void, which became stars, which became the sky, and the flare of green spread through the blackness, and began to dance, and down below, a faint reflection played across the unending white of the snowfield.

The air was sharp, clean, fierce. There! The scent of a living thing. In front of him, a shadow. He turned around and looked up. The Moon, silver-white, casting blue shapes across the snow, stared down at him. He loved it, and hated it. Then the scent drifted past, warm, familiar, a fire? Out of place here.

He had to find the scent. Out of place. He had to find it, and kill it.

He started to run, yelling -

Until Perry came in and shook him by the shoulder.

"Easy, boss, turn over, back to sleep."

And the knight sighed deeply and turned on his side.

Perry took note that another drop of valerian might be handy, assuming this was - He stopped thinking right there, and went back to his own place by the door.

***

The third day was a serious occasion. By the end, there would be a new master of the Sword of Destiny, or yet another white statue to stand on the cobbled streets of Westerings.

Eiswolf was not exactly nervous, because he knew he could win the battle. This time he would leave nothing to the vagaries of point-scoring; he was going to knock the little blighter out, stone-cold. But neither Perry nor Meroens had been able to get to the bottom of Sir Adelbon's strange self-confidence about surviving the Sword.

Perry shrugged, "Apparently he's talking about True Love as his defence."

"No special armour, then?" said Eiswolf. "He can't believe in Love alone, he's thick but not that thick, is he?"

"No," said Meroens. "The armour's all standard stuff. Nice, but standard."

"What about a trick, like the fairground men do with the dagger that disappears into the hilt?"

Perry shook his head. "The Warden would never go for it. He's a real believer, you can't get near the Sword unless you're in holy orders."

"There must be something," said Eiswolf.

Perry said quietly, "What if there isn't? What do we do then?"

Meroens laughed. "We? This is the boss we're talking about! The best fighter of them all! So grab the thing and run! We've got fast horses, we can be out of here before they can stop us!"

Eiswolf smiled.

But Perry felt sick, and would not look at Eiswolf as Meroens armed him.

***

In the piazza, the mood was sombre. The Hegemon and his group sat on the viewing stage, to watch the outcome for their Kingdom. The Glimmer Lord sat beside them.

Adelbon entered first, his entourage of pages and ladies now serious and almost wistful. He rode in on his great white horse, without his helmet, his eyes gleaming with an unearthly light, his golden hair creating a halo about his head, while his silver armour glittered like a thousand stars.

The Warden saluted him, holding up the Sword for the knight to see. "Be pure of heart, and the Sword shall know you!"

"I shall contest this Sword in the name of Truth and the Divine Right, and my Lady, the Eternal Rose!" Adelbon bowed his head. A squire handed him his helmet.

Well, no way could Eiswolf beat that. He rode on Storm wearing his helmet, because he did not have bright blue eyes and golden hair, and he knew the crowd was not in his favour. He even heard hissing. Meroens ran beside him as his squire at arms. Perry stayed back at the house with Pepper and Corsa, ready to make a quick exit.

Eiswolf rode up to the Warden. The man looked at the knight. He had been going to give him the truth and purity speech but a white glint caught his eye.

"What on earth is your device?" he said.

"It's a wolf," said Eiswolf, nettled.

"Oh. Are you sure?"

"Quite," said Eiswolf, tensely.

"Strange teeth. Never seen anything quite like. Anyway. The Sword of Destiny. You know the rules?"

"I believe so."

'Hm. Well, it's all up to the Sword in the end. Truth, purity, holy intent…" He squinted up at the mounted knight again. "Are you sure you want to do this?"

"Look, I'm only here for the Tests, so let's get on with it, please?"

"As you wish. Best of luck."

To which he did not add, 'You'll need it."

Adelbon rose to the occasion, Eiswolf had to admit. The silver knight was committed and strong, making up for less polished skills in energy of attack. Eiswolf was driven back to the rails more than once. But Storm was a well-practised tournament stallion and could turn like a snake to get his rider out of trouble. Eiswolf tried to take the battle to Adelbon, hoping inexperience would show and he would start to tire, but whatever hormones were flowing through the boy's veins, they kept his heart pumping and his nerves at top pitch for much longer than Eiswolf expected.

Time for another strategy. Distraction might work again –

"Have you thought further on Cymenshore?"

But this time, Adelbon did not even twitch. The lad took Eiswolf's advice and closed his ears.

Distraction, distraction. "Sir knight, what of the other Tests? This is not the end. "

Still not a twitch. This time Eiswolf was the one distracted, into letting his guard down. A heavy blow crunched into to his injured shoulder.

Surely Adelbon had to be getting tired? The Hegemon was watching very closely. And what did the Glimmer Lord want? But all these thoughts were a fog between him and his quarry, that silver toy, that glittering nonsense, that annoying thing in his way - Thing in his way - THING to hunt - HUNT SNOW PREY

Eiswolf's attack was stunningly fierce. His sword seemed on fire, his stallion screamed with excitement and terror, he slashed and stabbed and punched and hacked as if he did not need to breathe, or even see his opponent.

The Hegemon stifled a gasp. No man has ever fought like this. This is different. This man is truly dangerous.

What is this? thought the Glimmer Lord, revising his assumptions yet again.

At last, Adelbon started to suffer from the hurricane of blows, making moves that were a little uncontrolled, a little less than perfect. But that marginal decline was all Eiswolf needed.

He went in for the attack, blow to the head, and another, blow to the body to disturb balance, blow to the shoulder to change Adelbon's shield position, revealing, no, not quite - weak area under his arm, neck below helmet, clear view of chest - No, not quite - Blow to sword arm, raised to protect his head - underarm exposed - no, not quite - Chest better blow - NOT KILL, not here to kill - strike head, bastard won't fall off - Get thigh, less grip on horse, shield, swipe away - NOW!

Eiswolf punched though a massive blow to Adelbon's chest, unhorsing him. The boy landed heavily, and did not move.

The piazza was silent. Eiswolf sat frozen for a minute, two minutes, then seemed to come to and dismounted. He knelt beside Adelbon to take off the boy's helmet, before standing and removing his own. "By the grace of God, this knight lives! Warden, your judgement?"

The Warden, like the other spectators, was almost speechless. "Ah. A true - A true knight!" He looked wildly about him, but the other judges shook their heads. He swallowed hard and croaked, "In fair fight, this true knight has won the Sword of Destiny!"

But there were no cheers in the piazza.

***

The final ceremony of the Sword was to take place that evening. Eiswolf was to present himself, without armour, in the great hall of the Warden, where the Sword would make the final decision.

At the lodging house, Perry packed up the last of their belongings. Then he took them out through the rear yard, past the rubbish and a few dead dogs, to where Corsa waited to be loaded. He would have to support Eiswolf at the ceremony, but could not bear to imagine what would happen after.

As he came back into the house, one of Adelbon's pages was waiting. Perry decided to be friendly. "How does your master? I hear he fought bravely."

"He fought for Divine Right, without witchcraft," said the page. "My master wishes to parley with the werew… with Sir Eiswolf."

"I'll tell him." But the page had gone.

In the rear room, Meroens inspected Eiswolf's bruises and cuts. The knight took little notice.

"Did you hear that?" said Perry. "Adelbon must be on his feet and talking, anyway."

"Whatever," said Eiswolf. "Wonder what he wants?" But he spoke without tone. Meroens put him into a shirt, then a black robe over the top.

Adelbon entered, supported by two pages. He was pale, sweat stood on his forehead, his blue eyes seemed dimmer. "Sir Knight." He spoke in a low voice. "I fear you have been my end."

"I hope not," said Eiswolf, "for that was not my intent. You are a brave man and not many have fought as you did."

"I thank you, Sir Knight. But we both fought in the name of that most gracious lady, and she is a prize without compare."

For a second, Eiswolf genuinely did not know what he was talking about. "Oh. Ah! The Princess. Right. I bear her favour still." He pulled his shirt aside to show the necklace.

"And I also," said Adelbon. "For she gave her favour to me with many blessings and prayers, to wear always next to my heart, and swore it would protect me against all ills."

Eiswolf's ears began to prick up.

"And so," said Sir Adelbon, "as we both battle in her name, I would wish you to wear this favour in the time of your greatest test, for I know she would want you to be protected as I have been." He loosened his shirt and drew out a sort of necklace cum amulet.

A square of metal mesh like very fine chain-mail, measuring about the span of a hand in each direction, hung from a light steel chain around his neck. At the bottom of the square two more chains were attached to go around the body, to keep the amulet in place. Set into the mesh were many dull crystals, dark grey in colour, but not in any pattern or decoration that Eiswolf could see.

"Take this and wear it over your heart," said Adelbon, "and its Love and Purity shall protect you against all ill."

It had to be worth a try. Eiswolf put the metal chain over his head and allowed Meroens to pass the other chains around his body under his shirt.

"Exactly over your heart," said Adelbon. "She was most insistent."

"I thank you, sir knight," said Eiswolf.

And then the heralds arrived to escort Eiswolf to the ceremony, as much to make sure he did not bolt as to honour him. They brought a detachment of guards with them, just in case.

***

Everyone expected Eiswolf to become the next white stone knight on the cobbles of Westerings. The crowds on the road to the bastion were silent.

Eiswolf rode up to the hall on Storm. Meroens and Perry hitched their horses and followed on foot. But at the door, a serjeant at arms stopped Perry.

"Only those who are hale and whole may attend this sacred ceremony," said the serjeant.

"I am the squire of Sir Eiswolf!"

"That's nothing to me, nonce." The serjeant's lip curled. "Be off with you, you pathetic little freak."

"I shall report this to my master!" But a guard seized Perry by the arm and dragged him away.

"Report it to his corpse," grunted the soldier. "Out, you useless piece of dogmeat." He threw the squire to the ground. Suddenly, Eiswolf's protection meant nothing any more. Perry sat on a step, and waited. He shivered.

Inside the hall, the assembly stood quietly. Some wept, some prayed. A choir sang songs of distant hope, of the forgiveness of all things in the great vastness of life eternal. At the far end, the Warden prepared to do his terrible deed, assisted by two acolytes of his rite: one in red carried the Sword, the other, in blue, the sacred book of ritual. Behind him, five Weeping Nuns laid out a fine linen winding-sheet for the expected corpse. Three Zachorites clasped their hands in silent prayer.

Reality was coming home to Eiswolf. This town had killed dozens of great knights, many better fighters than he was. And they were certainly better men. None had escaped. He walked steadily towards the gleaming Sword, and he did not have a single idea of how to survive the Test.

He stopped in front of the Warden. "I am here."

The Warden gestured to him to kneel, then leaned forward and spoke quietly. "Sir. If you would part your shirt?"

"Sir, I…" Eiswolf could hardly speak, then found his strength. "Sir, I would not be seen to shiver, lest the people mistake that for the trembling of fear."

"Ah, I understand," said the Warden, and nodded.

Eiswolf knelt down.

Then the Warden turned to the crowd. "Be all of good understanding! We have been blessed by this Sword and its power, we will not put it in the hands of the unworthy! The Sword is not death, but ineffable truth and justice! We do this deed not from hate, but love!"

"Not from hate, but love!" the crowd repeated. The Weeping Nuns began to wail.

"Not revenge, but in the name of light eternal!" The Warden took the Sword from the red acolyte, raising it above his head for all to see, then turned the blade to point at the ground, and clasped the hilt with both hands. He took a step towards the kneeling Eiswolf. "Please lift up your head, sir."

Eiswolf raised his chin and tried, very hard, to keep his eyes open.

The Warden was now standing over Eiswolf. He held the Sword vertically, its point directly at Eiswolf's heart. The choir's voices rose in a great, sweet sigh. The Warden plunged the Sword down.

It would not go in.

Total silence.

The Warden lifted the Sword. Once more he tried to plunge the blade into Eiswolf's chest. The point would not enter, although the knight staggered a little from the force of the blow. Sweat ran down the Warden's face. Again he raised the Sword and struck with all his strength. Eiswolf rocked back on his knees but there was no doubt. The Sword refused to kill him. The Warden gasped, confused and agitated..

Eiswolf staggered to his feet and faced the crowd. "The Sword has spoken!" He grabbed the Sword from the trembling Warden and swung it about his head. "The Sword has accepted me as master! Do you deny me!"

None did.

Eiswolf strode through the hall to the people outside, to show the sign of his victory. Then he mounted Storm. Meroens and Perry ran to their horses, and they rode out of Westerings. Very fast. Before anyone changed their minds.

The Glimmer Lord watched him intently: but not half as closely as the Hegemon.

9: Temptations

"You have got to be joking," said the Princess.

"Not a word of a lie," said the Witch.

"Dear God!" cried the Princess. "Chloe, you are a ham-fisted bitch!"

In her defence, she felt lousy. Literally so, because one of the minty hounds had found a dead hedgehog and decided that the best place to hide it, now that the floors had no rushes, was in an open chest of royal robes. As is well known, fleas dearly love ailing hedgehogs and clean surroundings. Chloe was going though the Princess' long silver-gold hair with a nit-comb, not a pain-free process.

So the Princess was fuming. Apparently the dratted wolf-man was proof against poison AND magic blades. "What about the other chap, Adel-thingy?"

"Injured, your Majesty, and exhausted, and humbled, but he'll live."

Plan A had finally come through. Late, way over budget, God knew how much spent on sword-masters and armour and horses, arrogant. And failed. Adelbon had not won. But he was alive, so still in play.

"What did you make of him?"

"He is …" Jocasta searched for the right collection of words for 'he's as thick as two short planks but very pretty and would make a good disposable prince' without giving everything away to Chloe.

"He has a most noble person, gracious to all, noted for his generosity, and a stranger to intrigue."

"Ah," said the Princess. "Good."

"But, my lady," Chloe decided to butt in. "If the Knight of the Snow Wolf has won the Sword of Destiny, surely he can complete the rest of the Tests?"

The Princess frowned. "Do not speak of matters which do not concern you. Has the hair-tirer arrived? Oh, yes, and the man about the paint. Send them in, will you? Witch, we will talk later."

***

"You've never seen anything like it," said the Hegemon. "Never. Nightmare." He shivered.

"It'll turn out all right," said Marejah, but her voice betrayed her. For if her beloved Bevis was frightened, no sensible man could feel safe. "Please, try this, it's barley, a west-coast recipe…"

The kitchen fire gleamed over the walls of the warm little bakery, a memory to treasure in the darkness of the oncoming nights.

For the man was staring terror in the face. He had looked into the eyes of the Knight of the Snow Wolf as the Sword of Destiny plunged for the third time. He had seen that flat golden glint, that unearthly light, the one thing that Eiswolf could not play games with, the reality of uncanniness. And that shook him.

The Hegemon had progressed from draper's lad to the hidden ruler of the Kingdom by craft, guile, intelligence and damned hard work. At no point had he either relied on magic, or been unduly perturbed when it was used against him, as it undoubtedly had. His world was numbers and trades and bargains, not magic.

But what he saw at Westerings changed that. Maybe the old rules were dead. He needed a new plan, because otherwise he would only have a plot. As in, a place marked out in the graveyard. He had no illusions over what happened under a change of prince.

Above all, Marejah must be protected. And that meant she must be kept secret, sent out of danger, hidden…

He grabbed her by the hand. "Look, what about Wardur, I know people."

"Don't be silly! People will miss me here! And what about the bakery?"

"I'll see to that, please, Marejah, listen to me." His hands, sweating, grasped hers as hard as he could. "Please! Listen! Let me take care of you!"

She laughed, confused, drawing her hand away. "He's not king yet, is he? Loads can happen yet!" She leaned forward and kissed him on the cheek. "You'll find a way, you always do. And I'll be here, waiting for you. Right?" She smiled, her black curls gleaming in the firelight, her eyes full of loving certainty.

It was all he could do not to cry.

"Who's beaten me yet?" he said. "But humour me. If I ask you to go to Wardur - "

"Then off I pop! But I won't have to. You're my true hero."

She kissed him, and he tried to kiss her back.

***

A hero. But what sort of hero?

The Glimmer Lord sat back in his chair in his high tower, considering. The last bout had been the key. The way the man had fought, a kind of super-battle, a blitzkrieg. The knights of this world did not fight that way. The business with the Sword was impressive, undoubtedly, but equally undoubtedly the Glimmer Lord did not believe a word. There was a party-trick at its root. Put that man into a battle, though, and he not only won under his own terms, but adapted to almost any circumstance you could throw at him. A universal soldier indeed.

And what else beside?

The Glimmer Lord no more believed in magic than did the Hegemon, but he did know that there are more things in heaven and earth, and whatever else the old poet had to say about that. Eiswolf was plainly one of them. He was not human.

Having allowed that thought into his mind, the Glimmer Lord trapped it, and examined it. If he was not human, what else could he be?

The wolf did not come with the usual trappings, the business with howling at the full moon, or changing his skin, or betraying himself by waking among the corpses of sheep or men. He was thought to be a werewolf because of what people had actually seen, but could not understand. The werewolf idea was their nearest approximation to an explanation. That the man himself believed it, or in any case made use of it, was actually no evidence at all.

What sort of pet had Bess found herself? What sort of super-sub-alien being had lurched their way to her door?

Eiswolf might be more of a challenge than he had thought.

The Glimmer Lord poured himself a cup of wine, and considered deeply.

***

"Yow!"

"Well, stay still!"

"You're ruddy heavy-handed!" Eiswolf swiped at Bess.

"If you don't heal properly …" She left the threat unfinished.

He had come back less damaged than she feared, although the new injury to the shoulder was a concern. But, on the positive side, he had not taken any more serious blows to the head or damaged his back. The flesh wounds to his legs and upper arms, both new and older, were progressing well.

She dressed the bruise on his chest where the Warden had unsuccessfully tried to stab him through the heart. The mark was black and quite large, a pattern of scrapes and cuts showing where the mesh from the amulet had been forced into his skin, but as far as she could tell, neither ribs nor sternum were cracked.

"You were lucky," she said, slapping on a final layer of salve.

"Apparently, luck had nothing to do with it," said Eiswolf. "It's all down to Pure Love and this." He threw the amulet to her. The thing could not be magic, of course, so what else? "A hex? Doesn't smell of herbs or stuff."

Bess held up the finely-worked square of metal mesh. "It's steel. Very high quality, better than can be got here."

"What about the crystals? They're supposed to be special."

Bess inspected them; dark grey, octahedron in shape, like two pyramids glued together at the base.

"Remarkable," said Bess. "I wonder where these come from.'

"What are they?"

"Adamant. Men have died for these. Men will die. Countries will rise and fall, great pirates will trade them, queens will wear them."

"Those? Those grey things?"

"What's precious is not always obvious."

She held a king's ransom in diamonds in her hand: but no-one here knew how to cut them to release their fire, or how to use them except, occasionally, to cut other stone or engrave glass. Or, in this case, to reinforce a steel mesh enough to repel a stab, which they did very nicely.

Now, was this an accidental discovery among the cunning-men? Or superior knowledge? In which case, her mission could not be delayed much longer. She shivered.

***

The Princess' dungeon was a whirl of activity. The hair-tirer, a man much recommended, was a pragmatic craftsman, the son of a fisherman, and a huge relief after the usual run of elf-fanciers and sharp lads on the make. He created some really extraordinary looks for the Princess which had the advantages of being very hard to copy, arduous to produce, and enormously expensive. Which meant that the ladies of the Court and any competing royalty would really have to pull the stops out to get ahead of the Princess.

The painters were at work with white distemper, although muttering a lot about hoping this was one royal fashion that never caught on. That was as nothing, however, compared to the palace carpenters, dismantling the highly crafted work of centuries.

"It looks like a stable," said the Head Carpenter. "Don't you want no carving at all?"

"None," said Iris, in charge of workman relations.

"What about a nice little rebate, maybe a tiny hint of a bull-nose edge?"

"Nothing at all," said Iris. "We wish to honour the natural quality of the wood."

But the carpenter and his men had been through many years of training to make wood look anything but natural. Although it almost hurt them physically to do as the Princess asked, they knew this was nothing compared to the reality had they refused her.

The Princess also sent out for new Court robes, rich, complex, massive confections of velvet and brocade and satin festooned with taffeta ribbons and lace. She decided to broaden the colour palette a little, from white and flower-pinks towards crimsons, to show she was nearer to marriage. But she did not approach the palace wardrobe mistresses about her other ideas. She sent Dorcas down to the market to come back with a Southron woman. The seamstress frowned when she saw the choice of fabric, but was at least familiar with the style. The new clothes were quickly made, so the Princess ordered two sets each for winter and spring.

Now she felt more comfortable, at least within the confines of her own dungeon.

In privacy, she unveiled the Planning Hanging. All was in order, she understood every factor, every relationship. Apart from one huge, hairy wild card.

She knew how they were dividing the Kingdom. Maps covered the King's Chamber, in plain sight during meetings. Lawyers were lined up three deep every morning, as contracts and inheritances and property deeds were horse-traded. She had offered to help with records management, an offer not so far taken up. But she also knew that, impressive though Wolfie-thingy was in battle, many quite liked Daddy's low-key ways, because he was not strong enough to dictate but in control enough to prevent civil war. He knew when to keep his nose out of other people's business, in other words, and quite a few wanted to keep him, and the Kingdom, in one piece.

The Hegemon had gone quiet. He brought her no news, she had seen no sign of action against the Wolf, he had not declared for either King or Knight. A shame, as he really kept so many of the underpinnings in place, like taxes and militias and the boring stuff like roads and port authorities. Talking of which, Cymenshore –

THIS WOULD NOT DO.

She took off her heavy outer robe and hitched up her shift, took a hank of bright yellow wool, and put the little ladder against the Planning Hanging. A new piece of black velvet was pinned there, for the Princess had reports of the Glimmer Lord but had not yet met him. But he was definitely a new player in the game. He was connected to the Hegemon, who had met him at Westerings. She pinned yellow wool between them. And he had been sniffing around Wolfie-whatsit at the Tourney. Yellow wool there and there. So whose side was he on?

And if, let's try this one more time with feeling, if We remove the piece of white fur that represents you-know-who, what does that leave?

The Hegemon, too scared to make his move and a man with too many enemies. Adelbon, knocked about but still breathing, a possibility for Plan E but not a certainty. A number of no-hoper princes that Daddy discounted because of general imbecility. Ambitious earls and commoners like Black Al, who were also no-hopers because they might use her to gain the throne and dispose of her afterwards.

She climbed down and surveyed the map of relationships again. Could she and the Glimmer Lord possibly have interests in common? She would never know, unless she asked. She found a sheet of parchment, and a writing quill, and ink, and began to draft a letter.

***

Eiswolf had become restless in Bess' hovel, but this time was different, and disquieting. After the usual complaints and grumbles, he had become almost withdrawn, with none of the usual banter with Perry or horseplay with Meroens. Perry said he was throwing a moody, but Meroens was worried enough to approach Bess.

"Is the boss all right?"

She shook her head. "You can't take the battering he's had and just bounce back. He needs time, for body and mind."

"Right." Meroens still seemed troubled.

"Spit it out."

"Well, you know when he was fighting for the Sword, right, well, only," Meroens sought inspiration in his usual place, the roof. "Only, when he was, you know, fighting Sir Adelbon, I mean when he beat him, well."

"Well what? He got a clattering. I gather the boy was knocked even sillier than when he started." She laughed and started to clear away the supper dishes.

Meroens frowned and raised his hand. "No, Lady Boss, don't interrupt me."

And his tone halted her.

"You see, Lady Boss, I've been with the boss a couple of months, he's a nice-natured man, right? I mean, not soft or nothing but not mean or hard, a proper knight. Only in that last fight…" his eyes came down from the roof and met hers. "That last fight was…" He searched for the word, as if afraid to give the thought a form. "It was dark."

"Dark?"

He said no more.

Bess expected Eiswolf to stay at the hovel until the bruise on his chest reduced, but he was distracted, uneasy and short-tempered, and not simply eager for action. He had been thinking.

"Bess, I must take my place at Court. I must talk with the earls. I must take back the Sword. I do not want any false reports of how I won it after so much trouble in the getting."

Eiswolf had lodged the Sword in the royal armouries as proof of his success, but also for safe-keeping while he was weakened by injury. The Armourer took the Sword reluctantly, not even wanting to touch the scabbard. The thing had killed the greatest knights in the realms.

"What about the Hegemon?" said Bess. "He'll know what's happening at a political level."

"Not necessary. A commoner. Others can hurt me more."

Bess raised her head: she heard a new tone to her boy's voice, which she did not care for. "He's clever."

"Other men will seek to replace him, I have no doubt. They may be more useful to me. The immediate questions are the northern borders, the Marcher Earls are the key there. And Cymenshore. And then the Princess."

"Your wife, yes, she should be a consideration," said Bess, coolly.

Eiswolf sniffed. "She'll do as she's told, but her mother was a traitor, I can't take her loyalty for granted. She'll need to be watched. I must secure the succession."

Bess felt a chill. This was not her boy, not as he used to be. "Secure the - Dear me, boy, what language to use about your wife! I thought the point of all this chivalry was to rule well!"

"I won't rule at all if an assassin gets to me first." Eiswolf was brutal. "I can be sweetness and light once I can be sure of not getting killed. I can't just walk in with a bright smile and a mythical sword."

A flutter of realisation ran through Bess. "What about your true mission?"

He shrugged dismissively. "What true mission?"

"The one I have prepared you for!"

For a couple of seconds he studied her, calm, commanding, cool. Impersonal. "Which is what, Bess."

Her heart stopped as she looked up at her boy. No. The man. A man with hard eyes.

What did she want? What was so hard to say?

She wanted a murder.

She was not a murderer, of course not, what an idea, she was educated, liberal, a doctor! She wanted justice and light and right! But in the Kingdom, she knew there was no other way. These people had to be protected from a danger they could not understand.

The boy Eiswolf had been trained in the arts of war. But she did not have the words to tell him how wicked Gil was. So she had waited. Then he went questing, and won his spurs, becoming stronger and experienced, a rascal maybe but not desperate, not a man who took killing lightly, not an assassin. No knight would just murder a man, he'd be shamed. And hung. So she waited longer, until the danger from Gil was clearer.

Now, she had her killer. His expression told her that. But now Gil was the Glimmer Lord, a man of influence. Would Eiswolf kill him on her order? The world that Bess and Gil came from meant nothing to Eiswolf, their battle would be incomprehensible. He did not know 'totalitarian' was a word, or genocide or inquisition or eugenics or pogrom. And this new, cold, strange Eiswolf might think they were good ideas -

He took her by the shoulders and stared down into her eyes. "Face it, there will be no True Mission. It's a delusion, Bess. Frankly, I'm tired of hearing about it. This is now, this is real, this is power."

"This is not why I trained you!" She wriggled free. "Half this tin-pot little Kingdom? At best you'll be a petty war-lord!"

But she triggered the rage that now seemed to be permanently seething beneath his surface.

"What!" he yelled. "I do an impossible thing but no! Never enough! Go and do another impossible thing! And then, I am so special, I have a greater battle before me, so trot off, good doggy, and pull off another party trick! Well, NO!"

"Eiswolf!"

"No! I follow my Quest, I will win this Kingdom, no snivelling little plotters will take my destiny from me! Whether you wish it, woman, or no!"

He banged his hand with his fist and thrust his face down into hers. Now she felt the visceral snarl, saw that golden, unearthly - She pulled back in a reflex, then collected herself, trying to calm him, to be calm.

But his eyes were golden and blank and she knew he was on the brink of violence. And Meroens' word came to her. Dark.

"I was only waiting until you were ready." She went up to him and, for the first time in his life, he pushed her away in anger and hit her across the face, so hard she fell over. He stood over her and did not help as she scrambled to her feet. His voice was deep, harsh, not like him at all.

"You say power is about hard decisions. You're right. I go to the Palace tonight." He turned away from her.

She knew then. There would be no tale of the brave, good knight who killed the evil Glimmer Lord. There was no brave, good knight any more, no victor for Right and Light. Forget the wolf blood. This was a cold political animal on the long road to becoming someone else.

She stared at him in torment. "But I need you!"

He shrugged, and walked out of the hovel.

He was lost to her: and to her battle. Fourteen years of effort had been for nothing. But that was not why she cried so bitterly.

***

The Hegemon met with the Conclave, who were almost as unsettled as he. One of the older professors pushed the copy of the Manifest across the table, shaking his head.

"We are limited, my lord. Within the Manifest, only two Tests remain before the Wolf completes the Quest. In neither case is the result open to debate or challenge from ourselves. Now that he has the Sword, his path will be smoother."

"You believe in all that tosh?" The Hegemon almost spat the words out.

The black-robed academics swayed backwards, like a field of dark wheat in a wind. A bolder, younger professor answered him.

"Whether we believe or not is immaterial, Hegemon. What is important is that the people believe, and his opponents will believe, and those deciding which side to take, may believe. And do not underestimate the effect if the man himself believes. The Sword is a mighty weapon, even if no more than a piece of polished metal."

"Then what do we do about it!" The Hegemon started to pace. "You do understand! Instead of one, powerful Kingdom under the rule of law of our most gracious and peaceable King, we become a tender morsel for our enemies! However we chop the borders, our new neighbour will be led by a magical warrior. He will marry our Princess and maybe he'll find waiting for the old man to die is too tedious! You have not seen this man fight, but I have. In that dark soul is neither mercy nor patience nor, God help us all, humanity. My friends, this is the end of our peace."

The Conclave bowed their heads, and considered. The older professor raised his head to speak. "Then we must make our position known to him now. For he will have need of men of law and science..."

"NO!" And for the first time, the Hegemon yelled. "Are you deaf? He has no need of law or science or anything except the point of his blade! Who remembers the Wars of the Barons! You saw what happened to Cymenshore in the raid! When the earls start to sniff around, and foreign princes cut their deals, there will be no law or science or anything but destruction! All we hold dear, all that makes our society, will be gone, this court will be full of posturing toughs, our women raped and murdered, our children slaughtered at a whim, our dungeons will be full of the lucky, because at least they will not be in the piled-up heaps of corpses in the streets! The only law will be the law of a pack of rabid dogs!"

The Conclave watched this outburst in silence. "My lord," said the younger professor. "Kolras was a clever man. Neither of the last two tests depends on physical strength. He wanted to select a man who was intelligent, a ruler, not just a fighter. We can hope yet that by the wisdom of Kolras - "

The Hegemon sighed. "You really, really don't get it, do you. Who among you remembers Kolras?"

A couple of the most elderly academicians raised their hands.

"Did he strike you as a man of gentle good intent and virtuous goodwill?"

They shook their heads. "A difficult man," one volunteered. "But very clever."

"Yes!" cried the Hegemon. "Clever! No man has ever survived these Tests because no man was ever meant to! Kolras never foresaw this! I want - We need - The Kingdom demands - the right result! In the next Test, whatever happens, in case Kolras was not clever enough! Am I clear?"

"But, my Lord," said the younger professor. "That leaves us without a prince for the Kingdom."

"Let me worry about that," said the Hegemon. "Now get back to your books and your laboratories and bring me the right result!"

***

The King looked out of a window, in his usual vague way. He knew that the Hegemon met with the Conclave. In a couple of hours he would have to chair the King's Chamber, where the first item on the agenda was the dismemberment of his beloved Kingdom.

Because the King really did love his country. He had been brought up to take his responsibilities seriously. As a boy, he had been filled with the idea of monarchy as stewardship, law as the protection of all from the highest earl to the lowliest galley slave, and tradition as the concentrated wisdom of all those who had gone before. He genuinely believed that he had obligations as well as power, that naked power was like a strong spice, to be used sparingly from time to time, but never as a whole meal.

If only the Prince - He sighed. His son the Prince had been as misguided as the boy's mother. That silly woman. A headstrong boy, careless of others, narcissistic and cruel. The King told himself this could be amended, with guidance, in the way Kolras had guided him. But Kolras was dead. As the boy's adult character developed, the King's fears grew.

The court was full of young, ambitious men who befriended the Prince, commiserating with him, because his father, whom they said was a weak man with foolish ideas and no true courage, kept him away from real power. For the Prince was the sole heir: the Queen who followed the Prince's mother had not been around long enough to give the King a baby, and the third only produced a weakling girl. There would be no more heirs from her, either. One day the Prince would be King. The sooner, the better?

The King sighed now, as he had then. The Prince had grown up under surveillance. Like all Court children, he was allowed to believe that he had secret places and friends that nobody knew. But this was never true: a Prince lives in public, and it was a mark of his arrogance to think that the King, in his capacity as ruler, not father, would let him go unmonitored. The King's spies told their master all they knew, and he guessed the rest.

The King's eyes filled with tears as he thought of the day his son had disappeared; but they were tempered with his inner resolution, that the Kingdom must endure.

Now came this new man, this wolf, this creature that everyone agreed was quite, quite strange, who had every right to grab half the Kingdom. Eiswolf had already made contact with some earls. At what point would they suggest a coup? The King wished he could bet on at least one earl, let's say, Passfield, telling the rest to leapfrog waiting for the boringly tedious old buffer to die, and go straight to the vigorous new battle-leader, wolf or no wolf, who would then parcel out wealth and estates.

His thoughts went round in their insoluble circle. The King had no male heir. The Princess was not enough, no Queen had ever ruled, and the King had little appetite for a new marriage. At the back of his mind, he had never felt, let's say, comfortable about introducing a fourth Queen and a tiny vulnerable baby into a Court where his daughter… Well. He stared out of the window again.

The only way not to split the Kingdom was to marry the Princess to the wolf.

But the girl was being foolishly difficult. He had tried to explain that even if she did find another lord to marry and was safely fertilised, everyone would have to wait at least nine months for the succession plan to work. And what would the wolf, in his half-kingdom, be doing in the meanwhile? Not a solution.

What the King really needed was a new, young male heir and a spare, without the bother of splitting the Kingdom and handing it over to any werewolves. Or, indeed, anyone else. If the Princess did her duty with a couple of strong little boys, actually, there was no further need of her husband. The Kingdom could remain entire while the boys were too young to reign; the King would rule his half and the widowed Princess would be regent of her half in name but naturally, following his orders. That would buy the King time, for no boy born now would be suitable for the burden of rule for at least, oh, eighteen years.

Or, could matters be arranged for Eiswolf to be around for a couple of years to produce the heirs without getting involved in rule and then, somehow, not be there?

This seemed over-complex. Far simpler all round for Eiswolf just to die.

***

A couple of days later, Perry returned from an extended trip to the backcountry villages to get special herbs and crystals for Bess. He found her sitting by the fire outside the hovel. That was not unusual: but the way she sat, as if her body was too weak to hold itself up, told him something was terribly wrong.

She raised her face to Perry, puffed with tears. Perry's heart somersaulted.

"They're all right, aren't they? The boss? Meroens?"

Bess found a smile. "They're fine, Perry. I'm being silly." She got to her feet awkwardly, suddenly aged by twenty years. "Did you get everything?"

"Yes. Look, what's the matter? Where is everyone?" Because Perry now saw that neither Storm nor the charger were tethered near the hovel: only Pepper could be seen, absent-mindedly nibbling rough grass.

"Come and sit down, Perry. You must be tired."

Perry sat by the fire, and waited for the disaster.

"Eiswolf has gone to Court, and taken Meroens as his squire at arms. He seems to have a very good chance of passing the Seven Tests of Kolras. So he will become a Prince and, in due course, the King and the father of Kings. He's going into another kind of world, Perry." And despite herself, a hot tear appeared on Bess' cheek.

For a moment Perry could not believe it. The Boss had done it. He had fulfilled the duty of every knight, despite every challenge, every disadvantage, every trick of magic or craft or deception. He had done it.

"But he left a message? For me? He left a message, Bess?"

She shook her head. No message. And Perry could tell by her expression, no thought of leaving one, either.

The terrible thing had happened. The one he feared above all else. Perry did not exist for Eiswolf any more. Eiswolf had become - like the others. This was not his Boss, not the man who had saved his life and been a friend and bloody irritating and a joker and the bravest fighter he had ever seen.

Perry saw the bruise beneath Bess' eye, and another terrible reality dawned. This man had hurt Bess, and left her behind. His Boss would never have done that.

"He didn't wait." Perry stole a glance at Bess. "For either of us?"

Bess shook her head. "He has to act quickly."

"That quickly, eh?"

Perry did not cry, or yell out, or start a tirade about honour and loyalty and friendship and obligation. He simply sat quietly, watching the fire.

"He's not a bad man," said Bess. "Just tangled up in all this. It's my fault. All my fault."

Perry almost turned on her. "How can you possibly mean that!"

Bess wrapped her fingers together, then unwrapped them. "I always had other plans for him. A darkness threatens this world, Perry, I thought he was my best chance to fight it, I needed him so much but I could not tell him, he'd have been horrified but I waited too long. I made him too good a man, he is too good a man - And now he isn't - I never really listened, Perry."

Perry' was furious for her. For who had listened more? Had cared more? Who knew Eiswolf better than his foster-mother? But that meant tears, so Perry stopped. He clasped her hands in his and held them. After a while, he tried again. "And you're sure he's gone? So there's no point in me…"

"None." Bess sighed as if her body would burst.

"I see."

Perry poked the fire with a stick, sitting for an hour or so. Bess sat with him, sometimes crying, sometimes staring. Perry went into the hovel for food but found none, so he went to Corsa's saddlebag and took out some bread for Bess.

"Is there anyone you want me to take a message to?"

"Are you leaving, Perry?"

He looked around him; at the hovel, at the horses, at the second-rank armour which Meroens had been cleaning, at battles and quests and impossible feats, at the happiest five years of his life. All just shadows, now, faded to dust. Not real any more. Sparks in the wind, like the embers in the smoke from Bess' fire.

"I think so, Bess. For a while. You have Corsa, I'll take Pepper. I might go to Cymenshore, I know people there. But I will be back, I promise that. So keep this place ready for me." From somewhere, he found a smile. "Got to come back for the coronation, right?"

She, too, found a smile. "Take care, Perry. Take very good care, poppet." She stood up and, to his astonishment, she hugged him and kissed his cheek. Then he saddled Pepper, untied him, mounted, and rode away.

***

The earls were most agreeable. They agreed with a great deal of what Eiswolf said. They laughed at his jokes, were serious at his proposals for reforms for the modernisation of the Kingdom, or at least, the half he would rule in the short term, and enthusiastic about his ideas on future military campaigns. He had their full confidence and their total support.

Even Eiswolf was not that inexperienced, but why not let them think so. "We play the jackass," he muttered to Meroens.

"Right, boss," said the squire, mildly confused.

To show their fidelity and entertain their future Prince, the earls set up hunts and dances and feasts, attended by the most powerful men in the Kingdom and the loveliest ladies.

Eiswolf was a man of appetites, not averse to a roll in the hay, or, for preference, on a mattress, as he had to be careful of his back. But he had a predilection for finding his own bed-mates, not any woman thrust at him by fathers or brothers or, worst of all, husbands, with a desperate wink, and an expression of determination on the lady's face.

In short, he had not had sex for a while.

The atmosphere at the Palace was stifling. He met the Princess, adorned in truly extraordinary gowns, her hair dressed up like a whirlwind, or a sea-anemone, or the seed-pod of an exotic flower, but still had not exchanged more than a few dozen words with her. He met the King - that is, he bowed while the King muttered how honoured the Kingdom was to have such a splendid knight. He tried to see the Hegemon, but the grey man was apparently very busy with Conclave.

Eiswolf needed air. He needed to be free. He decided to go for a ride.

The squires and grooms at the castle were not happy, but Storm was a stallion with his own ideas. He bucked and whinnied as soon as Eiswolf entered the stables. The horse puffed and shuffled while the boys put him in his bridle and everyday saddle, almost screaming when he was led into the cobbled yard.

"As restless as I am." Eiswolf mounted the horse, which neighed happily.

"Where shall I say you are going?" said the groom.

"Out." Eiswolf spurred Storm to a gallop.

He rode through the yard gates, then the City, to the villages, on to the main route to the North. Then, after a couple of hours, he turned to a less well-travelled path to the west, through a wild wood, then a scatter of villages which had little to do to with the Palace or its politicking. Here the air was fresh, pine-scented, simpler. These were the people who might feel the difference if he were King, he told himself. Humble, poor folk, without a voice –

"What's that!" shrieked a lad.

"Dunno!" shrieked another. "Stranger!"

And Eiswolf found himself under a volley of stones. He galloped through the village and up a hill onto a grassy downland, open to the blue heavens. Here, he could breathe.

Then he saw them. In the far distance, half a dozen armed men on horseback pursued a dapple jennet that carried a tiny figure, a girl, crying for help. Immediately, he spurred towards her, for this is what knights did.

As he approached the group, some of the men halted. A couple turned back: but the girl galloped towards him until he could see her fire-gold hair, her huge green eyes –

"My Lord! My Lord!"

And she rushed up towards him, her horse panting its last, her eyes wild with fear, flushed with the panic of escape.

"Fear no more, Lady! For I am here!" He unsheathed the Sword of Destiny, feeling the power of ancient heritage, the assurance of success in battle.

The men saw this. He knew he had beaten them without striking a blow. They turned tail and galloped away.

He caught up with her horse and took the reins. She seemed on the point of collapse and so he halted the horses, dismounted, carefully lifting her from her saddle.

"My Lady! My Lady Mifanna?"

She looked up at him with her huge eyes, and nodded.

"Are you hurt? We can find a place of refuge -"

But she grasped his face, pulling him towards her, kissing him. Suddenly the rest of the world did not matter.

10: Cymenshore

The road to Cymenshore was straight, broad, and expensive. Tolls were due at regular intervals, approximately at the end of a day's travel for a man on horseback, or beside natural pinch-points like a bridge. A little cluster of taverns and stables surrounded each toll, tended by prosperous landlords and jolly, cheerful ale-wives. Given the rate at which they were coining it, they had every right to be so happy.

Perry tried to merge in with the crowd of travellers to the town but slightly-built Perry did not look right on a war-horse like Pepper. Perry had settled on the story that he was delivering the horse to his master from a distant auction. And yes, he had looked underneath. Yes, he did know the creature was missing some tackle. No, his master would not mind. Improves the temperament, for a travelling horse. Fancy that. Pepper neighed to let everyone know he was there, waiting until Little Two-Legs told him to walk on.

Cymenshore exerted a magic pull across many realms: people travelled for unfathomable distances to bring or buy luxuries like gems, silk, spices, music and sex. Occasionally, they also brought their feuds and tribal clashes. As a result, the city was an exciting place, if a little volatile.

A few years had passed since Perry last set foot in Cymenshore. The road had always been well-travelled but was now thronged, in a steady stream of people, horses, ox-carts and herds. He hardly dared ask about the town: he feared what he might be told. About two days away, he started to spin a tale to an innkeeper, who blanked him out and pointed to a man at arms who was drinking on his own. "Bart will tell you stuff. I've got a business to run."

Bart, fortunately, would talk to anyone for the price of a pitcher of ale. He was stuck outside the city, waiting for the other six men of his company to catch up, for they were all to guard a merchant caravan leaving Cymenshore in two weeks. "We aren't allowed through the gates with weapons and we're all on one passport, bloody Tad's got that, should never have trusted him with it. Even me, I'm born and bred here, just haven't got the token. So either my lads turn up and we go in together or I wait until the caravan leaves and join then. Bloody annoying."

"No idea they were so strict," said Perry.

"Oh, a new thing, they don't like armed men roaming the streets, with the raid and all. You know the place?"

"I used to. So, has much changed?" Perry hoped the tremble in his hands would be concealed by the way he held his mug.

"Well, it's been rebuilt down by the docks, that was all burned, a couple of the livery halls went, and the shambles and the greenmarket, but it hasn't taken too long. There's a new man in the Council."

"I've heard that. Richard of Clifton?"

"Him. He pulled things together pretty swift."

"And what about the other people? I used to know a family called Netley."

"Well, you could try to find them but them as didn't get killed, a lot of them left." Bart swigged his ale and took breath. "For a while people thought the place had a curse. Old Mortain Vendant was supposed to have made a deal with a devil and then reneged, which he would've, if he had. Evil old bugger, he was."

"So he's dead?" said Perry, quietly.

"Him and the whole troop, the two sons, their families, old Mortain's sister, Varla, the worst of the bunch."

Perry swallowed hard. "But Mortain was never the ruler by birth, was he?"

"Legally, I suppose, he was the regent. The Count was Pedric, his elder brother, he died a while ago. Pedric had a daughter, but she went mad and I haven't heard what happened. Killed like the rest, I think. No, a lot of blood flowed that night. Hey, are you all right?"

"Ah, tired," Perry gasped. "I need some air."

Perry struggled out into the back yard before throwing up. Then he dashed into the safe darkness of the stable where Pepper was tethered. His shaking was becoming uncontrollable, the icy sweat dripping from his face and running down his back.

The names, all the names. Mortain, Varla, Pedric. The ones Bart had not mentioned. Mortain's sons, Jano and Hannet: their wives, Mismay and Delitha; the captain of the guard, the chamberlain, the doctor, the advocate-general, the heralds, the ladies in waiting. All crowding in on him, pressing down, a dead weight. Dead. All dead. Perry could barely breathe, he was choking with all the dead, dead…

Pepper whinnied, shifting a hoof. The noise broke into Perry's nightmare, waking him up a little. Here were no cries, no crash of burning buildings, no terrified hands reaching out to him, no little girl crying for her mother, no dead baby dumped like discarded washing, no armed men striding from house to house, pulling out the men and boys and slitting their throats, then running to the women inside and the screams and then the sudden silence, the men coming out with bloody hands and laughing and joking –

Pepper whinnied again, pushing at Perry with his velvet nose.

Perry stood up and gave the horse a hug. "It's all right, big fella. I'll be all right. Swear I will. I know I'll come through. "

Because that had been the only thing keeping Perry alive, during the raid on Cymenshore.

**

Eiswolf was beginning to find his feet at Court. With the help of the Heralds, the senior civil service within the Palace, and having introduced himself to Conclave, the royal advisors, he began the delicate business of finding out the real stance of the oh-so-friendly earls and barons.

The Hegemon was still elusive. Of course, Eiswolf was a direct threat to his position, so Eiswolf did not really expect anything else. However you looked at it, the Kingdom would be smaller and weaker once half the territory came under Eiswolf's rule. As prince, he could make his own foreign treaties and alliances.

Eiswolf did not dislike the Hegemon. The grey man was effective, in his way. All the rumours about his dark and shadowy methods were likely to be just that, Eiswolf decided. The man he saw with the Heralds was astute and decisive, but not personally vindictive or vicious.

But the Hegemon regarded Eiswolf with bright, clever eyes and an unreadable expression, and never shook his hand. He stepped back when Eiswolf stepped forward, smiling through his lips when forced to be polite. The man smelled of fear, which was not helpful.

So, to keep the Court ticking over, Eiswolf decided to play a princely hand, as far as he could with his limited cash. The prizes from the tourneys and dragon-slaying supported him in comfort but were not bottomless. Meroens was not as canny a manager as Perry had been. But there was enough to pay for private feasting and merriment, which went down as well with chosen members of Conclave as with the nobility.

"My lord," said Eiswolf to one of the senior professors, over a particularly fine southern wine, "I am but a simple countryman, in awe of scholarship and wisdom. I must have men I can trust by my side, to help me as I learn the ways of princely rule. I would ever be in their debt, no matter how generously I rewarded them, and beholden to the Kingdom which has so nobly assisted me."

The word 'generously' probably swung the deal, he decided later. Earls and barons liked money but, as he swiftly found out, academics loved it. At the end of three weeks, he had signed up two professors, three senior lawyers and a herald. All of whom, naturally, also believed they were doing their duty by both the Kingdom and their new prince.

However, nothing would happen until he discovered what the final Tests would be. But here, Conclave simply pulled down the shutters. His professors looked shifty, while the lawyers put on their 'nothing to do with me, guv, I just follow orders' face. He tried pinning one of the troubadours to the wall to see what he knew, but the man wriggled free and shrieked, while making a hex sign and spitting over his shoulder.

Eiswolf made sure to meet the Princess at least every couple of days. They greeted each other graciously, then she whisked off to maidenly entertainment involving flowers or embroidery or singing with her ladies, giggling lightly the while. It was like trying to lay hands on a particularly irritating ghost.

But in quiet afternoons, in drowsy evenings, there was Mifanna. His heart lifted every time he saw the golden light on her hair, the clear water-green of her eyes, her smile, so shy and yet so open. She loved him. He was sure of that now, she was not just grateful for her rescue. She never drew back from him, she did not seem to care about his reputation as a werewolf. She listened to his stories, commiserated with his injuries, rejoiced at his victories, laughed with him, wept for him. Kissed him. He had never –

No, he had never. Never in his life had Eiswolf found a woman who simply accepted him and loved him. He had been in love a few times; but then the girl had been dragged away by her family, or found a more 'suitable' match, or balked at being outcast as a wolf's mistress. He had grown to recognise the flash of repulsion when they saw - whatever they did see - or the flinch of fear.

And after a while, he had not sought love. He was a lone knight, and would remain so. He now realised marriage to the Princess was about power. That was the only real reward of the Quest: love was irrelevant.

Which was why the greatest fighter in the Kingdom had no defences at all against Mifanna.

***

"How much!" Perry gasped.

The gates of Cymenshore were robust but not overly grand. They did their job, in an efficient, sober and straightforward manner. They were there to separate you from your money.

Perry had ridden through the Valley of Swords in the company of a small party of traders. He told them the tale of the name, that originally the Valley was called 'The Thousand Cuts' until the merchants of Cymenshore got tired of the joke, and transformed the name to the more romantic version. Perry and his companions did not quite pay a thousand tolls but the journey had been pricey.

But not nearly as expensive as getting into Cymenshore itself.

"Ten gold pieces," said the guard. "That your horse?"

"No, I'm delivering it for a friend."

"Right. Four for a stallion."

"He's not entire."

The guard squinted underneath. "Three then. Any weapons to declare?"

"No."

"Right, son, welcome to Cymenshore." The guard painted a small sign in ink on the back of Perry's right hand. "That's the property of the city. And if you've told us any lies, that stays here even if the rest of you don't. You get me?"

Once inside, Perry felt an overwhelming familiarity; the crowds and the smells and the sounds, the music from every corner, the squabbling and dealing and huckstering, the heavy spices and the rainbow of silks and carpets, the absurdly jammed stalls and the carts and wagons and sleds. And yet, as he rode into the town, it struck Perry like a hammer that everything was different. The streets had changed: he knew roughly where he was but the bell-tower was not in the right place if these were the Southron traders. Why didn't the road go straight down to the harbour any more? He tried again: surely that was where the Guildhall had been, and the pilotage house, and the barracks for the marines. Was, maybe. They were all gone.

"You look lost, son," said a voice from beside his knee. Perry looked down and saw a foot-traveller, an old man in dusty rags, his face concealed by a wide-brimmed straw hat.

"Sort of," he said. "It's changed."

"Where are you looking for?"

"The, er…" Suddenly Perry went blank, because in all the turmoil of getting here, he had not thought out exactly what he would do when he did. "The Guildhall. They still have one, right?"

"Oh, yes. Brand new, over there." The man pointed his walking stick. "You remind me of someone, have you been here before?"

"A long time ago.".

"The past is a different country," said the man. "Good luck with whatever you want." And then he walked away, head down.

So Perry rode to the new Guildhall, in time to see a procession of the Guild of Silver-workers. The grey-robed, fur-collared silversmiths walked down the street two by two. Their new Master, in his scarlet sash, waved happily at the crowd. At the door to the hall they halted, to be greeted by the Mayor in his heavy gold chain of office, and the aldermen. Yes. And Richard.

He looked well. The years had added to his bulk, but he was tall, he could carry it. His dark hair was as thick and curly as ever. He had the air of a man in control, a man of respect, a man who bowed to no other.

What now? Perry's heart raced. Did he dare to change their lives? Both their lives? Or was that too cruel, too late, too useless now, because everything had already changed. To come this far, go through all this, did he not owe - Perry froze. Richard of Clifton received the new master silversmith, the Guild went in to their feast, and the door closed.

Pepper shifted and neighed, wanting to know which way to go next. Perry roused himself and pointed the horse towards the harbour, for that was where the taverns were, which asked no questions.

***

"My lord! My lord!" Mifanna almost shone with happiness. She ran along the path towards Eiswolf.

"What is it, angel?"

They were in a secluded quadrangle outside the palace walls. Eiswolf had brought the girl to a hostel run by the Weeping Nuns, as he knew they would guard her ferociously. And here the couple met, talked, kissed. But no more, for Eiswolf was a noble knight, and she was of lordly blood. In any case, he would soon be betrothed to the Princess.

Love was permitted in Court, of course; only a foolish king would attempt anything else. But sex was another matter, because that was about money and power, which is why it was such a powerful political weapon. Love could be detuned into a pretty game of favours and poems and songs; sex got under the skin. Sex was animal and low-caste, and murder and deception and bastards. So knights and nobles could relieve their dangerous instincts with women who did not matter, like serving girls or prostitutes, but involvement with a woman of their own standing was different. And, of course, any noble lady caught in sex outside marriage was a hair's breadth from exile or imprisonment for life, if not execution, like the

Queens. So, however much he wanted to, Eiswolf knew he could not sleep with Mifanna, for both their sakes.

But she lit up his life. He had to meet her, had to, for his own sanity. She was all he lived for, the only woman he cared for, a beacon of love and beauty. He knew he was taking risks because the Princess had her spies. Mifanna was alone, his duty was to protect her, not expose her to more dangers.

"My lord! I have wonderful news!" She leapt into his arms and kissed him, laughing.

"Tell me, then. Tell me your secret!" He hefted her in the air.

"My lord, put me down!" She giggled tumultuously. "Please! I can't talk to you seriously like this!"

So he set her back down on her feet, they walked to a bench, she wrapped around him like ivy about an oak, then they sat and kissed.

"Your news?" he said.

"Wonderful! My great-uncle is coming to court! He's not dead, I have a family, Eiswolf! And an inheritance! I am become the Lady of the Black Fells again!"

That was wonderful indeed, but the news cut him in two. For what lady would be content with this shadow existence? Her uncle would undoubtedly want a good match for her. The whole sad rigmarole would play through once more. His love, his only love, would be lost forever. — He stroked her hair, such a wondrous colour, never could be another -

"You look sad, my lord."

"I fear this means we must part. I cannot stand in your way. You must find a husband, and that I cannot be."

"No!" She threw herself at him, weeping and desperate. "I will not find a family only to lose my love!"

"It must be so, for when I marry the Princess, all this must end. I cannot, I would not ask you for anything else."

"Meet my uncle." Her eyes were bright through the tears. "He's very clever, he'll think of something, he always does, please, please!"

Eiswolf smiled ruefully. It could do no harm, though not likely to do much good either. "All right. I'll meet him. What's his name?"

***

Down by the harbour, Perry found a low-profile tavern with stables, and paid the exorbitant rent for the week. He and the other tenants avoided each other's eyes, talking in low voices. But mainly, Perry sat by himself by the harbour wall, watching the ships and their crews, thinking.

He was here, after so long, after so much, a place of love and memory and horror, so why did everything now seem so - flat. This was not what he remembered. Maybe that could not be. That city was history. The people had changed. Perry had changed.

He had always assumed that when he came back, he'd find a way to pick up the pieces, maybe find old friends, build a life out of what remained, and, yes, he had hoped that Richard –

Richard had changed. He was a man of power now, a clean break after the horrors of the raid. He ruled well through the Council, according to the alewife at the tavern. He and his family, his wife Magret and their three little boys, were an example to the whole city of happy and contented family life, the way forward for Cymenshore.

Perry had no right to interfere with any of that.

"But what about the truth," muttered Perry. "Doesn't that matter?"

A test. Eiswolf had his Tests, this was one for Perry. A test to see if the truth did matter, if anyone could see Perry for what he was, who he was. Perry would test the truth. And if he failed –

He had no answer for that. But he started to walk towards the Guildhall.

***

Scents of cinnamon and butter swirled though the bakery as Marejah coiled dough into September spirals, an eastern speciality for the autumn equinox.

"He's making allies," said the Hegemon, bitterly. "Why can't they all see? You've seen it, haven't you?"

"They're blinded by gold, my love," said the baker. "That and ingratitude."

The Hegemon snorted. Did those idiots really think they could control that wolf-thing? He distracted them with a worn-out superstition, the Tests were some kind of trickery - But they said it was brought up by a witch? Maybe she had created it. He had heard of such a creature from the east, made from clay that could walk and talk like a living thing, with no heart, no soul.

He stopped himself. Eiswolf was flesh and blood, all right. He sweated, he ate, he bled. In the Chamber that morning, the knight had looked at the Hegemon as if he was being addressed by a curious, small, interesting prey animal. But then, as the Hegemon had turned to another lord, he saw a flash that was not a man, with hard golden eyes and a pointed face and grey-white fur –

Was the Hegemon really the only one to notice? "You have seen it, right, Marejah?"

"Seen what, my love? Hand me that bag of raisins."

"The wolf."

"You keep talking about it. I haven't seen that much of him. He's a big man, isn't he? Not exactly handsome, though." She sprinkled the buns with the dried fruit.

"Do you hear any gossip among the girls?"

"Nothing your spies don't already know. Now, what about ginger squares?"

He grinned. "With honey?"

"Naturally." She leaned forward and kissed him on the cheek. "For you, anything."

But the Hegemon could feel the way the lords were thinking. There was a momentum towards this thing of night - "I wish you would go to Wardur," he said.

"And what business would I do there? It's a poor place, by all accounts."

"All right. Cymenshore. What about that?"

She laughed. "You need more money than I have to buy a Guild licence! "

Now he laughed, too. "Money is the least of our problems." He grabbed her, amid the clouds of flour and spice, and kissed her properly.

***

Perry found himself outside the Cymenshore Guildhall in a crowd cheering a delegation from the east. The strangers rode even stranger beasts, apparently called camels, which were ugly and ill-tempered and had a habit of spitting. He heard the usual jokes about the mounts suiting their riders.

At such times, the Guildhall opened its doors to the town, so that the traders could see how friendly and welcoming Cymenshore was, and how safe, for no men at arms were visible in street or hall. Perry pressed forward with the surge to get inside for the ceremonies. These followed a set pattern: the aldermen officially welcomed the traders, with long speeches about how long they had waited for this moment, how long a journey the traders had undertaken, how long since their two mighty nations had decided on a closer relationship. And how long, dear God, Perry muttered, how long would all this take?

But eventually the aldermen ran out of puff. Fortunately the strangers had little of the language so they stuttered a few words, grinned, and shook hands instead. Then a herald presented them with a handsome sheet of parchment containing an inscribed 'freedom' of the city and a beautifully drawn coat of arms, so that was that: another official connection made.

The crowd broke up. Perry scurried towards the aldermen through the throng of petitioners taking their chance to nab a man of power in person. Perry pushed through the jabbering obsessives, the quietly desperate, the betrayed and the angry, close and closer to Richard.

Richard was adjudicating between cousins, always a tough call; their grandfather had played games with his will and now three factions fought within the family, all feeling severely badly done by.

Richard hushed their squabbling with a brief gesture of his hand. "My view is that in any will, the desire of the writer has to be supreme."

"Old bastard wanted to do me out of what's mine!" shouted one cousin. Richard closed his eyes for a second, an expression of patience under duress that Perry knew well. Richard did not lose his temper, but his judgement was as hard as granite.

"You." He pointed at one faction. "You have no case in law. You!" he pointed at the second. "You have been lucky when your grandfather died, for in another day he might well have changed his mind. You," to the third, "have done as well as you could have expected, so let this matter rest. I would have equalisation between you both," sweeping his hand across the first and second, "for I would not have a blood-feud over such a petty matter. If this comes before our courts, you will both lose your lands. Am I clear?"

Subdued, muttering, but frightened, the family bowed and left. Perry took his chance.

"My lord!" he cried. "I have a petition!"

Richard swung around, looking down at Perry. "Indeed. Your name, sir?"

Perry lost his voice. He made a half-strangled cough, then muttered, "I am known as Perry, my lord."

"I see. And your request?" He was staring into space over Perry's head, to see what other petitioners were waiting at the back of the hall.

"I had a connection here, in the Vendant household." Perry's voice trembled.

"Vendant? Oh, they're long gone," said Richard. "Vendant, eh? What, did they owe you money?" He laughed.

"My lord! I need to know…" and despite himself, Perry felt the tears start to well up.

"Look, you'll find all you need to know in the cemetery. That's where they are."

"But I heard…" Richard was beginning to walk away. Perry plucked his velvet sleeve. "I heard the Countess of Cymenshore still lived."

"It's news to me, then," said Richard. "She's been gone these eight years, and after seven she was officially declared dead. Leave go of my sleeve, boy, I have business to do!"

He strode away.

There had not been a trace of regret or sorrow in his voice, no emotion at all. For him, the Vendants were a closed book.

"Did you know them well? The Vendants?" said a voice. The old traveller from the marketplace stood behind Perry.

"Yes. I suppose I knew they were dead but it's still…"

"Still a shock," said the man. "I heard you asking after the Countess. She was a gentle soul. Badly treated by the family, I recall."

"Forgotten now." Perry started to leave, but the man caught his arm.

"Poor lady. They would not let her marry, in case a husband took control of the city. Some say that sent her mad, a cruel thing. There was a rumour of a lover, I think. But that was before the raid."

"The past is another country," said Perry, pulling away.

"The Countess, - what was her name, foreign, they had southern blood." The old man did not quite block Perry's way, but was inconveniently close.

"I don't remember," said Perry.

"Pervenche. Countess Pervenche? That means periwinkle, doesn't it?"

"I have no idea," said Perry, pushed past the man and forced a way out of the hall.

Countess Pervenche. A dead, mad, ageing woman.

Richard had not recognised - her. She had stood right in front of him, Perry/Pervenche, looking into his face. And yet he had not recognised the woman who risked everything, would have sacrificed everything, forsworn family and wealth and status, who would have moved heaven and earth to be at his side –

Eight years later, as if she had never existed.

RIP Pervenche. And now, not much reason for Perry to exist, either.

***

Mifanna was almost beside herself, running from Eiswolf to the door of the convent refectory and back again.

"You'll like my uncle so much, I know you will! He's really clever! My father said he's the cleverest man in all the realms! He says he's going to restore me to my rights, I know he can think of something! I can hear them!"

She dashed to the door again. This time a troop of horses were outside the convent, men were coming through the gate. Behind the guards walked a man in a black fur-trimmed robe.

Eiswolf smelled the expensive civet scent, and recognised the Glimmer Lord.

Mifanna ran up and hugged the man as if she wanted to break him. He smiled, stroked her bright gold hair, held her strong, elegant hands. Then he saw Eiswolf.

The Glimmer Lord bowed. "Well met once more, sir, I trust. Did I ever properly congratulate you on your adventure at Westerings? An extraordinary feat. And I understand I have you to thank for my niece's safety. I shall forever be in your debt. My pretty Mifanna is all the family left to me. I would break worlds asunder for her." He smiled at the girl. She laughed, and hugged him again.

"Sir, your niece brightens the life of all about her," said Eiswolf.

The Lord turned to him. "And yet you seem sorrowful. I know you to be a warrior beyond compare, and my niece tells me you are a great man at court. You will soon be a prince. Surely your life is as golden as any man could wish."

Mifanna waved at Eiswolf, mouthing "Ask him!"

Eiswolf cleared his throat to begin the most difficult speech of his life so far. "My lord, appearances may deceive. For I have found myself so entranced with your niece that I fear…" Eiswolf, normally not at a loss for words, was struggling. "I fear that we shall be - We cannot, I must fulfil my sworn Quest, it may be that your niece, although I would protect her from all harm…"

The Glimmer Lord let him stumble on. A man in love, all right. His eyes were unsteady, his mouth hung open like a farm-boy, a trace of sweat on his brow. Lord, what fools Love makes of men. Especially when stewed into a seething broth of ambition and sexual frustration and fear.

He waited until Eiswolf ground to a gargling, embarrassed halt. "My dear sir, I have every confidence in your good intent, and your regard for my niece."

Mifanna broke in. "Uncle, I love him. And he loves me. I would be by his side for all time, no matter what the cost." She softly went to the knight, to hold his scarred brown hand in her long white fingers.

The Glimmer Lord frowned. "My dear, you do not know what you say! For this man is to marry the Princess and be a King!"

"I know, Uncle. But cannot a King know love, like the commonest of his subjects? Say not that our love is forbidden, for my love is true for all time, I shall love no other!" She looked up at Eiswolf, the tears glistening on her cheeks.

The Glimmer Lord seemed overwhelmed, rubbing his face with his hand. "My child, what have you done? Sir Knight, have you done ill by her?"

"No! Never!" Eiswolf almost barked at him.

Mifanna went to the Glimmer Lord. "Uncle, this noble knight has ever treated me with respect and kindness. That is why I love him."

Eiswolf took a deep breath. "Mifanna, there is no way. I am bounden to my Quest, which I must complete within a year and a day or face an ignoble death. And I must marry the Princess. And I shall not betray that destiny. Whatever my personal feelings, my duty comes first, as your uncle knows. We must part."

"Then I must die." Mifanna said this so quietly, yet with such resolution, that both the men were shame-faced.

"Say not so!" cried the Glimmer Lord.

"I cannot live without my love, so I must die." She dropped her eyes, her hands covered her mouth, trembling.

"Your crown comes at a heavy price!" The Glimmer Lord glared, embracing the girl. "For she is all that is left to me now! I cannot lose her again, not the last of us." They clung to each other as the girl wept and the man held her close, as if she were drowning. He turned in fury to Eiswolf. "You talk of duty! Your foolish idea of duty would kill her!"

Eiswolf could barely speak. "You must not think of death, Mifanna. I will do all in my power…"

The Glimmer Lord, weeping, held tight to the girl. "Sir, I am an old man, I have many regrets, and I can tell you that to reject true love will burn your soul!"

"I am already in hell, sir," said Eiswolf, quietly.

Mifanna's life was once more in his hands. Only this time, by all his training, all the rules of the Court, he was expected to let her die. Or publicly dishonour her for all time.

The Glimmer Lord was almost beside himself. "I cannot let this be! I cannot! Mifanna, are you sure? Are you set in your intent?"

"Uncle, I have no desire to die!" Her tears, too, were flowing freely, like pearls on the down of her cheek. "But without my love, my saviour, what light is in this world for me? You take away my hope!"

The Lord sighed deeply. "Girl, you present me with a woeful choice. I would not lose you, but to become this man's love, you must renounce your family name, your reputation among the Court, you must strip yourself of all the honours and privileges of your rank. Will you do this for him?"

Her face seemed to glow. "Yes, my Lord. I will follow my love. Wherever he goes, I shall be, whatever he wishes, I shall become, joyfully and without reserve! I will be a beggar outside his door, I will be the dust beneath his feet, save only that I am near to him!"

The Lord sighed deeply, from his heart. "Then, Sir Knight, I offer you my sacrifice. Take my niece, to save her life, and yours, for what use is a family name once none are alive to bear it? What is a crown without love?"

"Sir!" Eiswolf was tormented almost past bearing. "This is not in my power!"

"Must we weigh true love against this bizarre quest, dreamt up by a bunch of old men? The Court cares nothing for love, or you, Sir Knight! Look at Mifanna, sir, my golden girl! What is the dead kiss of that cold princess compared to hers, that icy blood compared to this warmth, that stony gaze to this light of true love! Would you let the whims of the Court destroy the life of my lovely Mifanna?" The Glimmer Lord stroked her hair again.

Eiswolf was almost incoherent. "My Lord, I cannot do this with honour."

But the Glimmer Lord was relentless. "You speak of betraying the Princess, yet she comes from a line of traitors! What lord at Court does not have his sweethearts, his little honeys, all at his command? Why so pure, Sir Knight?"

Eiswolf cried out. "Not for my sake, but hers! I will not tarnish her name! And the Princess …"

The Glimmer Lord snorted. "She seems a sensible woman, I'm sure she no more expects your fidelity than you expect her warm embrace. Let Mifanna be known at court by the least of her titles as the Lady of the Black Fells, and your friend. That will be a reasonable solution for all of us."

Mifanna looked up at Eiswolf so bravely, that his heart almost burst.

"I shall - I shall …" Eiswolf stumbled. "I must think…"

Mifanna came to his rescue. "My love, whatever your decision is, I shall accept joyfully, for I know that will be for the best. For you are my brightest sun, I hope only to adore you in your glory! Go now!"

The knight bowed to them both, walked away down the cloister, then through the gate.

The Glimmer Lord turned to Mifanna and chucked her under the chin.

"Drama queen!"

And Mifanna giggled.

***

Perry swished the curry-comb over Pepper's broad flank. The horse was in good condition, which is more than could be said of its groom. Perry muttered to him.

"I can be a scrivener, they need people in the counting houses, take chambers above a shop, keep my head down, I can get by. I need a story, though, so I've been a squire, the Barons of Elderton are still useful, so why have I stopped being a squire?"

The horse shifted and clopped one of his mighty hooves.

"Maybe I'm sending money home to my silver-haired old mother. Nah, too many questions. All right, my knight got killed and I've realised a life on the road is not for me? No, too glamorous, the lads would want the details. Maybe I took an injury. Maybe I limp. Doesn't stop me scribing but means I can't go gallivanting. Hold still, you old sod."

Pepper snickered, nuzzling Perry.

"I've got to sell you. I don't want to but I can't afford to keep you. Anyway, what does a scrivener want with a warhorse?" She refreshed the curry-comb. "Where were we? So I was a squire, only my knight, did what? What about not being a squire?"

"What about a noble lady who was forced to flee in disguise and has travelled the roads these many years, hoping for word of her true love?" The voice came from outside the stable.

"No, that'll never play," said Perry. "Who's going to believe that?"

The old man in traveller's clothes came into the stable.

"Hallo, Octa," said Perry. "Sorry I didn't recognise you before. Must be in the air, not recognising people."

"My lady." The man bowed. "How good to see you."

"Yeah, well, I'm not anybody's lady any more, and I haven't been for a while. I take it the chamberlaining business is not what it was?"

The man shook his head. "Little call for it, when a court is no more. Why did you not return?"

She looked him in the eye. Octa had always been a competent chamberlain if rather stodgy. But the lines on his face and his ancient rags showed that he, too, had been forced into unimaginable ways, after the fall of the Vendants.

"I was having too much fun. Keeping away from mercenaries, getting burned out of villages and chased into wildwoods."

He shook his head, sadly. "But when the fighting was over?"

"Those who betrayed the town were still here. What did you want, I should ride in on a snow-white palfrey? I'd have been dead in a heart-beat." Pepper whinnied, because Perry was a touch too energetic with the comb.

"A clean break, then," said Octa. He nodded at her clothes.

"Survival," said Perry. "No more, no less. What about you?"

He laughed quietly. "So where have you been, and where does this mighty beast come from?"

"I'll tell you over an ale. We get this straight between us only, let's be clear. To everyone here I'm officially dead, I see no reason to change that. None of us can go back."

Octa nodded. As a lady of the Palace, she would have been deemed old, her complexion wrecked by the sun, her hair chopped like a slave's. As a lady of the Palace, she was over-bold, coarsened; ruined. But the way she stood, her confidence, the way she looked him in the eye was new. "You seem more alive, my lady."

"Been places and done things," said Perry. "Come on, I'm paying. This time."

***

Bess started to come out of her grieving after a couple of weeks, and no longer found herself ambushed by tears. She had villagers to treat, and the mare to look after, and plans to make.

Because her task did not go away without Eiswolf: it just became harder, and much riskier. Maybe the last thing she would ever do.

Know your enemy.

Well, she certainly did that. She had known the Glimmer Lord for what? Thirty years? From school to university to Veritas. But he had been called Gilbert Roche then, and she was Dr Bess Mulholland. And she had followed him into the Glimmer Project. Only then had she realised how far he would lie, deceive and destroy to achieve his aims. She continued to work at the Project, not because she believed in him, but because she did not: unknowing, he had invited his destruction inside.

In reality, on the first Glimmer expedition, nothing was as they expected. No model, no projection, can ever truly represent what happens in different - space. That had been their error. This was not merely an alternate dimension, the Kingdom was in literally different space.

Nothing had worked. All the technology they brought with them was useless. She picked up the full-moon amulet that Eiswolf had taken from Jocasta, who had once been Dr Martinez, ethno-biologist and biochemist. She squinted along the surface. The holographic image was still just about visible, but as a position locator, it was dead. Jocasta had never been entirely stable, and she slipped over the edge quite quickly when they discovered they were stranded. A lot of the others, once realisation set in, had some sort of psychotic break. Poor old Dave, Nico, Bridget –

Bess had realised it was time to adapt or die. The Kingdom could be an interesting place to live, even pleasant: the population density was low, a 'big town' might only have two thousand people. By definition, all food was organic, when available. People valued manners and traditions. Although religion existed, it was pleasingly disorganised: the idea of a pogrom or crusade was unknown. The downsides were obvious: you could be killed by an infected scratch, let alone malaria, cholera or meningitis; there was only the crudest surgery or dentistry, equality and human rights were not even a glint in a madman's eye. The closely-knit and usually closely-related people of a town could turn viciously on strangers. Bess had made her mistakes, until she realised the people needed a story that fitted their own ideas. So she became the Good Witch, without ever defining whether this meant good at witchery, or doing magic for the good. And, this being a simpler time in some ways, people took her at her word.

But Gil had been unstoppable, even after the shock of ending up in the Kingdom. If his original plan for society was blown away, no matter! He would build one here, in this medieval dimension. He called himself the Glimmer Lord and began to attract men and resources to him in exactly the same way as he had sweet-talked his way around the universities and government departments - and weapons companies - in the old days.

Then Eiswolf had turned up on her doorstep. If anyone could combat evil from another universe, then this boy, so obviously not entirely human, was it. He knew nothing of his origins, apart from the slip of writing about rime and snow and the gods of ice that he produced from a little leather bag around his neck. So she told him he had a new life with her, and she would help him. Eventually, he trusted her enough to believe her.

And so, now, she was punished. He had been a gift, a shooting star, but she had trashed that gift. The scalpel had stabbed the surgeon.

She brought down her books from the shelf, where she had written down all she could remember of the science from her old life, and began to study. Gil had to have a weakness. There had to be a way to stop him that did not involve Bess becoming an amateur assassin. There had to.

***

The Princess had a new idea. How wonderful, the creative freedom that one could find in a large white space! Who had known that this room was almost a perfect cube! Her dungeon sparkled; clean, echoing, brilliant, apart from the Planning Hanging and its covering curtain. Even the dragon's skull on its mount did not look quite so out of place. The girls complained that the new benches were rough but they looked right. Rugged and honest and natural, with all the stone and lime-washed white walls.

Anyway, her dungeon, her rules. A footstep sounded in the corridor beyond. Another advantage. No-one could sneak up on the Princess; every rustle created a reverberation.

"Your Majesty!" said the guard at the door. "The seamstress is here, with a tradesman?"

"Send them in," said the Princess. "Then close the door. This is a fitting."

The seamstress entered, bearing a large basket that rattled, followed by a short, wizened man carrying a small leather bag.

The big idea had come to the Princess after her experience with the hair-tirer. He had created wonderful styles, but putting them in place took a good hour or three, hardly an effective use of her time. What a pity, she said, that she could not do important work instead of sitting around.

A light came into his eyes. What about a wig? He could create one on a canvas cap, which could be pinned in place in a few minutes at most. And you could change them round or create new ones very easily –

The idea sold itself. Some ladies at court wore obvious woollen wigs to cover baldness, but the Princess' wigs were an entirely different concept, made of hair like her own, works of art in their own right (and priced that way, too). One problem solved.

Now for the gowns. The bigger and heavier the court robes became, the more structural support they needed: stiffened canvas, leather reinforcing bands, small strips of springy willow-rod, wiring, little weights to improve the way they draped, with multiple underlayers. The bigger they got, the more help the Princess needed to get in and out of them. Dressing, too, was starting to absorb a lot of time.

Unless she found another way. The Princess had been impressed by a jeweller who visited the court, who did wonderful things with wire. He had been a little surprised when he saw her plans, but today he had brought the prototype. The seamstress was there to wed technology to tradition.

"Now," said the Princess, "show me how it works."

And the guard outside her door heard an entirely new and mysterious noise. Something went "Sproing!"

11: The Ring of Power

Mifanna was not the only new face at Court. A frisson of excitement went through the town as a small group of riders approached the Palace. At their head, on a magnificent long-maned steed of creamy white, rode a young man whose hair glinted like gold.

Adelbon made his usual impressive entrance, but not in armour. He was dressed in sky-blue, for he came as a courtier, not a warrior. He rode through the palace gates, his golden sun device gleaming on horse-trappings and the tabards of his pages, his ladies glowing in all the colours of the rainbow.

But all was not well with Adelbon. As he dismounted in the castle yard, many noted that he needed help from a squire. His face was pale, although he carried his pain with a brave smile. Leaning on a page's shoulder, he slowly and carefully made his way towards the great entrance.

The Princess and her ladies watched all this from their regular window in the royal tower.

"Is that him?" said Dorcas. "He's younger than the other one."

"He's followed by a proper retinue," said Chloe. "That's more like a prince."

"Limping, though," said Iris. "You don't want a damaged one, surely. If you have the choice."

The Princess stared down at the boy with her gimlet eyes. She had never actually seen him in the flesh. Tall, check. Golden hair, check. Impressive horse, check. General air of doomed heroism, a touch of hope against all odds, check. Just as her scout Jannick of Netley had told her, when he had found the boy last winter. That was why she picked Adelbon for Plan A. She'd named the Plan after him. And although Adelbon had scored a blank in the battles against Eiswolf, as disposable princes went, he would do very nicely.

"Such a brave young man. He has travelled far to pay court to Us, and has suffered much in Our name. Set forth a lordly feast for him and his followers, for he is a knight who carries Our favour."

"Which wine?" said Hebe.

"Not the best stuff, how about the last delivery but one from Copsale? That'll do, don't you think?"

"And the food?"

"No boar, plenty of pigeons and a ham. Make that two hams. Mustn't be stingy. Oh, find Jocasta, will you?" The Princess went back to the window and watched Adelbon, his progress slowed by the number of people who came to bow before him or thrust flowers in his hand. Yes, he would do very nicely. Plan E was not yet abandoned.

***

"We have examined the Manifest most closely," said the professor. "We are all agreed that for the next part of the Quest, the wolf knight must obtain the Ring of Power."

"And this is a real ring?" said the Hegemon. "It's not a symbol or a metaphor?"

He and the Conclave were in a pre-meeting in a side-chamber, for the Hegemon did not want any surprises when they went to the King, or in later reports to the Court.

"No, my lord, the Ring was forged in the Depths of Despair and hardened in the Well of Loneliness," said a librarian.

"I know how it feels," said the Hegemon. "So what's the catch?"

The academics all looked guiltily at each other. "The Ring was forged by elves," said the young, bold professor. "You have to take it off them."

"That's hardly a problem, is it?" said the Hegemon. "Most of them would struggle to keep hold of a cream puff, they're not exactly fighting men."

"Well, some say these are not like our elves," said the young professor.

"No natural sense of style and a tendency to bicker?"

One of the old professors cleared his throat. "Those are elf-*fanciers*, my lord. These are Dark Elves. Sworn enemies of the fairies, don't you know. They set a riddle to win this Ring, because its mighty power must be wielded by one wise enough to listen to its haunting voice and yet hold fast."

"So who's got it now?"

The academics looked at each other, and shuffled. "The last holder was Loblolly the Mad..." The younger professor trailed off.

"And once our wolf gets hold of this, he has, what? "

"Huge power, my lord."

"And if he gets it wrong?" There had to be hope.

"Oh, he's doomed to the Portals of Stone for all eternity. The books are quite clear about that."

"Good," said the Hegemon. He led the Conclave into the King's Chamber to break the news to the King and the senior earls.

"We only have two chances left, I gather?" said the King. "I mean, two more opportunities for our brave knight to prove himself before his final victory?" But everyone had understood him perfectly well the first time.

"There is good news," said the Hegemon. "This is a test of the man's intellect, not his muscles."

The King raised his eyebrows. "Is he sufficiently dim, do we think?"

"Your Majesty." One of the professors bowed. "This knight has shown himself equal to trials of strength, patience, and courage. The Test of the Ring will be solved by a mere riddle, which I believe is within his compass." He smiled, comfortingly.

Right, thought the King. You've taken the wolf's coin, have you?

Another professor shook his head. "He has little training in matters of the mind. But, the price of failure is the same. Death." He said it, gloatingly.

One for me, thought the King.

"And yet," quavered an old lawyer, "might there not be another challenger?"

"Oh?" the King, rather sharply. "Who?"

Dear God, you spend nine years getting rid of every half-witted rival and pretender in the realms and just when you're getting on top of it all, two turn up at once.

"Why, Sir Adelbon," said a young professor. "A most worthy and virtuous knight."

The King looked confused. "But wasn't he knocked out in the Sword of Destiny business?"

"If, indeed, he was defeated by fair means," said the lawyer. Had he been able to get away with a wink, he would have.

"Ah." The King narrowed his eyes. "I see your point. And this knight is…"

"At the palace," said the young professor. "The Princess herself summoned him, and he will attend the ceremony tomorrow."

"Ah. Did she," said the King. "I see. We will do as the Manifest requires, then, and command our Knight to find the Ring of Power. The people expect a celebration, so tell all that we begin preparations for the wedding of our most beloved daughter, should he succeed."

And if that didn't bring every earl scurrying to Court to take sides and conveniently show the King who could be trusted, he was a monkey's uncle.

But Adelbon? What the blazes was the girl up to?

***

"Sir knight, although We are but a feeble woman, We ever have the welfare of Our country at heart, and the benefit of all Our people from the humblest to the most high. But We see you are weary." The

Princess nodded to Sir Adelbon, commanding him to sit with a flick of her splendid, delicate glove.

They were in the Great Hall for an official greeting ceremony, under the gleaming blue flag of the King and the rich red pennant of the Princess.

The gloves were the Princess' latest idea: expensive, beautiful, and incredibly impractical. No lady could do much more than hold a book while wearing them. Eating meant getting gravy all over the superb lace and leather, so there was an accompanying fashion for little divided spears of silver to convey any delicate morsel from dish to mouth. They satisfactorily absorbed the energies, and the fortune, of any lady who might think of challenging the Princess.

Sir Adelbon bowed, slightly stiffly. "Forgive me, your Majesty, my wounds are still fresh." He waved at a page, who helped him to a chair.

"So We understand," said the Princess. "We trust you will soon be recovered, for We believe you fought most bravely."

"As any man could, against a knight who…" Adelbon looked around the Great Hall. The only people there were the Princess' ladies and his own retainers.

"Who what, Sir Adelbon?"

"Who is not as other knights, your Majesty." Adelbon spoke carefully. "I have never contested a man so strong, so swift and so, um. Sneaky."

"Ah," said the Princess. "And apart from sneaky, you seem to hint of another power?" She raised her eyebrows.

The knight went pink. "Well, some have said, for I know he was raised by a witch, that he has special, um, abilities."

Dear heaven, this dance could go on forever. The Princess clapped her hands. "Ladies, We would have a private audience with this knight. You may leave. Jocasta, We would have you stay. Sir knight, have not your servants preparations to make for the morning?"

He smiled, smugly. "My people are well prepared already, I believe."

It took another couple of nods and a twitch from the Princess before the penny finally dropped.

And then the Princess was (almost) alone with her protégé. "Sir Knight, We have admired you for a while. Tales of your deeds of courage have reached this court from all the lands."

He blushed. He really, really did. "Your majesty is too kind. The reputation of your great beauty summoned me."

"Yes, quite. We have not seen you at court before?"

"No, my father trained me at home in knightly endeavours, we are but a poor earldom. But, by the grace of providence, this winter I saved the life of a rich merchant, Jannick of Netley, who was beset by robbers. In his gratitude, he has devoted his entire fortune to my training and tourneys. "

The Princess waved at him to stop. "A generous man." And a good actor. "We heard, which is why We sent you our favour. So you have proven yourself both in battle and in contest with the forces of magic?"

He looked a little uncomfortable. "Well, in tourneys, yes, for by the grace of your father's peaceable rule, we have not been troubled by war even in my father's distant lands. I, er, I think some of the other tales may have grown in the telling."

"What tale does not, dear sir?" She smiled. "And a brave show you made. Only to be disappointed at the last, in Westerings."

He rose to the occasion. "Having seen your Majesty's great beauty, my disappointment is the sharper."

Finally, a spark. She played with her glove. "But if, as you say, Sir Eiswolf only came into possession of the Sword of Destiny by enchantment, is that not yours by right?"

He looked nonplussed. "The knight who wields the Sword has great power, however he possesses it."

Jocasta broke in. "Did you see the spell by which Sir Eiswolf obtained the Sword?"

"I - No. I saw the Warden of Westerings strike him in the heart, and the Sword refused to bite. It struck right by your amulet."

Both the Princess and Jocasta froze.

"Say again?" said the Princess.

"Your amulet."

"What amulet?" said Jocasta.

"My Princess, the one you sent me? I saw that the knight wore your favour? The necklace? Birds and so forth?" He gestured to his neck, in a fiddly way.

Good grief, thought the Princess. Forgot all about that. "And so?"

"Well, after he prevailed in the last battle, it behoves a knight to act with generosity and forgiveness, even if he believes there has been foul play. So as your Majesty had also chosen him as your knight, I thought he should bear your favour into the great test, so I gave your amulet to him."

"DO WHAT!"

"The one you bade me wear next my heart." The boy was redder than red now. "Did I do wrong?"

***

Meroens took off his practice chest-plate and looked at the shield.

"That's what we technically call a bloody big dent," said the Armourer.

They were sorting out weapons and mail for Meroens. The bulky wrestler was not the easiest man to fit, so he was trying pieces on in the armoury, after his regular practice bout with Eiswolf.

"Yeah, bloody big." Meroens frowned unhappily.

"You seem down, friend. How the hell did you split this?" The Armourer poked a finger through a hole in a shoulder plate.

"I didn't. He did. He's very…"

Very.

"Very what?"

Meroens was deeply bothered. He sat on his worries, telling himself not to be stupid, or a coward, trying to ignore them, but they would not go away. The Armourer was a decent sort, so he put his thoughts into words. "You know, he's a good bloke. I mean, he was a good bloke before, only now it's different. I mean, he's still very nice manners and all, you should hear him talk with all them lords, long words and everything. But when he's fighting, I don't think it's just having the Sword, I seen swords, I don't think that one's no different really, it's more than that, like he's…" He ran out of thinking.

The Armourer, still assessing the damage to the shoulder-plate, noticed that Meroens had stopped. "Like he's what?"

"Dark." Meroens landed on the single word that encapsulated his fear.

Because he was afraid, a very unfamiliar feeling.

When he sparred with Eiswolf, the way the man fought had changed. He had an edge, as if one day he might forget they were only training. The moves were swifter, sharper, better, as they should be after so much practice, now his injuries were healed. But Eiswolf's sword-arm did not concern Meroens nearly as much as his head.

"Dark?" said the Armourer. "What's that, then?"

"Well, like, when I look at him, only not straight-on, like something's behind you, he's different?" Meroens screwed up his face. "Sort of it's his eyes, they're - Different. Like, er…"

"Dark?" said the Armourer.

"No!" Meroens roared. "This is important! They're hard! And they shine like that shield! And then he's like he don't know who I am, like he's not there any more, just this sword. And It Don't Care."

The Armourer, an old soldier, had seen his share of berserkers and psychopaths on the battlefield, so he nodded.

But this annoyed Meroens. "I seen those men when it gets to them, the ones as goes after the killing? Because they like killing? It's not like that. He's not trying to kill me, not as me. He can't see me. It's like that dragon."

The Armourer was completely lost. "What dragon?"

"One of the men what fed it said she didn't really see the goats. Not to see what they were, anyway. She chased anything warm what moved. That's what he does. He sees something move, so he kills it."

The Armourer put down a chain mail coat to look at the wrestler carefully. "Pal, if I was you, I'd get an injury. Sprain or whatever. Came on sudden this afternoon. Get my drift?"

Meroens sighed. Perry would have known what to do. But only God knew where he was.

***

The guard raised his hand, so the Hegemon stopped. They were walking very quietly along the corridor outside the Princess' dungeon.

The guard turned and whispered, "It's about here, where I hear the noises. Put your ear to the wall, my lord. Listen!"

At first, the Hegemon only heard his own heartbeat. Then he started making out noises. Strange noises. And muttering.

"Drat, drat, drat!"

That was definitely the Princess.

Rattle, rattle, clink, kerplunk. "Drat!"

A sound like a chain dragging. A heavy weight dropped on the floor. Tinkle, tinkle, splot.

"Oh, for the love of - Get in! Ouch!"

Crunch, sproing, sproing.

The guard looked at the Hegemon, raised his eyebrows and shrugged. "Any idea, sir?"

The Hegemon put his ear against the wall again, listening carefully.

Bang! Bang, bang, bang. Tinkle. "That's better!" More dragging sounds. "Oof!" Something dropped with a thud. "Right! Let's try again."

Then a cold chill went down the Hegemon's back, for he heard an unearthly hooting sound, like a wind trapped in the wall demanding to be let out. The noise stopped, then started again, louder. Then came more little hammer-blows, followed by a low, deep, mournful hoot.

He had heard enough. "Guard, keep me informed. Ah, no need to worry anyone else with this. I shall inform the King myself."

"Then you know what it is?" said the guard.

"Yes," lied the Hegemon. "But there is no call for men of the lower orders to trouble their minds. That will be all." He strode away.

One more entry for the worry-list. What on earth was she up to?"

***

At noon the next day, Conclave paraded into the Great Hall, which was full to bursting. Every nobleman in the Kingdom wanted to be here for the announcement of the next Test.

Eiswolf stood beside the King's throne, waiting patiently. As the man who was, increasingly possibly, the next ruler, he was dressed in rich blue velvet robes trimmed with white fur. At his side hung the Sword of Destiny, and under his shirt he wore the Princess' amulet, in case any freelance assassin decided to have a go.

In the crowd of nobles, he could see the Glimmer Lord, who gave him a nod. A skein of exotic fragrance hung in the air, lemon and anise and camphor. There was Mifanna, lovely in pale green brocade, her red-gold hair shining like a flame. She smiled and curtseyed to him, a secret token.

Then the trumpets announced the royal entrance. The King walked in, nodded at Eiswolf, and acknowledged his court. He sat on his throne. The Hegemon scurried into place on the other side from Eiswolf. Then came the Princess and her ladies, burdened with court dresses, wigs and gloves, carrying small masks of stiffened gilded canvas to conceal their loveliness.

The senior professor waved his arms wide. "Great King! Rarely have we seen such a time! In this day, the fates of the Kingdom and your lovely daughter may be determined! For by the wisdom of the most far-sighted Kolras, this knight has been chosen for the most important Tests of all! Sir Knight, do you come here in true humility, wishing only to serve this Kingdom, for only a knight of pure heart and innocent intent may be chosen?"

A flash caught Eiswolf's eye. Gold and sky-blue. Dammit, that boy Adelbon.

The professor coughed, like an apologetic goat. "Sir Knight?"

Eiswolf switched back to court mode. "Ah. I hear your charge. A humble man like myself has many faults and errors. Yet, for the love of this beautiful Princess," currently buried under a heap of brocade, buckram, false hair and a mask, "and in respect for this great Kingdom and its people," like the nobles in the Hall, all of whom would sell their own grannies for an earldom, "I shall endeavour to purify my heart, that I may succeed where so many others have failed."

Adelbon stared at him very hard. Sizing him up already?

The King smiled vaguely and waved at the professor, who unrolled the translation of the Manifest.

"Then, Sir Knight, you must pursue the Quest of the Ring of Power!"

A wave of shock ran through the crowd. Even the Glimmer Lord seemed taken aback.

But this was the professor's moment in the sun, and he milked it. "You must go to the dark North, to Hafon Swyno, to find this most dangerous and potent talisman made by Elves! But if you fail, you shall be as stone for all eternity! Do you accept this challenge?"

Eiswolf looked the King straight in the eye. "I accept."

The crowd erupted in cheers.

Most interesting, thought the King.

I wonder if he's up to it, thought the Princess, not meaning Eiswolf.

"Dear God!" whispered the Hegemon, for he had seen the flat, bright, deadly golden gleam in Eiswolf's eyes, and knew this was not an illusion. So they were going to hand the Kingdom to that thing?

**

A huge crowd came to see Eiswolf, Meroens and a dozen other men set out for the distant north, so they could tell their children and their grandchildren. Eiswolf smiled and waved, but went off at a canter on Storm, quickly leaving the people behind. He did not stop until three hours later, when he drew his retinue about him.

"This is a difficult mission. I don't want anyone who does not understand that. Forget all the hero stuff at the Palace, we might all die. If you're here because you've been ordered, leave now with my blessing, and your pay. If you think you're going to get glory, I can tell you now, you won't. Glory is what troubadours sing about. If we get back. This is the most important quest of my life. If any man gets in my way, I won't be distracted. I go through you, not round you. There will be no rescues. We have no facilities for wounded men. Is that clear?"

The men nodded, Meroens among them

"Then who chooses to leave?"

None of the men moved.

Eiswolf frowned. "I don't believe you. Meroens, you've seen these men in the practice grounds, pick out five - No, four. The rest of you, go."

So Meroens picked out the men he thought best suited; tough, unimaginative, grizzled horsemen. The others rode off. Most were angry.

Eiswolf turned to the wrestler. "Meroens, that means you, too. Do you think you're up to it? With that injury?"

"I'm up to it, boss, as long as I don't have to fight you."

The other men laughed.

So they rode past wood and moor, village and hamlet, over high fells and through deep gorges. In five days they reached the borders of the northern country. They travelled light, buying or killing the food they needed, silent for the most part, focussed on the journey. Eiswolf barely said a word. But at night when they bivouacked, he did not stay by the fire with the others but withdrew a distance away. Meroens appeared to doze but kept an eye on his boss, because Eiswolf wrestled dreams in his sleep. Sometimes he seemed to change, although in the blackness of a forest night, maybe Meroens' eyes played tricks.

They reached a lonely village, a string of half a dozen huts by the rough trackway. The people ran inside the huts when they saw the riders, but one of the horsemen dismounted and dragged out a man. "Is this Hafon Swyno? We come seeking the elves."

The man's expression of pure terror told them they must be close.

"Look." Meroens pointed to a track running up the side of a hill. A wooden post was splashed with bright reddish-brown. About a hundred metres along stood another.

The horseman dragged the peasant by his arm and pointed to the posts. "Is that them?" The man nodded.

"Then come on," said Eiswolf. He led the way.

They rode along the track for another half-day. The posts started to be splashed with white as well as red; in the gloaming, they glowed like torches.

"What are elves?" said Meroens. He began to shiver.

"No man knows," said Eiswolf. "Creatures not of this world."

"How are you going to…"

But Eiswolf was not in the mood for conversation. He made Storm gallop past the posts, down a hill and then up the other side to a small crest of rock. He stopped, staring fixedly, motionless on the horse.

Meroens caught up with him, peering into the evening mists. Then he, too, froze.

Below them the path wound down the side of the hill into a flat-bottomed green valley, where a small silver river curled and twisted. At one side stood a mound: as high as a hall, as long as half a plough-furrow, smooth as a river-washed pebble, and bright, gleaming white. It looked like a gigantic, half-buried egg, except that at one end, facing the setting sun, was a massive wall and gateway of stone.

Meroens could see snake-like patterns carved into the wall, red and white paint gleaming in the crevices. "Elves?" he said, finally.

"What else," said one of the horsemen.

"Wait for me here." Eiswolf rode down towards the mound. As he approached the entrance, a dim light appeared inside. He dismounted and walked in. None of his men expected to see him again.

***

"You disappoint me," said the Hegemon. "Guards, bring the torch closer."

The light glanced off the damp stone walls. There was nothing else; no daylight, no air, no nothing, except the jailers and their charge. This was the cellar that no-one knew, except the unlucky ones who were brought here. Few ever took their knowledge back into the world outside.

The Hegemon knew he had to save his Kingdom and his Princess from Eiswolf. There was no time for pleasantries.

In the cellar stood two chairs of simple design. The Hegemon sat on one, Bess was chained to the other. Behind her stood a guard with a torch. Two jailers stood passively, waiting for instructions.

"Shall we try again," said the Hegemon. "This creature Eiswolf. Tell me all about him."

Bess glared at him through bruised eyes. "I know nothing!" she spat.

"Jailer."

The man hit her again, with enough force to rock the chair backwards, plainly not using all his strength. He did not need to. He was very skilled at judging how much a prisoner could take. Bess, good witch or not, was a middle-aged woman, and the Hegemon wanted her to talk, not die. At least, that was what he wanted right now.

"Bess, I do not want to do this. But the Kingdom is in danger. You must tell me what you know."

"Little man!" She hissed with anger. "He's beyond anything you can imagine! You are nothing compared to him, nothing!"

And then the jailer hit her again, once in the face, once in the gut.

"We can carry on like this," said the Hegemon. "But I would prefer not to. Is the other ready?"

The other jailer pointed to a bucket of cold water beside his feet.

"Please, Bess. For your own sake. Tell me about the creature."

"No!"

Torture is not a sophisticated process. Torturers might like to believe that you need great intellect or understanding of the human mind or finesse. Psychopaths and sadists often take this as a proof of their superiority, while the stupid just like inflicting pain. But it does not take massive chambers full of special equipment to break a man or woman: fear, and isolation, and fire, and a bucket of water will do as well. And a man, or woman, willing to injure another human being again and again and again, and close their ears to the screams and their minds to what they are doing.

***

Eiswolf stood before the gateway to the mound. He could see into a tunnel under the earth. A torch on a long pole had been struck into the ground, so he picked it up to light his way. The torch smoked, letting off a strange incense-like smell.

The mound was chilly. The further he got from the entrance, the danker and darker the tunnel became. In the torchlight, the snaking patterns carved on the walls seemed to writhe like living things, creatures no man had seen, or perhaps should see. But Eiswolf went on.

At the far end was a faint glow. He made out ornamented pillars, then a square doorway, then a chamber. The room had a dim grey light, not like his torch, nor yet like daylight. Eiswolf put the torch into a holder by the doorway. He walked inside.

The chamber was big: the height of four men, curved walls made of smooth grey stones piled one on another up to a roof the shape of an upturned boat. Polished grey stone covered the floor: in the middle stood a table and two stools. On the table was a chess-board, and at the table sat an immensely tall figure, robed and hooded in black, stretching out a hand to straighten a chess-piece: a long, ivory-coloured hand. And a metallic odour -

"Sir Knight?" said Eiswolf.

For this was no elf, but the Dogstar Knight, the lover of the Queen of Faery.

The Knight looked up at Eiswolf. "Sit down. We have been waiting for you."

Eiswolf frowned. "Sir Knight, this is where I must win the Ring of Power, a charm forged by the elves."

"Forged by them, maybe, but no longer in their care. The Ring has its guardian, that is my privilege now. Would you contest me for this charm, as you put it?"

"Are we to fight? They said this was about a riddle."

The Knight pushed back his hood, revealing his ivory-coloured hair. He laughed. "You would like a riddle, Sir Eiswolf? Well then. What goes on four legs in the morning, two at mid-day, and three in the evening?"

That was easy. Why so easy? Bess told him this one. Eiswolf scoured his memory. "A man, who crawls on all fours when he is a baby, stands when he is grown, and uses a stick when he is old. Is that it?"

"Do you think that should be it? Shall I give you the Ring now?" The Knight held out his closed hand, as if he held the Ring inside.

This was wrong, all wrong,

"No. That's not enough, is it?"

The Knight laughed again. "Not nearly enough." His laughter echoed among the grey stones. "Sit, Sir Eiswolf."

"Then are we to play chess?" The chill was getting into Eiswolf now. He sat. The stool felt like cold steel. "I can play, although I am no expert."

"Do you think Kolras wanted a chess-player for a king?"

"No, I suppose not." Despite himself, Eiswolf could feel a shiver travelling over his limbs.

"What would he want?" The Knight leaned forward and fixed Eiswolf with that distant, brilliant grey stare.

"A man fit to be king."

"Precisely." The Knight moved a couple of the pieces: Eiswolf noticed that on his own side they were white. A queen of rock crystal, ornamented with gold, beside a knight in glinting white quartz, streaked with a dark mark like a lightning bolt. Behind them were bishops, castles and pawns, in ivory, marble and alabaster. On the Dogstar Knight's side, the pieces were in porphyry, bloodstone, serpentine, amethyst: and a king of carved ruby.

The Knight finished arranging the pieces on the black and white squares. "Let us start."

Eiswolf lifted a pawn, but the Knight frowned. He clapped his hands.

Suddenly all the black squares disappeared. The board was plain white. The Knight seized Eiswolf's hand holding the pawn, a touch so cold, it burned.

"Sir Eiswolf, what do you call a man who always takes the choice of the right?"

Eiswolf stared at the featureless board. A splinter of panic stabbed his mind. How was he supposed to play? What was the question, keep calm, think clearly. "A man who always chooses the right. We can all see the right, most of us. So he makes an easy kind of choice, but doing it is - " He stared at the board again. "Not so easy."

The Knight let go of his hand. "Well said." He clapped his hands again. Now the board turned black. "What do you call a man who always takes the choice of darkness?"

The black board seemed to absorb every trace of light, like a slice of nothingness on which the pieces hovered. Eiswolf was colder. His hands shook, not in fear, but simple physical stress.

"If he always chooses darkness." Think it through. "We all know we should choose light, so he is deliberately choosing what he knows to be wrong. That is a difficult decision."

"Indeed, What manner of man, then?"

"He makes a difficult decision but once made, doing it is easy. If he can forget his humanity, like a dog or a rat."

The Knight smiled. "But such creatures protect their young, cherish their mates, attack under provocation but not otherwise. Only man seems to find evil easy."

Eiswolf sat back. "We are not perfect. But most of us try." He could no longer feel his hands or feet: the unbearable cold crept up his body, inch by inch.

"Well, so the right is clear, and so is the dark choice. What then do we call this?" He clapped his hands a third time.

The board became grey, the pieces lost their colour and were indistinct. It was not even clear which side of the board was which. Eiswolf stared. The chill sat on his chest like lead.

The Knight watched him for a few minutes. "This is your final education. You should thank me for this."

But now Eiswolf was so cold, he could barely move his lips. "I am," breathe, "too stupid to understand," breathe, "help me, please."

The Knight laughed. "You ask for help? Why not kill me to get your Ring? It will give you power, so much power."

"No. No. I want to know the answer."

"Is that more important than power?"

Eiswolf could hardly breath, cold, so cold. But that deathly cold brought a kind of clarity. "Yes."

The Knight leaned forward. "For that, I'll give you this one. What shall we call this game. Oh, yes, I know." He tapped the grey board. "Life."

The Knight picked up the ruby king, pulling the little carved figure in two. A ring of grey metal dropped into his right hand. "This trinket is what you seek. But it comes at a high cost. For if you fail now, you shall never leave this mound. This is the Ring of Power that your wise men speak of. With this you may see into the minds of all mankind. With this, you can become king."

The cold seemed to pool about Eiswolf, crackling into his joints, his teeth, his veins . The ring was plain metal: no engraved message, no stone, no magical glow. It did not look much.

The Knight placed the ring in the centre of the chessboard. "What do you call a man who saves his friends and abandons them, who protects his household and rejects them, who has ambition but no thirst for power, who is merciful but kills without hesitation, who loves and cannot be loved, who boasts but despises himself as he does? Think well."

The cold pierced Eiswolf's heart. He knew, now, that the chamber was the last place he would ever see. All for nothing. Bess, Perry, the Quests, even Mifanna, all illusions, dreams, a scatter of smoke in the vast uncaring universe. Only death was real.

And truth.

He fought for control of his frozen lips. "Eiswolf. You call him Eiswolf."

A breeze flowed through the chamber, just enough warmth to let him breathe.

The Knight put his hood back up. "Well said, Sir Eiswolf. You have won your trinket. The Ring of Power, as forged by the elves. Will you not take it now?"

But Eiswolf had learned much on his quests, especially about those who lay claim to magic powers.

"I have not travelled so far for a forgery. I think I prefer the real thing." He darted forward and seized the Knight's left hand, on which glinted a grey metal ring. "This will do."

12: The Final Test

"Is he coming?" said the Princess, through her mask.

She sat in her echoing dungeon, her shell-pink robe carefully arranged. She was ready for her Knight in shining armour, who had been through such terrific tests to win her hand.

Only, he was keeping her waiting. All morning. She rapped her gloved fingers on the arm of her silver throne.

"No sign," said Iris, peering through the window-slit. "I think you can put that down."

So the Princess lowered her gilded mask. "What on earth is he doing?"

Chloe and Hebe entered the dungeon, having earwigged around the court. The Princess snapped at them. "Any news?"

Chloe curtseyed. "We have been told he stands without the city walls, your Majesty. Your father the King will ride out to him."

"And the Hegemon?" said Dorcas. Chloe nodded.

"And the Glimmer Lord," said Hebe.

The Princess frowned. "What's it to do with him? Why's he so important all of a sudden?" Sudden suspicion. "What's Daddy up to?"

"I hear," said Chloe, "that the Knight wishes to be invited into the City, not to arrive like an invading army. And the others are counsellors."

"H'm," said the Princess. "And everyone's buying that, are they? Where's Black Al? We mean, the King's Champion?"

"At the King's right hand," said Hebe.

"We see," said the Princess, darkly. "Well, eventually, We suppose, Wolfie-thingy will see fit to greet Us. But We shall not hold Our breath. Wine, We think? Oh, and find Jocasta."

After a very, very long time - nine and a half years, to be precise - matters were moving swiftly. Which meant Plan E would have to be even faster.

***

The King, astride his royal charger, waited while the noble knights of the Kingdom arranged themselves on their battle stallions, by precedence. The horses, excited, were kicking up and the whole business was taking longer than it should. The Hegemon perched uncomfortably beside the King on a small mare.

"Dammit," said the King. "I thought they said he couldn't do it?"

'They' were the Conclave, standing at a distance from the riders, looking very sheepish.

"We are in uncharted waters," said the Hegemon. "We seem to have reached the limits of academic knowledge."

"And a very short voyage that was. Once round the duck-pond. What now."

The King had a list of options, they were not many, and he hated, really hated, making a definitive commitment to any of them. In his experience, and he had been King for thirty-four years, going about making decisions was a very bad idea. They usually upset someone, and could not always be blamed on anyone else if they went wrong.

The parade formed up and, to the sound of drum and trumpet, the King went forward with his Champion and his senior advisors to meet the great Hero at the gates.

Eiswolf was on the big white horse, sitting very still, his rough-looking bunch of squires behind him. He was not in armour but black and red robes, trimmed in white fur. But the King could see the Sword of Destiny at his side, and presumably he was wearing the Ring of Power. Then came one of those odd shifts, like a flicker of light across the King's eye and he saw a golden flash - By God, Eiswolf could be a strange creature!

The Hegemon was obviously ill at ease, shuffling in his saddle and glancing from side to side. Poor Bevis, thought the King, all this was very hard on him. The Glimmer Lord, on the other hand, was almost smiling in a grim way. The King had met men like that, too. For the moment, better to have him inside the proverbial tent than out, him and his pretty red-haired niece or whatever she was.

The parade halted. The King put on a royal smile, lordly and yet generous.

"Sir Knight, we welcome you home from your Quest! Have you brought us the Ring of Power, as demanded by Kolras?"

"Yes, my Lord! Here!" And Eiswolf held up a glittering gold ring, its magnificent ruby glinting in the sunlight.

The crowd almost swooned, the knights applauded and a choir struck up a quick madrigal of jubilation. The Glimmer Lord looked carefully, and smiled. He knew the Ring, and that was not it. Deceptive creatures, Fairies.

"My King." Eiswolf rode forward, dismounted from Storm, and made a deep bow. "I ask you humbly for your permission to enter this great City. I present this Ring to you for your safekeeping, and the protection of this Kingdom." He held the ring above his head. "I am ever your subject."

Nicely played, boy, thought the King. Maybe there's more to you than I thought. But you can't have my crown yet.

What he said was, "Your courage is matched only by your generosity, Sir Knight! Enter, with our blessing, for we shall feast mightily today! Let all mark that the future of our Kingdom lies in his hands. Enter, Sir Knight, as our chosen Hero, and let our people rejoice!"

So Eiswolf got back on Storm and, followed by Meroens and the other men, rode calmly into the City. He raised his hand in salute to the cheering crowds, but did not smile, nor laugh. He was cool, and watchful, and prepared.

***

"I'm sorry, my sweet. If I could think of another way, I would."

"Daddy!"

The Princess was not taking it well. Good God, herding dragons would be easier than getting his daughter to make nice with that dratted man. She was glaring at him. Well, she was probably glaring at him, it was hard to tell through that blasted mask.

"My love, if he succeeds in the last Test, you'll have to do rather more than kiss him."

"Daddy!" The rising wail had a real edge, this time. "Don't be disgusting."

Sometimes the King wondered about the wisdom of keeping his daughter so insulated from the petty concerns of life. She was now a twenty-four year old virgin with a very high opinion of herself.

"We knew this day would arrive, my dear."

"Well, I ruddy didn't!" she snapped. "I was quite working on the principle that this day would NOT arrive! He's weird!"

"He's an unusual man, I agree."

She rapped his hand with her glove. "No! Daddy, unusual is short or a squint or a hump! Not a wolfie - cloudy - thingy - And he's hairy! He's got a tail, one of the girls heard! And he's all rough and insanitary! Ugh!"

The King sighed. "Look. Turn up to the feast, drink a glass of wine, give him a quick smacker, then you can get a headache. I don't want him cutting up and saying we're not keeping to our side. No excuses for a fight, my love. As far as everyone else is concerned, we're both absolutely delighted that our Knight has returned. Aren't we."

She muttered and rumbled but she knew he was right. "I suppose so. God, what I do for this Kingdom!"

"Small steps, my angel. The road to power is full of small steps. And he's a long way from the end yet. Oh, by the way. I know you like that Adelbon boy, but I'd be a little distant during the jollifications. Wouldn't want any rumours, would we."

"Daddy!"

"Would we."

More mutterings, but in the end she nodded. A chip off the old block, thought the King. Which is why the next thing he did was go to Black Al and raise the surveillance level on his lovely daughter.

***

Meroens sat in his place on a stool outside Eiswolf's chamber, and considered deeply. He stared at the back of his hands, a gesture he saved for the problems that could not be solved by staring at the ceiling. If things got really bad, he folded his arms and closed his eyes and whistled through his teeth, but he was not quite there yet.

This was all wrong. Yesterday in practice, the boss had nearly killed Pasquin, one of the hand-picked grizzled fighters. That could have been Meroens, except he was still pleading an injury. The flat golden stare was happening more often. Afterwards the boss was moody, not his old self at all. Grim, and he'd never been that before. But then he was a fighting man, Meroens had heard all about how many had died in the pursuit of the Tests, and how many Eiswolf had killed. That had an effect on a bloke.

Meroens kept a very careful eye on Eiswolf. An old sword master had once told him, a man could go one of three ways. He could take to killing for a pastime, or he could stop noticing that he was killing, acting without thought. Or he could be haunted by those he killed, and that could take a man beyond the reach of sanity.

So far, Eiswolf was not playing at killing, nor had his temper deteriorated into unthinking violence. But did the flat stare conceal madness?

"Meroens." His knight called from within his chamber. "Come in here a moment."

"Yes, boss."

Perry would know what to do. Or Lady Boss. But where were they when he needed them?

***

No sun. Black. A pale white glow. Why? Look up. The brilliant, brilliant stars, they move, they dance, so many, so many, many, many glinting on the snow, the infinite plain of snow, so far into the distance, without end, no end. A wind. Smell the wind. A cold scent, a live scent, smells warm. Food? Faint. THIS way is stronger. Heat. THIS way heat, not snow, not stars, heat, food maybe.

Hunger. Follow the heat. Run faster, scent stronger, run to - Small black. Moves? Yes. Food, then. Runs? No. Little movements, not running. Injured? Or will it fight, dangerous? Still alive, good food. Smell food. Smell blood.

Where to attack. Weak, little movements, no strength, no danger. See black against the snow, hand, five long thin - No danger. Weak. Approach to attack.

"My boy! Help me!"

Snap.

Fire. The smell of fire.

Hazily, Eiswolf came to. He stood in his chamber, staring at the Sword of Destiny glinting in the firelight. In the doorway, Meroens held out a fresh robe for him. The man looked terrified.

It had happened again.

"Just put that down, please," said Eiswolf. "I think I can about manage to dress myself. Have you checked on Storm?"

Meroens bowed and almost ran out of the chamber.

Eiswolf sat heavily on the bed. What was happening? What was he turning into? Where was Bess? Eiswolf broke into a sweat and almost vomited.

***

"Play the game carefully," said the Glimmer Lord. He sat in the grandest of the guest chambers in the royal tower, as befitted his status. Today was going to be a good day.

"Yes, my lord," said Mifanna.

"Do not let the King see too close an acquaintance between yourself and the Knight. The King and his daughter must not be shamed in public, he could send us into exile, or the earls might riot before we are ready. In either case, we lose control."

"Yes, my Lord." Mifanna curtseyed. "My Lord, if I could trouble you for some gloves? The ladies at court all wear them."

"Yes, my pretty, can't have you looking like a country bumpkin, can we." The Glimmer Lord took out a bag of coins. "Is that enough? Have you any information for me?"

"The Knight seems different. I think he is troubled by nightmares. The big squire no longer sleeps within his chamber and frowns a lot."

"Well, not every man takes kindly to marriage. Especially when it's Princess Ice-knickers."

"Ice what, my Lord?" Mifanna frowned prettily.

The golden gown suited Mifanna's hair very well. Eye-wateringly expensive but worth it, the Glimmer Lord told himself, a suitable frame for the picture that was Mifanna. Her elegant, graceful movements, the sweet husky voice that could also sing like a nightingale, the infectious laughter, all these made Mifanna perfectly irresistible. She was a vision of pure, ideal femininity, obedient, charming, modest, content to worship her knight, with no desires for herself. She made the ladies of the Court look grubby and clumsy.

But in the future, there might be a technical problem.

"When you dally with the Knight, this is pressing of hands and lips only? No further, for remember, you are a lady of noble blood?"

Mifanna flushed. "As you commanded, my Lord."

"Very good. We must maintain our mystery, my lovely Mifanna. Have any of the ladies explained what is to happen when you and the Knight do become as one?"

Mifanna went bright red. "My Lord, I know what passes between a man and a maid."

"Right. Well. Before anything does start to pass, as you put it, I'd be glad of a short conversation first. Nothing to worry about, just a precaution."

Mifanna curtseyed. "As my Lord commands. My Lord, one matter concerns me. The nobles at court have been most gracious. And their ladies. But, my Lord, what about the Princess?"

The Glimmer Lord smiled. "Don't be too obvious with her. You may even become her companion, I gather she has no great taste for our wolf-like friend and sharing the burden of the marriage bed could be welcome to her. In time. So be pleasing, helpful, charming, all you do so well. Above all, be respectful. Now, go forth, my little tyke, and sparkle!" He patted her on the head, she flashed a lovely smile at him, and ran out of his chamber.

Yes, today would be a good day. But one thing puzzled him. At the moment of Eiswolf's greatest triumph, where was that wretched woman Bess?

***

"They say he will become King," said Octa. "Where shall I put these?" He held up the rolls of parchment.

Perry had rented a room in the Eastern Quarter of Cymenshore, a respectable enough district, establishing himself as a scrivener. Himself, not herself: even in a peaceful town like Cymenshore, a lone single female was at risk, and a profession like scrivening, a copyist of legal documents with side lines as a low-level lawyer and archivist, was not open to women. However, scrivening paid considerably more than any woman's work such as laundry or weaving, so Perry went back to a life of deception. But, still feeling responsible for the old man, she had retained Octa as a general servant to fetch and carry. Out of her earnings, she paid for his board and lodging in a modest room downstairs.

"Put them on the window table," said Perry. "Who's going to be a king? Not Richard? Even he's not that big-headed."

A couple of months in Cymenshore had shown Perry the reality of the man she had once loved more than her life. Like most people, Richard of Clifton had his points, but he was not quite as amazing as her younger self had thought. For Perry, this was an unforgivable crime, taking into account all the events since then. The gilt was definitely off the gingerbread.

"I meant the knight, my lady."

"Perry." She was sharp. "I am now and will always be Perry the Scrivener." She was still concentrating on the number of wills and leases she had to copy. "Fourteen, I thought he said twelve. Knight, you say? Which knight?"

"The wolf, my lady? To become King?"

Perry froze. "Oh?" She busied herself with the wills. "Well, that's what he was all about, marry the Princess and get half the Kingdom."

"They say there is one more challenge to come. But they already plan the wedding. A great occasion, Mistress Langly and her sister say they will journey to the City to be in the crowd." Mistress Langly, a widow, was their landlady and a keen royal-watcher."

Perry smiled. "I bet they do. But we have better things to occupy ourselves, Octa."

"Is it true that he is a werewolf? Why would our King marry his daughter to such a creature?" Octa tutted to himself. "That does not befit a royal line. There are dark tales. They say he kills without mercy, and eats raw meat and has dealings with Fairies. This cannot be right for the Kingdom, my lady."

"Not our concern," she said, stiffly. "What else?"

The man held out a small bundle covered in a linen cloth. "I thought you might like these. Fresh, there's a new fancy-baker in town."

Perry sniffed the spicy perfume. "September spirals! I haven't seen those since forever! Where did you get them?"

"Beside the butter-cross. They're from a new woman, from the City. Pretty girl, very black hair."

Marejah. Suddenly, Perry knew. But why was she in Cymenshore? Who paid her Guild licence?

Her old life was crowding in on her. "Thank you, Octa. Maybe I'll introduce myself later. I'd like to hear what's happening up in the City. Maybe. Can you take these copies back to Notary Mark of Podmore, if he wants another set, I can do them tomorrow."

The man left.

Perry stared out of the window.

Eiswolf had won his princess, and a crown. He hadn't needed Perry. Well, of course not. He was a knight, and brave, and bold, and sometimes quite bright. When he wasn't an idiot. She missed him terribly, which is why she thought about him as little as possible. She missed the life, the fun, the jokes, the scrapes, the danger.

But the dark, hateful tales were growing, too. Even in far Cymenshore, men told of Eiswolf the savage, Eiswolf the killer. Stories like Octa's were all over the marketplace.

Perry heard them with a heart like lead. Because... Because they might be true.

She had always recognised a terrible possibility. Eiswolf might really be a creature of night and evil, though he himself did not know. A year after she became Eiswolf's squire, he had transformed to that terrifying, shifting-shape thing with golden eyes set in a sort of triangular mask. This time the change lasted more than a moment, for a couple of minutes, but he seemed to have no memory afterwards. Then, in a skirmish not long after, she had seen him fight in that unconscious, killer state, and it scared her.

Bess told the squire not to worry. She handed Perry a bottle of tincture of valerian, saying a few drops might help. Perry gave it back to her, and demanded the truth.

Bess hesitated, then decided to confide. "He's always had absences."

"It wasn't an absence! God, something was present! Horrible, strange."

"I know, I know." Bess took a deep breath, and grabbed Perry's hand. "I know you're loyal to him, and you're brave. Not many stay by him when they see how he changes. That thing he becomes is real, I've seen it, it's him but not - It's hard to explain but I think he had another shape before he came to me."

She took out a small square blue bottle, and gave it to the squire. "Perry, we must look after him and help him, but if he ever turns into that dreadful thing and doesn't turn back, then I - we - have a responsibility to the people here. He's my boy but if…" She swallowed hard. "Well. I won't let him get like that. I'd rather remember him as he is now."

They never said more. Perry got the message. Love can be hard, and cruel.

But that was long ago, in another city. Perry told herself she had no part in the goings-on at Court, she had no responsibility for her knight any more. Why she had kept the bottle, she could not truly explain.

Only now he was in terrible trouble, and she knew it, and could do nothing. And that broke her heart.

***

The betrothal feast went quite well.

The King's kitchen was adept at celebratory catering by now, turning a hand as easily to herons and peacocks (both stringy, if impressive when roasted and dressed back into their feathers) as the usual boar, venison, pigeon, rabbit and pork. To mark the betrothal, the head cook had let his imagination fly with pastry and marzipan, creating a bower of pink roses enclosing a cage of real white doves for the Princess, and an armoured knight on horseback for Eiswolf, containing an apoplectic falcon. The cook had not really set his mind to what would happen when the feasters broke into his 'subtleties', but actually, the nobles found great sport in watching the falcon take its frustration out on the doves. Anyway, it was the thought that counted.

Eiswolf toasted the earls, they raised their cups to him, and a few nudged their ladies in the ribs as if to remind them of other paths to power. The ambassadors nodded to him, observing with sharp, unsentimental eyes. The Princess –

Well. A large bundle of pink brocade was sitting on a small throne three chairs down, topped off in a sort of architectural arrangement of silver-gold plaits and ringlets, picking at a poached fish with a long silver prong. The gilt mask interfered with any assessment of her mood. He'd have to make the first move. A job for tomorrow.

Then a movement at a lower table caught his eye; a flash of red-gold. Yes. Mifanna chatted prettily with one of the older earls, then she looked up and caught his eye. His heart warmed. There could be a pleasant aspect to a prince's life, perhaps.

But Eiswolf was not the only one to catch that glance. The Glimmer Lord saw, and smiled to himself.

And the Princess? Well, who could tell what she saw or thought, behind her mask?

Then the trumpeters blew a fanfare. The feathers and bits of dove were swept away. The earls expected the King to announce the boundaries of Eiswolf's new principality: but the King had found a way to stall that unpleasant matter. Instead, the black-robed men of

Conclave processed into the Great Hall, headed up by the King's Herald, who bore Kolras' Manifest on a cushion for its final appearance, this time accompanied by a small slip of vellum. They were suitably serious.

The Herald's voice echoed back from the vaulted ceiling, as the hall became deadly silent. "Great King! My lords and earls of this Kingdom! Hear ye all, the final words of the most eminent Kolras, which shall set the fate of this Kingdom!"

"For Kolras, who served all the days of the Hermit King, after giving sage guidance to the Fighting King, and then again under the Splendid King, has left this Kingdom the incomparable legacy of his wisdom. In our time of need, as our enemies surround us, he meditated upon how a King should rule, in humility as well as pride, in peace as well as war, with a gentle heart as well as a strong arm. And so he devised these Seven Tests, for only such a man may become of the Blood Royal. Today, my Lords, we could be in the presence of such a man!"

The nobles in the hall cheered, but Eiswolf seemed fittingly unmoved. Then Meroens, from the bottom end of a lower table, looked at his boss a little more closely. The flat, golden eyes did not look back.

The Herald had only started, however. "In the times of the Fighting King…"

And on for another ten minutes of early modern political history: all of which proved that the King who currently sat at the High Table did indeed have every right to be there, his daughter was legitimate issue of his loins (skipping lightly over her mother's penchant for strapping young lads and ambitious earls) and so the King had every justification to strip down his Kingdom any way he chose. Eiswolf was not the only one with a glazed expression by the end.

"My Lords, the wisdom of Kolras now tells us that our new, young lord must learn the ways of monarchy! He shall do so under the tutelage of our Princess, who shall be his most loving and devoted wife." The bundle of brocade leaned forward a mite. "And the generous and selfless devotion of his father in royalty, our great King!" General cheers. The King smiled and waved vaguely, happily.

The Herald let the hubbub die down. Once again he became deadly serious. "But first, he must undertake the last and, some say, the greatest of the Tests. What this terrible Test is, no man may know but the man who must accomplish it. Sir Eiswolf, please accept this challenge with a heart as pure as the man who devised it."

The Herald bowed, offering the slip of vellum on the cushion to Eiswolf.

Snow. Snow, darkness, the lovely night, the blood-hunt, the hunger –

"Sir Knight?" The Herald whispered as loud as he dared. "Sir Eiswolf?"

Snap.

The hall. Hot. Smell of food, wine. He wore red. A man was holding out a purple cushion. The King's Herald? "Ah, my lord

Herald. So flattered am I by your faith in me, that you take my breath from me! This final challenge …" Nobody frowned, so that had to be it. "I accept this Test with all good grace, and I will stand by its demands."

"Even unto death?" said the Herald, still concerned by that distant expression.

"Whatever this Kingdom demands, I give freely," said Eiswolf.

Which seemed to go down well. He did wonder what he'd agreed to, though.

***

"So, what is it, then?" said the King, back in his private chamber.

"We can't tell you," said the oldest professor.

"Don't be foolish, man," said the Hegemon. "That stuff's for the crowd, not us."

The Conclave looked at each other, and cleared their throats.

"Actually," said the bold, young professor, "we can't."

"Or won't?" said the Hegemon. His voice had an edge.

"Can't," said one of the lawyers. "We don't know. Kolras arranged it so we can't know. He was a very wise man."

"Well, somebody bloody knows!" shouted the Hegemon.

"Only Albert," quavered a young lawyer.

"Who the hell is Albert?" said the King.

"Well, he's a toad."

By slow, painful steps - although not nearly as painful as the King and the Hegemon would have liked to make them - the

Conclave explained that the Manifest contained a list of possible tests, out of which the last was selected. In the presence of representatives of Conclave, Albert the Enchanted One chose the test by making a noise when a blind man pointed at it on the Manifest. An unlettered man then copied out the letter-shapes. (The stable where Albert lived in his bucket, tended by the little groom, had been quite crowded.) Once Albert had declared his choice, no educated man was allowed near the copy. Eiswolf had to be the first to read it.

"Can't you give us a clue?" said the Hegemon.

"I seem to remember a Mountain of Fire," said an old professor. "Or is that another story?"

"Wasn't the Great Morass on the list?" said another. "Ghastly place. Old Kolras had a very perverse sense of humour."

"I don't believe this," muttered the Hegemon. "Is there nothing we can do?"

"Apparently not," said the King. "Get me Black - get the King's Champion. I feel the need of more guards about me tonight."

***

Eiswolf shook off the heavy robe, warming himself by the fire in his chamber. The folded vellum was in his hand. The atmosphere smelt bad.

"Right, boss?" said Meroens. "So where are we off to next?"

"We aren't going anywhere," said Eiswolf. "I do this alone."

"I'm not happy about that. Look, boss, no criticism, I don't think you're well. You're getting that funny look."

"Know your place, squire!" Eiswolf snapped. "Do you dare tell me what to do?"

Meroens was silent, but not for long. His duty as a squire was to tell the truth. "If you go at this and you're not well, you could get killed. Right? Enough round here want you dead. If you ride out on your lonesome, it's like an invitation, right? So at least tell me. So I can watch your back."

But Eiswolf could not tell him. Why had Kolras decided - But then, Kolras had not decided. He had left everything up to the forces of chance, the accidental croaking of a toad. Which seemed a very cavalier way to test the next king of your realm. But then again, no man had ever got this far. Maybe Kolras had not thought it through.

"Before I leave, I would like to meet with the Glimmer Lord once more." Eiswolf meant Mifanna, of course.

"Not his pretty niece?" But all Meroens got for his attempt at humour was a bleak, fearsome stare from his knight, and a grunt. Meroens left to pass on the messages, more concerned than ever.

Eiswolf stared into the fire. This was the final step before he achieved all any knight could hope to gain. This was his reward for years as man at arms, courage on the battlefields, miseries as a poor knight, then, chosen by mere accident, the most extraordinary series of quests in history. This was his revenge on all those who despised him, called him wolf and worse, who had kicked and abused the little boy, had tried to kill the growing lad, who had turned their back on the man. Now he would be their king. And now, the black sky and the endless snow were always at the back of his mind, he straddled two worlds, under the hard stars of the world of ice. The howl of the Snow Wolf, who would one day eat the moon, deafened his mind; and he knew no way back.

***

"So, how did it go?" The Princess was working in her private study, surrounded by maps and treaties.

Chloe shed the wig, outer robes and gloves, putting down the gilded mask.

"He's weird," she announced. "But he kissed me so I suppose it's all official."

"Not on the mouth, I hope." The Princess was attending to the documents on her table. "Here, have a swig of brandy."

"No, a sort of scrape on the cheek. He doesn't shave very close," said Chloe. "I think your father might have noticed. He gave me a very funny look."

"Oh, I'll sort that out. Hardly really needed to be there, after all, so much stuff to attend to with splitting the Kingdom. Feasts take up a lot of time and I have better things to do. As long as 'A Princess' kissed wolfie-thingy, then everyone's happy, right?"

"I'm not so sure," said Chloe.

Jocasta hurried in, looking uncharacteristically concerned. She, too, had been at the feast and had heard worrying news among all the chit-chat. "Your majesty, I would advise you about Sir Eiswolf,"

The Princess snorted, but Jocasta continued. "My Princess, reports from the practice grounds say he is becoming stronger and more ruthless. Much, much stronger."

"Chloe, stop drooping, go and set out the robes for tomorrow. If We are to entertain this knight, We must look the part."

The girl curtseyed and left, gratefully.

"What are you saying?" said the Princess.

Jocasta poured herself a brandy. "He's turning."

"You said werewolves do not exist."

"They don't. I don't know what he is, there's a terrible anger in his eyes, all the men say so, they're afraid to spar with him. I thought he was just another ambitious fool but this is different. Every time he comes back from a quest, he's stronger, if he achieves this one…" Jocasta trailed off, and gulped her drink.

"I see. And you think he will be dangerous to me?"

"I think he's dangerous to the whole world," said Jocasta,

"Then we must move fast," said the Princess. "How is our golden-headed darling?"

Jocasta laughed. "Our pretty Adelbon is getting very exercised about the injustice of your Majesty's forced marriage. He sees himself as your saviour. No! Your hero."

"Good. I wouldn't want him to get cold feet. He will have to kill the wolf, though. Do you think he's up to that?"

"No. No man is. Not in a straight fight. Adelbon's strong but inexperienced. We have to find ways to strengthen his arm, or weaken the wolf's. I'll review our options."

The Princess nodded. "Agreed. Plan E it is. If the wolf could insult him, publicly, that would help. How can we do that?"

"We have a little planning time until the wolf returns from the last quest. Be of good cheer. It's still not impossible that Kolras might do our job for us."

But hope, as the Princess almost reminded her, is never a strategy.

***

Midnight: the fire burned low in the Glimmer Lord's chamber. He waited for Eiswolf calmly, almost happily. He had not intended to spend quite so long on this little scrap of territory, when realms and empires to east and south also needed attention, but it had been very satisfactory to manage matters to his own great plan. The legacy of Kolras had helped, painting the King into a corner, along with his snotty daughter. Eiswolf had been easily seduced, as so many are who have suffered much when young. Offer love to a man without it, give him hope and beauty and romance, promise him power, tell him he is a hero, how easily they fall.

Now, all scenarios were positive. Some were even entertaining. The Glimmer Lord applauded his own genius.

If Eiswolf was sensible tonight, he would come to a most agreeable and profitable conclusion, and rule under Gil's command. If he wasn't, Gil could use Eiswolf's love for Mifanna as a deadly weapon, for faithlessness in a royal marriage meant treachery to the King. And there was always the option of proving the man a werewolf; Gil had seen the flat golden stare at the feast. That would destroy Eiswolf completely, preferably taking Bess with him. Blast Bess! Without her meddling, he would not be in this god-awful, insanitary, draughty castle in this backward world! He could have been sipping a cocktail in the Caribbean, rich and famous. He'd always fancied Antigua.

But Mifanna was a masterstroke. Gil gave himself another pat on the back for that. Maybe he could have used the Princess to trap Eiswolf but she was an arrogant little bundle of self-importance, and setting her up would have taken time, while Mifanna was his creature entirely.

He did wish he knew what the final Test would be. He had no more luck than the King in getting Conclave to spill what they knew: on previous evidence about Kolras, the task would sound big and important and supernatural but probably turn out quite mundane. Eiswolf should get it out of the way fast, surely, the crown was so nearly in his grasp.

Mifanna slipped into the room, a fluttering, perfumed dream in willow-green and gold. "You sent for me, my lord?"

"Our knight wishes to talk to me. I'm sure he will want to bid you farewell in private. Make him regret leaving you, but fire him up to return as victor."

Mifanna smiled charmingly, with a touch of fearfulness, but also desire postponed. Then the expression disappeared. "Like that?"

"Exactly so. When he does come back, assuming he does, we must plan your role at court. Be visible but not conspicuous among the ladies, then by stages…"

"Oh." Mifanna twisted a piece of silk in her hands. "That sounds like a long time."

"We must not be impatient." Then the words struck him. "As if what will be a long time? We have to allow at least a year for a baby."

"Oh. Are we waiting for a baby, then?"

The Glimmer Lord looked carefully at Mifanna, glowing in the firelight. "A baby from the Princess gives him legal right to the whole Kingdom."

"Or say he becomes king anyway," said Mifanna. "Then he can choose a new queen. He could still keep the baby."

But not the mother. She did not say so but the Glimmer Lord did not need her to.

"So that's the idea? Queen Mifanna?" He almost laughed. "King Eiswolf and Queen Mifanna. What a lovely royal pairing that will be!" And then he did laugh.

Mifanna went bright red. "So what's wrong with that! Nobody needs her, she's like a wax seal on a document! And when the old man's out of the way…" Mifanna caught the Glimmer Lord's expression, and became more respectful. "As queen, I would make sure the wolf keeps to your Lordship's plans. The Princess might become difficult. My way is easier."

"Hm. Up to a point, lovely butterfly." But then they were interrupted by a knock at the door: a servant, announcing a visitor. Eiswolf entered the room.

He seemed bigger. Maybe the shadows from the fire across the dark chamber, or the folds of his black velvet court robe made him seem broader, maybe the glint of the Sword by his side reminded them both that this man had killed and killed again to become the hero who would soon be a king. Maybe he simply had the confidence of a man within a breath of his heart's desire.

"My lord." The Glimmer Lord bowed. Mifanna curtseyed.

"I may not come back." Eiswolf spoke clearly but quietly to a spot above the Glimmer Lord's head. "I have read the requirements of the last quest. This is a difficult task. Many would seek to stop me if they knew what I know. If I succeed, you may see by the blood on my Sword when I return. If I fail, I shall die there, neither I nor the Sword will be seen again. I have also sent this message to the Conclave. If I succeed, I shall return as Prince Royal and shall marry the Princess. I will then ask you, my lord, to be a counsellor in the Prince's Chamber, which I shall establish for the rule of my lands. My court will be in Wardur. You will be given houses and estates there. You, my lady Mifanna, will remain here and be lodged with the Weeping Nuns. No scandal will attach to your name."

"But my love!" Mifanna dashed forward, her face streaked with tears. "How can I live without you?"

"No scandal." There was a rough edge to Eiswolf's voice. "You will be a dutiful and respectful noblewoman of this Court, until such time as my Princess requires a new lady in waiting. She will then send for you. That is all I can offer."

The Glimmer Lord bowed. "You have been more than generous, my Lord."

Mifanna looked stricken. "How can I live without your love? My darling!" She ran forward and threw her arms about the knight, weeping into his broad chest. For a moment he almost weakened, his face twisted in pain.

"Never doubt my love!" he whispered. "My lord, keep her safe! I entrust you with the most precious thing in the world, will you give me your word."

"You have it, my lord." The Glimmer Lord bowed as if Eiswolf were already a king.

Then the knight kissed Mifanna tenderly on the brow, and swept out into the darkness, towards his destiny.

As soon as they were quite sure they would not be heard, Mifanna and the Glimmer Lord danced a little jig around the chamber.

"Slam-dunk, Queen Mifanna!" yelled the lord. "High-five!" He raised his hand in the air, palm outward. Mifanna had no clue what that was, he often spoke in strange words, but his meaning was clear. She grinned, and slapped his palm.

He winced. "Easy there, soldier, remember the Madame Butterfly act. Maybe you're right. The sooner we get you to be Queen, the better."

Before various things started happening that might be hard to explain.

***

The road to the Crystal Catacombs was long, and lonely. The November winds swept the remaining leaves across the muddy roads, the icy rain drove sideways through cloak and jerkin, even through chain-mail. When he set out, Eiswolf rode by day, as did most travellers, because a forest at night is a playground for bears, and wolves, and bandits. Although Eiswolf could defend himself, why waste the energy. His travelling hours grew short as the shrinking days of autumn turned to winter.

He rode north-east, across barren plains and into great fenlands where the only safe path was marked by white stones; on either side the morass sighed and breathed the stench of decay; small green flames flickered in the darkness. Then through a landscape of streams and gravel valleys, pretty in the summer but chill and echoing in winter, a land without settlements, the hills casting their cold black shadows where the sun could not rise above them.

He did not announce who he was: he paid his way, like any travelling man. He had been followed on the first few days by squires from the court, but as soon as they saw he took the road north-east, they fell back, because only one good trail went that way, with a limited choice of destination. They assumed he travelled to the most dangerous one: and they were right.

The challenge was simple enough; deceptively so. When his mind wandered to the black skies and the snowfields, it felt easy. He knew that Bess and Perry would have talked him through, pointed out the problems and potential pitfalls, but they were not here. In the day, he tried not to think of them, because he did miss them… No! A sign of weakness. What need did a true knight have of an old witch and an eccentric squire? Under the black sky, he did not even remember them.

The Quest was everything now, the reward nothing, meaningless. He did not quest for a crown, or the Princess, or for power, or fame, or a place in history. He quested because that was what he was.

His dream-journeys into the land of snow and black nights were becoming more frequent, guided by an instinct, not a thought, driving him on like hunger, like sex, like the beat of his heart, the stench of fear, the sound of tearing flesh and the scream of terrified prey. No-one to bring him out of those places, no friend to lay a hand on his shoulder and tell him to rest, no-one to bring him back to Eiswolf of the Kingdom again.

Now he began to travel by night as well, under the huge moon which hung yellow and low, his horse frightened and exhausted from lack of rest, he not eating, not sleeping, not thinking, driven on, beyond the Tests, beyond the quest. If he felt the Sword of Destiny on his hip, he did not always know what weighed so much: he might look at the Ring of Power, and wonder why he had it. He melded into the brilliant black sky, the endless snow, riding north-east, ever north-east, towards the pale winter sun, which weakened and died a little every day.

Then one morning, under a red-streaked dawn, he arrived.

His horse stopped. Storm had no more energy. The animal neighed and stumbled. Eiswolf knew he had to dismount before the horse collapsed under him. They were at the base of a cliff; he had been travelling along a gorge for two days, the crags above becoming higher and higher. Now, he saw a crack in the rock, as tall as a palace gate. On the side of the cliff, in the old writing, Eiswolf could make out a rough inscription: 'Sacred. Enter with a pure heart or not at all."

He knew he needed all the help he could get. The true Ring of Power was on a chain around his neck, because he had been fearful of wearing it. But now, he put it on.

The crack led to a dark, airless passage. Eiswolf needed light: he grabbed at bushes from the side of the gorge, cutting a hank from Storm's tail with the Sword of Destiny, winding the hair around the branches as tinder for his flint. He held the burning torch in his left hand, the Sword of Destiny in his right.

The passage was narrow, natural in origin but squared off as it twisted through the rock. Once out of reach of daylight, he noticed glittering, tiny crystals bouncing back the light from the torch, like little, faint stars. He walked on. The crystals became larger; odd, sharp, branch-like growths hung down from the ceiling, white and glistening; others, fatter, trunk-like, grew up through the path. When he kicked them, they rang like metal.

Ahead, Eiswolf could see light, dim, diffuse, not the flame from his torch. This had to be the Crystal Catacombs. By now, Eiswolf had no idea where he was, but a scent reached him through the dark, guiding him on, warm, musky. White calcite crystals glittered from wall and roof, faintly illuminated by a small sink-hole high up above. He reached a cavern. At one side was a white slab, roughly rectangular.

And on the slab was a knight, his armour burnished black from helmet to boot, the breastplate and greaves inlaid with enamel patterns in bright blue. A long sword lay down his body, the hilt on his chest in both hands, the blade stretching to his feet. A round shield rested at his feet.

He smelt alive. He was breathing.

The conscious part of Eiswolf recognised the legendary resting place of Sir Devlas, the original owner of the Sword of Destiny. But that man had lived centuries ago.

Sir Devlas had brought the Kingdom together, serving the Tall King through civil factions and challenges from foreign realms. He had fought fire-drakes, and serpents, and sorceresses, and creeping plagues, and the treachery of mistresses and the falsehoods of unworthy earls. He had been defeated only by enchantment, but not wholly: for his life was preserved in sleep, against the day when he should be called forth in the Kingdom's hour of need.

Eiswolf looked at the man more closely. On the breast-plate, sectioned across his chest into bands in the ancient fashion, he could make out engraving in blue enamel in the old letters.

"D-E-W-I-G-L-A-S".

As Eiswolf spoke out the name, the man seemed to twitch in his sleep.

All Eiswolf had to do now, was kill him. And then Eiswolf would become invincible.

Sir Devlas was the greatest hero of the Kingdom, the ultimate guardian, a legendary protector of the poor and weak. He had never turned his hand against another man in rage or meanness: he had never been known to turn his hand against a woman at all. He fought fair, so he fought with one hand behind his back.

And he was asleep, so killing him would be easy.

If you were a mere assassin.

Eiswolf held up the Sword of Destiny, then stopped.

So many dead already. The knights at the Tourney, like that boy Sir Dauntless, or fighting the dragon, like that poor devil Sir Frithwald. The battle for the Sword itself. So many dead because of the Tests of Kolras, not just the eleven knights, but all those that they had killed. Those men, and women and children, died not because of war, or threat, or invasion, but a kind of vanity. The vanity that drove a man to seek power no matter what, who did not care who died because if they got in his way, they were without value. A man who did not recognise the humanity of others. So many dead. And he had killed so many.

What was one more. But Sir Devlas had done him no harm. And to kill a sleeping man was the act of a coward.

"I'm here," he told himself. "This is the final step. This is the Quest. This is my destiny." He raised the Sword again.

The black night swirled above him, the hard, sharp white stars like knives, the cold drift of snow across the land, the blood, the hunger, the imperative. Kill. He looked down. The body slept at his feet. It needed to be killed. He felt the Sword in his hand, raising the steel blade, which glinted under the whirling stars, glittering across the clear black sky like a new galaxy, bewitching him with beauty, saying one word. Kill. Kill.

Kill.

13: Return of the Knight

"He's coming back," said Black Al. "He bears a bloody blade, I think we must assume that he has been successful. Are you well, sir?"

No, he was not. The Hegemon went pale, sweat started to pour from his hands. "I must see the King." But first he had to have another difficult conversation.

***

"He's coming back," said Jocasta.

The Princess, in her undress Southron-style pyjamas and without her wig, was in her side-study at her table of charts and treaties. She sighed. "Drat, flip and blow. You know, I don't think Kolras was as devious as everyone makes out."

"You have to allow the knight to pay court. The wedding is set for the turn of the year, you can't not, it looks odd, might make people suspicious."

"Really," said the Princess. "We'd better get weaving on Plan E, then." She rearranged a couple of the leases. "Adelbon to defend my honour and kill wolfie, with a little help from us. Any more thoughts?"

"I still think the best option is the 'other woman' ploy. That insults you and the royal line. It's common knowledge that he has been kind to Mifanna, Lady of the Black Fells. He saved her life, I believe."

"Remind me?"

"Red-haired girl, young, came to court with the Glimmer Lord, her uncle."

"Oh, her," said the Princess. "The one with big wrists. What, is he sweet on her?"

"What do you mean, big wrists?" Jocasta was genuinely puzzled.

"Big feet, too." Very little escaped the Princess about the ladies of her court. "Do you think there's enough for a rumour?"

"Yes, I think we can build a rumour."

"Then let's get busy." The Princess examined a lease. "Now, where on earth is Little Pootly, and do I want it or can Daddy have it?"

***

The King was also in his private chamber, pondering with Black Al, his Champion. "So what do we really know about this Adelbon chap?"

"Younger son of one of the northern earls, not a man who's been to court much, I don't think they have the money."

"So why, suddenly, can he turn up with a circus troupe of pages and ladies? That armour won't have been cheap, either. Or the horse."

"He has a backer," said Black Al. "He saved a rich merchant from robbers last winter and the man put his fortune at the boy's disposal."

"H'm. How uncommonly generous of him." The King was playing with the Ring of Power.

"Is it true about that ring?" said Black Al. "Can you feel the power?"

"No. For the very good reason that this is not the real Ring of Power."

"What?"

The King smiled, and made the red flash from the ruby play over the walls. "You go out and risk your life not once, but several times, on the promise of a kingdom. You are, at very least, ambitious. You win the means of becoming a mighty ruler. The Ring. You then give it away to a nice old buffer, because you promised to. Where is the logical flaw in that, my dear Al?"

"Oh." Al had assumed a knight would always be trammelled by the conventions of chivalry.

"Anyway, the backer. Is this merchant rich enough to support young Adelbon?"

"Well, he was. I gather he had a stroke of fortune just before."

"Ah. Just before he was robbed. Isn't that extraordinary. Fate gives, and Fate takes away. When was this, exactly?"

"About a year ago. Before the turn of the year, anyway."

Which was about when the Princess had persuaded the King to sell one of her manors so that she could finance improvement works on a distant estate in the far east. So distant, that the King had no way of finding out whether any money had been spent at all. "And who is this merchant?"

"Jannick of Netley, your Majesty."

"Ah. I believe we have met." A weasel-eyed man, a Cymenshore trader, who looked at margin first and proprieties later —

In a way, he was proud of his daughter. An apt pupil. He would let her little gambit run a while longer. Who knew what the girl might have stumbled on.

"Let's invite young Adelbon in for a chat. Interesting chap. Certainly looks the part, eh?" And the King laughed, punching Black Al in the shoulder.

***

"I don't want to do this, Bess," said the Hegemon.

In the stinking darkness, something moved.

"You must help me, Bess. He's coming back. He's dangerous, you know that. Tell me what he is."

The heap of rags quivered. "I don't know."

"How can I believe you? You protected him. You nursed him. You know him."

He crouched down beside her in the filthy straw, stroking her hair. She shuddered but did not move away.

"He's a danger, Bess. I won't have that. He's a danger to the Kingdom, and my Princess. You know that, too."

She mustered every molecule of strength she had left. Her mouth was as dry as leather; but her resolution remained. She took a huge, impossible gamble. "Bevis, think! For the sake of Marejah, think what you are doing!"

He sprang back, as if stung by a wasp. "I can kill you!"

"I know. But that is not the man Marejah loves."

Stillness. Either he would stamp her to death here and now. Or maybe, she could get though to him –

She heard him move, a shuffle of feet, perhaps. "This Kingdom is under threat. You have information I need. I'm sorry, Bess. My personal feelings don't count."

"But they should," whispered Bess. "They should. Or what are you fighting for?"

He marched out. The door slammed on the lightless cell. "They should," she murmured.

***

Mifanna, resplendent in gold and blue, perused a drawing; she had ordered an artist to create an emblem for her. The existing flag of the Black Fells was white divided by a black stripe, very boring compared to the Princess' white rose, or the Snow Wolf, now interpreted by an artist who was a) competent and b) had actually seen a wolf.

"So you see," she explained to the Glimmer Lord, "I am a beautiful butterfly, as you have so often called me, but with a sting in my tail." The creature in the drawing did indeed have a stinger, and what might be interpreted as a crown. "Oh, and my lord, I think I should be more generous at Court."

"Indeed so, Mifanna? But my fortune is not inexhaustible." Or at least, not sufficient to pay for the cohorts of troubadours and pages that Mifanna seemed to have employed; but then, not all the wealth in all the realms was enough for that.

"Oh, my Lord! How shall I make myself respected at Court, if I am kept a mere beggar!" She pouted.

"Now you know that doesn't work on me. Draw in your horns, my pretty butterfly. Concentrate on the return of your Knight."

"He will see me, and die of love for me!" Mifanna twirled in her gorgeous dress.

"I hope not," said the Lord. "Or we'll have to start this whole charade all over again."

That was a thought, though. When Eiswolf died, who next? What did he really know about the boy Adelbon?

***

Eiswolf rode through the gates of the City to a kind of stunned silence. Before him he bore the Sword, streaked with the red-brown of old blood. He was weary and shabby with travel, his face haggard and fierce. The return journey had taken two weeks, and he had not rested on his way. He rode up to the Palace into the courtyard, then dismounted from the exhausted Storm.

"Where is the King!" he yelled. "Bring me the Conclave!"

The black-clad scholars ran out into the yard, followed by the Hegemon.

"Here!" yelled Eiswolf, waving the Sword in the bright winter air. "Here is proof! Take this to the King, for I have done all that Kolras demanded. I claim my reward! And let no man deny me." He glared at the Conclave. They drew back in fear as if his glance burned.

The Hegemon came forward quietly. "Let me take the Sword. You are our champion, Sir Eiswolf. All is prepared for your victory."

The knight swayed, near collapse, but steadied himself with the scabbard from the Sword. "Tell the King that I demand audience. You, Hegemon. Let your mistress know that her husband comes to claim her."

The Hegemon bowed, then walked carefully back to the royal tower. Meroens, who had joined the crowd in the yard, ran to support his knight: but Eiswolf looked at him as if he did not recognise him, and pushed him away. Two barons came to support the knight to his chamber instead.

***

"Dear me," said the King. "And whose blood is it?"

The oldest professor, tears on his cheeks, struggled to talk. "Sir Devlas. That animal has killed the bravest, noblest knight this Kingdom has ever known! If I had realised, if they'd let me look at the Manifest, if they'd asked me, Kolras cannot have meant this!"

"Dear me," said the King. "So Sir Devlas won't be galloping to our side in our moment of greatest need, then." He put the Sword down on a table.

"The Sword has been bathed in the blood of virtue!" The old academic quavered. "You know what that means!"

"This is a tragedy!" The younger lawyer spluttered. "This creature of blood and cruelty, he cannot become our King!"

"I'm afraid I must disagree," said the King. "He can. And, under the laws of the Seven Tests, he will. Gentlemen, I have a request. Can you make absolutely sure that all the Tests were undertaken absolutely as Kolras demanded, and that the results are not in doubt?"

But so frightened were the academics, he could not be sure they had taken his heavy hint. They scurried out, muttering and twitching, but the Hegemon remained behind.

"You can't do this, sire," he said. "You can't let this go on."

"Oh, Bevis, of course I can. Look, if he marries the Princess, and we hear the patter of tiny paws in a year, well, then the Kingdom has an heir. And if, say, an accident happens to our wolf lord, men of battle don't make old bones, then the Princess becomes regent under my guidance, the Kingdom would still be as one until the pup grows up and inherits. Or whatever."

"But your daughter, Sire! Can you condemn her to such degradation?"

The King swivelled round to face his friend, his colleague, his subject. "None of your business, Bevis. The baby is the important thing."

"Babes do not always live, your Majesty! And that creature is hard to kill! He could be on his throne for years!"

"A baby." The King became ruminative. "You know, once the Princess is away from court… Maybe I was too quick to dismiss the obvious. It is not completely impossible that I should marry, Bevis."

"What!" The Hegemon could not believe his ears.

"Why not. I may have a son myself. Say she doesn't produce an heir, and she, well, dies, the wolf has no claim on my half of the Kingdom. Always an option."

"Sire!" The Hegemon almost exploded. "You cannot mean that! Kill your daughter?"

"Now, Bevis - "

But the man was beside himself. "An heir? You're too old! You've left it too late!"

"What!"

"Sire, I will not allow it! You are fifty! A son won't be ready for the throne until you're seventy! Do you really think the earls will settle for a dribbling old fool and a boy? This is madness! You must make the Kingdom over now, to a man you can trust, who loves - who loves this land as much as you do, who loves your daughter!" He tailed away, betrayed by his tears.

"I see." The King's eyes were blue ice. "Or what, Hegemon? Do you think the men who promised to follow you will come through? I fear you will be disappointed." He walked to the door and called to the guard. He turned back to the weeping Hegemon. "I thought I knew you better than that. Bevis, the price I pay to rule this Kingdom is vast, but I pay it. A King has neither friends nor family. A King must assume that all advice, however well-meant, is tainted, and that all allegiance is temporary. I wear mail under this robe, always have. I do whatever this Kingdom requires, and no individual can be more important than its fate. I hope you understand. Guards, take this man away." He paused. "And I suppose you'd better return that sword to its owner. He will be asking for it."

***

The atmosphere at Court was odd, but not because of the absence of the Hegemon. He had been called to a distant town for a legal dispute, they said. Few missed him: he was hardly a star in the social firmament.

No, the oddness was the Princess and Sir Eiswolf, and their very strange, long-distance, bloodless courtship. Everything happened in public, graciously, elegantly; notes were passed, gifts were exchanged and circulated among the cognoscenti for comment. Toasts were made at feasts: the Princess even danced a few steps with her husband to be (well, Eiswolf guided a masked bundle of brocade around the floor for a few seconds. She had changed her perfume to jasmine, and he also reconsidered his judgement of her as a natural blonde: the eyebrow behind the mask was definitely dark.)

So far, so good, the ambassadors sent their reports to their rulers. But other currents ran below the glittering surface; the Princess was developing Adelbon's position as a potential prince, while Mifanna was making sure of her victory over Eiswolf.

And eventually, the lines crossed. The Princess discovered Mifanna entangled around Eiswolf in a quiet corner during a feast, and showed her displeasure. Oh, did this ever displease her. One hundred decibels of shrieking's worth. The whole court could be in no doubt that she felt slighted.

Eiswolf discovered that the Princess had given Adelbon a fiery new stallion, a pure-bred horse from the palace stables. The silly young twit flaunted the beast in Eiswolf's face in the exercise-yard. He watched the boy do his jousting exercises, and growled.

The Princess started to cold-shoulder Mifanna in public, saying the little ginger tart from nowhere was far too disrespectful: the ribbons alone on one dress had cost more than the Princess' best robes. And because the Princess was being such a bitch, naturally Eiswolf took Mifanna's side very satisfactorily, pleading with the Princess in person to be more understanding of a young girl who had been through so much: which was the chatter of the Court within the hour. He promised Mifanna he would protect her, no matter how high-born her enemies.

All very entertaining to those who were not involved, but the Glimmer Lord was getting worried. There was definitely something up with Eiswolf. He was in Mifanna's grip but seemed increasingly distant and odd. The Princess was picking fights with Mifanna for no good reason, as if creating a feud, but Mifanna was being insanely reckless, while the Adelbon alternative was not ready for deployment.

The Glimmer Lord had set his considerable mind to working on Adelbon. The boy looked good and made the right noises, and was pleasingly suggestible, altogether a much more amenable option than Eiswolf. Adelbon was flattered by the Princess' attention, but seemed clueless about what to do about it. The Glimmer Lord started to imply that Adelbon should take the advice of an older man, an experienced courtier and diplomat, and he was willing to be that mentor. Adelbon had begun to listen. Trust was growing, but not yet absolute: not the surrender that Gil wanted.

And then one night, Mifanna came to the Glimmer Lord in a temper. "She insulted me and Eiswolf did nothing!" she announced. "He told me to grow up! He should slap her silly face for her! Oh, my Lord, please, let's get rid of the Princess and put Eiswolf on the throne! All the lords would follow him, you know they would!"

"Patience, Mifanna. It's not that easy."

"Yes it is!" she yelled. "Why are you so scared, you're a sorcerer, you can do it! I've seen your books, you've got poison and black magic, you're the same as that Jocasta woman!" Then she was very silly. "I could tell people things."

***

Meroens made shift to be useful in the armoury. He was no longer Eiswolf's official squire. As a prince, Eiswolf had no need of squires as such: he had a household of servants and lesser nobles to see to his needs. So Meroens, tough, experienced, and a good sparring-partner, became a fixture in the exercise yard and the training arenas, a reliable man around the junior knights. And he, too, paid special attention to Adelbon.

The boy was vain, and prone to make errors because of that. He over-estimated his stretch, his strength, or his endurance. Meroens and a couple of the other old-timers made sure he did not get away with too much. He was young, tall and strong, all huge advantages. If he added skills as well, he might be unstoppable.

Ladies of the court came to watch him at practice, including Chloe, Iris, Dorcas and Hebe, and Jocasta. Once or twice the Princess herself had come, joining in the genteel applause when the boy won a bout.

Meroens was helping the Armourer polish the endless rows of armour and weapons in the equipment shed. "You know, he's not a patch on the wolf. He really isn't. He's pretty to look at, all the moves come straight out of one of your books." He gestured at the Armourer's lavishly illustrated fechtbuch. "But he doesn't really know why he does half of it. Now Eiswolf, he knows before he goes in what he expects to come out."

"When he's in his right mind," muttered the Armourer. "Did you see what he did to poor old Beltrap last week?"

Meroens put down his polishing. "I heard that was an accident."

"You heard wrong. Look, I know you're loyal and all that, but Beltrap's lying up in the hospital with the nuns. God knows if he'll ever come out. I saw him. Your man went for the death."

Meroens fell silent. The man who had returned from killing Sir Devlas was different.

"I still don't think he's like that," he said, after a while. "His old mother the Witch could sort him out, heart like a lion, she has. He's not like that."

But both he and the Armourer knew that men could change.

***

The Glimmer Lord had decided: now was the time.

An accidental meeting would be more to the point than another discussion arranged through servants, which therefore became general knowledge. So he bumped into Eiswolf in one of the Palace cloisters.

"My lord, such a pleasure! I hear much of you from Mifanna!" He played the fond uncle for all he was worth.

But the Glimmer Lord was not designed by nature to register warm-hearted affection, even if he had felt it. Eiswolf, in his strange state between the stark black sky and the cold shade of the echoing cloister, smelled his uncertainty and his fear.

The Lord looked at Eiswolf's hand, and a sudden chill went over him. "Ah, sir, I see you wear a ring of the Fairy style." No response. No flush, to show that the true Ring of Power had been recognised. Which was not the gewgaw in the King's treasury.

The Glimmer Lord forced himself to go on. "Fairies. Interesting people. Not of this world, they say."

No response. Nothing.

"Do they," said Eiswolf.

"Ah," said the Glimmer Lord. "I hope my niece is good company? I know you give her much favour, I thank you for that." No response. "Anyway, you have greater matters to hand. We all await the naming of the day of your accession. And of course, your marriage."

Not a shiver. The Glimmer Lord had pressed every button he could think of, but the man might as well be made of stone. Had Gil lost his own power? Had it been taken, with the Ring?

"We have already talked of what comes next," said Eiswolf. "But know that my actions will be governed by the needs of my realm."

"You have given thought to your court in Wardur, my Lord?" Back to the strategy: like, when will you announce your official mistress, maybe?

"Thought, yes," said Eiswolf."

"I hope you have relented, and that my poor niece may adorn your court. Her trust is in you, my lord. She is a most passionate and devoted creature, her heart is given for life."

What do you know of passion, thought Eiswolf.

Because the man's mind was laid bare.

Since wearing the Ring, Eiswolf knew that nearly everyone who approached him, did so because they believed he had power. Their souls were naked. The ring stripped away all the subterfuges and disguises, leaving only that ugly hunger. He had power, they wanted some, and they would do anything to get it. This was one reason for his peculiarly distant manner.

And then, Mifanna. Finally, oh so reluctantly, even he had to face reality. The lovely, frightened girl was no more than a spiteful court lady, demanding and foolish. Her pretty ways were settling into an unpleasantly predictable pattern: Mifanna seemed determined to drive him into conflict with the Princess. The girl tried to bend him to her will as if he were a horse to be broken, to make him show more favour to her than the woman he was to marry. And she no longer seemed to care who saw it.

If she had been acting alone, maybe that's where Eiswolf's considerations would have stopped: with a silly girl. But now, faced with this crafty, cunning man and his naked ambition, even Eiswolf could no longer ignore the truth.

Or the game that Mifanna and her uncle played: the royal mistress, and the power behind the throne. It would not be the first time a kingdom had been stolen that way.

Well, not his kingdom.

"I make my own decisions, my lord," said Eiswolf. "Tell your - niece - that as the old saying goes, she should be careful of trusting princes."

Eiswolf turned to walk away. The Glimmer Lord was speechless. In a second, his world had crashed.

Game over? Already? The Glimmer Lord swore to himself. No, impossible, not game over. A blip, nothing! In the real world, what had happened? Had that silly tart Mifanna pushed too far? He seized Eiswolf's sleeve.

"I fear my niece lets her enthusiasm outrun her sense."

"Oh, I doubt that, my Lord. You share too much blood."

There, there, the golden flicker in the eyes. The Glimmer Lord held the sleeve a little tighter.

"I am ever your lordship's servant, I wish only to please…"

"Unhand me, leech!" Eiswolf yelled. The cloister caught his rage and repeated it on the stones. "Take yourself and your whore out of my sight! By God, if you come near me again, I'll run you through!"

He strode away towards the King's Chamber. His rage boiled inside, love deceived, power under threat, the creature under the black sky and the unmerciful stars. He raised his head and roared, the unearthly sound echoing through the cloister's columns. All who heard it, shivered.

***

"Is there anything we can do?" said the King, pale and unnerved.

Previously, Eiswolf had seemed well-mannered and quite civilised, but his last meeting had not been like that. Eiswolf stood over the maps and demanded (Demanded!) some of the richest lands in the Kingdom, then told (Told!) the King that the princely court would be in Wardur, a huge castle built for battle, not display. Then Eiswolf growled that the Kingdom must pay him and his army if they wanted his backing, or face unpleasant consequences, Oh, and he wanted privileged status at Cymenshore. He would not pay port dues to the Kingdom. Or there would be trouble.

And then, with another floor-shaking snarl, he walked out.

"Alas," said the oldest professor. "Must we allow such a creature…"

"Gentlemen, I made an error," announced the King. "No, no," for Conclave went into a flurry of loyal denials. "I allowed my respect for Kolras to blind me. Is there nothing in Kolras? What happens if you get the right result but the wrong man?"

"He has the Sword," said a lawyer.

"He is a mighty fighter," said another.

"Tell me something I don't know!" yelled the King. "Sorry. Sorry. This is getting to me."

"He is protected," said the oldest professor, holding up a book. "The Sword has been bathed in the blood of virtue, no man may overcome him, by fair means or foul."

"H'm." A sharp-eyed young lawyer grunted. "Let me look at that? H'm. I might just have spotted wiggle-room."

The King exploded. "I don't care if you've spotted the seven-domed palace of the Genie of the East, find me a way!"

***

The ploy had failed. Even if Mifanna got the wolf back under her spell, it would be risky to assume this was permanent.

The Glimmer Lord's next candidate had to be in place, fast. Fortunately, Adelbon was coming along nicely. News of Eiswolf's noisy attack had spread; an hour ago the boy actually came to the Glimmer Lord to see if he was all right. Adelbon had practically offered his sword, should the Lord need a defender. Gil politely waved that away, but allowed an expression of deep concern to flicker across his face. He explained that he was now worried that Conclave's interpretations of wise Kolras might have led them to the wrong conclusion, for alas, the Kingdom, and the Princess, would be the sufferers.

The boy went red, and swore on his sword to defend the Kingdom and the King and Princess from any harm, supernatural or not.

"Wisely said, young man." The Glimmer Lord gave him a sweet, sad smile. "You may yet be called upon to fulfil a greater destiny. Let me meditate with my books, and confer with men of wisdom. Prepare yourself for death, Adelbon, but also for glory!"

Cooking nicely, in other words.

**

Mifanna was in her chamber, and bored, and therefore tetchy. As the Glimmer Lord had shut his purse to her for the moment, she was not surrounded by adoring troubadours and cooing ladies. So she took it out on the dressmaker.

"No, you idiot! Tighter! I must have a smaller waist!"

The dressmaker was equally exasperated. "My lady, how can I fit you if you will not remove your shift, or at least wear a lighter one?"

"Hold your tongue!" shrieked Mifanna. "This makes me look fat! I will not be a laughing stock!" Now for her newest threat. "Shall I send my protector, Sir Eiswolf, to deal with you?"

The woman shivered involuntarily. "No, my lady. Please, breathe in?"

A few minutes later, the woman left, with many apologies and scared for her life. A satisfactory result all round for Mifanna. She was treated like royalty already, so she took every opportunity to behave in an unpleasantly regal manner. The progression to an actual crown should be very smooth indeed.

"My lady, my lord Eiswolf wishes to speak with you." The page bowed.

She waved graciously and the boy went. Right, into Operation Butterfly. Mifanna started to breath in short gasps to make her skin flush, carefully arranging herself in a frail but determined pose, like a lily on a long stalk. She disentangled one red-gold curl to fall negligently across her white neck, finding a spot where a shaft of sunlight from the window fell across her hair, but washed more delicately over her face.

"You may enter, my lord," she cooed.

Eiswolf filled the doorway. Time for the butterfly to flutter.

"My lord! My lord, how many centuries since we last met! I have counted every second!" She danced up to him and tried to embrace him, her heady exotic scent enveloped him - He stepped back.

"Is my lord displeased? How may I cheer your spirits?"

He half-snarled. "You make yourself notorious."

"My Lord?" Mifanna looked up in hurt, green-eyed innocence.

Dark-faced, he came into the room and pulled her over to the window. "Mifanna, you are young, I have given you more licence than I should. My association with you is a matter of gossip, that you rule me through my animal desires." He swallowed hard, for the next part. "That is not fitting for a prince. Mifanna, this must end."

She was genuinely stunned. For once, she did not have to act.

He stared into her face, her eyes, trying to find the ideal girl who had caught at his heart, his soul, every longing in his body and mind. Where was she?

He had told himself she grew wilful because of the influence of court, the unfamiliar surroundings. With maturity she would calm down. Then came the shouting matches with the Princess, her demands, her lies, her petty, vindictive nature, beating servants, throwing threats and insults –

But she had been the one bright light in his life, she was why he wanted to live at all –

Yet again, the truth plunged a dagger into his heart. The longer he looked down into her freckled face, the clearer reality became. The Ring of Power could not be denied. This was the real Mifanna, a spiteful, vicious, reckless creature. Vulnerable? Or conceited and aggressive? Mysterious? An over-rated idea. Pretty in a troubadour's story, highly undesirable in reality. They had met by accident, and accident is no way to plan a prince's life.

She looked up at him, and his love-light had gone. She had lost him. She started to cry.

"My lord, how can I live without you? How can I please you, only tell me! If I have been foolish!" She threw herself to her knees, "I swear to make myself worthy of you! Please, my Lord!" And, weeping, she tried to embrace his feet.

He took a step back, his legs were lead and his body was melting like ice before a fire. "No, Mifanna. This is at an end. I shall see that you are provided for. But you must leave this court, nor must you ever come to Wardur. This is the regret of my life." His voice was breaking. "Go and get a fine rich husband, and be happy."

Eiswolf turned away from her, because he could feel himself weaken, for one last kiss, one last embrace, one more day… This could not be. So he set his face like stone, and walked out of the chamber.

Mifanna stayed on her knees until she heard his footsteps recede down the stone corridor. Well, that was no good. She wondered what had triggered the confrontation: nothing from her, surely.

Then she heard a slight movement by the door.

The Glimmer Lord appeared. "Well, Mifanna, we have a disaster."

"How did you know?"

"I had an uncomfortable conversation with our friend. Hard to manage, isn't he."

"Not impossible," said Mifanna. "I have love potions. It's a temporary setback."

The Glimmer Lord went to the window: he could see the courtyard beneath. "How are you getting on with Adelbon, by the way?"

Mifanna sniffed. "He's a pompous brat. He won't dance and he knows nothing of flirting, I've tried telling him about my terrible past but he's really not good at listening. He ignored me totally at the feast yesterday. Look, we can manage the wolf, I know we can. Give me a couple of days. He was crying when he left here, wasn't he?"

"Let me think deep thoughts, dear Mifanna. By the way, be careful how you let sunlight shine on your cheek. Your upper lip?"

"Oh." And Mifanna leapt back into the shade.

***

"Wiggle-room," said the King. "You interest me strangely."

He had recalled Black Al and those members of Conclave who had not been reduced to utter panic. They were led by the sharp-eyed young lawyer who, with his team of students and juniors, had spent a torrid three hours going through the data.

"Your Majesty, this has been a tough one," started the lawyer.

"It will get a damn sight tougher for all of us if you don't find a solution," said the King. "I gather he has threatened the Glimmer Lord, my chief councillor. None of us can feel safe."

"Indeed," said the lawyer. "Well, Kolras and the texts are quite clear. The Sword, once bathed in the blood of virtue, protects him from attack by any man of woman born."

The King's eyes lit up. "And just what exactly do they mean by 'born'?"

"Surgical removal from the mother is included," said an older lawyer. "We checked. Only if the man was created without a woman can you get round that one."

None of them could think, at that moment, of a knight who had come out of an egg.

"But this is all swords, isn't it? What about poison?" said the King. "That peculiar woman Jocasta is supposed to be good at that."

"Apparently he is immune to the strongest poisons. We did ask her," said a professor.

"Falling from a horse? Attack by a bear?"

"The man killed a dragon, Your Majesty," said the old professor.

"Only one of royal blood who is pure of heart can challenge him," said the young lawyer.

"So where, pray, are you wiggling?" said the King.

"Ah, well, the texts say a *man* can't do it. If we could find a *woman*..."

***

The Princess was not impressed.

"Why are you all looking at me?".

The Conclave, Black Al, and her father, all shifted from foot to foot, and stared at the scrubbed stone floor of the Princess' dungeon.

"If I had another way..." her father started.

"Do shut up, Daddy. This is the silliest thing I have ever heard. I don't know one end of a sword from the other!" She flounced, and put down her mask.

"We can train you, your Majesty," said Black Al. "I have the best men in the armouries, they could teach a one-armed granny to fight!" But then he caught the Princess' expression. "Saving your Majesty's grace! I meant only..."

"And can they make me grow taller by a head and shoulders, give me the muscles of a bear and the reflexes of a viper? I think not! Daddy, I will be clear. I love this Kingdom, I will do anything for it. But I will not commit suicide!"

The mask went back up, the Princess rose and signalled to her ladies. They processed out towards the Royal Tower, for more dancing, games, and being very, very annoyed at this ludicrous situation.

"Good try, chaps," said the King. "What can I say? Keep searching. There may be a half-blood princess we've all forgotten about. Hopefully she's a big strong girl with a bad temper."

The Conclave left the dungeon, depressed. The King was about to follow when Black Al took his arm. "Sire, I think you should see this." They waited for the rest of Conclave to leave, then Black Al led the King towards the wall covered in the blue silk curtain.

"And? It's a curtain. I prefer tapestry myself, it's warmer."

"This." Black Al drew the curtain aside, revealing the Planning Hanging in all its bizarre, complex, multi-coloured glory.

"What the blazes is that?" said the King. The Hanging looked as if a huge, demented spider had spread a web all over the old tapestry. Dangling at various points were scraps of fabric, like the bodies of flies drained of their life-blood.

"If you look carefully, Sire, I believe you can make out the heraldic colours. The Barons of Elderton, and Earl Passfield, the Council of Cymenshore. "

"White fur?"

"I think we all know who that means."

And the King needed no clue about the sky-blue and gold scrap, or the pathetic piece of grey flannel that represented the Hegemon.

"That's part of my royal banner," said the King.

"Indeed, Sire. I'm there too, you see, the black leather. I gather, from some of the ladies, that Her Majesty refers to this as the Planning Hanging."

"Really," said the King.

"What I want to know is, who's she planning to hang?"

The King said nothing. He returned to his chamber. But he was beginning to wonder what on earth he had done in a past life to deserve all this.

***

That night, the King and his Chamber supped in private. Eiswolf did not attend the King's party: he had sent word that he needed time for thought, and would be alone. This was greeted with a sigh of relief: it was hard to entertain a man while you plotted his death.

So everyone made the best of it. The King found the spirit to make jokes, while the Princess deigned to put her mask aside within the Chamber although still deeply displeased with her father. Lanterns burned brightly in the winter night, troubadours sang, and ladies began to dance. The court was subdued, but still a court in splendour.

And then, as all prepared for sleep, a dreadful shriek rang through the Palace. Everyone froze. Guards poured through the corridors towards the noise. Then came another shriek, and loud, terrible sobbing.

The King sent his daughter to the safety of her dungeon and, with Black Al, walked towards the sobs, pausing only to arm himself with a sword from one of the guards.

"Dear God, what now." The King and his Champion followed the noise up into the guests' chambers, to the room currently given over Mifanna.

They found a scene of horror. In the dark, lit only by the torches, they saw two figures, one on the floor, the other crouching over it. But the room was slippery, reeking, gleaming with –

"Blood," said the King. "My God, it's like a slaughterhouse in here."

The weeping figure put out its hands: hands dripping with dark red. "My King! See what he has done to my girl! Murder! Justice, my King! For she will never come again, my brightness, my lady, my girl!" And the distraught figure stroked the red-gold curls, spread out on the floor behind Mifanna's head.

Black Al ordered his men. "Seal off this tower. The killer might still be here. Bring a doctor. She's beyond help but her uncle needs assistance. Sir," Al crouched down beside the Glimmer Lord. "Sir, we need to look at your niece, to discover what has happened. I don't think you should be here for that. I will send you to another chamber, a doctor and the nuns will care for you. Please allow us to help you."

The Glimmer Lord let Black Al lift him to his feet, and guards escorted him away.

Then the King and Black Al and one of the doctors from Conclave examined the slight body. The green and gold dress had been ripped to shreds, as had the stout linen shift beneath. The men in that room had all seen death, lots of it: cut throats, heads cracked open, bodies sliced apart. This was different.

Black Al carefully removed the rags of cloth, but all he could see was a mess of dark blood and stinking intestines. The doctor leaned over his shoulder. "Move that leg. Ah, yes. Gutted."

"What?" said the King.

"The throat has been ripped out but whether before or after death, I cannot say. The main injuries are between collar-bone and thigh, the body has been eviscerated, something has tried-"

The King gasped. "Something?"

"These injuries are jagged, not smooth cuts like a knife. I have seen similar wounds when a bear caught one of our woodsmen."

"A bear?" said Al, mind racing. "In here?"

"A beast," said the King. "A beast roams this Palace." He straightened up. "I can think of only one. She was his particular playmate, was she not?"

The room went silent, chill despite the torches. "My men heard them arguing," said Al.

"I don't think we need to look further afield," said the King. "Find the man, seize him, and bring him to the place of interrogation. Clean this room and lay out this girl so that she may appear decent at her funeral."

**

Black, so black, yet so bright, the wind shrieking across the snow-field, the cold cutting, tasting, wrapping itself around him. Which way now? The red veils in the sky above danced and reformed, shifted and vanished; the green glowing and vivid, curl, shimmer, stretch, shudder into movement then fade, fade away, a whole heaven of dancing green flames, then beyond all, the piercing stars, his stars, where the gods of ice looked down on this desert of snow, this creature, stranded in the vastness, he looked up –

Noise. Scrabble, shuffle, footsteps on paving. The scent of the air changed, not clean any more, damp, ancient stone, a warmer wind but old air, tinged with - Fear.

Eiswolf smelled the panic before he heard the guards calling out in a hue and cry. In this dim chamber with only a single rush-light, away from the din of court, where he had come to think without interruption, he listened carefully. An intruder. A murder. He grasped the Sword of Destiny, for he should go and help them, that is what knights were for –

He opened the door to the corridor. Two guards rushed past in the darkness. One turned and yelled to men behind, "Keep an eye out, he'll have the Sword of Destiny, and maybe the Ring." They were looking for him: he should join them.

But the man's voice was wrong. Even as Eiswolf opened his mouth to call to them, he hesitated. One of the men, far away in the darkness, yelled back.

"Do we kill him?"

"No, take him to the King. They'll rip him apart, like he did that girl. "

That made no sense. But the men laughed.

"Here, wolfie!" yelled another voice, whistling. "Wolfie, wolfie! Come and see what I've got for you, you murdering bastard!"

He could smell the fear, and the fury. They were hunting. They had the blood-hunger.

He took a risk. Standing in blackest shadow, in a rasping voice, he cried, "I've just got here! What's he done?"

"The girl Mifanna! Ripped her apart!"

"We're going to skin him alive!"

The shock almost froze him. He grasped the Sword harder. The men from the rear party were getting closer. They might not see him in the shadow.

"A torch!" the man cried. "I've got a torch, I need a fire."

Another said, "I can smell burning. That chamber ahead."

Eiswolf strode into the corridor and drew part of his robe over his head. He walked with determination, far enough behind the first men to be obscured by darkness. The men behind stopped for a few seconds to light the torch.

"Here! You!" A man called. "You, up ahead! Get the men from the Third Tower, get everyone."

Eiswolf waved back. But the guardhouse of the Third Tower was on the floor above, he needed to be out of here, down, across the courtyard. No. That would be full of men by now. Which way, which way. He reached the spiral stair, a stone helix set into the wall, and climbed up out of sight of the men behind. They ran past, he waited until the echoes died, then slowly came back down.

A way out. A way out that did not go through the main gate. He edged along the corridors, closer to the kitchen blocks and the stables, past little store-rooms and cubby-holes. Everywhere he saw more torches, heard more men. He descended a level, then another, but the clatter and yells were loud and desperate, he could hear doors being wrenched open and slammed.

"Not here!"

"Not here!"

Then he smelled the night air. He must be near one of the servants' doors into the small courtyard by the armoury - Too close! Too close to the chambers where the nobles were, he was going towards the armed men, not away from them.

He could not fight them all and win. The Sword of Destiny might make him invincible - in a fairy-tale. Here, he would not win. They would not take him to trial, for a wolf was vermin. They would flay him then and there, and nail his skin to one of the great gates, as they always had with wolves. If he was still alive afterwards, they would set fire to him.

Then out of the darkness, a hand grabbed his sword arm. Eiswolf turned like a falcon in flight, ready to take at least one with him. He could not see the man in the dimness, he smelled sweat and fear. But familiar? He hesitated.

"Boss!" hissed a voice. "It's me, boss!"

"Meroens?" Beyond belief, trust - "What do they pay for a wolf!"

Meroens angrily shoved Eiswolf in the chest. Then he whispered, "Boss, shut up and follow me. Kill me then if you like."

What could he lose? Eiswolf followed the wrestler in the darkness, through an alley into the exercise yard, then along the wooden rails towards the armoury, past the equipment shed into the stables. Storm stood bridled and tied to a post. The white horse whinnied, but Meroens grabbed Eiswolf and dragged him to another stall, containing an anonymous bay stallion. Quickly, he untied the horse and threw a blanket over its back: to get a saddle meant going into the tack room, but the torches were too close.

Eiswolf sprang onto the horse's back. Meroens threw him another blanket for a cloak. "Get out now!" he whispered.

"And you too!" said Eiswolf. "Don't come after me. I'll find you. I will find you!"

Meroens slapped the horse on the flank and it trotted into the yard. Eiswolf rode through the milling guards, then saw the palace gate was still open. He yelled, "King's orders! Reinforcements from Wardur! King's orders!" and, bowed over and holding the blanket close, cantered through the soldiers.

A guard stood in his way, about to raise a torch to see the rider. Eiswolf rasped again. "King's orders! I go for reinforcements! God's sake man, the thing's inside the castle, not out here!" He persuaded the horse to rear. "King's orders!"

And the guard stood aside.

Eiswolf galloped through the panicking town, then the gate in the walls, out into the grey, bleak night.

***

In the cold dawn, the King addressed his nobles in the Great Hall.

"We have suffered a grievous loss this night. A most gracious lady has been murdered, and we have discovered the depraved evil lurking in the bosom of one whom we treated as our son. This creature cannot live. But as a being of enchantment, Conclave informs me that no ordinary means will destroy it. I have therefore commanded my heralds to journey to every corner of our Kingdom, there to announce the reward for the death of the abomination known as Eiswolf, and how this may be compassed. I have been greatly aided by a man who has suffered most of all." He nodded at the Glimmer Lord, who, bowed and tear-streaked, took his place beside the King.

The Lord raised his head, and his voice. "While we may not kill the wolf by sword or arrow, yet shall no man assist it. All men shall refuse to give it water, food or shelter; any who help will suffer a most terrible death."

"What if we find the thing?" yelled Adelbon. "Shall we not attempt its life?"

"By all means," said the King. "And with God's grace, you may succeed. But the one sought by the Heralds must also do their part. By any means, we must kill this thing!"

And that, he said to himself, includes the bands of brigands and pirates about to be unleashed by Black Al, because the King did not trust to any magical rubbish about pure-hearted virgins. Eiswolf was dead: he just did not know it yet.

14: Last Deception

Uncooked cakes lay scattered across Marejah's table. The girl wept uncontrollably, her black curls over her face, her cries filling the little bakery.

Perry had come in for fancy buns and another chin-wag over old times, but immediately went to her side. "What is it?"

"Oh, Perry! Look what he's done!" Marejah pointed to four small canvas bags on the table: they were full of gold coins. "Something terrible's happened! He's sent me no message for weeks then he sent me this! I don't want his money, I want him!"

Perry managed to calm her down for long enough to get events in order. 'He' was Bevis, the Hegemon. He had said Marejah would be safer in Cymenshore, she did not know why. He'd written to her about Eiswolf's quest, and his return, and Mifanna, and the Princess. Then, without warning, the letters stopped. A guard from court had arrived with the gold, but no note.

"He said he'd look after me and this means," she gulped, "this means he can't! Oh, Perry, what's happened to him?"

"Let me see his last message."

Tales told by a frightened man; a situation beyond his control, a ferocious, demonic presence darkening the Kingdom. Perry dropped the letter.

Unexpectedly, Octa arrived at the bakery with a message. All men of standing were commanded to gather outside the Guildhall. Perry persuaded Marejah to put the bags of gold in a flour-sack until she returned. At the Guildhall she joined a crowd of traders, scribes, merchants, craftsmen and a scattering of minor nobles: the important men of Cymenshore.

Richard of Clifton and the aldermen stood, looking strained, behind the King's Herald, the senior man from Court. By his manner, he bore bad news.

"Men of Cymenshore. Listen to this proclamation from your King. The creature Eiswolf is now revealed as a thing of evil and enchantment, who has foully murdered a defenceless lady. This creature Eiswolf is declared condemned, out-law, and wolf's head. No man may aid it on pain of a traitor's death, together with their families. The bounty is a thousand gold pieces."

A very decent amount. Some merchants were obviously making mental notes.

"But also know," said the Herald, "that Conclave has determined that no ordinary man may kill it. The King would not lose his bravest knights in useless assault. We seek one of purest heart and royal blood."

Not a problem, Perry could almost hear the merchants think, who would check on their purity and whether daddy married mummy if they do the job?

"And that person. Er." Oh, the tricky bit. The Herald had been rehearsing this in his mind for days and the words never came out right. "This person must be a woman."

Silence. Absolute, stone silence.

Finally, an alderman stirred. "What?"

"A woman," said the Herald.

More silence.

"We're screwed," said a voice from the crowd.

The Herald bowed and went into the Guildhall with Richard and the aldermen.

Everyone dispersed. Perry was rigid with shock but Octa managed to guide her away. He took her back to her chambers.

"My lady, you have a decision to make."

***

The Herald took wine with the council of Cymenshore. All were despondent. The council listened in increasing gloom as the Herald told them of a Court in a state of siege, the future of the Kingdom in the balance. Trade would undoubtedly suffer.

Richard stared up at the lists of past mayors, freshly painted on the Guildhall walls, and at the glorious stained glass in the huge new windows. "This is a strong town. We've endured much."

"Not this creature," said the Herald. "It ripped that girl to pieces. We need it dead, now. We've looked through our almanacs of nobility but they are not complete. What about here? Is there no noble family with a candidate?"

The men looked at each other.

"The closest we had were the Vendants,. But they died in the raid."

"All of them? Our Conclave says all we need is royal blood to the fourth degree, I'm not saying you're hiding a princess, surely there's a cousin or a cadet branch?"

Richard cleared his throat. "Actually, no. The last Count was Pedric and he died a few years ago. His brother Mortain was regent but he and his family all died in the raid. I know that because I identified the bodies. I was a steward in the household at the time."

"There was an heir," said an alderman. "A woman, never married, went strange in the head, they say. "

Richard cleared his throat again. "Countess Pervenche. She disappeared in the raid, hasn't been heard of for eight years. I'm afraid Cymenshore cannot supply what you need."

Which was when the door to the hall flew open, and a nun strode in.

Well, as Perry had always told Eiswolf, if you're going to make an entrance, make a big one.

She had cobbled together an all-purpose nunning outfit from a loose dark robe belted with a rope, a slightly floury white napkin from Marejah over her short hair, and a linen snood over that.

"My lords!" she cried. "Be of good cheer!"

Every man's mouth hung open.

Perry marched forward, reminded herself that the woman was supposed to be a nun, not a brigand, and adjusted her step. "My lords! By the grace of God, I was in the marketplace, buying - Stuff! For my convent which is - Very distant! And we knew not what passed at Court."

She stole a glance at Richard, who was open-mouthed like the rest. Still he did not recognise her. What was he, thick? "But now, my Quest has come upon me!"

"Who the hell are you?" said the Herald, finally. "Who is she? Local lunatic?"

"No!" cried Perry. Here goes nothing. "I am Countess Pervenche of the House of Vendant, I come to rescue the Kingdom!" Strike pose, look heroic, chin up.

Dead silence.

"Rubbish," said an alderman.

"Not so fast," said the Herald. "The lady you speak of is dead." He approached Perry.

She curtseyed as best she could remember, deeply, if rather shakily. "Not so, my lord! For I was - er - Knocked out during the raid. Borne away by - er - Priests! And taken for my safety to a convent, where I recovered my wounds but not, alas, my memory until a year past. And I heard of the good rule of these men in my beloved Cymenshore, so I left the - er - glorious but, in the end, meaningless exercise of power to those better suited than I, a weak and feeble woman." She curtseyed again, and sweated.

"Who knew this lady?" said the Herald. "You, sir, you said you were a steward." He glared at Richard.

"It has been many years," he said, faintly.

Not that many! Perry shrieked to herself. Idiot!

"Has she no distinguishing features, no birthmark, maybe a scar?".

"Aha! Have so!" cried Perry. "Tell them about the bird! Popinjay!"

Richard's eyes clouded over. "Oh, my God."

"What bird?" said the Herald.

"Evil brute," said an alderman. "The old Count gave her a red parrot, big bad-tempered creature, beak like an axe, bit everyone. Nearly took her finger off."

And Perry held up her left hand, with the scar across the knuckle where Popinjay had been too playful one day.

"Oh, crap," said Richard. "It's her."

"Told you she went strange," said another alderman.

"And do you have royal blood?" said the Herald to Perry.

"Great-granny on my mother's side, sister to the Limping King, yep. You've got to let me at him." Perry took a step forward. "Look, for serious, I'm the only one who can help you. You see, I know him."

The Herald peered at her a little more closely. "My God. You. Well, I'll ask no questions here. Will you do it?"

"She can't!" Richard exploded. "She's a woman! She's too -"

"Weak?" cried Perry. "Idiotic? Easily deceived? Easily forgotten, maybe!" She glared at him. "I have survived much, I can survive this. Go home to Magret, Richard, wait for news of my success."

Then she turned on her heel and followed the Herald out of the Guildhall. Oh, that felt good. A bit silly, but good.

The Herald's men brought her a riding mule, but Octa had been to the stables and retrieved Pepper, so the Countess of

Cymenshore rode out of town in a nun's habit on a huge black warhorse, followed by her elderly, fussy squire on the mule.

Once back on the road, the Herald rode up to her. "I do recognise you, squire. Funny thing. Your voice. I never bought into that Barons of Elderton business, your voice should have rasped or not been affected at all, not just husky. You two did stand out, the werewolf and his eunuch."

"What the devil's been going on?" said Perry. "How did it all get this bad?"

"Will you kill him? He was your knight."

"Have I a choice? Let's ride together, tell me everything."

***

The King sat with the Glimmer Lord in his chamber, as he had with the Hegemon in other days. How comforting to talk with an older man who had been through almost as much as the King, who shared certain views about the world, who was proving to be very helpful indeed in running the Court.

Meroens busied himself at the armoury, keeping his ear to the ground, not letting on by word or deed about his friendship with Eiswolf, not least, because he was not sure the man was a friend. The tales around Court were exaggerated or plain lies, he knew that. But he had seen the man change, had seen him fight. Poor old Beltrap was still in the hospital. And he had killed Sir Devlas. Meroens was confused. He kept his mouth shut.

The Princess managed to swallow her own shock at how close she had come to marrying a monster. No-one would tell her how Mifanna had died but she felt as if Death had flown over her, breath ice-cold on her cheek. The man was strange but that? Never. Never, never. So she filed that fear and revulsion in a very dark corner of her mind, only to be allowed out during nightmares.

Then she turned to current concerns and insisted that Adelbon continued his training, although the boy was itching to confront the wolf. When asked, she declared that if he lived, Adelbon could challenge for the Tests next spring. Her own plan to dispose of Eiswolf was still poison, as a direct win in battle looked ever more unlikely. However, that had to wait until they located the man. The Heralds and Black Al would flush him out, a task best left to them.

Her more immediate concern was the Glimmer Lord, or 'Weasel-face' as she called him. He hung about her father like a bad smell, not only in the King's Chamber but Conclave as well. But he had not courted her either personally or politically; he had never responded to any of the proposals she had made, in their mutual interest. Indeed, he seemed to be excluding her. She was still the heir; so what was he up to?

And her wondering went up a level or two when Jocasta reported back a few days after the murder. The laying-out women had called on the witch, because she had a reputation as a wise-woman and they were unsure who else to tell.

Mifanna's body was arranged on a stone slab in a cool cellar, ready for her winding-sheet. But when the women had removed the ripped and bloody clothes, and dealt with the exposed internal organs, the body was not - right.

"How do you mean?" said the Princess. "I hear she was torn apart."

"No, your Majesty," said Jocasta. "For a wolf, this was curiously neat. Throat crushed, the rest of the body opened up but very little removed, apart from an area around the pelvis. Mifanna had no breasts."

"What?"

"And she was also very fuzzy. More hair than usual."

"Ugh. They would have suited each other, then."

"Especially on her upper lip. Very slim hips, not much waist. The dressmakers said that, too. "

"Ah. Oh!" The penny dropped. "And big feet. And knees. "

"Quite, your majesty."

The Princess frowned. This was beyond even her plotting. "So either Wolfie's a bigger box of tricks than we thought. Or …"

"Or the Glimmer Lord is." Jocasta frowned. "Your Majesty, Mifanna was ever associated with the Glimmer Lord. But boys grow fast at that age, the deception could not have lasted much longer."

"So, the wolf was deceived? Reason enough to kill."

Jocasta shook her head. "No. The injuries were specific, total and controlled, not about anger but removing evidence. The Glimmer Lord could do that. Not rage, cold, cold…" Because that was what Gil was, ever since Jocasta had known him, which was a long time.

"But she was his niece?"

"My lady, I can tell you for a certainty that the Glimmer Lord has neither niece nor nephew. I'd assumed she was a mistress, but Mifanna was always an out and out deception."

The Princess sat back. A plot that was bigger and more complex than hers? How dare he! "So he set up a trick but for whatever reason it was not going to plan, so he decided to cut his losses and make the wolf take the blame. But is that enough to prove the Glimmer Lord a murderer?"

Jocasta chose her words carefully. "Ask yourself. What game did he plan with Mifanna and the wolf. And now he's making himself indispensable to the King. I would be very, very careful around the Glimmer Lord."

The Princess looked straight at Jocasta, who seemed genuinely upset. "I understand. Good work. I shall see this body for myself. Pay my respects."

The story at Court soon spread: the Princess, out of her compassion, sat beside the body of the unfortunate girl, ordered the finest brocade to line the coffin, and paid the laying-out women well. She kissed the dead girl on her brow (and, while that close, noted the golden down on the lip and the coarser hair beginning to grow in front of the ears on the edge of the jaw, wondering at just how dim men could be. Well, presumably even the wolf would have noticed by the time 'she' started singing baritone).

The Princess stored the information.

***

The King received his unlikely saviour in private. He saw no point in alarming the whole court, let alone alerting the ambassadors. So the Herald brought Perry, tidied up and in a borrowed gown, into the King's Chamber, where the junior lawyer, two senior professors, Black Al and the Glimmer Lord were also assembled.

"Your Majesty." She curtseyed deeply.

No-one seemed to recognise her, fortunately.

"This is the maiden?" said the King.

"I am Pervenche, Countess of Cymenshore, your Majesty. I was rescued from the raid and taken to a convent, where I have lived all these years. Only when I heard of your great quest was my memory restored to me."

"A miracle," said the Herald. "Countess Pervenche has been sent to us by Fate."

They all stared at her.

"Not very big, is she?" said the King. "Eiswolf is a large man and a great fighter. How do you propose, well, not getting killed?"

"The justice of my cause shall protect me." Perry curtseyed, then a thought struck her. "Oh, and armour, I fight in armour, right? Swords and stuff, I'm not stupid."

The old professor cleared his throat. "The texts are clear. You have royal blood?"

"She does, my lord," said the Herald.

"And you are pure of heart?"

Perry grinned. "Absolutely. Pure as a, er, pure thing."

"Then the texts say she can overcome any enchantment." The professor nodded and smiled, paternally.

The King sniffed. The enchantment did not worry him, the damn big warrior with a sword, did.

Black Al was practical. "Can you fight?"

"My convent is a fighting order," said Perry. "We have regular fixtures against the Weeping Nuns."

"Ah," said Al. "Tough competitors, they are."

"Let us not waste time on talk," said the King. "Herald, take our lady to the armoury and equip her royally."

Perry curtseyed, then left with the Herald.

"I give her two minutes," said the other professor. "Anybody here think different?"

"Not that long," said the King. "A very brave lady. Foolish, but brave."

They shook their heads. Even with the best armour, and months of training, and all the twists and techniques that Al and his men could teach her, and throwing in a spell or two for what that was worth, there was no way that the Countess could beat the wolf. They went into a huddle, to work out the real plan for a kill.

**

Meroens looked once, then twice, then three times, as the Countess came into the equipment shed. The Armourer stared as well, but not because he recognised her.

The Herald took charge. "This is Countess Pervenche of Cymenshore, who has been chosen by Fate to fight the wolf and save the Kingdom. We require armour and weapons for her, of the greatest magnificence."

Meroens found his voice. "Er, miss?"

Perry marched up to him. "That's Countess Pervenche to you, servant!" She hacked him on the shin in emphasis, then gave the biggest, slyest, most secret wink she could.

"Oh. Oh! Oh, many apologies, my Lady." Meroens bowed.

"And do you intend to use a sword?" said the Armourer, his voice rising to an incredulous squeak. "I fear these will be too big for you. Maybe a lance? That'll keep him at a distance …" He trailed away. His imagination failed.

"You got a horse?" said Meroens. "I mean, you got a horse, my Lady?"

"I have a black destrier of the best breeding. Yes, Armourer, I will use a sword. I have seen knights smaller than myself in the lists."

The Armourer was about to explain that dwarves did not count, because they were short but broad, but her expression made him change tack. "It's your funeral," he said, then immediately bit his lip. "You got a device for your shield? I mean, has my Lady …"

"Yes. I am the Knight of the Periwinkle." The men looked blank. "It's a flower, bluey-purple." They still looked blank. "Like a rose shape but blue. On a silver background."

"Ah!" said the Armourer. "I'll get my men going, then. Nice choice, squire. Blue rose it is." He walked happily down to the limner's, and the Herald bowed and left.

"Bugger me, Perry," said Meroens. "What the hell do you think you're up to?"

"I'm the one. I'm the Blessed Maiden Knight."

"But you're not any of those –

"Don't push it."

"Bloody hell." Meroens tried to absorb both the information and the sight of Perry as a lady.

"Look sharp about the armour," said Perry. "I don't want to hang around here too long."

"You going to do it? Really kill the boss?"

"If I have to. Dear God, this is horrible. This business about Sir Devlas, and the girl. Did he do it? Is he mad?"

***

In the lightless cell, the Hegemon wept quietly.

For the first week, he had been convinced that the King would realise his error, that the Hegemon was too valuable, he would miss what the Hegemon did –

But he didn't. The guard gave Bevis bread and water, then left him in the dark.

He could hear quiet groaning from the cell next to him. Both had doors leading onto an unlit corridor, a barred slot at the top. Noise could travel, although muffled. In the second week, as he realised the King had forgotten him, he started to whisper.

"Who's there? My name is Bevis. Who are you?"

After two days, he got an answer. It chilled him to the bone.

"Bess."

He was silent for a day. The bread and water arrived. He called to the guard. "You know who I am?"

"A prisoner."

"I am a man of wealth and power."

"Not in here, you're not." The guard went away. Bevis heard a squeal from the next chamber. The man muttered, "Witch!" and slammed the door.

He tried again the next day. "I can pay you."

"How?" said the guard.

"I have hidden gold. Take it to someone in Cymenshore, keep a bag for yourself." He knew he could not buy himself out, Black Al had his men too well-trained. But Marejah -

"Tell me where," said the guard, who knew very well who the Hegemon was.

"Water!" He heard the faint whisper form the next cell.

"Shut up, witch!" said the guard.

"Why does she want water? I left orders!"

"Yeah, but you're not giving orders no more, are you? No-one's got any orders about her. This gold…"

The Hegemon sat back, hard. Again he heard the faint whisper. "Water!"

He had reached his limit. He could not do it.

"Guard, another bag of gold to you, make sure she gets water and bread."

"Can't do that. Have to make my mark for it, see? Strict rations."

The Hegemon stared into the blackness. It could no longer matter.

"Then take half of mine. But do it now, and make sure you do so every day."

"You'll die. She's on her way out. What's the point?"

"Do it," the Hegemon said to the darkness.

The next day, he heard a louder sound. "Thank you, Bevis."

And then they talked. He told her about his childhood, and the little town, and the merchant, how he came to court, how he admired the Princess beyond reason, but Marejah was the woman he looked forward to seeing. And she talked back. Most was beyond his understanding. He caught that she had been trained as a doctor, and went to an ancient university in a place called London, which was like the Conclave, and had learned much about the world and the universe.

"We all trained together, me and Bridget and Jocasta and Nico and Rishi and Ali, there was a whole bunch of us and it was so exciting! And then we heard about Gil, he was setting up something called the Veritas Project, to go … Well. Outside Time. "

"How can you do that?" said Bevis.

"I don't know. It's complicated. We were learning to sail the ship, not build it. The project was dangerous, we knew that, but we had all the technology. They told us the trip might be one-way but I'm not sure anyone believed it. Not - not until it happened."

"What about the wolf?" As they weakened, there was little else to do in the dark, but talk.

"He came to me. He was lost, only a boy, he was so lost."

"What is he?"

"I don't know. But if I and my friends came through here, maybe there's other worlds that can. He's not evil, Bevis. I know he isn't."

"He's not like us."

"No." Bess sighed. "You and me, he's not like us. I would have made a good man into a murderer, a weapon, and I told myself I did not care. You let the end justify the means and so did I. He wouldn't do what we have done. "

She sighed again, hugely. "Tell me about when you first came to court. That must have been exciting."

***

The Herald sent his men to the four corners of the land, to proclaim that the Knight of the Periwinkle challenged the Knight of the Snow-wolf to a fight to the death, for the preservation of the Kingdom. A tale of magic and sorcery, of right against the forces of evil, of a lost heir giving up a life of holiness to return to defend the land she loved so well, to save the Princess from a fate worse than death. A damn good story, actually. Perry was quite proud of it.

"Lost heirs always gets them going," she said to the Herald. "Hint of religion, hint of sex."

"What will the wolf think?"

That was harder to say. In the old days, he'd have smelt a rat straight away. But if he really was insane - Perry had tried to send word to Bess, but the messenger came back saying the hovel was deserted, and had been for a while. Perry had a black feeling in the pit of her stomach. The time she had always dreaded was approaching. If he was truly lost to the darkness, she knew what she had to do. Horrible beyond tears, but necessary, a last act of mercy for a man who had been her friend.

In the armoury, Meroens was off finding a small mail shirt. Perry looked at the blue bottle Bess had given her, all those years ago. She had never asked what it contained, never dared to open it even for a sniff. She could not kill Eiswolf in fair fight, she knew that. She just had to get close enough to open the bottle and get the stuff on his skin and into his mouth or eyes. The chances were that she would die too, but then, what did that matter?

***

The noise of the troop accompanying the junior herald echoed through the countryside. So many soldiers to deliver a message! But the terrified people took comfort that the shadow across their lives was going to be removed.

Eiswolf smelled the horses trotting through the winter woods before he heard them, and withdrew back into his bracken shelter. He had been living off the land and stealing, a little, from the villages, because he knew if he showed his face, he was dead. Unless he killed the villagers and thus confirmed his character as a monster.

The horror did not end. But the most horrible thing was that he could not remember. He had been angry with Mifanna, very angry, disappointed, hurting terribly, but not enough to kill. Well, not in his right mind. Could he have done that? Under the black sky?

He spotted the herald: what message from Court could be that important?

He slunk through the wood, edging behind a barn towards the small clearing that acted as the village marketplace. The troop stopped and the herald dismounted. A knight had been found to challenge the wolf for the Kingdom. Straining, Eiswolf could just hear the courtly words.

The villagers listened in silence. "What if the wolf wins?" said one.

"Then he may return to the Palace, to be rewarded for the Seven Tests of Kolras."

Perry had insisted that Eiswolf needed a reason to come forward. As she pointed out, this would cost the King nothing, because Eiswolf was going to die.

How odd. Eiswolf heard the message but it was - odd. Not the way he would have done it. They must expect him to win, obviously. So who was this Knight of the Periwinkle, stupid name, wonder which lady thought that was a good name to stick on her knight, he could think of three winkle jokes right now?

One of the villagers obviously shared his thoughts, and asked. The Herald coughed. "The Knight is the bravest Lady of this Kingdom, and will win by divine favour and purity of heart."

"Lady?"

Lady? They had to be joking. A woman?

Now he knew something was adrift. Possibly the King had gone nuts, or that damn Conclave had come up with this lunatic scheme. They were insane enough to believe it. But there was only one way to find out.

When you make an entrance, make a big one.

So he roared out from behind the barn, shaggy and dishevelled, a true wild man of the woods. Small children burst into tears and a pregnant woman fainted. The men of the village formed up to defend their families (good for them) and the herald looked as if he had just had a personal accident.

"I am Eiswolf, the last and lost! Descended of Rime and Storm, the North Wind and the Northern Lights, faithful to the Gods of Ice! I hear your challenge! I accept!"

"Oh," said the herald. "Um. Oh." He stared.

"I think you'll find you have to tell me where to go?" said Eiswolf. "For the fight?"

"What?"

"Directions?" But the man stared blankly. "When they gave you the proclamation, didn't they say where - "

"Oh. Er. Ah!" The herald scrabbled around in his satchel and brought out another piece of parchment. "Here we are. Yes. You must present yourself at the Dale of Doom. Erm. It's off the Cymenshore road."

"Doesn't ring a bell."

"Behind the tavern of the Golden Fleece, you can't miss it, next to the really big blacksmith's, Old Tom's place."

"Oh, right. You've got a time?"

"Not really, when you're ready." The herald smiled helpfully.

"Well, let's say noon, day after tomorrow. See you then." And Eiswolf went back into the greenwood.

Nobody spoke for a couple of minutes.

"H'm." The herald cleared his throat. "That went quite well, didn't it? Pleasant manner." His mouth was trotting out polite phrases because his brain was still playing catch-up with what had just happened.

Then they raced back to the Palace.

***

The short winter day broke over the Dale. A pale glow slithered down the dirt-track road, over the smithy's soot-darkened chimney where a fire burned blood-red day and night, and glanced across the tavern of the Golden Fleece, whose landlord stood ready to live up to his pub's name when the spectators arrived for the fight.

The locals had built a small arena with a wooden stand to seat the King and his Conclave and the other lords away from the mud. The winner would be the knight walking off the field. No-one expected the fight to last very long.

At mid-morning, Perry rode in on Pepper, accompanied by Octa on his mule and Meroens on his charger.

"Not happy about this," said Meroens.

"My lady knows what she is doing," said Octa.

"You bet," Perry lied.

"Remember his left side, where he had the shoulder injury," said Meroens. "If he, you know, if he does that thing, like, with his eyes, well, get out of the way, right? Don't be stupid."

"I won't," said Perry. "I've used up all my stupid just being here."

They reached the centre of the temporary arena, where the Herald waited.

"Are you prepared?" he said to Perry.

"As I'll ever be."

"The sign for commencement will be when I drop this red flag. No noise, nothing else. There are no judges or umpires other than myself. Your men cannot help you if you fall and are not allowed into the arena. This has to be clean, clear and without dispute. Do we understand?"

They all nodded, then Meroens and Octa rode out of the arena. The Herald watched them until they dismounted as well.

Perry waited, shivering inside her badly-fitting armour. The Armourer had done his best, but good plate is made to measure: she had to take what he had. The old-fashioned cuirass was too roomy across the back and tight on her chest, and the waist was too big. The helmet felt vast. She could see through the slit in the visor, but it was not well-aligned with her eyes, it felt cold, but sweaty as well. Oh, well. One way or another, she would not be in there for long.

She heard the hoofbeat before she saw him. Eiswolf rode in on a borrowed horse, carrying a plain shield. He had been fully, if grudgingly, armoured by the blacksmith, and the man's wife had rigged up a black surcoat. The mail shone bright under the watery winter sun.

He rode to the centre, where the Herald gave his speech about judges.

Eiswolf seemed huge. Perry had, for some reason, never realised how big he was. Unless she had forgotten. Or because he was on a horse. Or did her fear make him seem big?

"Sir Knight!" he cried out. "Or, should I say, my Lady! I have no desire to fight a woman! Reconsider this madness!"

Oh, boy, he wanted to chat. One of his better ploys. "Sir Knight, I come here to fight, not toy frivolously in a passing fancy like a spoilt Palace sweetheart!"

"Pardon?"

Oh God, the damn helmet was now full of spit.

"Lady, in all my years at Tourney, I can tell you one thing!" He rode a pace closer. "A good big 'un beats a good little 'un any day of the week. Get lost, squirt, no-one will blame you."

"Get on with it!" Perry turned and rode to the edge of the arena. Turn again. Face the opposition. Ride straight towards them. Jink, if you were going to, at the last moment. Right. She had taken Eiswolf through these manoeuvres so many times, had sparred with him so often. But the real thing was different. Terrifyingly different.

Eiswolf and his horse sauntered over to the arena rail, he adjusted his gauntlets, arranged the surcoat, checked his spurs, shuffled his helmet about, tested the straps on the bridle –

She shrieked "Bloody hell, man, you're lovely enough! Just fight!"

He turned towards her. Then he got off the horse.

Perry exploded. "What! What! What now!"

Eiswolf approached the Herald, muttering. The Herald looked a little surprised, then came over to Perry.

"My Lady, the knight has informed me that his horse has a sore tendon."

"Sore tendon my arse! I'll give him a ruddy sore tendon!"

"Calm, please, my Lady. The knight wishes to fight on foot? We may find another horse but the knight must approve it."

"God, we'll all die of old age first! Look, whatever he wants, do it. Right?"

So Perry dismounted. Oof. The armour seemed a lot heavier when you weren't sitting down. But not too heavy for fighting. Running, maybe not, especially with the shield, but otherwise fine. She checked her belt and the little pouch holding the bottle. Fine. Let's go.

God, he's a big bugger. Blast. Right. He's head and shoulders taller than me and a longer reach, too. Oh. Off the horse, I've given him a bigger advantage, blast. He's standing there but any minute now, he'll do that funny dance step to the side –

It's a lot further than it looks. Seem to have been walking for ages. Is he walking backwards, the bastard? Yes, he is!

"Stand your ground, coward!" she yelled.

"Pardon?" he yelled back.

"Stay still!" She waved her arms. Not a good idea. The shield slipped. On the horse, she had rested it on the saddle but it was too big to hold easily. Her left arm was tiring already. Oops.

He yelled. "I'll wait till you pick that up! Want a hand?"

"No!" She wrestled the shield back into place, and assumed the position. By God, he'd moved back another ten paces. She'd clatter him when she caught up with him -

She marched forward, swiftly and determinedly. He stood still until she was within five paces, and then stepped back, raising the Sword of Destiny. Then he dropped it to his side again.

"Do you really want to do this?"

"Oh, yes! Do I ever." She raised her own sword, ready for the first blow.

"This isn't fair, kid. How much fighting have you done?" He was resting on his sword, now, the bastard. Like he didn't even need to take up the position.

"Enough," growled Perry. And she took a big swipe at him.

He leaned back a little, as the blade whistled in front of his helmet. "Nice one," he said, encouragingly. "If you'd been a pace closer, maybe."

She swiped again. And he deflected the blow with his shield almost without moving. "That's better. But you're going at it like a bull at a gate. This could go on for hours."

"No, it won't!" yelled Perry, and attacked again, and again, and again –After four minutes she had managed to run out of breath and strength but not sweat or spit. Inside the helmet was getting very wet.

Eiswolf stood patiently, twirling the Sword, resting his shield against his leg. "Want a breather?".

Then Perry spotted the Herald walking towards them.

"His Majesty wishes to know what the problem is? There does not appear to be a great deal of fighting happening?"

Eiswolf turned to him and in a different, fearsome voice, said, "If his Majesty wishes to come down and take up the fight himself, he is most welcome."

"Ah." The Herald bowed, and returned with the message to his master. They both saw the King twitch slightly.

"Fireside warriors," said Eiswolf. "Come on, then. Your best shot. Come on lad! I mean, lass!"

So Perry swiped and stabbed and hewed; and even when she made contact, she knew the blow was not a good one.

"You been at this game long?" he said.

"Eight years!" she growled.

"Now, you see, you're dropping your left arm again, I can get in, like this!"

He hit back and the blow swept her off her feet. She landed on her back with a thump. "Damn!" The helmet shifted again and now she could not see a thing.

"Problem?"

"Helmet," she said, faintly.

"I'll give you a hand." She felt him unlace a strap. "Perry! What are you doing inside there?"

She stared up into sky. "Not Perry."

He helped her to her feet. "Yes, you are."

"I mean, not just Perry." She recovered enough to take a stance. "I am Countess Pervenche of Cymenshore, I am here to defend the Kingdom!"

"Really? Blimey, you kept that quiet. You want your shield?" He picked it up. "It's too heavy, I'd never have given you one that size."

"Shut up, you great, big, noisy…" She grabbed the shield from him, almost beside herself.

"Sorry. You know, if you had issues, you could have just talked to me." He sounded mildly hurt.

She spotted movement from the stand. "Oh, cripes, here comes the Herald again."

The man took his long, deliberate walk towards them. "I should point out to you two - knights - that if one loses a helmet, then both must, or you must restore that helmet to the Countess."

Eiswolf peered into the helmet. "God, what have you been doing in here, Perry? Yuck. You want this thing on your head?"

"No. Tell his Majesty we will fight without helms."

"Well, that will speed everything up," said the Herald. Only idiots and madmen fought without armour to the most important part of the body.

Eiswolf removed his helmet.

"Good grief," said Perry. "Now that is scary. What's with all the bristles?"

"Oddly enough, barbers are not a feature of the greenwood." Eiswolf was acid.

The Herald interrupted. "Can we start, please? I'd like to get this over before the New Year?" And he walked back to the stand.

"Right," said Perry.

"This is really stupid," said Eiswolf.

"Look, raise your Sword at least or Sir Play-by-the-rules will be back."

So they raised their weapons and circled.

"I didn't do it," said Eiswolf. "Mifanna was a conniving bitch, but I didn't kill her."

"Not what they say," said Perry through gritted teeth. "Ha! Oh." The blow missed.

"You're too short, you know. Was it bad?"

"Horrible. Ripped apart. Ouch!"

"You're supposed to get out of the way. Look, I'll whistle at you when I'm coming in."

"I don't need you to - Ouch!"

"Like this." He made a thin high-pitched noise. "Right?"

"Well, if you didn't, who did it? Oi, you didn't whistle!"

"Give me a really big haymaker or they won't know what's taking so long. Yow." Eiswolf staggered, mainly acting but a little bit for real.

"Big enough for you?" Perry began to prance around. "Well, who wants you out?"

"Everybody," said Eiswolf. "God dammit, I don't want their poxy Kingdom! I'd be a terrible king, makes you think black thoughts. High level attack coming in. Hey, remember that ploy with the double twirl? Always looked good. Useless, but pretty."

"Like Adelbon?"

They nearly giggled, but sobered up in time. The manoeuvre went well: an 'ooh' came from the stand.

"Look, on your honour and Bess' life, did you kill that girl. Truth."

"No. Truth. I'll knock you down, you lie still, I go in, then you roll away."

"And lose my shield?"

They stood still for a second.

"Trust me," said Eiswolf.

"All right," said Perry, and went down like a felled tree. More gasps from the stand, then a small cheer as she rolled out and stood, sword in hand. "Oh, crap, crap, crap. I can't kill you!"

"Too damn right," said Eiswolf. "Whose cockamamie idea was this?"

"Look, mate, I can kill you all right, I just don't - It was Conclave. I'll go for your knee."

"Whatever you can reach, Shorthouse. Oof! That's not my knee!"

"That greasy sod the Glimmer Lord is really tight with them." Bang, bang, parry, thrust, miss. "What about Sir Devlas? You killed him."

"No! Do I go about killing sleeping men?" Crunch, swish, small hand to hand struggle, bang.

"There is blood on the Sword."

Fast as a snake, out of sight of the stand, Eiswolf peeled back the sleeve of his mail. A gash ran across his arm. "Perry, you know me better. A damn huge horrible bluff but if I didn't, they'd kill me for failing the Test. If I did, I'd be a murderer. There's no good choice! I lied to serve the truth."

"Oh, hell, Eiswolf, how are we going to get out of this!"

"Haven't you got a really clever underhand piece of tomfoolery? Here comes a big one." He arced the sword over his head and barely missed Parry's ear.

"Aha! Take that, varlet!" She darted in towards his armpit. "You wearing Adelbon's amulet whatsit?"

"Why?"

"Look, I come in, you slip on one knee and drop the Sword. Closer to the stand."

So they worked their way over towards the audience, hacking and slashing, knocking each other flat often enough to satisfy the appearance of injury, then Perry got in her 'lucky' stroke.

Eiswolf went down heavily on one knee, the Sword slithering across the muddy field. Perry raised her blade to the heavens, then aimed at Eiswolf's throat. "Prepare to die, wolf!"

He dropped his head in defeat.

She cried, "Bare your breast to me, creature, that I may stab you with my silver dagger."

"You what?" he whispered.

"Trust me," she whispered back.

He pulled down the tattered surcoat and the mail beneath. The steel square with little grey diamonds glinted in the remaining daylight.

"But what is this!" cried Perry. "For I have seen this before! In my convent, where we cure poor wretches of enchantments!"

Suddenly, the Glimmer Lord took notice. He had not really cared which way the battle went: the man would be killed now or afterwards, although he had not expected the woman to make a fight of it. But this was not in the playbook.

Perry unlaced the amulet, and held it up. Eiswolf groaned deeply, sinking heavily onto his knees.

"My King!" cried Perry. "This is an amulet of great and wicked power! A sorcerer's work! This brave knight was under an evil spell, confused and tormented! "

Astonishment among the nobles.

"What!" yelled the King. "But he murdered that girl!"

"Sir Eiswolf!" yelled Perry. "Where were you on the night of that lady's death?" She muttered in a low voice. "For God's sake, make it good."

Eiswolf looked up at the King, playing a man exhausted and forlorn. "Confused as I was, I prayed for guidance." He scanned the crowd, very fast. "I went to strengthen my arm against the Kingdom's enemies. By a passage of arms with my loyal squire! Meroens!"

Meroens, sitting on the back row, tried not to look too surprised.

"Is this true?" said the King. "Squire, why did you not come forward?"

"I, er, I…"

Perry stepped in. "Meroens! Were you not afraid that if you did, the evil sorcerer would attack you and your family? For you are but a poor, simple man, stronger in body than mind."

"What she said." Meroens crossed his arms. "All that."

"Then we must find this sorcerer," said the King. Damn, blast, who would credit it, how the blazes? The Princess would be livid.

"Sire." Eiswolf stood, as if slowly recovering his strength. "I am now in my right mind once more. I awake from a long nightmare! My liege, I was enchanted into a false love to shame our lovely Princess, and seduced into that rage which so alarmed the Court. All this to force me from your favour. But I see the sorcerer before me, one who has most craftily obtained your confidence. Your majesty, I fear you are deceived - in the Glimmer Lord!" He pointed at him.

"Was he not found beside the body!" cried Perry. "Was he not the pimp and protector of the girl!"

Now, had the Glimmer Lord been a popular man among the nobles, matters could still have gone his way. But the Princess was not the only one to find him weaselly, for those who rise without trace are often resented. Gil took one look at the faces around him, and ran. He reached the horses before the guards had time to react. For a man of his age, he was a fast runner, and a good rider.

"Sir Eiswolf, we have been most grievously deceived!" said the King. "Welcome back to our Court! Countess, we owe you a most enormous - Debt."

***

"You are joking," said the Princess.

"Unfortunately not," said Jocasta. "Wedding's back on."

The Princess sighed heavily. Well, onto plan H, whatever that might be.

"The King wishes you to congratulate the knight," said Jocasta. "You need to keep them both sweet. Look, it need not be for that long, just until you fall pregnant."

"I do not want to start to imagine any of that," said the Princess. "Oh, say to him, this afternoon. After midday? We can meet in the dungeon."

"The King insists you are alone," said Jocasta. "And no sliding out because of a meeting, or urgent messages, or feeling ill."

"Oh, all right," said the Princess. "Dear me, what a fuss."

So, finally, Eiswolf, newly shaved, washed, trimmed and generally made to look like a knight rather than a dead dog dragged out of a sewer, as Perry had put it, met his future queen.

He came into the dungeon cautiously. A minty hound trotted past, sniffed, then snarled. They tended to do that; all dogs, that is, not just minty ones. The room smelled bald, cold, more like a tomb: he was astonished at the King's cruelty, to deny the Princess any rushes, or tapestry to warm the wall, or even furniture. There were pieces of rough-sawn wood but nothing he could identify as chairs. A skull glared menacingly from a post. There was a slight, odd, oily odour he could not place. At the far end, in front of a blue silken curtain, the only softness in that bleak room, the Princess sat in a swathe of cherry pink, silver-gold hair in a sort of birdcage, gloved, and behind her gilded mask.

"May I approach, your Majesty?"

"Certainly, Sir Knight. Stand where We may see you!"

He stepped into a patch of sunlight about five paces from the Princess.

"We must congratulate you, Sir Knight. You have passed every Test, proven your valour and destroyed an evil sorcerer."

"All for the Kingdom," he said. "But now, your Majesty, we must fulfil our joint destiny."

And he still meant it, but frankly, after Mifanna, romance was not high on his life-list. Neither was half the Kingdom; at least, not while everyone still thought he was a wolf. He could almost feel the plots twining about his ankles. But avoiding this marriage would give his enemies more of a pretext. So he made a graceful bow, preparing to seduce.

"Your Majesty, now we are in private, how may I address you?"

"Pardon?" said the Princess.

"How may I address you? What shall I call you?"

The little pink figure did not move. "Your Majesty," she said.

"Er, no actually, er, no-one else is here, so what do I call you?"

"Your Majesty?"

"No, er, what do your friends call you?"

"Your Majesty," said the little figure, as if talking to one of very limited intellect.

"Don't you have a name?" This was going nowhere fast.

"We have many names, Sir Knight. Fifteen, We think. But you may call Us your Majesty."

"But in bed! We are to be as one, Your Majesty. Have you no pet name?"

The little head went on one side, like a bird's. "We are not a pet."

Right. This was going to be tougher than even he had thought.

"Madam, I would wish to be a most fond and attentive husband."

"Oh, we're not having any of that," said the Princess.

"Then how, madam, do you propose to get pregnant?" He began to lose his cool, just a touch.

"There will be occasions for the, ah, necessary," said the Princess. "We will give you some dates. Our people will talk to your people, and so forth."

No. No, this was not how it happened. Plainly she needed to be swept off her feet by a real man, he bet no man had ever dared to touch her, she did not know what love and passion was! He was a wolf, not a pathetic minty hound!

He strode forward to the little figure, to rip aside the mask and kiss her.

A wailing, mournful hoot raised every hair on his back for a second, but he recovered and seized her. Oh. Hard, heavy, stiff. He could feel rods and wires. She must be tiny, she seemed to be mainly clothes. He went for the manoeuvre where he swept her into his strong arms -

And fell flat on the floor, her wig came off and bowled across the stones, followed by the mask and the gloves.

Sproing. She fell apart.

"Aargh!" He dropped everything immediately. What sorcery was this? He looked in panic around the dungeon, for this was surely a cursed place –

"Drat, drat!" The words were indistinct, as if behind a door.

"Princess!" he yelled, scrambling to his feet. "Are you enchanted?"

"Oh, do be quiet, you silly man."

A side-door opened, revealing a study with a big table covered in documents. A small, slight woman stood in the doorway, her pale hair cropped at jaw-length, in simple black garments of an odd design: loose leggings to her ankles, and a sort of shirt without a collar.

"You?" said Eiswolf.

"That damn voice tube wasn't strong enough. Why did you have to pounce like that? Women don't like it." She started to pick up various bits of princess scattered over the floor.

He stared. "Were you ever actually…" He peered at her eyebrows. "You are a natural blonde. So who…"

"Oh, I don't have time for all that flapdoodle, I have work to do. Kingdoms don't run themselves, especially now the Hegemon seems to have disappeared. No, I was there if it was important. What?"

He stared at her. A small, slight, pale, sharp-featured woman. Intelligent, certainly. A great beauty? No. Queenly, maternal? A wife? "Er. Well. Um." Deep breath. "Madam, we are to be married and so…"

"What?"

He was lost. "Am I pleasing to you, then?"

"Frankly, you're not my type, can't abide chest-hair, but that's hardly important."

And she meant it.

This was ridiculous. "Look, lady. Have you thought there might be a way out of this? For both of us?"

She looked up into his eyes for the first time. "You mean that?"

***

The King's Chamber was solemn. The Conclave sat on their benches on one side, in their black academic gowns. The earls and senior barons sat on the other, in their brilliantly coloured robes: a few wore mail. The King entered, and sat in the centre on his golden chair, holding the sceptre of justice. The King's Herald brought the meeting to order.

"Let all here assembled listen to the words of our King, and abide by the judgements found in this place."

They all nodded.

"Gentlemen," said the King. "These have been times of turmoil. I cannot recall a time when the Kingdom has been in greater danger. But, by divine grace and the wisdom of many here, and of course, the blessed memory of Kolras, who got us into this mess in the first place, God rot his soul," (but he did not say the last part out loud) "the Kingdom has been preserved. Our daughter wishes to approach this chamber, with her knight, and the Countess of Cymenshore, also lately restored to us."

The King signalled to the guard by the door. In came the Princess, in a relatively modest wig and pale pink gown, followed by Eiswolf, in sober black, then Perry, in her nun's getup.

The women curtseyed and Eiswolf bowed, in silence.

The King spoke to his daughter. "My dearest Rose, Eternal in your fidelity, apart from what I think is an assassination plot on that damn hanging of yours" (the King did not say that last part, either) "you have requested an audience. What is your wish?"

The Princess was a very fast study. Perry had been impressed. She was word-perfect within three rehearsals, better than Eiswolf. Show-time.

"My beloved father, great lords, wisest counsellors, in this Chamber I put aside my royalty and stand before you a simple girl, wishing only to serve this great Kingdom as best I may. This Knight," the Princess nodded to Eiswolf, "has most bravely accomplished all that Kolras required, and is now entitled to my hand, and half this Kingdom. I would give my hand willingly."

Hello, thought the King. Would?

"But now, a greater Quest must be fulfilled, and so I must wait in patience, with sorrow in my heart and yet, such love, for my Knight to return." She drooped.

"So you're not getting married at the turn of the year?" The King extracted the bones of the argument. "Why not? The people expect it."

Eiswolf took a step forward, and bowed. "Your Majesty. This Kingdom is still in great peril, for the Glimmer Lord is at large, and may be plotting more destruction on all of us."

Good point, thought the King, but not the whole story.

"This Kingdom has enemies," said Eiswolf, "and we must prevent this sorcerer from gathering these dogs into a pack which might overwhelm us and all we hold dear. My King, I will hunt this creature down and destroy him." He bowed, deeply.

"All very well," said the King. "Why not get married first? What about this afternoon?"

Eiswolf did gulp slightly. "Alas, my King, I would not leave your daughter a widow, or a child of ours fatherless and defenceless. Let me achieve this, my greatest Quest, and return in victory to enjoy a lifetime of happy marriage to our most beautiful Princess." He actually went down on one knee and kissed her hand. Perry had thought that was too much but the Princess explained that Conclave, which had a high proportion of old bachelors, was sentimental about that kind of thing.

"Right," said the King. "But what about while you are away? Or if you don't come back? For example?" His blue eyes bored into Eiswolf's face.

"My King, I shall not leave my Princess without a champion. I nominate Sir Adelbon to be her protector, and shield of this kingdom while I am gone."

Well, thought the King. You're not as thick as you are wolf-looking. She seems pleased with herself, too. One in the hand, one in the bush. But the King did wonder how much Adelbon knew about his future role as Patsy-in-Chief. "Sir Adelbon is a noble knight. So my Princess must wait a little longer? Not too long, I hope. The peaceful succession of this Kingdom is a matter close to my heart."

The Princess curtseyed. "The Crown shall pass without war or discord, that I promise you, father. And, with my prayers to protect him, my Knight shall return in victory. Farewell, my brave love!" She wept copiously, assisted by a good dose of pepper up one of her sleeves.

The King turned to Perry. "And what of our valiant Countess? Do you return to Cymenshore?"

Perry had thought about that long and hard. She had been brought up as a noble lady and although not expected to rule, she had been trained in the arts of diplomacy and court life.

The Princess had asked her the same question during rehearsal.

Perry had shrugged. "I feel like I ought to. But I've been out on the road a long time, I'm not sure I could go back to court again, not as a countess, anyway, Richard and his chaps are doing all right. Would you, if you were me?"

"Oh, yes," said the Princess. "But I like everything clean and neat. Your hairy friend, frankly, gives me the shivers, not that he's rude or anything, he's been very nice to me. He's a bit innocent about women, though, isn't he?"

"Innocent?"

So the Princess explained what she meant.

Perry stored the information. Court ladies do that a lot.

And now the King was asking her.

"My King, I too have a higher quest, for my convent needs me. But I shall ever be at the call of my people of Cymenshore, in their hour of need."

"Oh, right," said the King. "I'm sure Richard of Clifton will be relieved. About the hour of need business. Well. That would appear to be all. Let us drink to the future of this Kingdom, to these noble ladies, and this brave lord. For they, and only they, have brought us all to where we find ourselves today."

Then the members of the Chamber broke up into smaller meetings (and cliques and plots) as usual. Eiswolf and Perry, not being members of the Chamber, bowed, and left.

The Princess came over to her father. "Daddy. I'm going to be part of the Chamber now, aren't I."

"How can I keep you out?" He smiled, indulgently. Better to have her under his nose, so he could see what she was up to.

"Only, it's all got very slack, recently. I know he's only a commoner, but the Hegemon really keeps on top of things. Where is he?"

"Poor Bevis. Yes, he did."

She squinted at him. "Daddy. Have you done something very silly?"

***

They carried the little man out into the evening air when few were in the palace courtyard, swiftly taking him to the house of a discreet doctor to rest and recover.

But before he was brought from the cell, he grabbed the arm of one of the guards, and whispered hoarsely, "Take her, too! Take Bess! I shall not leave here without her!"

The guard called to Black Al. "He says there's a woman here."

"Well, nothing to do with us," said Black Al. "Anybody know about her?"

The man who had taken the bribe coughed. "She's in the next cell. But I think she's dead."

They looked; the small heap of rags hardly moved, but Bevis resolutely insisted that they move Bess first, so he could see they did as they promised. "Where do we take her?" said Al.

"That woman Jocasta's a witch," said another guard. "That's what this one needs. A doctor won't be much good."

So Jocasta came from the Princess' chambers, which was still the dungeon but now renamed. And nearly died of shock when she saw her old friend Bess.

"Who did this?" But she knew there would be no answers. "You can't let the wolf see her like this. He'd kill you all."

Jocasta, a biochemist, had also trained as an emergency medic for the Glimmer Project, with a special emphasis on 'hardship' without technical support. She found a small bed-chamber within the Princess' apartments, and called up a couple of the less scatty wise-women. The Princess came to visit; she was curious about Bess and, in her own way, was shocked. But she knew that rule, whether her father's or the Hegemon's, might mean doing horrible things. She had been brought up in that culture.

"We need to look after her for a few weeks," said Jocasta. "If she hasn't been too damaged, we can get her rehydrated and dry out these wounds, the bruises will go down too. Bess, can you hear me?"

The figure on the bed lifted a hand.

Jocasta grasped it. "I'm here, I'll help you. God, what have we become."

"Gil," whispered Bess.

"Gil's gone. I've asked Bridget to come. We'll get you better."

"Bridget?" said the Princess.

"The Pontifex. The Neuts of Bladbean?" Jocasta started to giggle and cry at the same time. "It's a really bad pun. In Latin. She was a Dublin convent girl, at the lab she was always telling these really bad jokes in Latin…" And then she burst into tears. That life was gone.

Slowly, Bess improved. A few days later, she managed to sit up and recognise Jocasta.

"Hallo," said Jocasta. "Welcome back."

Where was the cell? Where was the voice? Had they killed him? "Where's he? Where's Bevis?"

"Calm down, he's fine, they're looking after him. You concentrate on you."

"He's not a bad man." Bess started to weep. Then she looked about again. "Where is he?" And this time, the desperate look in her eyes could only have one meaning.

"Eiswolf's at the armoury with his squire. He's fine. You can see him soon."

Bess looked down at her arms, felt the tenderness and injuries on her face and body. "Not too soon. He's all right?"

"Yes. He knows you're ill, we've told him you need to rest, we practically had to fight him to keep him out, but he can be quite sensible. He's really brave, isn't he. Whatever he is. But ... he won't be marrying the Princess."

Bess smiled. Then she laughed. "The scoundrel!"

And Jocasta laughed too.

***

The Hegemon came back to Court a few weeks later, after recovering from his illness, which they said he had caught while travelling to a distant land on the King's business. He immediately started whipping systems back into shape. He reported as much to the Princess as to the King, in her new role as Secretary to the King's Chamber. The baked fancies at Court were much improved by Marejah's return from Cymenshore. Trade boomed in the port.

Sir Adelbon slid easily into his new position as the Princess' Champion, which gave him plenty of time for improving his fighting skills and a free pass into most tourneys. The Princess was also most attentive in persuading him to learn the gentler arts of courtly life; dancing, singing and flirting. The more intellectual stuff, like lying, plotting and deceiving, she decided, would have to wait.

Jocasta and Bess declared a truce. Jocasta wanted to go back to her little cult in the woods; they might be ridiculous but they were at least honest, in their way. But she did promise not to kill any more knights. As it happens, between the conclusion of the Seven Tests, the end of Sword of Destiny ceremonies at Westerings, and the reduced level of dragon-slaying (the Keeper was far too fond of Mavis to let anyone kill her) the opportunities for knights to let rip had declined.

Jonno and Nev leapt into the gap, declaring a Series of tourneys for the next year, to be decided at a massive Triumph meet come midwinter, although Colin was still very sniffy about battles that did not end in death. However, he agreed to officiate as Herald to the new contest.

The King was happy, because now he had an Enemy. Every king needs a really big enemy, but a supernatural one is best of all; such a wonderful excuse for cracking down on, well, almost anyone and anything. The Glimmer Lord could not have been better if he had been invented. The King patched things up with the Hegemon by explaining that he had been under the sorcery of the Glimmer Lord. The King would not have recognised a kitchen sink if you put one under his nose, but he knew how to use one.

"My dear chap, how can I apologise! Awful business, truly awful. But we're all right now, aren't we?"

The Glimmer Lord also got the blame for a bad onion harvest and a flood at Wardur as well.

Bess was escorted back to her hovel. The guards told her village she had been seized by brigands, who held her hostage and abused her most mercilessly. A troop of the King's men had discovered her in the forest, and rescued her. The hovel was warm, dry, comfortable, she had her books and her own medicines, the villagers were welcoming, after a week or so to get used to the idea that she was back, and it was only a day's journey to the Palace.

Eiswolf, Perry and Meroens met Bess there before setting out on the quest to find the Glimmer Lord.

"I don't like leaving you on your own," said Perry.

"I'm not on my own, Octa will look in on me, I've got my clients. Anyway, everyone knows I'm under the protection of the great Eiswolf." Bess smiled up at him, and he grinned back.

"You got everything?" said Meroens. "We'll be back soon. Like, when we've sorted this bloke out. All right?"

"All right," said Bess. "Come here for a kiss, you big lump."

So Meroens got a kiss, and so did Perry, now travelling as Pervenche's illegitimate half-brother (who also seemed to have been through the hands of the Barons of Elderton, but the backstory was still in development). As Eiswolf got his hug, Bess made an announcement.

"Eiswolf. This is hard for me to say."

She stared around at the band of oddballs and misfits, for this was now her life, and she knew she had to measure up to them.

"Eiswolf. I am so sorry for what I did to you. No, quiet, let me speak. I was going to - My God, what I would have done to you, I apologise." She took a deep breath. "You are all much better people than I am. If you knew, you would not forgive me. I wanted you to be a weapon!"

The men exchanged glances.

"Listen, I'm not crazy. I promise to do better."

She had to stop, to swallow a sob. The others stood silent.

"I will. I won't forget what's important. Oh, come closer. Listen. Let all hear and understand - Meroens, stop fidgeting - that by the laws of this land, and with a pure heart, I recognise this man

Eiswolf as my son as if he were my own flesh, with all the legal duties on me which that implies. Eiswolf, I say you are human. I will swear to this under law, no matter what the penalty. If you want it. Is this your will?"

Eiswolf nodded. He could not speak.

"Well, off you go. Make sure you come back. Son."

***

The winter landscape was harsh in black and white, the smell of snow on the wind, under the dark sky with its brilliant stars and the huge moon. Eiswolf trotted ahead on Pepper, smelling out the path.

"So he didn't kill Sir Devlas?" said Meroens, for the third time.

"No!" Perry was beginning to lose patience.

"Won't you miss being a woman?" he said, pressing the other button.

"I am still a woman," she growled. "I have always been a woman. I always will be. Nothing has changed."

"But we know now," said Meroens. "Here, do you fancy me?"

"No."

"Do you fancy him?"

Well, actually... No. She suddenly saw that, well, she knew far too much about him. His deceptions, petty dishonesties, terrible jokes, poor personal hygiene on occasion, hangovers and moods -

And the golden eyes.

Bess had explained his strange fits away. "He's had a huge dose of psychotropic drugs this year, one way and another. What with Jocasta, and I'm sure that torch in the mound, then that massive blow to the head, they give you flashbacks, like really real bad memories." Which might explain what he saw, but not what Perry saw.

But she still had the blue bottle.

Eiswolf, riding ahead, sniffed the air, happy to be on the hunt again. He had checked all the bags for the trip himself, not because he did not trust his squires but because he was cautious, and wanted to be sure. And in Perry's satchel, he had found the blue bottle.

He knew what it was. He had seen Bess use it around the hovel. She had impressed on him when he was a boy that he should never, ever, go near it unless she was there. "It's tincture of aconite. A few drops can kill you. I don't really like having it here myself, but it's fatal on rats and suchlike."

"Fatal?" he said, immediately fascinated, as all boys of his age would be. "Like, really, really fatal?"

"You feel cold, your heart goes funny, then it hurts, then you die. So never go near this, or the tall purple flowers in the garden. I'll show you them. They're called wolfsbane."

So when he found the square blue bottle in Perry's satchel, he knew what it meant. He had sprinkled the contents on a rat's nest in the stable, then rinsed the bottle out carefully and filled it with water. Then he put the bottle back in the satchel.

On the road, he waited for the squires to catch up with him and Pepper. "Hear this, world! Ready or not, here we come!"

And they laughed as they rode out to their destiny.

******

About the author

Born in what was once the ancient Kingdom of Northumbria, later the Palatinate of the Prince-Bishops of Durham, at university I studied English, including Old English and medieval texts. Today, I work as a business consultant.

I have a lifelong interest in weird science, alchemy, cosmology, ancient and medieval history. Sports interests include fencing and steeplechase racing.

My influences are Jonathan Swift, Daniel Kahneman, Terry Pratchett and Vladimir Nabokov, films by Studio Ghibli and the Coen brothers, and intelligent action movies (I'm a big Ron Howard fan).

Eiswolf, Quest for a Hero is the first novel in the sequence. To follow soon:

Eiswolf: the Return of the Prince

Eiswolf at the Court of Love

For more about these books or others by New Stane Street Books, contact

newstanestreetbooks@btinternet.com

For a reading list on Arthurian texts and the medieval take on chivalry (not the Victorian one), ask me. The Eiswolf stories date to about 1150 to 1250 in our universe, or Anglo-Norman to Angevin. But as you will know if you've read this far, Eiswolf's world is not ours.

For my take on speculative fiction, **Charles and the Visitors** is also on Amazon/New Stane Street Books.

Printed in Great Britain
by Amazon